Una-Mary Parker li
Drawing extensively on her background as a former
social editor of *Tatler* and a prominent member of the
social scene, writer and broadcaster, Una-Mary Parker
has crafted a dramatic and compulsive novel of
suspense. Her previous international bestsellers, *Riches*,
Scandals, *Temptations*, *Enticements*, *The Palace
Affair*, *Forbidden Feelings*, *Only The Best*, *A Guilty
Pleasure*, *False Promises* and *Taking Control*, are all
available from Headline and have been extensively
praised:

'A compulsive romantic thriller' *Sunday Express*

'Deliciously entertaining' *Sunday Telegraph*

'Scandal . . . saucy sex and suspense' *Daily Express*

'This novel has everything – intrigue, romance,
ambition, lust' *Daily Mail*

MARION

A Dangerous Desire

Una-Mary Parker

HEADLINE

First published in 1997
by HEADLINE BOOK PUBLISHING

First published in paperback in 1997
by HEADLINE BOOK PUBLISHING

10 9 8 7 6 5 4 3 2 1

ISBN 0 7472 5140 1

Typeset by CBS, Felixstowe, Suffolk

Printed in England by
Clays Ltd, St Ives plc

HEADLINE BOOK PUBLISHING
A division of Hodder Headline PLC
338 Euston Road
London NW1 3BH

One

Lucy had always loved fast cars. There was something so sleek and sexy about them, and the sensation almost of flying, as she accelerated, thrilled her. Speeding along a motorway to the beat of loud pop music with the wind whipping her long hair through the open window was her idea of heaven. It was like shaking off earthbound shackles, being gloriously free and powerful even, so that she had the feeling she could circle the sky and go anywhere she liked. This particular evening, though, Peter was driving. Not that she minded. He too drove with dash and style, loving the new car they shared, a flashy scarlet Mitsubishi Carisma, as much as she did. Humming along with the music, he pressed hard down on the accelerator, overtaking cumbersome lorries and leaving the sluggish traffic behind. Eventually he'd have to turn off on to a secondary road to reach the village where her parents lived but meanwhile, like a golden runway in the evening sunlight, the M3 stretched ahead and she suddenly felt a burst of elation. This was a weekend she'd been looking forward to for a long time: the formal announcement of their engagement. Tomorrow her parents were giving a barbecue party and Tilly, her younger sister, had got an exeat from school. Already the glint of a square-cut emerald surrounded by diamonds flashed on her finger, and glancing at Peter's regular profile, she felt a glow of deep contentment. Two years together, one of which

1

she'd lived with him in his flat, had assured her they were right for each other. In the summer they'd have a traditional country wedding and then it would be a case of living happily ever after. Dreamily she stared ahead, content in the knowledge of having the rest of her life planned. She laid her hand on Peter's thigh and he took his eyes off the road just long enough to turn and smile at her. Lucy smiled back. She'd never been so happy in her life.

The traffic was getting heavier now, vehicles lumbering towards the south coast like mindless metal lemmings, spewing out choking fumes. Peter overtook an articulated lorry, the hub of its giant wheels thundering level with Lucy's face. At that moment the lorry accelerated, forcing him to push the car to the limit, gripping the wheel as he concentrated on the road ahead, finding himself involved in combat with a mighty opponent, a race to get ahead. Lucy braced herself as the Mitsubishi's engine screamed and the car hurtled forward like a projectile. The lorry roared aggressively, only inches away, determined to keep up, to overpower them, and she felt as if they were a small beetle about to be squashed by a giant's foot. Side by side they raced as other vehicles, anxious to distance themselves from impending disaster, pulled back. Lucy realised her left foot was pressing down hard on an imaginary brake. She was suddenly scared by the risk Peter was taking. Then, just when she thought they would crash, the lorry surrendered. The roaring monster was being reined in. With a smile of triumph Peter shot ahead. The winner! Relieved, Lucy looked at him. He was flushed with triumph.

'What a dickhead,' he said lazily, turning up the volume on the cassette player. 'People like him cause accidents.'

As they cruised on, the sunset turned to a richer gold, casting long shadows over fields and trees veiled in the first fresh green of spring.

Suddenly Peter spoke. 'Look at that! God! What's happening?' He looked aghast as he stared through the windscreen. On the other side of the motorway a cloud of dust was bowling along like a giant ball. It came hurtling forward, growing larger and denser, gathering momentum by the second. He slammed on the brakes, narrowly avoiding the car in front. Behind them, the giant lorry's engine screeched as the driver tried to bring it to a halt. Mesmerised with fear, Lucy wondered what the spherical mass would look like as it passed them on the other side. Only it wasn't passing. It was storming the central reservation that divided the motorway, a dark threatening shape, looming out of the earth it was gathering as it spun forward. And it was coming straight for them.

Then everything seemed to turn to slow motion. Lucy watched, petrified, as the object took shape, became a large estate car, rising up over the central barrier like a giant porpoise, soaring up . . . up . . . out of the spume of dust, arching high in the air over the car in front of them, somersaulting with slow grace towards them.

Then it was fast forward – too fast. No way of escape. No time to think. An instant later the sickening impact as metal crunched against metal . . . glass shattered . . . rubber screamed . . . chrome clashed with heavy resonance . . . and then the hurt, the stinging pain and eventual agony took over and everything turned to monochrome. The sky, the grass, the wreckage around them, Peter's face. The world had turned into a black and white photograph and the thought that flashed through Lucy's mind at that last second was, So this is how I'm going to die.

Diana glanced at her wristwatch. Lucy and Peter should have arrived at least an hour ago. Lucy had phoned as she was leaving the City Radio studios where she worked as a researcher to say they were setting off in fifteen minutes. That had been two and a half hours ago. Allowing for the Friday night exodus from London, they should still have been home by eight o'clock. The aroma of roasting lamb garnished with rosemary filled Eastleigh Manor and, slightly irritated, Diana feared it was going to be overdone at this rate, along with the roast potatoes and the parsnips laced with honey and sesame seeds. Restlessly, she wandered from the kitchen back to the drawing-room and poured herself a glass of wine. Where on earth were they? Not that Nigel was home yet either, but he was often late. His commuting to London and back every day meant she could never be sure when he'd turn up but Lucy and Peter were usually very punctual. Surely they'd have phoned if they'd been delayed?

Tilly strolled into the comfortably furnished, chintzy room, changed out of her grey and navy school uniform into tight black cord jeans and a pale pink tee-shirt. Tall for fifteen, and with a luscious rosy bloom that promised great beauty when she was older, she flung herself on to the sofa facing the fireplace and looked expectantly at her mother.

'When are we eating, Mummy? I'm starving.'

'Lucy and Peter aren't here yet. Neither is Daddy.' Usually Diana looked younger than forty-six but tonight there were dark shadows under her eyes, like crushed moths, and her mouth was tight.

'I think I'll ring Daddy on his mobile,' she said distractedly.

Tilly strolled out of the room. 'I'm going to get myself a banana,' she called over her shoulder. Tilly felt rather out of it these days. Although she came home most weekends from Woldingham, so many things seemed to be happening in her absence and life at Eastleigh Manor was altering so rapidly, she often felt out of kilter. Though Lucy was six years older, they'd always been close. Then Peter had come on the scene and suddenly Lucy was on another planet, talking about curtains and cooking, and acting as if she couldn't wait to get away from her family. Even Diana seemed to be excluded from this new world which only Peter inhabited. At times Tilly thought Lucy was being jolly unkind, putting him before them all. They were a family. Flesh and blood. She wasn't even sure if she liked Peter all that much and the thought of having him as a brother-in-law wasn't appealing, but Diana had told her they must all make him feel welcome for Lucy's sake. Tilly peeled back the skin of the banana and bit into it hungrily. When *she* got engaged she'd jolly well make sure it was to someone the whole family liked.

In the drawing-room, Diana dialled the number of Nigel's mobile. He answered immediately, his tone terse.

'Hello?'

'It's me. How long before you're home, darling?'

'God only knows.' He sounded impatient and weary and she could just imagine him at the wheel of his BMW, briefcase open on the passenger seat beside him so he could glance at his papers while he was stuck in a traffic jam. Over and over again she'd suggested they move back to London so he wouldn't have to commute but he refused to consider the idea, saying they could never afford a house like Eastleigh Manor if they lived in town.

'Traffic bad?' she asked, trying to sound cheerful.

'It's at a standstill. I'm still on the M3. There's been an accident a mile or so ahead. God knows how long it will take now. I'd go ahead and start dinner if I were you.'

Diana was no longer listening. Her mind had latched on to the word 'accident' and a wave of freezing presentiment surged through her body.

'Lucy and Peter aren't here yet . . .'

'I expect they're stuck in this bloody jam, too.'

'I suppose so.' Her voice was hollow, verging on panic.

'What do you mean, Di?' A shaft of uneasiness made him sound angry. 'Where the hell do you think they are, then?'

'I don't know but they should have been here over an hour ago.'

'If they're only an hour late, I don't know what you're fussing about. I'm probably going to be *two* hours late. Why don't you ring them?'

'You know Peter refuses to have a mobile phone; he says they're too intrusive.'

'Bloody stupid!' he sighed, and then said more gently: 'Don't worry, sweetheart. They'll have got held up. I'll get back as soon as I can. Don't worry.'

Diana said goodbye and wished she had a calm personality like Nigel. She'd called him her Rock of Gibraltar for twenty-three years and knew she could never manage without him. He was strong, dependable, and had never looked at another woman. Sometimes she wondered what she'd done to deserve such a good and loving husband. Pouring herself another glass of wine, she strolled out through the French windows into the garden. The sun had almost slipped below the horizon and an atmosphere of melancholy hung in the air like a gossamer shroud, waiting to wrap up the departing day. Diana wished she could rid herself of the premonition that something was wrong.

Thirty minutes later Nigel had progressed, inch by inch, some three-quarters of a mile along the road. Cars were being waved on past the scene of the crash in single file, but the morbid curiosity of the other motorists made the going painfully slow. What in heaven's name made people want to gawp at the tragic aftermath of an accident? he wondered. But as he drew nearer the tangled mass of vehicles, the ambulances and police cars with flashing lights, the cordons roping off the area, the spilt oil and dripping radiators, and the teams of uniformed rescue workers, he too felt a compulsion to look. He *had* to look, if only to reassure himself that no one he knew had been involved.

The sight that met his eyes shocked him more than anything he had ever seen. The central barrier had been destroyed as if by an armoured tank smashing its way through, bending and buckling the metal fencing, turning it to scrap. All around the tangled remains of ten or more cars lay scattered across the motorway, indistinguishable from each other, coalesced into mere heaps of metal. Grotesquely, a large black estate car stood on its bonnet, as if it had taken flight before plunging, headfirst, into an oncoming lorry. No one, Nigel reckoned, could have got out of this alive. Feeling nauseous and cold, he was just about to ease his car forward when he saw the front of a scarlet vehicle jutting out from under the wreckage. It couldn't be . . . it wasn't . . . please God, don't let it be! But it was. He recognised the registration number. He also saw there was nothing left of the back half of the Mitsubishi.

'Keep moving, please,' commanded the young policeman who was regulating the slow progress of the traffic.

With a tight feeling in his chest, so that he feared he might be about to have a heart attack, Nigel leaned out of the car window.

'That's . . . my daughter was in that red car . . . where . . . which . . . ?' He was floundering, his voice choked, a look of desperation on his face. 'Can you tell me . . . ?'

The policeman – just a boy, he thought, a clean-shaven, baby-faced boy – came nearer and leaned over to talk to him.

'They've taken the casualties to Guildford General Hospital, sir.' He reached for his walkie-talkie. 'I'll get a car to escort you there. Just hold on a moment, sir.'

Nigel could sense the drivers behind him, already frustrated, were becoming impatient. One of them sounded his horn. The policeman spoke urgently into the mouthpiece, hurried to the front of the car to give the registration number, and then came back to the side window.

'A police car will be waiting for you at the next intersection. Exit number four, sir.' And he waved Nigel on.

His first thought, as he followed the police car with its wailing siren, was to find out exactly what had happened before he phoned Diana. She was alone in the house apart from Tilly, and if the worst had happened . . . but here his mind shied violently away from that possibility. Whatever had happened, Diana mustn't be alone when she was told. He'd have to get hold of her mother, who lived in a cottage in the grounds; they were very close and Diana would need her. And what about Tilly? She was going to be devastated if . . .

Nigel was almost blinded by the tears that welled in his eyes and trickled in itchy rivulets down his cheeks. How could Lucy and Peter have survived when their car had been all but pulverised? The young bobby had referred to 'casualties'. Did that mean some people were still alive? The dead weren't 'casualties', were they? But there must have been several fatalities. What about the driver of the estate car, the one with its bonnet plunged headfirst into the cabin of that huge lorry? If Lucy and Peter had got out alive it would have been a miracle. Nevertheless he clung on to the thinnest thread of hope because that was all that was holding him together at this moment. Then he remembered that he and Diana were not the only ones whose lives would never be the same again. Peter was an only child, his mother a widow. Who would tell *her* her son had been killed? For a moment he contemplated leaving it to the police. They were trained to impart bad news, counsel the bereaved, give professional help where it was needed. But then he knew he couldn't. That would be the coward's way out. He'd have to tell Miranda Beaumont himself.

Suddenly the police car took a sharp left turn and, following it, Nigel saw in a heart-stopping moment the dull red brick of Guildford General Hospital. They'd arrived and the siren was silenced, fading away with a final wail. Then the policemen climbed out of their car and came over to him. They'd got here so quickly he wasn't prepared, wasn't ready yet to . . . 'This way, sir.' They were helping him out of the car as if he were a very old man. He *felt* like an old man. Then, on legs so suddenly weak he thought he'd collapse, Nigel walked to a large entrance marked CASUALTY. Ambulances, their back doors open, were parked outside, and there was a lot of activity going on.

Inside he was hit by the sickening smell he always associated with hospitals and the feeling of panic increased. He looked around wildly, a part of him hoping to see Lucy, another part of him knowing that was impossible.

'Take a seat, sir, and we'll find out what's happening,' a constable said in a voice filled with the reassuring overtones of authority. Nigel sank gratefully on to a tubular metal chair, suddenly afraid that he was going to pass out. His skin felt cold and his heart was juddering. Gazing at the floor, he saw nothing. The noisy activity of a busy casualty department whirled around him but he heard nothing.

'If you give us your daughter's name we'll find out where they've taken her, sir,' the other policeman was saying.

With a growing sense of unreality, he gave them Lucy's name. They also wanted to know her age and a brief description as well. Nigel didn't ask why.

They seemed to be gone a long time and someone brought him a cup of tea. Nurses scurried to and fro, and a drunk, swearing loudly, was brought in from the street with a bleeding head. Just as Nigel thought he couldn't stand it any more he felt a hand on his shoulder.

'Mr Howard?' It was a nurse with red hair and a scattering of freckles across her pale face.

Nigel nodded, unable to speak.

'Would you come this way, please? The doctor would like a word with you.'

Diana Howard dialled Nigel's car phone. It was now ten o'clock and she'd heard nothing. After a minute the recorded voice told her, in maddening tones of disinterest, that the number was unavailable. 'Please try later,' it advised.

'Oh, God, what can have happened?' she exclaimed in desperation. 'Why isn't he in his car?'

Tilly plumped herself down on the sofa beside Diana, tucking her long legs under her. 'It'll be all right, Mum. Perhaps they've all met up, and as the traffic's so bad, they've taken a round-about route.'

'Daddy would have let me know.' She ran both her hands over her face in a washing gesture. All she wanted was her family to be home, safe and well. 'Something must have happened.'

Tilly said nothing, not knowing what to say. She had a nasty shaky feeling in her own stomach, but she didn't really believe anything could be wrong. Accidents happened to other people's families. Any minute now, they'd hear the cars coming up the drive, and there would be Daddy, and Lucy with Peter, all laughing and explaining that the traffic had been so awful they'd thought they'd *never* get home. Then Daddy would pour himself a stiff whisky, and Lucy would follow Mum into the kitchen to chat to her while dinner was being dished up, and Peter would hang around politely, asking Tilly how she was getting on at school.

Suddenly the phone rang, startling them with its loudness. They looked at each other and Tilly was the first to her feet, dashing into the hall to answer it.

'Hello?' she gasped breathlessly, relief sweeping over her.

'May I speak to Nigel Howard, please?'

Dashed by disappointment, she said curtly, 'He's not here.'

'Well, when will he be in?' The man's voice sounded impatient, desperate even.

'Any time now. We're expecting him any minute.'

'Tell him that Oliver Stephens rang. I'll call back later.' There was a click then silence.

'Who was that?' Diana called from the drawing-room, anxiety making her voice sound harsh.

'Someone for Daddy and he was jolly strange, too. Hanging up on me like that,' Tilly retorted.

At first she wondered why she was lying in the rain. It was trickling down her face, sliding into her ears, running down her neck. It didn't smell like rain, though. It wasn't a clean fresh smell; there was something cloyingly sweet about it . . . where had she come across that particular smell before? She frowned, but for some reason it hurt, sending a shooting pain across her brow. She tried to open her eyes, see where she was, watch the falling rain, but her lids seemed to be stuck down.

Panic overwhelmed her. She couldn't breathe. What in God's name was happening? Had she been blindfolded and gagged? She had to get away from here . . . wake up from this nightmare. Gingerly, although it was painful, she licked her lips and then realised in a terrifying flash that what she was tasting and smelling was blood. Her blood? Or someone else's? There seemed to be a weight across her chest . . . perhaps she was lying under someone who was bleeding? She tried to speak but found her lips couldn't form words: tried to move but seemed paralysed. Then she heard the chilling sound of a dog, howling in agony. It was only when she felt a hand on her shoulder that she realised with horror it was her. Shocked, she struggled to sit up, find out what the hell was going on. Why was it raining blood on her face? She struggled, trying to concentrate, trying to pin down even one coherent thought, but she was lying in a black tunnel and couldn't find a way out.

'Just lie quietly, dear,' she heard a woman's voice say. 'You're going to be all right. You've got some nasty cuts and bruises, but we'll soon have you cleaned up.'

Why did she have cuts and bruises? she wondered wildly. What had *happened*? Peter! She remembered something about Peter . . .

'I can't see,' she cried out, wild with terror. 'Where's Peter? What's happened? Where am I?'

'The doctor will come and see you in a moment,' another female voice informed her soothingly. But before he could a great dark wave swept over her and carried her away on its undertow.

'I'm afraid my husband's still not home,' Diana said, truly agitated now. Each time the phone had rung her hopes had risen; she'd been certain it was Lucy to say they were sorry they were late, the traffic had been terrible, they were on their way now – and each time it had been this man she'd never heard of, wanting to speak to Nigel. 'I don't know when he'll be back,' she added.

'I was told he'd be back at any minute,' he said anxiously, 'and that was half an hour ago.'

'I know. We thought he would be. He's obviously been delayed . . .'

'Could he still be in London?'

'What? Oh, no. When I spoke to him he was on the motorway, stuck in bad traffic. An accident was holding everything up.' Diana wished to God this man would get off the line in case Lucy or Nigel was trying to get through to her.

'If you'll excuse me, I must . . .'

'Will you tell him I called?' Oliver Stephens said urgently. He had a strong, rather loud voice. 'It *is* urgent.'

Perhaps she should take a message? she thought. If this man wanted to talk to Nigel about an important business matter, her husband would be furious if she didn't appear gracious.

'Can I take a message?' She tried not to sound too desperate with impatience as she reached for the memo pad and pencil on the telephone table.

'He'll know what it's about. I need to talk to him.'

'All right. I don't know when . . . it might have to be in the morning . . . it's nearly half-past ten now . . .'

'Yes. I see. But if you could ask him . . . please tell him to call me.'

'Yes, all right,' said Diana, hanging up quickly.

'Who *is* that dweeb?' Tilly demanded, coming into the hall, having listened to her mother's side of the conversation.

Diana shook her head. 'I haven't the faintest idea, but I think it's very inconsiderate of him to keep phoning at this time of night when we're obviously anxious to know where Lucy and Daddy are.' As she spoke she started to dial a number.

'What are you doing now?' Tilly asked.

'I'm trying your father's mobile again. This is ridiculous.

He *must* be in his car.' Tears sprang to Diana's eyes. 'What's happened? Why aren't they all home?' she wept, exhausted by nervous tension.

'Mr Howard?' The Indian doctor looked at Nigel sympathetically. He was small and slight, and had dark liquid eyes which must look sad even when he was pleased with life.

Nigel nodded, unable to speak. The blood was roaring in his ears and he felt as if the life was draining out of him.

'Well,' Dr Kapoor began, hands deep in the pockets of his white coat, 'I have been attending your daughter and in a moment I will take you to see her . . .'

'She's alive?' Nigel rasped in a choked voice.

The doctor paused for a fraction of a second before answering and in that moment Nigel knew for certain that the news was bad.

'She *is* alive,' he said carefully, 'and she was conscious when they brought her in, but we suspect she has a fractured skull because she slipped into a coma a little while ago.' He paused, and looked at Nigel intently as if sizing him up to see how much bad news he could stand.

Nigel nodded slowly, determined to keep a grip on himself. 'What now?' he asked, amazed at the steadiness of his voice.

'We will be operating to remove what we believe to be a blood clot on the brain.'

Nigel nodded again, feeling like a marionette having its strings jerked.

'There are other injuries, too. Her left arm is broken in two places, and she has several cracked ribs . . .'

'But she's going to be all right?' Nigel's eyes were beseeching.

'It's a miracle she wasn't killed,' Dr Kapoor said gently. 'We are doing everything we can.' He paused, considering the best way of telling this distraught father everything he should know.

'What is it?' Nigel asked intuitively.

The doctor frowned, looking genuinely distressed. 'I'm afraid her face is badly damaged.'

'How badly?'

'We can perform plastic surgery, although the blood clot on her brain obviously takes priority, but she will need further corrective surgery in about six months' time.'

But she is alive, Nigel thought. *That's all that matters* . . .

'Can I see her?' he asked.

Dr Kapoor nodded, his dark eyes sympathetic. 'Prepare yourself for a shock.'

As they walked along the brightly lit corridor, Nigel suddenly remembered Peter, and was instantly mortified to realise that in his concern for Lucy, he'd forgotten all about his future son-in-law.

'The young man who was in the car with her . . . how is he?' he asked.

The doctor raised thick black eyebrows. 'I didn't know she was with anyone. I'll find out for you. What is his name?'

'Diana?' Nigel managed to make his voice sound calm and steady.

'Nigel! I've been going out of my mind with worry. Where are you, for God's sake? I've been trying to get you on your car phone for *hours* but you haven't been answering! Why aren't you home? Where are Lucy and Peter? Don't you realise, I've been frantic?' Relief that he'd finally phoned her made Diana erupt in anger.

'Chill out, Mum,' Tilly warned in a whisper.

Nigel sounded strange. 'I'm at the Guildford General. Lucy and Peter were involved in the accident . . .'

'Oh, God! Are they all right?'

'They've had a miraculous escape, considering.' He tried to break the news gently. 'Lucy is in the operating theatre now . . .'

'What's happened to her?'

'She's got some broken bones and a lot of cuts,' he said carefully. 'And they're doing plastic surgery on her face.'

Diana was already sobbing. 'Oh, my baby! Is she going to be all right?'

How, he wondered, was he going to describe his daughter's once lovely face? The purple bruising, the bloody lacerations? The eyes red swollen slits, the mouth a great gash that stretched across her cheek? How do you tell a mother that her daughter's nose and cheek look as if they have been pulverised by rocks and that the jawbone, gleaming white, protrudes through the skin?

'I must be with her, Nigel.' He heard Diana speak as if from a long, long way away.

'I'll come and pick you up, darling. Get your mother to stay with Tilly.'

'All right. What about Peter? How is he?'

'I'm still trying to find out. Then I'll have to get hold of his mother, before the police frighten the life out of her.'

'Oh, God. How terrible.' Her voice broke on a sob.

'I'll be with you in twenty minutes,' she heard him say.

As Diana hurried across the lawn, to the pretty gabled cottage where her mother, Susan Butler, lived, Tilly scampered by her side, badgering her with questions.

'What's happened, Mummy? Is Lucy badly hurt? Why are you going to see Granny at this time of night? Isn't Daddy coming home?' And getting no answer: '*Mummy!* What's happened?'

Disjointedly, she tried to answer Tilly's questions, but in

her shock and distress she hardly knew what she was saying. When Susan Butler came to the door, Diana burst into tears again, shaking all over, unable to speak.

'There's been an accident, Granny. Daddy just phoned, and Lucy and Peter have been hurt . . .' Tilly gabbled, scared by her mother's lack of emotional control. She'd always supposed all grown-ups were strong, like her father, and it was unnerving to see Diana cracking up like this.

Susan Butler showed no surprise. 'I knew something was wrong,' she said calmly. 'That's why I stayed up.'

Diana looked at her mother searchingly. Susan had always claimed to have second sight, and this wasn't the first time she'd seemed prepared for bad news.

'Can you come over and stay with Tilly, Ma?'

'Why should I need anyone to stay with me?' Tilly demanded indignantly. 'Anyway, I want to go to the hospital with you.'

'Darling, no. You're too young.' Diana sniffed. 'And God knows how long we'll be.'

'I'm not too young, and Lucy is my sister!' Tilly, always argumentative, never gave in easily.

Susan put her arm round her granddaughter's shoulders and hugged her. 'Darling, why don't you and I man the phones? There are sure to be people ringing up to ask what's happened, and if your father tells us whom he wants informed, we can make the calls. We can be far more useful here than we can at the hospital.'

Being made to feel important, Tilly capitulated at once. 'OK, but can I go and see Lucy tomorrow?'

'We'll *both* go tomorrow,' Susan assured her. Then she looked sympathetically at Diana. 'How bad are they?'

'Nigel didn't know about Peter. Lucy is being operated on now. Oh, Ma! I'm so scared.'

They walked slowly back to Eastleigh Manor, the three generations, each lost in their own thoughts.

'I'm sure everything is going to be all right,' Susan Butler said, looking up into the darkened sky which was now dusted with stars.

'God, I hope you're right, Ma.'

'Granny's always right about these things,' Tilly commented robustly.

Susan Butler smiled at her granddaughter but said nothing. The remark had been made for the benefit of Diana, always the frailest of the family.

The lights were on in all the ground-floor rooms of Eastleigh Manor as Nigel turned in at the gates and parked the car in the drive. On any other occasion the house would have struck him as looking festive and inviting, with its richly decorated rooms glowing like jewels through the deep mullioned windows, but tonight he could feel a sense of unease about the place. Diana would be waiting for him, waiting to be comforted and reassured and he wished she would not lean so heavily on him. She seemed to have no idea what a strain it was having to be the strong one all the time. The one who had to make all the decisions. The one who must never show weakness or falter when faced by adversity.

Getting slowly out of the car, he walked towards the front door, and heard the enthusiastic scrabbling of their black labradors, Muffie and Mackie, who always recognised the sound of his car. At that moment the door was flung open, the dogs rushed out, hysterical with delight, and Diana stood silhouetted against the glittering chandelier which illuminated the hall.

'Thank God you're back!' she exclaimed, flinging herself at him. 'I've been frantic. How's Lucy? What's happening?

18

Are they still operating on her?'

Nigel held her close for a moment, and caught a drift of the perfume she always wore, then he gently disentangled himself and turned to Tilly who was standing, still and pale, looking up at him.

'Are you all right, Daddy?' she asked anxiously.

The fact that at this moment she should be thinking about *his* welfare made him want to weep. He put his arm around her and hugged her tightly. 'Would you like a drink?' she asked solicitously.

Nigel looked into her sweet sympathetic face. 'I would, but I can't because I'm driving. I'd love a cup of tea though, darling.'

'And some bread and cheese? The lamb's ruined but you must be starving.' Tilly was as practical as ever.

'Thank you, sweetheart. That would be marvellous.'

'But we mustn't be long. I've got to get to the hospital,' Diana pointed out.

Susan came through from the kitchen carrying a tray.

'I thought tea would be a good idea,' she said. 'Tell me what's been happening, Nigel. How *is* Lucy?'

'I'm afraid she's . . . she's rather badly knocked about,' he replied, following her into the drawing-room.

'And Peter?'

'He has internal injuries. He's in intensive care.'

Diana gave a little scream and covered her face with her hands.

'Oh, it's too awful!' she said tearfully.

'They are going to be all right, aren't they?' Tilly asked, twisting her hands nervously.

'They're in very good hands,' said Nigel, wincing at the cliché as he spoke. 'Everything is being done that can be done.' He sat down in his favourite armchair to drink his tea, and Susan thought he looked as if he'd aged twenty years since the morning. His skin was a ghastly colour and his hands shook. She'd seen men come home from the front lines during World War II looking like that: stunned, as if the terrible sights they'd witnessed were forever engraved upon their memories.

Diana sat hunched in a corner of the sofa.

'How did it happen, Nigel? Were they going too fast?'

'No. I gather the driver of an estate car, going in the opposite direction, skidded and mounted the grass verge of the central reservation. The car cartwheeled before somersaulting into the oncoming traffic, hitting several cars before landing on top of a lorry.'

'Dear God!' Susan looked deeply distressed.

Nigel nodded sombrely. 'It was terrible. Both sides of the motorway became involved, one way or another. Crashed cars everywhere. It was like a battle zone.'

'Gross,' Tilly breathed.

'We must go to Lucy now,' Diana said, getting to her feet. 'You told her we were coming, didn't you, Nigel?'

'She was unconscious when I saw her,' he said carefully. 'They're operating to remove a blood clot . . .'

Diana gazed back at him, stricken, and sank into the sofa again, her legs giving way beneath her.

'Unconscious? You never said! Why didn't you tell me? Was she hit on the head? Oh, God . . .'

'Listen, Diana . . .'

Susan interrupted him in a calm practical voice. 'Modern medicine is so advanced they can do anything these days, often by micro-surgery. Lucy will be all right, Diana. She's young and strong. You'll see.'

Nigel gave her a quick glance of gratitude before turning to Diana. 'Ma's right, darling.' He finished his cup of tea.

'Let's go. I don't know when we'll be back, Susan, but we'll keep in touch.'

'There was a telephone message for you, Daddy,' Tilly said, suddenly remembering. 'Mummy wrote it down on the pad.'

Susan looked at Diana sympathetically. 'Off you go darling. Give Lucy my love.' She followed Nigel into the hall where he was reading the message. 'Is there anyone you want us to ring?'

'Not at the moment. I've already phoned Peter's mother. She's meeting us at the hospital,' he replied absently, stuffing the piece of paper into his pocket.

'Poor Miranda,' Susan observed. 'Peter is her only child, isn't he?' Then she put her arm around Tilly as if she were suddenly very precious. 'We'll visit Lucy tomorrow, won't we, darling? And meanwhile we'll keep each other company.'

Tilly nodded dolefully, too upset to speak.

Nigel and Diana drove to the hospital in silence, each preoccupied with their own thoughts. Nigel was entering the phase of detached calm that is often induced by shock, while Diana, still in turmoil, was wondering why such a dreadful thing should have happened to them all? A few hours ago everything had been perfect; Lucy and Peter were announcing their engagement and planning to marry in the summer. They'd found a bigger flat near the City Radio studios which would be perfect for Lucy, and Peter had just formed a partnership to start a financial consultancy, something he'd wanted to do for a long time.

'If only I could turn back the clock,' she murmured wretchedly. Just a few hours, that was all. She felt Nigel's hand, warm and strong, on her knee.

'I know, sweetheart.'

'It seems like only yesterday Lucy was a little girl,' she said brokenly. 'She is going to be all right, isn't she, Nigel? I couldn't bear it if . . .'

He tried to hide from her how full of despair he felt.

'She's going to need us to be strong, Di.' He thought of her lying there in a coma, her face mutilated, her poor young body broken. 'We mustn't let her see our alarm. It's most important that when she regains consciousness . . .' He faltered for a second, desperately trying to quash the thought that maybe she would never come out of the coma. 'We must be cheerful and assure her there's nothing to worry about.'

'That's going to be so difficult.' Tears had sprung to Diana's eyes once more. 'I wish I was strong like you. I don't know if I'll be able to . . . she's just a baby, Nigel. Our baby.'

'I know, I know.' But how strong am I? He reflected silently. And then he remembered that Oliver Stephens had called and left a message.

Two

Diana and Nigel sat on hard metal-framed chairs in a small windowless room, waiting for news while drinking endless paper cups filled with a watery fluid from the dispensing machine in the corridor labelled 'Coffee'. The atmosphere was claustrophobic. It was after midnight and in this part of the hospital there was an uneasy silence as patients slumbered in the darkened wards, watched over by tiptoeing night nurses. A senior nurse had informed them that Lucy would eventually be brought down from the operating theatre and placed in a side room set aside for intensive care patients. Until then, there was nothing to do except wait, bracing themselves from time to time as they heard footsteps coming in their direction, feeling sick with relief when they passed.

When they'd first arrived at the hospital Nigel had led the way back to the casualty department, to find out where Lucy had been taken. As he made enquiries, Diana overheard snatches of information about the crash. Six people had been killed, including the driver of the estate car. A young mother travelling with her two children had died on arrival at the hospital, but her little sons had survived. The traffic on the motorway had been disrupted for three hours while smashed vehicles were cleared away, the oncoming darkness hampering the operation. Eleven people had been badly injured.

Diana heard a porter who was ending his shift say to a

nurse who had just come on duty: 'One of the victims is a young woman who has practically lost her face. They don't know if she's going to make it through the night. You've never seen such a sight.'

Half fainting, Diana staggered over to where Nigel stood at the reception desk.

'Have you found out what's happening?' she asked weakly.

Turning, he put his arm around her shoulders.

'She's still in the operating theatre,' he replied gently. 'There's no news yet.'

'Oh, God, Nigel. I don't think I can bear it.' She repeated the remark she'd overheard, certain it was Lucy they'd been talking about. Her eyes were filled with panic and grief. Nigel could see she was near breaking point and he'd just been told it could be hours yet before there was any news.

'Would you like me to take you home again, darling? There may be a long wait before we hear anything.'

She rested her head on his shoulder. 'No, I want to stay with you.'

Now, as they sat in the waiting room, he glanced around for some distraction; the newspapers on the small central table were two days old, the magazines even older. It was one o'clock in the morning and he was beginning to feel desperate. Any news would have been better than this nightmare state of limbo, he thought.

'I wonder if Miranda has arrived yet?' he remarked suddenly. 'She said she'd drive down from London right away.'

'Poor Miranda. She must have been terribly shocked. I wonder how Peter is?'

They'd heard that he, too, was being operated on, for suspected internal injuries and a shattered right leg.

Miranda Beaumont had reached an age when the hot flushes

of the day combined to make her feel languorous and in a permanent state of arousal at night so that in her sleep she moved restlessly, pressing herself against the pillows and the mattress, dreaming . . . dreaming . . . sometimes until an orgasm awakened her to a fresh tumult of frustrated desire. A sense of longing permeated her all the time, and gave her grey eyes a hungry look and her painted lips a yearning pout. Her breasts ached and her hands fiddled nervously with her mane of tawny hair. She longed to be touched.

Widowed three years previously, after thirty years of glorious sex with her husband, Miranda had now entered her fifties and all the desires of her youth had come flooding back to taunt and tease her and remind her that old age was approaching, lying crouched and waiting on the horizon with its threat of sexual drought. The days were shortening and she knew she must gather in the last blooms before it was too late, before winter came with its dry impartiality, and the flowers withered away.

Her eyes flickered over Roger's body, lingering on his rounded buttocks and his crotch. Desire licked through her like a flame. He was twenty-nine, and in return for dinner in a good restaurant, willingly gave her what she wanted. In her menopausal years, and without a husband, she'd discovered that sex could be an expensive pastime.

Swaying her hips as she walked, so that her black silk culottes flared gently around her ankles, she went over to the lacquered Chinese cupboard on the far side of her spacious drawing-room.

'Brandy, darling?' she asked, her voice husky.

'Thanks.' Roger stood with his back to the modern fireplace, hands sunk deep into the trouser pockets of his pale grey suit. Flamboyantly good-looking, with ruffled dark hair and eyes that were sexily knowing, he had the eager expression of a man with a permanent erection. Just to look at him sent waves of desire sweeping through Miranda, making her wonder if they hadn't better skip the brandy and go straight to the bedroom.

At that moment the phone rang. She picked it up lazily. A minute later she turned to him with stricken eyes.

'It's Peter! There's been an accident. Oh, my God!' Her voice was shrill, face white.

Roger raised thick black eyebrows. 'Anything I can do? Is it bad?'

Miranda hesitated for a moment. No one knew about her relationship with Roger because she was sure that other people would be shocked. She'd even kept his existence secret from Peter, yet right now she desperately needed someone to take her to the hospital in Guildford. She couldn't bear to go alone. Nigel Howard had said it was a serious accident.

'Will you come with me, Roger?' she begged as she rushed to pick up her bag and evening wrap which she'd flung down when they'd returned from San Lorenzo.

'Sure,' he said easily. 'Shall I call a cab?'

'We'll have to take the car. Oh, where did I put the keys?'

'Where are we going?' He watched her scrabble among the papers on her desk, her long dark red nails flashing like rubies.

'Guildford. Ah, here they are! Thank God. Quick, let's go.' Clutching the keys, she hurried out of the room.

'*Guildford?*' Roger repeated in a stunned voice. 'Hang on a moment.' Then he paused, remembering all the lavish dinners in restaurants and the occasional gifts of gold cufflinks and Cartier knick-knacks. No point in alienating Miranda by saying he didn't fancy a drive down to Surrey on a Friday night. 'Hadn't you better change?' he asked instead.

'What?' She glanced down at her exotic black outfit. 'Damn!

I suppose you're right. Here, take the keys and bring the car round to the door, will you, darling? I'll go and change.'

Roger took the keys, saying nothing. He did not enjoy being treated like a chauffeur. Sometimes he wondered if it wouldn't be easier just to get a job.

As Susan Butler went to bed in the spare room at Eastleigh Manor she remembered that tomorrow her daughter and Nigel had invited nearly fifty people to a barbecue lunch, or an indoor buffet if it was cold or wet. Diana had already got in all the food, the wine was ready to be chilled, garden tables and chairs were in position on the lawn and sacks of charcoal stood in readiness. Susan clambered out of bed again and padded on bare feet down to the drawing-room, where with any luck, she thought, she'd find the list of guests on Diana's desk. First thing in the morning she'd have to start ringing around to tell everyone the party had been cancelled. Tilly could help. It would give her something to do.

There was no sign of the list anywhere. Perhaps it was on Nigel's desk in the study? It must be somewhere because Diana had read it aloud to her a couple of days ago. Susan turned on the light in the pleasant book-lined room and walked over to the large partner's desk that stood in the window. As usual, it was a mess; Nigel forbade anyone to touch it, even Mrs Warren wasn't allowed to dust it, and as Susan gazed at the jumbled chaos of files and loose papers, receipts, scribbled memo pads, stamps, elastic bands, a ruler, a pencil sharpener and an ashtray spilling over with paper clips, she knew it was hopeless. She'd never find it among this clutter. She turned to go, but the sleeve of her dressing-gown caught the edge of a jumbled stack of files and they slid sideways, disgorging some of their contents across the desk.

'Damn and blast!' she swore, shuffling the papers back as

best she could. Then something caught her eye. It was a letter, handwritten in green ink. How unusual, she thought, pushing it back among the other papers. Then, in spite of herself, she looked again. It began 'Darling Nigel . . .' Her heart skipped a beat and then turned to ice when she saw the signature.

'How's Lucy?' Susan immediately asked when Diana phoned home the next morning. She'd spent a sleepless night, desperate with worry, not only about her granddaughter but about the letter she'd found. Instinct forbade her from mentioning it to anyone at this juncture; better to wait until Lucy and Peter were on the mend. But its existence lay like a heavy weight over the heart, and the burning questions that filled her mind upset her deeply.

'She's still in a coma,' Diana replied, her voice flat and lifeless with worry and exhaustion. 'Peter's out of danger and Miranda is here.'

'You'll be staying at the hospital until Lucy recovers consciousness, I imagine?'

'Yes, we'll stay here.' Diana paused. 'She's terribly badly hurt, Mum. Her face is covered in dressings and they've shaved part of her head. Her arm is in plaster, and her ribs are strapped up. I'm so scared. Supposing she doesn't come out of the coma?'

Susan forced herself to sound strong and positive. 'Don't even think like that, darling. Of course she'll pull through. She's strong and fit, and it's amazing what powers of resilience the young have. Now, listen Diana. This barbecue party today . . .'

She heard her daughter gasp. 'Oh, God! I'd completely forgotten! What shall we do?'

'If you can tell me where the list of guests is, Tilly and I will ring round and put them off. And if there are any we can't get hold of, we'll go ahead and give them lunch.'

'Oh, Mum, would you? It's behind the bread bin on the kitchen dresser. I'd be so grateful . . .' Her voice trailed off.

'Leave it to me. Are you all right, darling?'

'Yes,' Diana replied in a small voice.

After she'd hung up, Susan realised she'd not asked after Nigel or how he was coping. Ever since she'd found that letter last night her mind had been filled with terrible suspicions. And if those suspicions were correct, how was she going to handle the future so far as he was concerned? Would she try and keep the truth from Diana, who was so naive? Who depended on Nigel, and looked up to him almost as if he'd taken the place of her late father. Who relied on him and trusted him utterly.

Of course she would say nothing. Pretend even to herself that she'd never found the letter. That way she'd be protecting Diana . . . or would she actually be betraying her?

'What's happening, Granny?' Tilly asked, bouncing into the kitchen at that moment. She'd washed her hair. It hung limply down her back like a fall of black silk.

'You and I are going to phone everyone to tell them the barbecue's off. Do you want my mobile? I can use the house phone.'

'Great. How's Lucy? Can we go and see her?'

'She's still unconscious, but let's see what your mother says later. We've got a lot to do here. It's nearly nine o'clock.' Susan waved the list. 'If we don't make these calls now, people will have left home. Let's get going.'

Miranda crossed her long legs, aware that her black leather trousers clung to her body like a second skin. Her red suede jacket clashed with her russet hair, but the whole effect was sexy and she knew it.

Nigel glanced across the hospital waiting room, where he and Diana still sat like zombies.

'Is there anything I can get you, Miranda?' She'd already spent several hours sitting by Peter's bed, and now she was waiting for them to complete more tests, before she returned to his ward.

'I shouldn't think so, unless that dreadful machine in the corridor dispenses brandy or whisky,' she said drily. 'As soon as I'm sure Peter's all right, we'll go back to London.' She glanced at Roger. His face was rigid with boredom, and he had spent a lot of the night pacing up and down the corridor, jingling the car keys in his pocket. 'Roger has things to do in town,' she added by way of explanation.

At the mention of his name, he forced a smile. 'I'm in no hurry.'

'Even so . . . I'm sure you have things to do.' Miranda paused, wondering what Diana and Nigel thought of him. She'd introduced him merely as a friend who'd been kind enough to drive her to Guildford. Nigel had looked at her without surprise and Diana, eyes bleary with tears, registered neither interest nor curiosity. But then, in her opinion, they were a boring couple. She'd never understood why Peter liked them – unless, of course, he was just putting on an act until after the marriage.

'Do you think the doctors will allow Peter to be moved to a London hospital?' she asked Nigel, who sat slumped in his chair gazing blankly at the floor.

'I shouldn't think so,' he replied wearily when he registered she was talking to him. 'Even when he's out of intensive care, I'm sure they'll want him to stay here.'

'I suppose so.' Her eyes flickered hungrily over Roger.

Although she thanked God that Peter hadn't been killed, the thought of trailing down to Guildford all the time was not her idea of fun.

'I'll ask them anyway,' she said stubbornly. 'He'd be much better off at the London Clinic.'

'That's up to you,' Nigel remarked shortly. 'This is a first-rate hospital. I can't see the point of moving him. Anyway, won't he want to be near Lucy?'

Diana suddenly burst into tears again. 'They were going to celebrate the engagement today . . .' She covered her face with her hands. 'I'm so frightened she's not . . . she's not . . .'

'Of course she's going to get better,' Nigel said robustly, putting his arm around her. 'You mustn't even think like that.'

Miranda looked at Roger, her plucked eyebrows raised. 'I think we should be going.'

He jumped to his feet, a look of relief on his face. 'Yeah. Right.' He glanced uncertainly at Nigel and Diana, who sat huddled close together.

'I'll be back later,' Miranda promised in the tone of voice used to pacify children. 'And of course I'll keep in touch by phone, but there doesn't seem to be much point in my staying while they complete the tests on Peter. I might as well go home, have a hot bath and a change of clothes, and then see if I can get him transferred to the London Clinic.'

Nigel nodded absently. For all he cared Miranda could clear off back to her hedonistic existence, her toy-boys and her selfish lifestyle. She hadn't even asked if she could see her future daughter-in-law and that made him wonder how much she really cared for Lucy.

At that moment a nurse put her head round the door and addressed Nigel and Diana.

'Would you like to sit with Lucy again? The doctor has carried out further tests and there's no change, but it would

31

be nice if you could talk to her. That helps, you know, if the patient is in a coma.'

They nodded eagerly. It was wonderful actually to have something to do after hours and hours of sitting, waiting for something to happen.

'Granny?' Tilly put her hand over the mouthpiece of the mobile phone. 'Mr and Mrs Winnington want to know which ward Lucy's in? They want to send flowers.'

Susan Butler put a tick against another name on the list and looked up. 'Tell them it's the Guildford General Hospital. I don't know which ward she's in. And thank them very much.'

They'd managed to get hold of most of the people on the list, with the exception of half a dozen couples.

'We'll have to go ahead and entertain them, won't we?' Tilly asked. 'I wish Dad was here to light the barbecue. He's the only one who knows how to get it going.'

'We'll cheat,' Susan asserted cheerfully. 'We'll cook everything in the oven and take it into the garden on big platters. After all, people won't expect much under the circumstances.'

'They're lucky to get anything.' Tilly sounded wistful. 'I wish Mummy would phone and tell us what's happening.'

'She will, as soon as there's news.'

By ten o'clock Mrs Warren, who lived in the village and came to Eastleigh Manor each day to clean, had arrived to give a hand. Susan had phoned her earlier and she was agog with curiosity to know every detail of the accident.

'Well, I never,' she kept saying.

The first guests arrived shortly after noon. Tilly, changed into clean jeans and a pale pink shirt, with her hair in a French plait, was ready with a jug of Pimms and a swift and breathless explanation for her parents' absence. Her voice trembled from time to time and her hands shook, especially when anyone sympathised. She was thankful when her grandmother appeared after a few minutes, as well groomed and calm as if she had spent the whole morning getting ready.

'My dears, I'm sorry everything is so chaotic,' she graciously told the assembled company, who were sipping their drinks in horrified silence. 'I tried to put everyone off for their own sakes . . .'

Some new arrivals strolled across the lawn, their innocent smiles indicating they had no idea what had happened.

'Hello, Susan!' The husband, Edgar Anderson greeted her with a kiss. His wife, Nancy, kissed her too, and without pausing said animatedly, 'Susan! It's so good to see you again. Isn't this fun? I hope nobody minds, but we brought a friend who is staying with us.' Nancy Anderson grabbed the arm of a tall, very tanned young man, who was smiling warmly. 'This is Simon Randall. Simon, this is Susan Butler, Diana Howard's mother.' Then she looked around expectantly. 'Where are Diana and Nigel? And where are the happy young couple? This party is to celebrate their engagement, isn't it?' she gushed, unaware of the sudden silence all around her.

'I'm so sorry. What must you think of us?' Simon said to Tilly. Lunch was nearly over, and they were sitting on a wooden bench in a secluded part of the garden. He'd found her there, blowing her nose on what looked like a strip of green loo paper, and it was obvious she'd been crying.

Tilly sniffed and gave him a watery smile. 'You weren't to know. Granny and I tried to get hold of the Andersons this morning, but you must have already left. Not that it matters now.'

Simon nodded ruefully. 'We left London after breakfast

because they wanted to show me Hampton Court on the way here.'

'You're from Australia, aren't you?' she asked shyly. It wasn't only his accent that had been the clue; he looked much healthier in an outdoor sort of way than other young men she'd met.

'Yup. I'm from Sydney.'

'How long are you over here for?'

'If I can find work, I'd like to stay for a year or so. I have an English grandmother in Suffolk; my father emigrated to Australia thirty years ago so I'm half British anyway.'

'Do you like it here?'

'So far I love it. Have you been to Australia?'

Tilly flushed, gratified at being treated like a grown-up. She felt amazingly at ease with this young man who did not treat her in a patronising way.

'I've hardly travelled at all,' she replied honestly. 'Actually, I'm still at school. Apart from family holidays in France or Portugal, I've been nowhere.'

Simon's smile deepened, showing even white teeth.

'You'll soon catch up once your studies are over. There's just you and your sister in the family, then?'

'Yes. Lucy is six years older than me. She's a researcher for City Radio. It's a new station but it's going awfully well, and she wants to become a producer in time.'

Somehow, talking about Lucy in a natural way made her feel better. Of course her sister would recover, said a voice in her head. In no time at all, she'd be telling Lucy all about this cool Australian and how they'd got talking right away, as if they'd known each other for ages. Tilly smiled gratefully at Simon, glad that he'd come for lunch after all.

'Great. She must be bright.'

'Oh, she is,' Tilly replied earnestly. 'She got ten GCSEs

and three A-levels. I know I shan't do nearly as well.'

'I bet you will! What are your subjects?'

They were still talking an hour later when the Andersons came looking for him.

'I think it's time we were heading back to London,' Nancy said, much subdued after her earlier faux pas.

Tilly walked with them to their car, wishing that Simon could stay.

'Will you let me know how your sister gets on?' he asked, while Nancy and Edgar said goodbye to Susan. 'Really, I mean it. I want to know. You've got the phone number, haven't you? I'll be staying with the Andersons for at least another week.'

'OK. I'll let you know.'

Simon's hand briefly touched her shoulder in a gesture of support and encouragement. 'She'll be fine. I'm sure of it.'

After they'd gone, Susan walked slowly back towards the house, her arm linked through Tilly's. 'That was tough, wasn't it, darling? Having to talk to all those people? You were brilliant. I don't know how I'd have coped without you.'

'Oh, Granny.' Tilly rested her head on Susan's shoulder. 'Lucy *is* going to be all right, isn't she?'

Susan's eyes looked troubled. 'God, I hope so. Usually I can tell . . .' Then she shook her head. 'I honestly don't know.'

'You knew she'd been in an accident?'

'Yes. I had a strong feeling about that. The news didn't really shock me at all.' She stopped and looked up at the sky as if searching for inspiration. 'Now . . . I'm not sure what's going to happen.' Then she sighed. 'Perhaps I'm trying too hard. These feelings come to me out of nowhere. The minute I *try* to feel what's going to happen, it's no good.'

'Have you always had second sight, Granny?'

'Unfortunately, yes. It's my Scottish blood. My grandmother was extraordinary. She knew exactly what the future held.' Susan laughed softly. 'In another day and age she'd have been regarded as a witch and burned at the stake!'

Tilly regarded her grandmother with round eyes. 'Do you think I've got the gift?'

'For your sake, my darling, I sincerely hope not.'

At that moment, they heard the telephone ringing in the house. They looked at each other, then Susan spoke.

'You get it, Tilly.' Her voice was shaky. 'You're quicker on your feet than I am.'

Miranda had assumed Roger would be staying with her. She stood on the pavement outside her apartment block, looking at him in anguish.

'Aren't you coming in?' It had never occurred to her that he'd want to go back to his own small flat in Islington after what she'd been through the previous night. Hadn't the trauma of Peter's terrible accident brought them closer? Cemented their relationship?

Roger had the grace to look slightly shamefaced. 'I need a change of clothes, Miranda, and if I don't get a few hours' sleep I'll be no good to anyone.'

Her lips tightened and she suddenly looked old, the lines round her eyes deepening, jawline sagging. In the morning light he could see her grey roots emerging under a wild tumble of orange-red hair that made her look young from the backview but became a grotesque parody of youth when she turned round.

'Why don't you have a bath and a sleep here?' she protested, a desperate note creeping into her voice.

'Thanks, but I really do have to get back. I'm expecting some calls.' He handed her the car keys with a forced smile. 'I'll get a cab. Ring you later, right?'

'You'll come for dinner tonight, won't you? I thought we'd

dig into that large tin of caviar. We could have it with vodka. And I'll get in some tournedos steaks and grill them with garlic the way you like . . .' Miranda knew she was begging but she couldn't help it. There was no way she could bear to be alone today, tonight, tomorrow, the day after. Tears rose to her eyes and a feeling of panic threatened to engulf her. She looked into Roger's eyes, hoping to tempt him with the basics of life: good food, good drink and good sex. She was generous with what she had to offer and all she asked in return was someone to be there, and to pretend, if nothing else, to care for her.

'Thanks, Miranda, but I'm going out this evening. Anyway, don't you think you should be with your son?'

It was like a slap on the face, and an icy wave of shock and misery swept through her. Her face looked pale and pinched. She turned and strode on her high-heeled boots towards the apartment entrance.

'Then don't fucking bother to come back at all!' she stormed over her shoulder. 'You're nothing but a fucking gigolo anyway!'

Once inside her own apartment on the third floor, she sloshed a large measure of vodka into a tumbler and added some tonic water, not minding that it was flat and tasted disgusting but swigging it back greedily. It was eleven o'clock in the morning and she didn't care. All she wanted was something to dull the pain; an agony that was more to do with what was happening in her own life than what had happened to her son.

The vodka hit her blood stream with a delicious rush, making her momentarily dizzy. Then, draining her glass, she poured herself another drink. Where did she go from here? Tears stung her eyes. Roger had been so unsympathetic. Didn't he realise she needed him? Quickly, she downed her second drink and poured herself a third. She knew she shouldn't, but what the hell? She needed to be cheered up.

For a moment she thought about her late father. It was the first time she'd recalled him in years. She'd been Daddy's pet. If he were alive now he'd have looked after her, made sure that she was all right. When she'd been a little girl, so pretty in her white organdie party frocks, he'd always swung her up in his arms and gazed at her proudly, calling her his 'little angel'. Her memories, idealised and romanticised by the passing of time, now became more than she could bear. Instead of making her feel better, the vodka seemed to have buried her under a black avalanche of despair.

Miranda threw herself down on the bed and broke into loud sobs. The sound of her weeping filled the flamboyant, satin-draped room. With her clenched fist jammed in her mouth she cried for her own lost youth and jaded looks, for her dead husband and father and for her injured son, but most of all she grieved for herself: for the unbearable loneliness she must face from now on. For the empty nights and the aching desire that never seemed to be assuaged. For a life that was no longer pleasurable and a future that looked bleak. Everything seemed to have gone from her.

'Hello?' Tilly clutched the phone, her heart pounding so hard she could hardly breathe.

'May I speak to Nigel Howard, please?' Relief flooded through Tilly. She had been sure it was one of her parents calling with news of Lucy.

'Mr Howard is unavailable,' she replied politely. 'May I take a message?'

'When will he be home?'

'I'm afraid I don't know.'

The voice became anxious. 'What do you mean? Where is he?'

'There's been an accident, and he is at my sister's bedside. She's in a coma and we don't know how long . . .' Her voice faltered.

'He can still be contacted, can't he?' the man asked after a slight pause. 'What's the number of the hospital?'

Susan had followed Tilly into the room and saw her distressed expression.

'Shall I take it?' she asked.

'It's a very rude man. He wants to talk to Daddy.'

Susan took the phone from her. 'Can I help you?' she asked. 'Who is this?'

'My name is Oliver Stephens and I would like to speak to Nigel Howard.'

Susan paused for a moment before replying, 'I'm afraid he's not here and I don't know when he will be returning. Goodbye.' Then she slammed down the receiver.

Tilly looked at her in amazement. 'Why did you hang up?'

'He's obviously a business colleague of your father's,' Susan replied shortly. 'Whatever he wants can wait. Now let's help Mrs Warren clear away. And what are we going to do with all those sausages?'

Without waiting for an answer, she hurried back into the garden, anxious to distract Tilly. In Christ's name, how long had this man been on the scene? And should she let Nigel know she now knew of his existence? The only trouble was, admitting her knowledge also suggested she condoned what was going on. Better, surely, to forget about the whole thing, and if the name Oliver Stephens ever came up, feign ignorance.

'Shall we put this food in the deep freeze, or give it to the dogs?' Tilly asked, holding a platter of cooked hamburgers and sausages, cold now and unappetising.

'The dogs,' Susan replied without hesitation. 'They'll think all their Christmases have come at once.' She turned to call the two black labradors who lay stretched lazily on the lawn in the sunshine. 'Mackie! Muffie!' With a bound, they came lolloping over, tails wagging.

While Tilly tenderly offered them succulent morsels with her fingers, which they took with dainty relish, Susan went indoors. The stress of all that had happened was suddenly too much. If she didn't sit down quietly for a few minutes to compose herself, she knew she'd start breaking up and then she'd be no use to anyone; just a seventy-year-old grandmother, another liability. Hurriedly she wiped her eyes and took a deep breath. Just when she'd thought she could put her feet up and worry about nothing more arduous than how the roses in her little garden were doing, everything had started falling apart. It was obvious Diana was going to need her even if Lucy recovered.

Three

Three days had passed and there had been no change in Lucy's condition. Diana and Nigel, increasingly distraught, kept a vigil by her bedside, taking it in turns at night, so that one of them at least could get some sleep in the 'on call' room along the corridor, which the nurses had put at their disposal. It was a tiny box-like room, with no windows but air conditioned, and it became their little haven, a retreat from the sight of so much medical equipment surrounding Lucy. There was just a bed, a chest-of-drawers, an armchair and a wash basin in the corner, but the bedside lamp had a red shade which cast a warm glow and it was blissfully quiet and free from hospital smells. On one of his quick trips back to Eastleigh Manor to fetch clean clothes, Nigel brought back a bottle of gin, some tonic water and a couple of glasses.

'People will think we're alcoholics,' Diana said, when he placed it on top of the chest of drawers.

'They can think what they like,' he replied. 'We've got the stress of sitting and waiting for Lucy to regain consciousness. They haven't.'

'How long is this going to go on, Nigel? I feel as if we're in limbo. We can't make plans for her return home, we can't do *anything* except sit and wait.'

He nodded. 'I know.' He didn't add that the doctor had warned him that morning that the longer Lucy remained in a

41

coma, the worse were her chances of making a recovery.

Diana didn't know how she was managing to survive the long days and the longer nights, but much to her surprise she seemed to be growing stronger instead of weaker. It was Nigel who was wilting, sinking into despair at times, although he kept saying they had no real need to worry. Then he'd slip off for a quick gin and tonic in their little room. Once she caught him making a phone call from the public pay phone in the corridor. He was talking rapidly and anxiously, but when she asked to whom he'd been talking, he brushed her question aside and said something vague about its being to do with the office.

Meanwhile Lucy lay swathed in dressings which almost completely covered her face and Diana longed to see just how badly injured she was beneath. But no one would tell her, beyond saying, 'She'll need some plastic surgery in due course, but it's wonderful what they can do these days.'

Not much comfort, she thought. But at least Lucy was still alive. Sitting by her side, hour after hour, Diana held her hand and talked softly to her about their plans for the future: her wedding, the flat she and Peter were buying, the way they were going to decorate it, the babies they would eventually have. On and on Diana talked, hoping something she said would rouse Lucy and bring her back to them.

'. . . and next year, darling,' she continued on the fourth morning, 'Daddy and I will rent a villa, in Portugal again, or maybe in the South of France, and we'll all fly out and have the most wonderful holiday and . . .'

'Peter?'

Diana caught her breath, looking at the still form of her daughter lying on the narrow hospital bed.

'Lucy?' she said urgently. Had she spoken? Nigel wasn't in the room at that moment, neither was any of the nurses.

'Lucy?' she said again. If only she could see into her eyes, see if she was regaining consciousness from her expression.

'Peter?' said a small voice again from under the bandages. 'Where's Peter?'

Diana pressed the bell, long and hard. 'Peter's all right, my darling. Everything's all right,' she said, almost shouting in her eagerness for Lucy to hear.

A nurse came hurrying into the room, eyes scanning the various instruments and dials, fingers encircling Lucy's wrist. 'Lucy!' she said, loudly and clearly. 'Lucy, how are you feeling? You've had a nice long sleep, haven't you, love?'

Diana held her breath. Supposing she'd imagined Lucy had spoken? Supposing she'd even dreamed it?

'. . . thirsty.'

'All right, love. We'll get you a nice drink in a few minutes,' the nurse said in a robust manner. 'Your mum will sit with you and I'll be right back.' She winked at Diana and gave a broad grin. 'She's back with us again,' she added in a low voice. 'I'll get the doctor to have a look at her.'

Clasping one of Lucy's small slim hands in both of hers, Diana experienced as great a surge of joy as on the day Lucy had been born. She was going to be all right! That was all that mattered. Her child had regained consciousness and she was going to live. A moment later she felt an arm around her shoulders. Nigel was bending over both of them, his face pink and suffused with emotion.

'Thank God! Oh, thank God,' he whispered. 'Lucy, my darling, you're going to be all right. Mummy and Daddy are here with you.'

'I . . . I can't see . . .' she quavered.

Diana shot Nigel a look of panic.

His smile deepened in understanding. 'That's just because you've got bandages over your eyes, sweetheart. Your eyes are fine.' He nodded to Diana, assuring her he spoke the truth. Lucy seemed to relax but only for a moment.

'Where's Peter? Daddy . . . I want Peter.'

'You'll see him presently, darling,' Diana cut in swiftly. 'Peter is fine. Absolutely fine. Don't worry about a thing.'

Lucy was quiet for a while, holding on to Diana's hand as she'd done as a small child, but from time to time whimpering pitifully, 'When can I see Peter?'

Although the doctor and nurses assured her that Peter was all right, but couldn't come and see her because his broken leg was strung up on a pulley, she still kept asking for him, refusing to believe he was alive. She seemed unconcerned about her own injuries although she kept asking for the dressings to be removed from her face, but all she wanted was Peter.

'Would you like to talk to him on the phone?' Nigel asked with sudden inspiration.

'Yes . . . yes, Daddy.'

Ten minutes later Nigel held his mobile phone to her ear. Peter spoke from his ward in another part of the hospital, having been briefed.

'Lucy? How are you, sweetheart? It's good to be able to talk to you at last.'

'Are you all right, Peter? I've been so worried.' Her voice was faint and whispery. His was surprisingly strong.

'I'm absolutely fine. I'm told we've both been very lucky.'

'Have we? I can't see, Peter. My face is covered in bandages.'

'Poor babe. Never mind. I'm sure they'll take them off soon. I wonder which of us will be well enough to visit the other first?'

'I hope I'm well in time for the wedding . . .' Lucy's voice drifted off shakily.

'You will be, babe, I promise. I may be on crutches, but

you'll be OK. Take my word for it.'

She tried to smile, but it hurt too much. There was a tight pulling pain and the bandages seemed stuck to one side of her mouth.

'Oh, Peter,' she sobbed, and felt her mother gripping her hand in an effort to comfort her. 'When can I see you?'

'As soon as they let me visit,' he replied cheerfully. 'Who knows? Once you get the bandages off, they may allow *you* to come and visit me. After all, I'm probably only a couple of hundred yards away. Silly, isn't it? I wonder if they'd let us have a double room? Not that I'd be much good in the sex stakes at the moment, with my leg tied to a frigging pulley!'

Lucy realised he was trying to cheer her up with his light-hearted banter, but she was beginning to feel ill again, trembly all over and slightly nauseous.

'I've got to go . . . I feel sick . . .' she said plaintively.

Diana took the phone from her and spoke. 'Peter, Lucy's very weak. She'll talk to you again, later.'

'Right. Don't worry, Diana. She doesn't sound too bad.'

'I'll come and visit you presently. Then we can talk.' She looked anxiously at Lucy. Her hands were shaking and her breathing seemed rapid. Seeing Diana's look of anxiety, the nurse smiled reassuringly.

'She's just very weak, and in shock. Don't worry. What she needs is complete rest.' She adjusted the saline drip that went into Lucy's good arm, the other being encased in plaster from above the elbow to her knuckles, and then took her blood pressure again, pursing her lips.

Diana looked at her with raised eyebrows.

'It's a bit low but that's to be expected.' She laid a hand on Lucy's bare shoulder. It felt cold and clammy. 'Are you chilly, love?'

'I'm hot,' she murmured. 'Baking hot.'

The nurse said nothing, felt her pulse for a minute, and then left the room.

Diana looked with concern at her daughter, wishing again that her face could be uncovered. It was as impossible to communicate with her as if there was a curtain hanging between them. The expression in a person's eyes revealed everything and this was being denied her. As Lucy lay silent now, breathing more quietly, Diana had no way of knowing if she was frightened, still felt sick, in pain, or reassured now that she'd spoken to Peter. There was only one way to find out and that was to ask, but she didn't want to worry her daughter with questions. It was enough, for the time being, that she'd regained consciousness.

'Why didn't you phone me yesterday? I waited in the *whole* day. You *promised* you'd call, Nigel. What the hell happened?'

'I'm at the hospital all day and every day at the moment, you know that. The last few days have been the worst in my life. For God's sake, you must understand, I've been frantic with worry. Anyway, I've told you, it's over. Finished. You've got to accept that.'

Nigel spoke from his car phone as he drove back to Eastleigh Manor later that day, in need of a bath, and some clean clothes. Thank God, he thought, he'd changed his mobile phone number. At least Oliver hadn't been able to get hold of him at Lucy's bedside, with Diana sitting there listening! The thought brought on the beginnings of a headache as his neck muscles tensed. What on God's earth had made him go for Oliver in the first place? And how he regretted it now. Christ, what a fool he'd been! It had only happened three times in his life, this insane burning passion for another man, when caution and consideration had been swept aside for the sake of lust, and the wild notion that this was what he'd always been looking for. Fool! Mad, crazy fool! It had ended in disaster every time, right from his first experience when he'd been eighteen.

He'd fallen in love with another student at Oxford. Jonathan had been blond and blue-eyed too, a music scholar with a large collection of classical records. To a background of Beethoven and Rachmaninov, the affair had blossomed and deepened until the night they'd slept together. After that there was no turning back. They had sworn to spend their lives together, travel the world, appreciate all the finer things of life . . . until the day Jonathan dumped him unceremoniously because he'd met someone else: a young man who played the clarinet with the Royal Philharmonic Orchestra. Nigel couldn't compete and gradually began to see the funny side of the whole affair.

What a fool he'd been! It would never happen again, of course. He was basically as heterosexual as the next man, and set out to prove it by wining and dining a succession of girls until he'd met Diana. Her sweetness and dependency on him made him fall deeply in love with her right away, and seemed to confirm that of course he was straight. There was no doubt about it. Sex with her was wonderfully tender and fulfilling. He adored her utterly. All he wanted was to marry her and have babies. Never again would he look at another man.

It was only when Tilly was on the way, eight years after their marriage, that he once again experienced that dark magic of a love he should have resisted . . . but couldn't. Diana was fat and heavily pregnant and found sex uncomfortable at the time, and Michael was tall and slim, athletic and blond – the most beautiful man Nigel had ever set eyes on. He found himself drawn into the relationship as if by a magnet. The temptation was too great, the love too powerful. At one point he almost thought he'd have to leave Diana, because the strain of keeping up a pretence and two separate lives at the same time made him feel like a juggler with a dozen plates spinning on sticks. He rushed from one to the other, frantically trying to keep them all spinning, for if one were to fall and crash, the whole act would be over.

Tilly was born and Michael decided to go and live in America. Nigel nearly had a nervous breakdown as he pretended to be the happy new father whilst in reality being once again the deserted, heart-broken lover. It had taken him two years to get over it and to find his way back to being a loving husband to Diana. Not that things were ever the same again but he put a lot of his stress down to problems in the finance company in which he worked, and as Diana was so involved with her new baby she accepted his explanation. Over the years he'd managed to rebuild his marriage, basing it on real affection, respect and friendship. That was until he met Oliver Stephens, who was in the army and stationed at barracks in London. Nigel had fallen headlong once again and had rented a small flat in town where they could meet unobserved. Sex had been wonderful.

Oliver was an adventurous lover, and an experienced one too. For a while Nigel exalted in his newfound love; he was nearly fifty but suddenly he felt young and virile again. He was able to say pressure of work kept him in London until late some evenings, and Diana was so engrossed with the prospect of Lucy's engagement and forthcoming wedding that she hardly seemed to notice. Anyway their love life had settled down by now and she seemed content with loving cuddles in bed and verbal assurances that he still loved her. Which he did, very much. It was just that he wasn't in love with her any more, and she no longer excited him.

Then he went to the rented flat one day and found a packet of Benson & Hedges cigarettes and a gold lighter on the bedside table. He'd never smoked in his life and neither did Oliver. In the showdown that followed, he told Oliver he never wanted to see him again then demanded his set of keys to the flat. Oliver flounced out in a rage, calling Nigel 'a mean old queen', but that wasn't the end of it. Overnight, he became obsessed, distraught at being given the push, and now he was hounding Nigel as possessively as a love-sick girl, as dementedly as someone suffering from paranoia. He kept apologising for taking someone else to the flat, swearing it hadn't meant anything to him, repeatedly saying it was Nigel he cared about, and no one else.

'How can it be over?' Oliver was crying down the phone now. 'You said there was no one like me! You said you'd love me for ever. You can't do this to me!'

'I can and I have, Oliver. No one cheats on me. You behaved badly and as far as I'm concerned, you're history.' With a firm click Nigel switched off the phone. He was entering the drive of Eastleigh Manor and, hearing him, Mackie and Muffie came bounding out of the house, slavering with delight. Nigel patted them in an absent-minded manner, his thoughts elsewhere. Oliver had become a serious threat. Nigel wished he'd just leave him alone, once and for all. The thought of Diana finding out what had been happening appalled him. Especially now. She wouldn't be able to stand the shock, coming on top of Lucy's accident.

Tilly came speeding out of the house and flung her arms around his neck. 'Hi, Dad! How's Lucy?'

Hugging her, he explained that she'd come out of her coma. 'She's even spoken to Peter on the phone,' he added with a tired smile.

'That's brilliant! Wow! Cool!'

'It's going to be a long haul,' he warned.

'Granny!' Tilly shot back into the house, shouting: 'Lucy's

49

going to be OK! Daddy says she's regained consciousness. Isn't that great?'

Susan emerged from the drawing-room into the hall. As always, she was elegant and groomed, in a wine-coloured skirt and blouse worn with pearls, her grey hair perfectly arranged.

'Is she really out of danger?' she asked. Nigel noticed that although she addressed the question to him she didn't look in his direction but instead gazed ahead, like someone who cannot see.

'Yes, they're very pleased with her,' he replied.

'And she's already spoken to Peter on the phone,' Tilly interjected breathlessly. 'Dad, how soon do you think she'll be home?'

'Some time yet, I suspect. Her arm is in plaster and her cracked ribs are strapped, but that's not the problem. It all depends on her face. They've done all they can for the time being, but she is going to need further surgery.' Nigel closed his eyes for a moment, trying to shut out the terrible memory of Lucy's injuries. He wouldn't even have recognised her if he hadn't been told it was her. And he dreaded, more than he could say, the moment when Diana realised how bad it was.

'They don't like keeping patients in hospital a minute longer than is necessary these days,' Susan observed, still avoiding eye contact with him. 'She may be home sooner than you think.'

As he bathed, lying in the hot pine-scented water to ease his aching limbs, he wondered why Susan was behaving so evasively. Had Oliver called the house again? Maybe he ought to get the number of the house phone changed and have it made ex-directory, too. But how would he explain that to Diana? Wearily he closed his eyes, longing for sleep and longing even more to be rid of the nagging worries that were going round and round in his head. He was beginning to feel he was on a video loop, repeating the same scene over and over until he went crazy.

Downstairs, Tilly was hopping around, her energy restored by the good news. 'Do you think Daddy will allow me to go to the hospital now, Granny? And you, too? Aren't you just dying to see Lucy?'

Susan's expression softened. 'Yes, I am, but let's wait and see what your mother says. Lucy mustn't get overtired. I'm just longing for the moment when she comes home. Then we can spoil her like mad.'

Tilly perched on the edge of the kitchen table, watching Susan spoon coffee into the percolator. 'Do you think they'll still get married in the summer?'

'Where are we now? The beginning of May.' Susan pursed her lips doubtfully. 'Somehow I think it's a bit unlikely. Peter will probably be on crutches still, if his leg's as bad as they say, and Lucy will be having further surgery. No, darling, I don't think so. Maybe they'll get married in the autumn. October is a lovely month. Your grandfather and I were married in October, and it was wonderful. All the trees were gold, and I remember the sky was blue – a really strong azure blue.' She smiled at the memory. 'It was a dazzling day.'

'You and Grandpa were very happy, weren't you?' Tilly asked softly. 'How long were you married? Forty-three years? Wow! Not many people stay married as long as that, nowadays.'

'We were blissfully happy. It was a marvellous marriage and I was very lucky.'

'Mum and Dad have a wonderful marriage, too, don't they?'

'Absolutely,' Susan agreed with more firmness in her voice than she'd intended.

'I'd *die* if they ever broke up.'

Her grandmother fixed a bright smile on her face. 'Well, as

that isn't likely to happen, I think you can look forward to a very long life.'

Darling Nigel . . . love ya! Ever, Oliver. The memory of green ink and rounded feminine handwriting on a white sheet of writing paper swam before Susan's eyes, causing her to spill the milk as she poured it into a jug.

'Watch out, Gran!' Tilly said.

'How stupid of me,' she mumbled. 'I really should wear my glasses all the time, I'm getting as blind as a bat.'

Nigel strolled into the kitchen at that moment, refreshed after a shave and a change of clothes. 'Is that coffee I smell?'

'It'll be ready in a few minutes. Do you want anything to eat?' Susan enquired.

'Shall I make you an omelette, Dad? I make jolly good omelettes. Or you could have scrambled eggs?' Tilly jumped down from the kitchen table, eager to make herself useful.

Her father looked at her fondly. 'My angel,' he said, putting his arm round her. 'Aren't you a kind girl?'

''Course!' She grinned at him. 'What's it to be? How about scrambled eggs with smoked salmon? We've got some smoked salmon, haven't we, Granny?'

Nigel caught Susan's eye, and in that split second he realised she knew. It was like a flashing signal passing between them, and although they both instantly averted their gaze, the knowledge hung in the air like a poisonous vapour.

Miranda switched on the large white television set in her bedroom and, reclining on her king-sized bed, settled herself against a mound of pillows. There was a programme she particularly wanted to watch, and for once she was glad she was alone. Not only was she exhausted, having driven down to Guildford and back to see Peter and pop in on Lucy, but she wanted to learn all she could about keeping young, or more importantly, keeping young-*looking*. She'd been taking Hormone Replacement Therapy for a couple of years now and that had certainly helped. Her skin had a healthy glow, her hair was still glossy, providing she had the roots dyed every three weeks and lots of conditioner applied after, and so far she didn't have a problem with her weight. But if she was going to keep up with Roger, who was being more attentive at the moment, she was going to have to do something drastic in the foreseeable future.

The screen blossomed into colour and, fascinated, Miranda switched off her phone so she wouldn't be disturbed. This was going to be worth watching. She could learn a lot.

Silvie Jacardy sat posed for the TV cameras by the swimming pool of her luxurious Hollywood villa, her blonde hair falling like glimmering gold to her tanned shoulders, her exquisite blue eyes sweeping provocatively over Matt Hillier, who was interviewing her for CBS. She crossed her shapely legs and smiled warmly as the lens zoomed in for a close-up. Matt, sitting facing her with his notes pinned to a clipboard, had a look of growing incredulity on his face. Silvie Jacardy was the most beautiful woman he had ever seen. Her drop-dead exquisiteness was something else. Unreal. Of course, it *was* unreal, he told himself. He cleared his throat and spoke.

'So tell me, Silvie, you say you owe your success in Hollywood, and the fact that you've starred in three films, to a plastic surgeon?'

Silvie's smile became broader, showing perfect white teeth. 'It's great,' she gushed. 'Dr Dick Kahlo is a wonderful person. He's done so much for me . . . given me confidence, you know . . . made me the person I am today.' Her voice was whisper-soft. She put a hand that did not look nearly so young as the rest of her up to her neck. Her nails were crimson talons.

'What has he actually done for you?' Matt coaxed.

Miranda, lounging on her bed, refilled her glass of wine, turned up the volume and snuggled back among her massed white lace pillows. This was *fascinating* and she didn't want to miss a word. She felt sure Silvie Jacardy was at *least* forty but she didn't look a day over twenty-seven.

'Well . . .' Silvie paused, tilting her head to one side as if to show her face at a better angle. 'Dr Kahlo did my nose. It was kinda large, so he lopped off an incy bit. Then he took a little tuck under my chin, right here.' She indicated the spot and gave a coy smile.

Matt seemed mesmerised. 'Did he do anything else?'

She giggled. 'My eyes kinda drooped, so he took a little nip out of my eyelids . . .' She tossed her head with a seductive movement and her hair swept across one of her shoulders with an almost audible swish of silk.

Matt's tone was deceptively gentle.

'Did you really need all that done? A beautiful woman like you?'

Silvie's smile was dazzling. It was as if she'd been injected with a substance to give her an instant high.

'Oh, I *wanted* it done! He more or less remodelled my whole face, and I just can't tell you how thrilling it was!' Then she glanced down at herself, shapely and curvaceous in a cut-away black swimsuit that seemed to make her legs go on for ever. On her feet she wore high-heeled white sandals and round one ankle a fine gold chain.

'He gave me bigger breasts,' she breathed. 'Can you imagine anything better than that? It was just wonderful. Then he flattened my tummy.' She laid a hand reverently on her own stomach. 'And he hitched up my butt a little bit.'

The camera cut to Matt's face. He looked stunned. 'And you're pleased with the results, Silvie?' he asked in a hollow voice. 'You really feel it's helped your film career?'

'Oh, yeah! It's changed my life. I'm just so grateful to Dr Kahlo. You know, he's a really great human being, and he's done the best he could for me. Why, it's like I've been reborn! Isn't that just the most marvellous thing?' Her blue eyes were totally sincere as was her voice.

'Sure . . . but did you want to be changed? Didn't you feel just a little bit insulted that he wanted to make so many . . . well, so many alterations?' *Jesus, what a lousy script*, Matt thought. *I feel like I'm talking about a fucking building.*

Silvie's giggle was ingenuous. 'I always knew he was doing it for my own good. I never felt bad about it. I think it's nice to be made beautiful, don't you?'

He side-stepped the question. 'Wasn't it all very painful?'

Silvie hesitated for a fraction of a second, then her perfect red-painted mouth formed a smile around perfect crowned teeth.

'It didn't hurt at all. I had the operations done in Dr Kahlo's own clinic, in the most wonderful high-tech operating theatre. Then I spent a little while recovering, which was like staying in a five-star hotel. Dr Kahlo believes that relaxing in a luxurious setting is an important part of the recovery programme. He likes to spoil his patients.'

'And was it expensive – this complete makeover?'

Her delicately reconstructed nose scented the air as if searching for an aroma that might bring with it the answer.

'I guess around a few thousand dollars,' she said at last.

'And now you've made several films?'

'That's right. My latest film is *Raging Rocks*.'

'And are you married? Do you have children?'

The smile looked fixed now. 'My children are my little dogs – Tai-Tai, Smoochy and Kiss-Kiss. Otherwise, I'm divorced.'

Matt's expression, on camera again, was inscrutable.

'Ah,' he said drily. 'And do you ever go in for a rebore?'

The blue eyes blinked in hurt surprise, the glossy mouth fell open. Then she shifted position, recrossed her legs and thrust forward her breasts, almost aggressively.

'From time to time I might have a little adjustment done,' she replied with studied calm. 'Maybe the odd silicone injection, or a little tuck.'

When the interview came to an end, Matt Hillier was pictured alone, standing against a panoramic view of distant hills, with the Hollywood sign in the background.

'Women, it seems,' he said looking directly into the camera, 'will go to any lengths to alter themselves. But is this because they are dissatisfied with the way they look, or because they a e anxious to retain their youth? There are always doctors who are willing to pander to a woman's vanity and, in Silvie Jacardy's case, enable her to further her career. Thousands of women pay millions of pounds every year to plastic surgeons, such as Dr Dick Kahlo, in order to change themselves. We have to ask ourselves the central question: is it worth it? Or are these doctors modern-day Frankensteins?'

The credits rolled, and Miranda reached for the *Radio Times*. *What* an interesting programme. She searched for the item in that day's listings, wanting to know more. Where was this fantastic clinic? Who was Dr Dick Kahlo? And how much exactly did all this cost? It didn't say. It had been the last part of a documentary called 'New Women', and was a repeat of a programme which had first been shown five years ago. Miranda threw down the paper sulkily and reached for a mirror. What she saw made her deeply discontented.

There were lines around her eyes, and also around her mouth. Her jawline had definitely lost its elasticity and her neck looked like beige crêpe paper. When she frowned, more wrinkles showed up on her forehead. Oh, God! She *was* showing her age. No amount of make-up or false eyelashes or hair dye was going to disguise the fact that she was growing old. Tears filled her eyes. She wasn't really *old*; women older than her found love again, even got married. But her image had always been young, sexy and raunchy. Unfortunately that image didn't adapt well to a woman of fifty-four. Roger was probably the last attractive man who would ever take her to bed. Unless she paid for it – and she didn't mean just by paying the bill in expensive restaurants. Some women actually paid men, in cash. The thought made her feel very sorry for herself. Tears spilled down her cheeks, dripping on to her leopard-patterned leotard top which she wore with tightly fitting black leggings. Not even her best friends could say she was ageing gracefully. She was past her prime and supposed it was time she changed her lifestyle, but, oh, it was going to be hard!

Four

Could he trust Susan not to tell Diana? That was the thought that burned in Nigel's brain all that day. He was back at the hospital, sitting by Lucy's bed while Diana went home for a rest, and asking himself a thousand times: should he tell her himself, before she found out? But what the hell was he going to say? A dozen scenarios flashed through his mind, none of them the truth. He could tell her Oliver Stephens was after a job in his firm and angry because there was no opening. He could say Oliver was a friend who wanted money for a gambling debt and was pressing him for a loan. He could say Oliver was a distant cousin who was mentally disturbed and given to making wild accusations. Or he could tell her Oliver was a homosexual who fancied him and wouldn't take no for an answer.

Nigel tried out all these explanations in his mind, and other ones too, as he sat by a sleeping Lucy, but he had a feeling Diana might not believe any of them. She was gullible but she wasn't a fool, and if her mother were to hint at the truth, Diana just might put two and two together. The thought made his face crumple as if he were in pain. Diana didn't deserve this new agony and he'd do anything to spare her. Certainly he'd never get involved in anything like this again. It had brought him a few fleeting moments of ecstasy but a great deal more pain than pleasure, and now he regretted ever meeting Oliver.

Lucy stirred. 'Mummy?'

Nigel reached for her hand. 'I'm here, darling. Mummy's at home having a rest.'

'How's Peter?'

'He's getting on extremely well. I saw him a little while ago. He sent you his love.'

'When can I see him, Daddy? I wish they'd take off these bandages.'

'They will, as soon as they can. Do you want to talk to him on the phone again?'

She squeezed his hand. 'Yes, please. Are *you* all right, Daddy? You can't go on sitting by my bed, night and day. You and Mummy must be exhausted.'

'As soon as they take off the bandages and you can sit up, we'll catch up on sleep. Right now I want to make sure my girl's OK.' He leaned forward, kissing her hand and looking at her with tender eyes. 'As soon as you're stronger we'll take you home, and then Mummy and I will spoil you something rotten.'

Lucy giggled, and the sound was the most beautiful thing Nigel had ever heard. There'd been a moment, in the past week, when he'd thought he'd never hear that sound again.

'We'll have to look after Peter, too. He'll be on crutches.'

'Of course we'll look after Peter,' Nigel declared stoutly. 'We'll set up a private nursing home at Eastleigh, if you like! With you and Peter as our VIP patients.'

She giggled again. 'When will they take off my bandages, Daddy? I want to see what my face is like.'

There was a long pause. This was the moment he had been dreading, but he'd already told the nurses that Lucy was on no account to be given a mirror.

'I'm not sure when they're coming off, darling,' he said with forced casualness.

'Sometimes it's terribly painful, Daddy. I can't even talk or move a muscle then. That's when they give me painkillers.'

'I know, sweetheart.' The doctor had told him they were giving her morphine every four hours. 'Just try and be patient. The great thing is you're alive, and you haven't lost a leg or an arm and neither has Peter.' *So how do you tell your beautiful twenty-one-year-old daughter that she's virtually lost her face?*

'That's true.' She nodded and her bravery broke his heart. 'They say I'll need some plastic surgery. I suppose Peter and I will have to put off the wedding?'

'Postpone,' he corrected her. 'Peter won't want to hobble down the aisle on crutches, anyway. We'll postpone it until you're both fully recovered.'

'I did so want a summer wedding, Daddy,' she said sadly. 'And I don't want to wait until *next* summer.'

'You may not have to. Anyway, don't let's worry about it now. I'll put you through to Peter.' A minute later he handed her the mobile phone and then slipped out of the room so she could talk to him in private.

'Are you feeling better, Peter?' asked Lucy. 'Does your leg still hurt dreadfully?'

He sounded cheerful. 'It's not too bad, Squiggles.'

She tried to smile as he called her by his pet name for her, but it hurt her mouth and cheek and she winced with pain.

'Are you all right?' he asked, concerned. 'You sound funny.'

Lucy tried to stifle the tears. 'My face is sore . . . and tight . . . and they haven't taken off the bandages yet, so that sometimes it itches.'

'Poor babe. Itching is a good sign, though. It means the skin is healing.'

'Does it? God, I hope it heals up soon. I honestly don't know how much more I can take, Pete.' She was sobbing now. 'And the worst part is not being able to see you.'

61

'Oh, Squiggles.' He was hoping the doctors would allow him to visit her in a wheelchair within the next few days, but didn't say anything as he didn't want to raise her hopes. 'You'll be up and about in no time, sweetheart. At least you'll be able to walk, which is more than I can.'

Lucy lay there wishing with all her heart that she could turn back the clock. Everything had been so perfect before the accident. Why did it all have to go wrong?

'When will we be able to get married now?' she wept. 'It could be ages before we're both OK again.'

'It shouldn't be all that long. There's nothing to stop us making all the plans, either. Drawing up lists, getting invitations printed, booking our honeymoon. You know, all that stuff.'

'Fixing a new date at St Mark's . . . but we don't know when the wedding will be now, do we?'

'The doctors should be able to give us some idea,' he pointed out. 'At least it will give us a target to work towards.'

'You're so brave, Pete. I know I'm wallowing in self-pity but I can't help it. It's lying here and not being able to *see* that's so dreadful. Whatever do people who have been blinded do?'

'God knows. You're feeling miserable because of shock. It's only natural.'

'Is it? Are you in shock, too?'

'Of course. I keep seeing that car somersaulting towards us, over the central reservation . . . Christ, we were lucky not to be killed.'

'*Were* some people killed?'

'I don't know, Squiggles.' He did, of course. One of the nurses had told him all about the fatalities but he didn't think it would help Lucy to know. She sounded so frail and he could just imagine her lying in her hospital bed, thin and white and deeply traumatised.

'Get some rest now,' he advised. 'I'll talk to you later. Thank God for mobile phones. This way we can be in touch all the time.'

'I know, it's wonderful. I love you, Pete.'

'Love you lots, sweetheart. Have a little sleep. Take care.'

'You too. 'Bye darling.'

''Bye, Squiggles.'

''Bye.' Lucy felt for the off switch, comforted by their conversation. Peter was always so positive. Of course they were only going to have to postpone their wedding. Maybe only by three or four months. Surely her face and his leg would have recovered by then? Pleasantly drowsy now, she lay back and planned her wedding dress. White taffeta, perhaps, with a full skirt and a train, she thought dreamily, and sleeves with ruffles . . . and her grandmother's lace veil. In a few minutes she was in a deep sleep, induced by morphine, exhaustion and shock.

In his room in another part of the hospital, Peter read the newspapers, watched television and made a few phone calls to his friends, conscious that he'd got off lightly considering the severity of the accident. What the doctors had feared might be internal injuries had turned out to be severe bruising only. His badly broken leg was a bore, but it could have been worse. Even if he had to be immobilised for a while with his leg strung up to a pulley, he could still enjoy life. Right now he felt hungry. He pressed the bell. Perhaps he could persuade that cute little red-headed nurse to get the tin of caviar his mother had brought him out of the fridge. That and a few crackers and a squeeze of lemon should see him through until dinner time.

'We're taking off your dressings today,' the nurse told Lucy the following day, 'and this time we won't be putting on any more.'

'Oh, I'm dying to see how I look,' she replied eagerly. She felt much better today, and although she was still on painkillers and had been told she couldn't go home yet, to have her face free of bandages was, she felt, a great step forward.

Gently, using sterilised water to ease off the dressings that had got stuck with blood, the nurse removed the gauze pads, the lint and the bandages. Lucy watched her closely, waiting to see the reaction, but her expression was impenetrable. With deft hands she revealed Lucy's features and showed no more emotion than if she'd been removing the skin of an onion.

'How does it look?' Lucy asked eagerly. With her good hand she reached for her cheek but the nurse grabbed her wrist.

'You mustn't touch,' she said, 'or you might get an infection. The doctor will be coming round in a few minutes to have a look at you.'

'Have you got a mirror? My mouth feels funny . . . sort of tight on one side, and my nose is blocked, but I don't think I've got a cold.'

'I'm afraid I don't have a mirror,' the nurse said abruptly as she gathered up the soiled dressings. Lucy looked around her hospital room, seeing it for the first time, and was amazed that while she had been in the terrible darkness of her bandages, she was in fact in this bright little room, with pale blue curtains and flowers on every surface. Her eyes, blinking in the sudden light, took a few moments to adjust to the sunshine pouring into the room and then she looked, amazed. There must have been at least twenty bouquets, some tied with big ribbon bows, others arranged in baskets. There were long-stemmed roses, arum lilies, Icelandic poppies and amaryllis, mixed with carnations, delphiniums, larkspur and peonies. Lucy had never seen such wonderful flowers in her life and couldn't believe they were all for her.

'How beautiful!' she gasped. 'Where did they all come from?'

The nurse handed her the little pile of cards that was on the window sill. 'These will tell you who they're from. Your mother has even written a description of the flowers on the back of each card.'

'Oh!' So touched she felt tearful, Lucy started reading them. '*Get well soon. Love, Aunt Moira.*' '*Heaps of love, Miranda.*' It took her several minutes to look at them all. Her work colleagues at City Radio had sent two dozen carnations. Tilly and Granny a large posy of sweetpeas. Friends in the village had sent several of the arrangements, and her old schoolfriend, Carol, who was going to be a bridesmaid at the wedding, had sent a huge basket of yellow roses. The last card was the best of all. It was from Peter, and although his mother must have ordered the bouquet from her own florist, he had written on the card himself.

'*Sorry to have got you into bed in this way. All my love for ever, Peter.*'

Lucy smiled, tucking the cards under her pillow. Then she reached for the mobile phone which she kept permanently at her side.

'Mr Beaumont's residence. Can I help you?' asked a man's voice, heavy with dignity.

Lucy started giggling. 'Peter? It's me. Thank you for the flowers. I've just seen them. Get it? *Seen* them?'

He sounded jubilant. 'You've got your bandages off, Squiggles? That's great. How do you feel?'

'It's marvellous to be able to see again, but my face feels very strange and there aren't any mirrors here, except the one above the wash basin, but I can't get out of bed to have a look because I'm strung up to various drips.'

'Does it still hurt?'

'Yes. They're still having to give me painkillers, and they won't let me touch my face because of infection.'

'Never mind, sweetheart. You're on the way to recovery now. You might be allowed to come and visit me before I can get to you! Think of that.'

'Wouldn't that be great? Oh, Pete, Mummy's just arrived. Can I ring you back?'

'Well, I'm not planning to go anywhere. Give your ma my love and I'll talk to you later.'

'Yes. 'Bye.' Lucy switched off the phone and looked at her mother with concern. 'Are you all right, Mummy? You look dreadful.'

White-faced, Diana dropped down into the leather armchair by Lucy's bed, praying she wouldn't faint. This was her first glimpse of her daughter's face and she was appalled. The surgeon who'd operated had talked to them about Lucy's condition, and counselled them on how they should react when in her presence, but Diana hadn't been prepared for this. She felt physically sick as she looked at the angry scars, one running from the corner of Lucy's mouth across her cheek. And her jaw! It looked as if it had been cobbled together with bloodied stitches. Her left cheekbone was black and swollen, her eyes scarlet puffy slits, her forehead deeply grazed; even her nose seemed to be at a strange angle.

With a deep sense of shock Diana realised she would not have recognised Lucy. Her beauty was shattered, her once fine skin deeply scored and bruised. Even her hair was darkened with matted blood, the crown partially shaved where they'd operated to remove the blood clot. This had been a girl with a flawless face, Diana thought as she tried to get a grip on herself. Then Lucy struggled to smile, but it was a lopsided grimace, painful to watch, revealing that even her front teeth had been pushed inwards and to one side.

'Isn't it great they've taken the bandages off, Mummy? They were so tight, but they told me they had to be, to prevent too much swelling.'

Diana fought back her tears with a superhuman effort. Lucy must not be allowed to know that her looks had been ruined. At least, not yet. Not until she was stronger. Not until she was well enough to be able to come to terms with what had happened.

'How do I look?' There was a pitiful eagerness in her voice. 'Have you got your compact? I'm dying to see how I look.'

'It's in my other bag, darling,' Diana said weakly. 'Does your face hurt?'

'Not really. They keep giving me something to take the pain away.'

At that moment, the surgeon who'd talked to Diana, Mr Maurice Clark, came into the room, smiling cheerfully and smelling of soap and freshly laundered white linen.

'Well, young lady,' he greeted Lucy jovially, 'and how are you today? Glad to have your bandages off, eh?'

She smiled carefully. 'Very glad.'

Mr Clark looked fixedly at Diana. 'Isn't she healing well?' he demanded. Then he bent to look closer at Lucy's face, examining every inch of it with obvious satisfaction. 'These contusions are going down nicely, and so is the swelling around your eyes. We should be able to take out the stitches on your jawline. The ones inside your mouth will dissolve by themselves.'

Straightening up, he went and stood by the end of her bed, his hands resting on the rail, his manner purposeful.

'Right, Lucy,' he began, reminding her of the geography teacher she'd had at school when he was about to deliver a lecture; alert with the desire to impart knowledge and given to outbursts of irritability if you didn't pay attention.

'Your face is coming along nicely, but you must realise you got quite a bashing and skin takes time to heal itself. So do bone and muscle and gristle. In time it *will* all heal, and you can have further surgery, of a cosmetic rather than life-saving nature, to restore your looks. But you must be patient. And don't be disheartened when you first see yourself. Rome wasn't built in a day. The nurses will tell you how to look after your face when you go home, how to clean your skin and all that, but be patient and we'll have another look at you in a few months. All right?'

Diana, who had heard the spiel before, watched Lucy's reaction. She was taking in all Mr Clark was saying and only looked despondent when she heard the words 'in a few months'.

After he'd gone, she said bravely, 'Well, at least Peter and I can *plan* the wedding, can't we?'

Diana struggled for self-control. 'Of course you can, darling. Would you like to watch some TV now? That's what Peter does. He says it really helps him pass the time.' She rose and went over to the small set which stood on a corner cabinet by the wash hand basin.

'I think I'd rather listen to the radio. I want to hear what City Radio are doing. I was working on several programmes when this happened. I wonder when I can get back to work?'

'Don't worry about that now, darling.'

'But I have to keep working, Mum. Peter can't manage the mortgage on the new flat all by himself.'

'I'm sure Daddy will help, until you're better.'

Lucy screwed up her face and it distorted as the injuries pulled it to one side, reminding Diana, to her horror, of a gargoyle.

Lucy winced. 'What's that?' Her fingers touched the ridged and angry scar.

68

'It's just a cut . . . and stitches. Leave it, sweetheart.' Diana spoke hurriedly. 'Didn't they say you mustn't touch your face because of infection?'

Lucy sighed. 'Do bring a mirror next time, Mummy. Or get Daddy to. It's so frustrating not knowing what I look like. Who knows? Peter might take one look at me and run for his life!' She giggled complacently, secure in the knowledge that nothing could come between them.

'Has Miranda been to see you again?'

'Not since the first couple of days. She's not very good at hospital visiting, is she? She spent the whole time telling me what a wonderful time she was having, going to lots of parties and restaurants and buying new clothes.' Lucy shook her head gingerly in case the movement hurt. 'I don't think she's had a day's illness in her life, and there was I, lying bandaged to the hilt, unable to see anything, while she told me how much her new outfit had cost and did I think it was nice? Honestly! How did Peter ever come to have a mother like that?'

'He obviously takes after his late father. Now why don't you have a little rest? Maybe a sleep, even? I'll be here if you want anything.'

Lucy closed her swollen and bloodshot eyes and snuggled down in the bed. 'Thanks, Mummy. Is Daddy coming later?'

'He'll be here this afternoon.'

'And Tilly? And Granny? I'd like to see them.' She was already beginning to feel drowsy as her most recent dose of morphine began to take effect.

'Of course, darling.' *I must warn them or they'll get a shock like I did*, Diana thought, amazed that she'd been able to hide from Lucy the reason for her initial near collapse. Although she'd been told what to expect, the reality had been infinitely worse and she doubted that even the most expert plastic surgery could restore Lucy's face to what it had been before.

* * *

'I can't believe you kept the truth from me,' Diana whispered to Nigel as they stood in the hospital corridor, along from Lucy's room.

He shrugged in a helpless way. 'Darling, I didn't want you to get upset. I was going to tell you before you saw her without the dressings, and believe me, she looks better today than she did immediately after the accident. I didn't know they were going to take them off so soon. It's wonderful what the . . .'

'But her face is *terrible*, Nigel!' Diana responded in distress. 'I nearly passed out when I saw her! Mr Clark never told us she'd look as bad as *that*! I'm not sure Tilly should see her at the moment.'

Nigel looked tired and strained. 'Lucy will think it odd if Tilly doesn't visit her. We should all try and act as naturally as possible. And not let her have a mirror for the time being.'

'What's Peter going to say when he sees her? Shouldn't *he* be warned?' Diana fretted. She couldn't help feeling protective towards Lucy, wanting to hide her away from the startled stares of others. Although never conceited about her looks, Lucy was nevertheless going to be devastated when she saw just how badly she'd been injured. Any young girl would feel the same. Especially on the eve of getting married to someone as attractive as Peter.

Feeling weighed down with despondency, Diana drove home, wishing she could change places with Lucy. She was forty-six, had been happily married for nearly twenty-five years, and had achieved everything she'd ever wanted. A wonderful husband, two children, a beautiful house in the country and a gracious standard of living. *It wouldn't have mattered if it had been my face*, she thought, as she gripped the steering wheel fiercely. Who would have cared? Nigel would still have loved her, her children would have felt compassion, and her mother would have been supportive. The best years of my life are over, she reflected sombrely. But how can I give Lucy's best years, yet to come, back to her? The need to make some sacrifice was great. At that moment she would have given everything she possessed, including her own soul, to have Lucy restored to the way she had been before. Hot tears stung her eyes for the child she loved so much. Her firstborn. Her baby. Grown now into a young woman of intelligence, humour and charm. If only . . .

She was crying so much she had to stop in a lay-by for to continue would have been dangerous. 'Why did it have to happen?' she said aloud, resting her head on the steering wheel. What had Lucy ever done to deserve this dreadful calamity? It was several minutes before she could continue her journey.

Diana brought the car to a standstill in the drive and hurried straight to her mother's cottage at the far end of the lawn. Susan had basically moved back into her own home, but they were still in and out of each other's houses several times a day.

'Mum?' Diana pushed open the front door which led into a small square hall. The rooms always smelled of flowers and wax polish, an aroma Diana had known and associated with her mother since she'd been a child.

'I'm in the kitchen,' Susan called back. To soothe her frayed nerves she was cooking, an occupation she found therapeutic. Spread out on the scrubbed tabletop were the ingredients for chicken casserole. 'I'm making masses,' she remarked, as she peeled off the golden skin of a Spanish onion. 'It will save you cooking.'

'Thanks.' Diana shot her a grateful look. Susan observed her more closely.

'What's wrong? Lucy's not worse, is she?'

Then Diana told her, trying to spare her the worst of the details. 'But her face is really bad, Mum,' she concluded. 'When you go and see her, don't let on that you're horrified.'

'Of course I'll hide my feelings but if we keep it from her completely, isn't she going to get an even worse shock when she sees herself in a mirror?' Susan asked sensibly. 'She knows she's got to have corrective surgery, doesn't she?'

Diana nodded, unable to speak.

'Well then,' Susan continued, 'why don't you talk to the doctors and ask them exactly what has to be done, so that when you talk to her, you speak from a position of knowledge. You can reassure her. Remind her how most of the women in Hollywood have been completely *reconstructed*. Take a positive attitude, Diana. Tell her that this is the moment when she can have all those little touches every woman seems to crave for, done while they're at it! Hasn't she always said her nose was a fraction too long? Well, this is the moment when she can do something about it.'

'I suppose you're right.'

'I know I'm right. She'll only fall apart and think her beauty is gone for ever if *you* think that. When she's stronger, make a few jokes about having a facelift yourself, to keep her company! Be as sympathetic as you like, but be positive, too. She mustn't be allowed to wallow, no matter what.' As she spoke, she sliced the onion deftly, and tipped the pale translucent slices into a pan. 'And if you think I'm weeping,' she added stoutly, as she wiped her eyes, 'I'm not. It's these bloody onions.'

'Where's Tilly?'

'Gone over to play tennis at the Tennants'. Oh, by the way, you know the Andersons brought a young Australian to the barbecue?'

'You did mention it.'

'He wants to stay in this country, and he's looking for a job to tide him over until he gets himself organised. Apparently he's good at gardening. Nancy Anderson says he's transformed their garden, but it really isn't big enough to justify their employing him. She wondered if you'd like him, here? Especially at the moment as Nigel doesn't have the time and old Herbert is past it.'

'Yes, I'm afraid it's too much for him now.' Herbert, who lived in the village, had helped Nigel for several years but his arthritis had almost crippled him the previous winter and now he could only hobble around.

'Sounds like a good idea,' Diana said. 'He's nice, is he?'

'Charming. A very nice type of young man, as your grandmother would have said,' Susan assured her. 'He can stay in my spare room, if you like? That way, he'll feel more independent than if he stays with you. I'll give him a key and he can come and go as he likes.'

Diana smiled. 'And you'd rather like his company?'

'I'm never averse to the company of young people,' her mother replied spiritedly. 'Shall I tell the Andersons that you'll take him on? Then he can phone you and fix everything. His name is Simon Randall.'

'Great. Nigel will be delighted. He was complaining about not having time to do the lawns last night.' Diana rose to go back to her own house.

'I'll bring the casserole over later, unless you'd like to eat here?' Susan suggested. 'It might be cosier.'

'That would be lovely. Thanks, Mum.'

Back at Eastleigh Manor, Diana let Mackie and Muffie into the garden while she listened to the messages on the answerphone. There was one for Nigel, from a man calling himself Oliver. He said he'd phone back later. Diana made a note of it on the message pad, remembering that he'd called on the night of the accident. Vaguely, she wondered what it was about.

Miranda had booked a table for one o'clock at San Lorenzo. It was crowded as usual, but because she'd told them she'd be entertaining Amelia Harrow, they'd given her one of their best corner tables, set under a jungle of hanging plants and creepers. The name of the actress still meant a lot although she hadn't been in a major film for twenty years. Miranda, arriving early because it would have blighted the whole lunch if she hadn't been there before Amelia, ordered herself a vodka and tonic. As usual the restaurant was crowded. She craned her neck to see if there was anyone interesting lunching today. This was the haunt of celebrities. Her only reward was a glimpse, through a palm, of a has-been pop singer and a fairly well-known model in a micro-mini kilt. No Princess Diana. No Joan Collins. She sighed in disappointment, but then remembered that she was hosting a major celebrity herself. The thought cheered her up so much she ordered another vodka and tonic.

At that moment, Amelia burst upon the crowded restaurant like a beacon of light. Dressed in a dazzling white suit and a hat with a soft floppy brim, she glided forward, the sheen of the pearls round her neck, the gloss of the scarlet on her lips, causing several people to turn and stare at her.

'Darling!' she shrilled, flinging up her white-gloved hands as she made a dive for Miranda.

'Darling!' gushed Miranda, as they touched cheeks and kissed air. 'How *are* you? It's been an age!'

'Exhausted, darling. I've been to a party every night since I arrived. You're looking well, sweetie.' Amelia settled herself with much wriggling and adjusting of her skirt and jacket, and then took off her gloves. 'Is Peter better? My *God*! What a terrible thing to happen.'

While Miranda answered her, and ordered more drinks, and asked for the menu, Amelia kept up a flow of chatter while her eyes darted around the room to see if there was anyone she knew, or, more importantly, anyone who might be useful.

'So when is the wedding going to be held?' she eventually asked. It was obvious it took a great effort on her part to concentrate on what Miranda had been saying.

'Darling, I've no idea. The last time I saw Lucy she was absolutely *shrouded* in bandages. I believe her face is wrecked.'

'*Oh, no!*' For the first time Amelia looked really interested. 'Her *face*! Christ! How does Peter feel about *that*?'

Miranda shrugged. 'I don't think he knows how bad it is. Nigel told me she's got to have *massive* plastic surgery. Isn't it awful?'

'Awful,' Amelia agreed, fastidiously wiping the corners of her mouth and smearing her table napkin with streaks of scarlet. 'Who's she going to go to?'

Miranda purposely sounded vague. 'I haven't a clue. Who is there? I did see a programme on the TV about a Dr Dick Kahlo. He sounded quite good. Maybe she should go to him?'

Amelia leaned closer and dropped her voice. 'He's the *best*. I've got dozens of friends who've been to him and I know him quite well.'

Miranda was dying to ask if he'd used his skills on Amelia's face but she didn't dare. 'Oh, well, I'll recommend him. Where is this clinic of his anyway?'

'Just outside New York. Give me Lucy's address and I'll write to her and give her an introduction to Dick. He doesn't take just anyone. He's a very dedicated man, and a serious plastic surgeon. He much prefers treating the victims of accidents to doing purely cosmetic surgery.' As she spoke she was reaching in her handbag for a snakeskin address book and a gold pen.

'That's not the impression I got from watching this TV programme. A starlet called Silvie was boasting that he'd reconstructed her from head to toe. She was a walking advertisement for everything from silicone breasts to a hitched-up bum!'

Amelia laughed, amused for the first time. There was no one in the restaurant whom she needed to impress so she could relax. 'Of course he does all that, and it does make for a more interesting TV show than serious surgery. He once did a massive amount of work on his wife, Rita, because she wanted to get into films too, then the spoilt bitch walked out on him and went off with a beach bum.'

'Does he charge much?' Miranda was aching to know everything about Dr Kahlo, as each glance in the mirror convinced her more and more that she needed to have something done about her face, if not her body although it was lean and supple and in fairly good condition. But her eyes! Her sagging jawline and neck!

'Plastic surgery is never cheap, so you're probably talking three or four thousand dollars for a small op. In the case of Lucy, if her face has been really badly injured you might be talking a lot more. It's far more expensive in America than it is here, but it's also more advanced. Dick has new techniques that haven't even been tried out in England.' Her pen was poised. 'Lucy . . .?'

'Lucy Howard, Eastleigh Manor, Near Godalming, Surrey,' Miranda replied, tight-lipped. This hadn't gone the way she'd wanted at all. What she'd really been after was the address and a few details about Dr Kahlo so she could write to him about herself. Mentioning Lucy had merely been a way of bringing the conversation around to plastic surgery.

'Great.' Amelia looked triumphant, tucking away her address book again. Then she sipped her drink, sucking the vodka and tonic through a floe of crushed ice. 'So what's your news, Miranda? Still seeing that young man?'

'Roger. He's fine,' she bristled. *What the hell did Amelia mean with that taunt about her young man?* 'Let's order, shall we?' This lunch was going to cost her over a hundred pounds so she might as well enjoy the food if nothing else.

Once again, Nigel returned Oliver's call from the mobile phone in his car. This was going to be the last time. He was not going to take any more from the man he had once loved but who had now become an insupportable menace, capable of ruining his life.

As soon as the telephone exchange at the barracks put him through to Oliver's office and he heard the familiar clipped voice say, 'Lieutenant Stephens speaking,' Nigel took a deep breath and launched on to the offensive.

'Why do you keep calling me?' he demanded. 'I have nothing more to say to you so you're wasting your time. And mine.'

Oliver's voice was shaky and anxious. 'I have a lot to say to you, Nigel. Please don't be like this. I'm sorry for what happened . . . I never meant to hurt you or upset you.'

'Then you should've thought of that before taking someone else to the flat, shouldn't you! We're finished, Oliver. You betrayed me. I will not be treated like that. Now get the hell out of my life.'

'You don't want your wife to know about us, do you?' Oliver asked. 'I could tell her, you know, if you refuse to see me again.'

'I'll see you dead first,' Nigel burst out, fear striking him like a blade through the heart.

'But we had so much going for us,' Oliver pleaded. 'You can't throw it all away now. I love you, Nigel. And I know that in your heart of hearts you feel the same way.'

Panicked, Nigel put his foot flat down on the accelerator and he held the steering wheel in a fierce grip. 'Just leave me alone. Believe me, if you go anywhere near Diana, you'll live to regret it.'

'I'm not going anywhere.' Oliver was angry too, now. 'You're so afraid of upsetting your miserable little life, with your dull suburban wife and your boring two point four children. Jesus Christ! With *me* you had fun! You *lived*! If you refuse to see me again I will talk to your wife, tell her about us.'

'And one more word from you and I go straight to your commanding officer,' Nigel roared as he took the bend in the country lane at eighty miles an hour.

'We're getting rid of all these today,' the nurse announced the next morning, removing the drips from Lucy's good arm. 'You don't need them any more.'

'What bliss. Now I'll be able to sleep on my side instead of being stuck on my back,' she observed in delight.

'We'll give you a nice blanket bath in a few minutes. That will freshen you up. Do you think you could manage a little breakfast?'

'It hurts to eat.' Since she'd regained consciousness she'd been drinking liquids through a straw. Her front teeth ached and her jaw was sharply painful when she opened her mouth.

'Then how about a nice cup of Complan?' As she spoke the nurse put her arm around Lucy's shoulders and eased her forward so she could slip another pillow behind her back. Lucy let out a thin wail.

'Ouch! Oh, my ribs!' The strapping round her middle was tight but to move was still agonising. 'I'm falling apart,' she said, trying to make a joke of it. 'What with my face and my ribs and my arm . . .'

'You could still dance. There's nothing wrong with your legs.'

'True.' Lucy's smile was wry. Then she went suddenly quiet. A thought had just occurred to her but she decided not to give voice to it. Better to wait until she was on her own.

It wasn't until an hour later, when she'd been washed and had her hair brushed, with promises that she could have it shampooed in a couple of days when her stitches were removed, that she very slowly and carefully swung her legs over the side of the bed. For a few minutes she sat on the edge, feeling sick and dizzy. The plaster, from her left armpit to halfway down her hand, seemed suddenly heavy and alien. Her face throbbed while a splitting headache made her long to lie down again. But she couldn't. She wasn't going to give in now. Curiosity overwhelmed her. She *must* see her face. Gingerly she rose to her feet, gripping the metal rail of the bed with her good arm. For a moment she stood quite still, waiting for the weakness in her legs to subside. Then, taking a deep breath, she started shuffling towards the wash basin, bent forward like an old woman.

Another wave of nausea swept over her, leaving her bathed in a chilly sweat. Reaching the basin, its rim struck cold to the palm of her hand as she grasped it to stop herself falling. The effort to pull herself up straight nearly made her faint. Black dots danced before her eyes. Bile rose to her throat. But at last her face was level with the square of mirror that was screwed to the wall. Bracing herself, she took a long hard look at a face she didn't recognise, at a countenance so distorted by injuries that for a wild bewildered moment she thought it must belong to someone else. Where had she gone? Surely this grotesque creature couldn't be her? Through swollen red slits a pair of terrified eyes looked back at her, beseeching her to prove them wrong. This gargoyle *couldn't* be her, could it? Lucy watched as the eyes filled with tears and the torn puffy mouth trembled, and in that second realised her face, as she knew it, was destroyed.

Clinging to the basin, swaying over it so that her forehead touched the mirror, she sobbed with grief and shock. No one had prepared her for anything as bad as this.

'What are you doing out of bed?' The nurse paused in horror before hurrying over to Lucy.

'Now come along. Back to bed. You shouldn't be walking around,' she continued bossily. She put strong arms around Lucy, and half guided, half carried her to the bed. 'There you are. Now I'll fetch you a nice cup of tea.'

Lucy continued to weep inconsolably. Curled up on her side, with her plastered arm lying heavily on her hip, she cried as if her heart would break. The nurse patted her shoulder sympathetically.

'Have a good cry, love. Let it out. Then you'll feel much better. And it's not the end of the world, you know. You're seeing your face at its worst today. Within a week or so the bruising will have gone and you'll begin to look like yourself again. And if any of the scars still show, a touch of plastic surgery will soon put that right.'

Lucy wasn't listening. Only one thought filled her mind. She couldn't inflict herself, hideously deformed as she now was, on Peter. Not that he'd wanted to marry her for her looks but how could she expect any man to want to be burdened with someone who looked so *frighteningly* damaged? It made her wonder how her parents had been able to compose themselves when they'd seen how badly she'd been injured. And why had no one warned her?

After a while she stopped weeping, more from exhaustion

80

than anything else. Relieved, the nurse tucked the blanket around her shoulders and told her to have a little sleep. She'd bring her a nice drink in a while, she promised, but Lucy had already fallen into a heavy slumber, her mind blocking off what she was not yet ready to face.

Five

It was difficult to write with one hand, but Lucy managed by wedging a corner of the pad of blue Basildon Bond under the heavy plaster on her left arm. The voluntary aide had brought in the writing paper and envelopes for her that morning.

'I want to thank everyone who sent me flowers,' Lucy had said the previous afternoon, when Mrs Haines had come into her room asking if there was any shopping she'd like done.

'Of course, my dear. Would you like a newspaper, too? Or some magazines?' She was an elderly widow who drew great personal solace from attending those who were less fortunate than herself, and she had a particularly soft spot for Lucy. For such a devastating accident to have happened to this charming young woman on the eve of her engagement filled Mrs Haines with sorrow.

'Just some writing paper . . . and a biro, please,' Lucy replied, giving her one of the five-pound notes Nigel had slipped into her locker drawer for expenses.

She decided to write the letter immediately; do it, get it over with, put the past behind her. In case she weakened and changed her mind. Not that she would, though. From the moment she'd seen herself in the mirror she'd known what she must do. There was no turning back. She signed her name with a flourish, the 'L' large and clearly defined. Then she somehow managed to tear off the sheet of paper, fold it in half, and stuff it into one of the matching envelopes. When one of the nurses came into her room with her lunch tray, which consisted of a bowl of soup, Lucy handed her the letter.

'I know it's an awful thing to ask when you're so busy but could you get Mrs Haines, if she's still here, to deliver this for me?' There was a catch in Lucy's voice. The nurse glanced at the envelope. It was addressed to Peter Beaumont in Room F2, Mansfield Ward.

'I should think that would be OK,' the nurse replied brightly. 'Isn't your phone working any more?'

'I think the battery's flat,' Lucy lied.

Nigel and Tilly came into the room at that moment. It was Tilly's first visit to her sister, and she'd been warned what to expect.

'Hi, there!' she exclaimed glancing around with admirable nonchalance. 'What is this? A hospital room or a flower shop?' She plonked a box of chocolates and the latest edition of *Vogue* on Lucy's lap. 'Your black eyes make you look like a panda!'

It was the right thing to say. Lucy shot her a grateful look.

'Thanks,' she said drily. 'Perhaps I should patent this exact shade of black and purple as the latest thing in eyeshadow.'

Tilly put her head on one side and regarded Lucy critically. 'With a tinge of yellow as well, I think.'

Lucy gave her new twisted smile. 'Oh, definitely. And a ruby hair rinse. That's vital.'

'To be applied to the roots only,' Tilly agreed.

Their father looked nervously from one daughter to the other but it was all right. The young had their own way of understanding and communicating with each other and Lucy seemed to have brightened at the sight of her sister.

'How are things, darling?' he asked. He'd heard the night before that she'd got out of bed to reach the mirror.

'Not so bad,' she replied carelessly. 'I'm going to insist on going home tomorrow. There's no point in my staying here.'

'You mustn't go until the doctors say you can.'

'But what's the point in staying? My arm's going to be in plaster for months, and there's nothing more that can be done to my face. I can just as easily stay in bed at home as remain here. And I'd rather be at home.'

'And I can fetch and carry when I'm home at the weekends,' Tilly interjected with enthusiasm. 'And Granny will be in her absolute element cooking special treats for you. She sent you her love, by the way. She couldn't come today because she's having our new gardener to stay and she's got to get the place ready, but I expect she'll come tomorrow.'

But Lucy wasn't listening. She was staring into space, her thoughts a few hundred yards away in Room F2, where by now Peter would probably be reading her letter.

'My darling Peter . . .' he read with surprise, and automatically reached for the phone. Why on earth was Lucy writing to him? Come to think of it, they hadn't spoken since the previous day but that was because the physiotherapist had spent ages giving him exercises he could do in bed, and by the time she'd finished, he'd fallen asleep, exhausted.

'. . . Although it breaks my heart to do so I am writing to break off our engagement because . . .' What the hell was this? He punched out her number, but a disembodied voice announced a moment later that the number was unobtainable. So Lucy had switched her phone off. '. . . because my injuries make it impossible to go ahead with the wedding,' he read on. 'It will be years, if ever, before I will be in a fit state to face the world, far less get married. Please try to understand. Dad has my engagement ring in safekeeping but I will see that it is returned to you. I'm sorry about this, but there's no way I can marry you now.' It was signed 'Lucy'. Nothing else. No word of love. No sign that she still cared.

Peter lay back against his pillows and tried to think rationally. Of course she didn't mean it. The shock and the pain she'd suffered had brought all this on. He must talk to her. Try and get her to see she was being silly. Of course they must be married as soon as they'd both recovered. They loved each other. They'd made such wonderful plans. Lucy couldn't go chucking the whole thing overboard just because of a car accident and a few scratches on her face! She'd got to be made to see sense. He must get his mother to talk to her. In frustration, he tried phoning once more. Lucy's mobile was still switched off. Then he punched the number for Eastleigh Manor. Maybe he could get some sense out of her parents.

Diana sounded shaken. 'I'm sorry Peter, I don't know anything about this. When did you say you got Lucy's letter?'

'At lunchtime. I've been trying to get hold of you all ever since, but Lucy's switched off her mobile.'

'We've been with her all afternoon. We only got home a few minutes ago.'

'I tried to get one of the nurses to take a message . . . anyway, what's happened, Diana? What's made her change her mind?' He sounded frantic. She spoke with care.

'I think she got a big shock yesterday when she saw her reflection in the mirror. Maybe she feels unable to face you, looking as she does at the moment.'

'But that's no reason to break off our engagement,' he protested. 'I love her. I don't care if she *has* got a few scars. No one's perfect. I'm an ugly old thing myself.'

Diana warmed to Peter's disparaging description of himself; he was in fact very attractive with laughing grey eyes and a lean tanned face.

'Give her time, Peter. She's suffering from severe shock, both physical and emotional.'

'As she's switched off her phone, I'm going to write her a note telling her not to be silly. But can you talk to her, too? Tell her she can't throw everything away, our whole future, because of this?'

'Lucy has a mind of her own, you know.'

'Yes, but she's over-reacting. She's got to be made to realise I still love her, no matter what. I thought she loved me, too. I didn't think anything would split us up.'

'I expect it's because she loves you that she doesn't want to inflict herself on you. She won't want your pity, you know, Peter.'

He sounded outraged. 'Why should I pity her, for God's sake?'

Diana paused. 'She *has* been very badly hurt,' she said at last. 'Give her time. Let her come to terms with what's happened and don't rush her.'

'Oh, I won't! I just want us to stay together, loving each other. I don't want us to part.' His voice quavered and Diana realised he was more distraught than she'd imagined.

'All you can do is tell her how much you love her, and assure her you're still there for her,' she said gently.

'I will. God! It's so *frustrating* being tied up to this bloody pulley thing. If only I could go and see her and explain how I feel. I suppose there's no chance of her being able to come and see me, is there? Couldn't she be brought to me in a wheelchair? I know if I could only talk to her, I'd be able to persuade her to change her mind.'

Diana felt a premonition of disaster like a cold hand being laid on her heart. What *would* Peter's reaction be if he saw her?

'I'll talk to the doctor and see what he says,' she replied evasively.

'So will I. There must be a way. Meanwhile I'll write her a note telling her how much I love her.'

Tearing a blank page from the back of a novel he'd been given, he began to write using a biro he'd borrowed from one of the nurses.

My darling little Squiggles

Please, *please* don't even *think* of breaking off our engagement. It doesn't matter what's happened as long as we have each other. Of course we're going to get married. I love you, love you, love you, Squiggles. Never doubt it. I don't care what you look like; you are you and *nothing* will ever make me feel any differently towards you.

You mean the world to me – we are made for each other. It's bad enough having a broken leg, but don't break my heart as well. Please switch on your phone again so I can tell you how much I love you and how I long for us to be together again. And put the ring back on your finger. I want everyone to know how much I long to marry you.

Loads of love, P.

When Lucy read the note she wept. Peter was the kindest, most loving man she'd ever met and it was typical of him to want to stand by her, no matter what. Perhaps he still did love her and maybe that love was strong enough to withstand the terrible thing that had happened to her, but right now she couldn't risk putting him to the test. If he were to reject her now she didn't think she'd ever recover from the hurt. Far better for her to put an end to their relationship and refuse to see him, because that way she'd at least keep her pride intact.

She read the letter once again and then with tears streaming down her cheeks, she folded it very carefully and put it in the envelope where she kept her money. Maybe one day . . . No. She wouldn't even let herself think about what might happen in the future. When Nigel came to visit her that evening she was sitting up in bed, her manner resolute.

'Daddy, I want to go home in the morning. I must get out of here as soon as possible.'

He frowned. 'Why the sudden hurry? I don't think they'll release you yet.'

'Release me? This isn't a prison, you know. As long as I rest when I get home and have old Dr Sutherland drop in to see me from time to time, I surely don't need to stay here? I *can't* stay here, Daddy. I *must* go home.' She sounded desperate, he thought. Diana had told him about the call from Peter but was Lucy so anxious to avoid a confrontation that she was prepared to discharge herself from hospital against doctor's orders?

'Not if the doctor says you can't,' he said firmly.

'I *must*!' Tears rolled down her purple cheeks, plopping on to her cotton nightdress. Her uninjured hand was clenched in a tight fist as she jammed it against her misshapen mouth. 'I *must*, Daddy. I can't let Peter see me like this and I'm so afraid he'll find a way . . . and then I'll be stuck in bed here . . . unable to get away . . . while he has a good gawp at my face. Please, Daddy. Tell the doctor I'll be well looked after at home . . .' She broke off, sobbing.

Nigel took her hand, gently prising open her slim fingers so that he could hold it between his own.

'My darling, don't upset yourself so. I'll do anything you want,' he promised. 'I'll talk to the doctor. See what can be arranged. We'd *love* to have you home with us, more than anything. I just want what is best for you.'

'I know.'

He kissed the crown of her head and the stench of stale blood filled his nostrils.

'Thanks.' Lucy squinted up at him in gratitude. 'There's no way Peter can get out of bed and come and visit me here, is there?'

'No way, I promise. The poor bugger is strung up to the ceiling like one of those turkeys you see in butchers' shops before Christmas, hanging upside down. He can't even roll on to his side.'

Lucy gave the flicker of a smile, more with relief than anything else.

After he'd kissed her goodnight, Nigel strolled along to where Peter lay, incarcerated.

'How are you doing, old chap?'

Peter switched off the TV set with his remote control and looked at Nigel anxiously.

'Have you been with Lucy? What does she say? I wrote to her earlier today, telling her we simply couldn't call off the engagement, but I haven't heard from her again.'

Nigel lowered himself on to the edge of the narrow wood-framed armchair by the side of the bed. The seat was cluttered with books and magazines and he eased himself carefully backwards until he found a more comfortable position.

'She needs time and space right now. Let her be for the moment, and I'm sure things will right themselves eventually.'

Peter spoke fretfully, his brow puckered. 'I don't understand why she's behaving like this?'

'Don't you?'

'We've survived the most awful ordeal and miraculously escaped with our lives; it should have brought us even closer together. Why doesn't she love me any more? Why does she want to end everything?'

'Try to be patient. You know her face was badly damaged, don't you?'

'Yes. My mother said she was all bandaged, but so what? I don't mind if she has a few scars. She's underestimating my feelings for her if she thinks that's going to make any difference.' He sounded quite offended at the thought.

'I think it goes much deeper than that, Peter. Just give her time to get her strength back and I'm sure she'll think differently.'

Thank Christ there hadn't been another squeak from Oliver, Nigel reflected as he left the hospital and walked briskly towards the car park. Perhaps threatening to go to his commanding officer had scared him off. Oliver had, for some reason, been on his mind all day. He hoped it wasn't telepathy. In the past, when they'd still been together, there had been an intangible link between them, a communication of thoughts and feelings that was almost eerie. He'd be thinking of Oliver in a vague sort of way, and the next thing there'd be a phone call or Oliver would turn up at his office.

'I thought I'd give you a surprise,' he would say, and in those days it had been a delightful event in Nigel's otherwise humdrum day. Then he would suggest they went somewhere for lunch or perhaps a drink. Often they took a cab and went to his secret flat.

Other times he'd contact Oliver on the spur of the moment, only to find his call was expected. They'd revelled in this mutual unexplained communication of thoughts, confirming in their own minds the closeness of their relationship.

Now, as he unlocked his car, he looked around almost furtively, as if he half expected Oliver to jump out from behind another vehicle. A moment later he realised with sick apprehension that he'd been right. Telepathy still did exist between them. The light indicating there was a message on his car phone told him that, without doubt, Oliver had been trying to get hold of him. The familiar and once loved voice spoke briefly, and what he said was to the point.

If Nigel didn't agree to seeing him again he'd tell Diana exactly what sort of a man she was married to.

Susan Butler waved her hand expansively. 'It's a small kitchen but I think I've got everything. And if you're hungry at any time, just help yourself. There's always plenty of bread and cheese, and a basket full of fruit.'

Simon Randall grinned with appreciation as he looked round the cheerful little country kitchen, with its Welsh dresser, gaily painted collection of pottery plates and mugs, and cosy seating arrangement in a window recess overlooking the garden. To have got himself fixed up as a temporary gardener with the Howard family was one thing; to find himself staying with Mrs Howard's mother, in her delightful cottage in the grounds, was really landing on his feet.

'This is very good of you, Mrs Butler,' he said gratefully. 'I'll be sure not to get under your feet and be a nuisance, but if there's anything you want fixing, just let me know and I'm your man.'

Susan looked at him circumspectly. He had an open-air appearance, tanned, his curling fair hair windswept, his body strong and muscular in faded jeans and a checked shirt. She could just imagine him riding the waves on a surfboard. Best of all so far as she was concerned, his expression was honest, humorous, and without guile. She decided she liked him immensely.

'Why don't you sit down and I'll make us some coffee? Then you can get unpacked and I'll show you around the garden. As you know, my eldest granddaughter has had a bad accident and life has been chaotic. My son-in-law hasn't had a moment and the weeds have taken over in a big way.' As she talked, she put on the Cona coffee machine, her rings glinting on her arthritic fingers as she spooned in the grounds with surprising dexterity.

'How is your granddaughter . . . Lucy's her name, isn't it? I remember Tilly telling me . . . how is she getting on?' He sat astride one of the wooden kitchen chairs, arms resting against its back.

'I hope she's coming home today.' Susan sank into the chair opposite and he realised how tired and strained she was behind the bravely bright exterior.

'So soon? I had the feeling she'd be in hospital for months. That's great.'

'Personally, I think it's too soon, but they don't keep people in hospital like they used to. In my day you were kept flat on your back for a month if you had your appendix out!'

'Yeah. Well, she must be chuffed to be coming home. The weather's so glorious she can sit out in the garden and that will do her a lot more good than lying in some stuffy hospital room.'

'Of course you're right. Nothing like a bit of fresh air. It'll be wonderful to have her back, too. She's been so badly hurt, poor darling.' Susan's voice dropped to a sad whisper. Then she made an obvious effort to sound more cheerful. 'Now tell me about yourself, Simon. Which part of Australia do you come from?'

'Sydney. We live right near the harbour. Originally my parents came from Scotland, but I was born in Australia and that's really my home.'

'Are you an only child?'

'I'm the youngest of five,' he replied with a laugh. 'We're scattered all over the world right now. My eldest brother David is in Hong Kong, my second brother Keith works in New Zealand. My two sisters are both married, one living in Kenya and the other in America.'

'Good Lord!' Susan adjusted her glasses and looked at him in horror. 'Your poor parents! They must miss you all dreadfully!' Involuntarily she glanced out of the kitchen window, seeing Eastleigh Manor at the far end of the lawn. 'How spoilt I am, with my daughter living a hundred yards away. I shall never complain about being lonely again!'

'My parents have got each other,' Simon pointed out. 'That makes a big difference. I'm sure if Ma was on her own she'd come and live with one of us.'

Susan looked at him, her smile warm in spite of her weariness.

'It sounds to me as if you come from a very nice family.'

'We get on OK.'

After they'd drunk their coffee, Simon went up to his bedroom which had sloping ceilings and overlooked the orchard. It was a bright little room, with birds nesting outside the window under the eaves, and an old-fashioned patchwork quilt covering the cherrywood bed. Plain white walls, a chair and a chest-of-drawers completed the cosy yet simple atmosphere, fulfilling his childhood fantasies of everything in the old country being small and quaint and picturesque.

It didn't take him long to unpack because all he had brought with him were a couple of pairs of jeans, several shirts and sweaters and a pair of strong leather boots. When he'd finished he sat by the window contemplating the next few months of his life, until, hopefully, he found a suitable job in engineering. So far he had only met Mrs Butler and her granddaughter but he liked them both. The old lady was not unlike his own mother: spirited, warm, strong and capable. The type of woman who would have thought nothing in the outback of defending her home with a gun. Tilly was an average sort of schoolgirl but with the promise of beauty. She reminded him of a gypsy: dark-haired, with eyes like shining olives and skin like a dusky peach. He wondered what Lucy was like, the adored eldest child. Destined to make a suitable marriage, he presumed, judging by the exterior of Eastleigh Manor and the obvious affluence of the Howard family. He was sure she was the sort of young lady who wouldn't be *allowed* to make an unsuitable match. These upper-class English families were funny about that sort of thing.

At that moment he saw a white vehicle in the distance, turning in through the drive gates. As it drew nearer he realised it was an ambulance. It pulled up outside the entrance of the big house and after a few minutes he saw someone in a wheelchair being pushed inside by a middle-aged couple. So Lucy had come home.

'Oh, God, it's so wonderful to be back,' she said, as Diana helped her into bed. 'I began to think I was going to be stuck in hospital for ever.' She lay back against the pillows and closed her eyes. Exhausted after the short ambulance ride, all she wanted to do was snuggle down and sleep but first she looked appreciatively around her room, comforted by the familiarity of everything. The pale green curtains, patterned with lily-of-the-valley, the old rocking chair with its white lace cushions, her little oak desk that had been her eighth birthday present, her pictures . . . all represented memories of a secure childhood.

'Is there anything I can get you, darling?' Diana asked.

'No, thank you, Mum. Just make sure Peter doesn't come anywhere near me . . . not that he'll be able to. At least not for a while anyway.'

'Don't worry about it. Now try and get some sleep. You know the doctor said you must stay quiet for the time being.'

'I know.' They'd given her instructions about bathing her face, and her eyes, too, and told her to avoid bending forward as this would exacerbate the bruising. At least she'd had her hair washed by a nurse that morning, leaning backwards over a basin which had hurt her neck. But now her head felt wonderfully clean, freed from the dried blood.

'Most important of all,' said Mr Clark, when he came to say goodbye, 'don't, on any account, sit in the sun. Don't let it anywhere near your face. Wear a hat with a large brim at all times, and dark glasses, and maybe a scarf as well.'

Lucy had looked astonished. 'I'd have thought it was the best thing! Surely the sun will help the scars to heal and give me a nice tan? When I had spots when I was younger, the sun always helped to clear them up.'

The surgeon had closed his eyes in mock horror. 'That's the *worst* thing you could do now. The sun will coarsen your skin and make the scars much more prominent. You must be very, very careful.' Then he winked at her to lighten the mood. 'It's very ageing, too! You don't want crow's feet at thirty, do you?'

Now, as she lay in her own bed, Lucy wondered how long it would be before life returned to normal. She'd been warned her arm would remain in plaster for three months and that her cracked ribs would be sore for the next few weeks. No one had told her, though, exactly what could be done for her face. It was going to take more than a little adjustment here and there to make her look even human again, she figured. Meanwhile, she would hide from the world. No one outside her immediate family must see that she looked like a parody of a horror mask.

Simon came down from his bedroom, having had a bath and changed his clothes. Susan was taking him over to the manor to meet Diana and Nigel, and he wasn't sure what he was supposed to wear. Just how formal were the Howards, living in that grand house of theirs? He'd been invited for supper and had visions of sitting at a candle-lit table, glittering with silver, and eating elegant portions of exotic food – whilst being the only person in the room wearing jeans and an open-necked shirt.

'We'll go in this way,' Susan said, heading for the back door. 'Diana's bound to be in the kitchen.'

Mackie and Muffie greeted them ecstatically, tongues lolling, tails wagging. Susan patted them affectionately and then they clustered round Simon.

'Diana, this is Simon Randall.'

Diana shook his hand and smiled graciously. He thought her a pretty woman, but in a faded way, like a sepia photograph, with her pale brown hair and eyes and lightly tanned skin. She went back to stirring a large saucepan of soup, from which emanated a delicious aroma of onions.

'I want to thank you for coming to our rescue,' she said. 'The garden is rapidly turning into a wilderness. We just haven't had a moment since my daughter's accident.'

'How is she? She came home today, didn't she?' he enquired politely.

'Shall I do the drinks?' Susan cut in. 'You look exhausted.'

'Yes, thanks!' Diana sank on to a kitchen chair by the central table. 'Do sit down, Simon. What would you like to drink?'

'A beer would be great. Thanks.'

Susan, he noticed, seemed as at home in her daughter's kitchen as she was in her own. While she fixed the drinks, he turned back to look at Diana.

'How's your daughter getting on?' he asked. 'Your mother told me she had just got engaged and was getting married at the end of the summer.'

'She was,' Diana replied sadly. 'I think the situation is rather on hold for the moment.'

'I'd say it was not so much on hold as totally cancelled, from what I gathered when I talked to her this afternoon,' Susan remarked drily, as she placed a tin of beer and a glass mug on the table in front of Simon. 'She was adamant that she neither wants to see nor hear from Peter again.'

'Was she?' Diana sounded fretful. 'Oh, dear, I'm afraid she thinks he'd go off her if he saw her like this, but her face *will* get better in due course. I'm sure of that.'

'It must have been a very worrying time for you,' Simon remarked sympathetically.

'It's been awful,' she admitted. 'Thank God the worst is over.'

Tilly, home for the weekend again, came swinging into the room, her long legs covering the distance from the doorway to the kitchen table in a few strides. Under one arm was her tennis racquet; around her waist she'd slung her pullover with the arms knotted in front.

'Hiya!' Plonking herself on a chair, she grinned at Simon. 'How's it going? Have you settled in yet?'

'Just about,' he replied. 'I see you've been playing tennis? Are you any good?'

'So-so,' she replied. 'Our neighbours have a court and they invite me over to play from time to time. If you'd like a game I can easily fix it. We could have a doubles match. You and me, and Anthea and Timmy. They're brother and sister and really cool.'

Simon spoke hesitantly. 'Well . . . er . . . I'm here to work. I don't think . . .'

Diana interrupted him. 'You're not expected to work *all* the time.'

'Quite,' agreed Susan. 'Consider yourself one of the family.

After all, the Andersons are friends of ours, and so that makes us friends, too. We don't go in for any of this employer-employee nonsense.'

Simon felt pleasantly surprised. Somehow he'd not expected an older English lady to be so outspoken and up-front.

'Good. Then I'll fix it,' said Tilly. She rose and stretched and he noticed her round young breasts showing through her tee-shirt. When she saw him looking, a red flush stung her cheeks and she dropped her arms quickly. 'When's dinner, Mum? I thought of having a bath first.'

'In about half an hour,' Diana replied. 'I've done a huge rack of lamb with roast potatoes, French beans, courgettes . . .'

Tilly stooped to fling her arms around her mother. 'Rack of lamb!' she exclaimed in delight. 'I'm *starving.*' She closed her eyes and sniffed the air in ecstasy. 'Where's Daddy?'

'I'm not sure. He had to meet someone on business.' Diana sounded vague. 'He said to start without him if he was late.'

Susan looked up sharply and stared at Diana for a moment but she seemed perfectly relaxed and if there was anything to suspect about Nigel's absence this evening, it had not struck her. But then she was used to Nigel's getting home late. He'd been coming home late for years.

'This is a double betrayal,' Nigel pointed out bitterly. 'First you cheat on me, in *my* flat, and then you threaten to spill the beans to my wife.'

He'd met Oliver in a discreet little pub near Richmond, where they'd had secret *rendezvous* at the height of their affair. In those heady days they'd been stirred by the romantic view of the river from high on Richmond Hill, and by the olde worlde atmosphere of the Three Feathers. That was due more to a figment of their imagination than anything else, because the establishment was strictly pseudo with its fibreglass beams and fake lead-paned windows.

'I don't care what you call it.' Today Oliver was sullen, bitter at being rejected. 'You're such a prissy old queen! Whoever said anything about fidelity? What age do you think you're living in? If you think a relationship bars you from seeing anyone else, that's your affair. You can count me out on that one!'

They were alone in the bar at this hour, seated by the 'inglenook' fireplace, but they kept their voices low and Nigel kept glancing nervously at the barmaid to make sure she wasn't listening.

'I had thought we cared for each other,' he said painfully. This was hurting him more than he'd expected. He'd fallen heavily in love with Oliver and, idealistically, had thought that love was returned.

'You obviously don't care for me enough to forgive and forget,' Oliver retorted. 'Why are you making such an issue of the one quick fling I had?'

'I expected you to be faithful.'

'As you've been faithful to your wife, I suppose?'

'Let's leave her out of this.'

'On the contrary, I'll make sure she's very much a part of this, if you walk out on me,' Oliver said defiantly.

'Oliver, it's over. Please try to understand. I don't want a show-down. I don't want to have to go to your commanding officer—'

'I bet you don't!'

'But I will if you threaten to tell Diana. She's been through enough in the last few weeks; she doesn't need this now. I'll do anything to protect her.'

'Maybe you should have thought of that before you embarked on an affair with me.' A look of desperation had come into his eyes and he was sweating. 'You promised me we'd always stay together. You said we had a real on-going relationship. And then just because . . . Christ! You'd think I was HIV positive or something, the way you're behaving now.'

Nigel looked stricken. 'You're not, are you?'

'What's it to you?' Oliver suddenly jumped to his feet, knocking over his glass. Nigel couldn't be sure whether Oliver's blue eyes blazed with anger or unshed tears as he turned and stormed out of the pub.

Lucy read the letter again, encouraged by its helpful and friendly tones. She'd never heard of Amelia Harrow who introduced herself as a friend of Peter's mother, but she explained that Miranda had told her all about the accident and, on hearing corrective surgery might be necessary, she was happy to recommend the most wonderful plastic surgeon in the world. She knew him personally, he had looked after many of her friends in Hollywood, and specialised in treating people who had been injured rather than those who just wanted to be beautified:

> His name is Dr Dick Kahlo. He has his own clinic on Long Island and I can promise you, the results of his work are astounding. When you are better, why don't you come and stay with me in New York, where I have an apartment, and maybe we could meet up with him? As he is an old friend and you have been in an accident, I'm sure I could arrange a special fee . . .

When Diana came up, Lucy handed her the letter.

'What do you think, Mum?'

'Amelia Harrow!' she exclaimed in an impressed voice when she saw the signature.

'Who is she?'

'*Who is she?*' Diana repeated incredulously. 'She's only one of Hollywood's biggest film stars. I suppose she's a bit past it now but she used to be terribly famous. Have you never seen *Now and Forever*? Or *The Favourite Child*? My God, I went to see all her films when I was young.' She skimmed the letter with growing interest. When she finished it she looked up at Lucy, and for the first time since the accident her daughter was really smiling.

'Doesn't she sound nice? Imagine her inviting you over to America so that she can take you in person to this doctor? That's so kind. I can hardly believe it.'

Lucy suddenly looked depressed. 'I don't suppose she'll want to help me when she knows I've broken off my engagement to Peter. She is a friend of Miranda's, after all, and that's why she's being helpful.' It broke her heart that Peter had been writing to her every day, begging her to reconsider her decision, but she'd remained adamant. How could she possibly let him be burdened for life with a woman whose face would shock everyone who set eyes on her? She was a *mess*, there was no denying it. There was no guarantee she'd get to look better in time, either. This Dr Kahlo hadn't even *seen* her. Hadn't assessed her injuries.

'I'll talk to Miranda,' Diana said, rising and smoothing the bedcover. 'I wonder if she's been to him herself? She's the sort of woman who would go in for facelifts, isn't she?' Then she remembered Susan's advice. 'Mind you, why don't I have the bags under my eyes removed at the same time? Perhaps we should go to this clinic together?'

Lucy smiled, knowing her mother didn't mean it. Diana was all for growing old gracefully. She didn't even wear much make-up.

'Anyway,' Lucy remarked, 'it was kind of Miranda to

mention it to this Amelia Harrow or whatever her name is. I'll write and thank her. I don't suppose we could afford this clinic, anyway.'

When she was alone again, she climbed out of bed and, going into the bathroom, sponged her face carefully with witch hazel, as she'd been told to do. This she accomplished, including brushing her teeth, without looking in the mirror. Then she padded to the window and looked out. After being so long indoors she longed to get out and breathe the fresh air. It was a nice day. Warm but not too sunny. If she wore a big hat and dark glasses, surely she could sit out for a bit? Someone was crossing the lawn. She leaned out further to see who it was. She saw a tall young man with fair curling hair striding towards the house. He was carrying a spade and looking purposeful. Then, as if he sensed he was being watched, he glanced up at the window, saw her, and grinned.

'G'day, Lucy,' he called out cheerily. 'Are you coming out? It's a beaut day.'

She withdrew in alarm, hiding her face behind the curtain. Who the hell was he? Disappointment welled up inside her as if from a cold dark spring. Now she wouldn't be able to go into the garden because he'd be there and she didn't want to be seen. Much later, when she'd finally dressed herself, hampered by the rigidity of her plastered arm, it suddenly struck her that the young man *had* seen her. Seen her and not seemed to notice her face. Of course her family would have told him about the accident. Warned him to pretend not to notice her injuries. That was why he'd acted as if it was the most natural thing in the world to see a girl hanging out of a window, her face like a gargoyle's.

Tilly found her struggling to do up the buttons of her favourite blue and white striped shirt.

'Here, Luce, let me,' she offered. 'Are you coming downstairs for lunch?'

'I don't know.' She sounded doubtful. 'Who's that young man in the garden?'

'That's Simon Randall. He's our new gardener and he's living with Granny in the cottage.' As she talked she buttoned Lucy's shirt and straightened the collar. 'That's better. Do you want to wear your blue belt?'

'No, thanks. My ribs are too sore. I suppose he knows about the accident.'

'Who? Simon? Yes, of course he does. Everyone knows. It's the talk of the village. Everyone keeps sending their love.'

Lucy slipped her feet into her canvas garden shoes and with her good hand reached for her sunglasses. She decided she *would* sit in the garden. But if this Simon what-ever-his-name-is expresses sympathy, she thought defensively, I'll tell him to mind his own business. She would *not* be pitied. Picking up a silk scarf that was hanging over the back of the chair, she tied it under the chin, well forward so that it covered the lower half of her cheeks. Then she put on a large straw hat she'd bought in Portugal the previous year.

'Are you ready?' Tilly had been hovering, anxious to be helpful.

'As ready as I'll ever be,' she said irritably. Then she made a little grimace which further distorted her face. 'Oh, well! Here Comes the Bride, I suppose,' she added drily.

Her sister pretended to wax lyrical. 'You look dark and mysterious; a woman with a secret past! Inscrutable, sphinx-like . . .'

'More like the Bride of Frankenstein,' she responded, 'with a face that could launch a thousand plastic surgeons.'

'Darling, how lovely to see you,' Diana exclaimed, when Lucy came into the kitchen. She'd been talking to Mrs Warren about cleaning the silver, but now they both started agitating around Lucy, offering her a chair, a drink, food, anything she wanted.

'Don't fuss, Mum,' she replied good-naturedly. 'I thought I'd sit in the garden for a while, but I don't want to have to talk to that new gardener you've got.'

For a moment Diana looked confused. 'Oh, you mean Simon?' she exclaimed. 'He's a friend of the Andersons'. Just helping out until he gets a proper job.'

'I don't want to see him,' she said stubbornly.

Tilly and Diana exchanged glances.

'Well . . . OK, darling,' Diana said. 'Shall I get a deck chair and put it under the chestnut tree? It's lovely and shady there.'

'Thanks, Mum.'

Tilly was rummaging around in the fridge. 'Want a coke?'

'Yes, please.'

While Diana hurried off to the garden, Lucy wandered around the ground-floor rooms of the house, seeing them from a new perspective. This was the first time she'd come downstairs since arriving home and everything looked strange and different, smaller somehow, and neater, as if the place had been deserted for several months. Yet it was only . . . what . . . three weeks since the accident? It seemed like a lifetime ago. By now the study desk should have been piled high with lists of guests, wedding invitations waiting to be sent out, estimates from florists, caterers and wine merchants, and all the paraphernalia of preparing for a country wedding. In the drawing-room there should have been copies of *Brides* magazine, piled up on the coffee table for she and her mother to pore and giggle over some of the wedding dress designs amid a clutter of fabric and lace samples. By now, she reflected sadly, the atmosphere should have been filled with excitement and expectancy, not this melancholy gloom as if someone had died. Even the vase of flowers her mother always arranged on a table in the bay window looked tired and wilting. But, of course, something *had* died: her future with Peter . . . or had it? She still loved him, still kept that first letter he'd sent when she'd broken off their engagement, still harboured a lingering hope that one day . . . maybe after her surgery . . . but, no, those were dangerous thoughts. Peter was an attractive young man. He could have any girl he wanted . . .

'There you are, darling,' Diana greeted her, as she stepped through the drawing-room French windows into the garden. Lucy glanced around rapidly, shrinking behind her scarf, hat and dark glasses. It was all right. She felt safe. There was no sign of the gardener anywhere.

Six

'Maybe she's right. Maybe it would be better if you didn't get married.' Miranda looked across the hospital bed to where Peter still lay, his leg no longer strung up to a pulley but protected from the weight of the bedding by a wire cage.

'I don't see why.' He looked pink and fretful and ruffled. 'At least she could come and see me now, and we could talk about it.'

'She's up and about?' Miranda's carefully painted eyebrows arched in surprise.

'So I believe. She's been home for a couple of weeks now and there was never anything wrong with her legs . . . unlike me.'

'Then you haven't actually seen her since the accident?'

'You know I haven't. What the hell difference does it make anyway?' Peter was rattled. It annoyed him that when his mother did come to see him she spent her time peering into the mirror of her compact, dabbing at her face with a tiny powder puff, adding another layer of gloss to her mouth, so it looked as if she'd smeared strawberry jam on her lips.

'So you don't really know how she looks now?' Miranda observed darkly.

'Does it matter?'

'Well . . .' She dragged out the word. 'If she's got to have a

107

lot of corrective surgery, she's probably no oil painting, is she? Thanks to me, Amelia Harrow wrote to Lucy and got a very full letter back from her. She described some of her injuries. Apparently, whatever it costs, Diana and Nigel say they'll pay for her to go to America to see this famous plastic surgeon. It was all my idea actually. I saw a documentary about him on TV. I've half a mind to approach him myself.' She raised her chin and smoothed her jawline, imagining it firm and smooth once again.

Peter looked at her in amazement. 'You? It's hardly worth it, is it?'

'Peter!' She felt devastated. Whichever way she took his remark, it was deeply hurtful. She felt tears sting her eyes.

'What do you mean? You make it sound as if I'm not going to live long enough to enjoy the benefit!'

'No, I didn't. I meant, it's probably very expensive and painful, and for what? Everyone grows old. It's not a disgrace. Why pretend to be younger than you are?'

'But I want to look good and continue to enjoy life.' Miranda bit her lip, sensing his lack of sympathy. Her good looks meant *so* much to her. They represented a way of life she was not prepared to give up. Not for years yet anyway. Apart from which, what had it got to do with him?

'When will you be getting out of here?' she asked to change the subject.

'Not long now, I hope. Jesus, I'm bored! I suppose I'll have to go to a convalescent home or something.'

'I suppose you will. It's a pity my flat doesn't have a second bedroom or you could have stayed with me.' A shaft of guilt penetrated as she realised with thankfulness that what she'd said was true.

'If Lucy hadn't broken off our engagement, I could have stayed with her at Eastleigh Manor,' he retorted.

'Perhaps it won't be long before you can go back to your own flat?'

'With all those stairs? You have to be joking.'

Miranda sat there, in her beautiful burgundy-red suede trouser suit, and wondered why she'd bothered coming at all. She and Peter had never been close and now that he was incapacitated his patience seemed strained to breaking point.

'Well, what do you expect me to *do*?' she asked in a martyred voice.

'Nothing.'

'Shall I go and see Lucy and try and get her to change her mind?'

'That would be fatal. You know how stubborn she is.'

Miranda made a final attempt at appeasement. 'I'm so sorry you've had this wretched bad luck, sweetheart. Why don't you come and stay with me? You can have my bed and I can easily sleep on the sofa. Then I can look after you . . .' He has no idea, she thought, what a sacrifice I'm making. But I'm prepared to do it because people will judge me a bad mother if I let him go to a convalescent home, and I need their approval.

She felt dashed when he retorted shortly: 'That would cramp your style though, wouldn't it? What about Roger? I can't see him enjoying a threesome of that sort.'

'You don't understand. Since your father died I've been lonely. I need friends, Peter. Roger doesn't interfere with your life, so why should you mind my going out with him?'

'It's bloody embarrassing, having a mother who's dating a man only a few years older than myself.'

'Don't be absurd! In this day and age . . .' She wasn't sure whether to laugh at him for being old-fashioned, or weep because his criticism had wounded her. Weren't mothers supposed to be regarded with respect and admiration by their sons? But in her heart of hearts she knew she wasn't acting like a conventional mother. But what the hell! She stood up and smoothed the soft suede of her trousers over her hips. If she didn't fill the stereotype of a mother in her mid-fifties then it was too damn' bad. This was her life, too. She'd bloody well do as she liked, and if Peter objected that was his problem.

'I'll be off then,' she said breezily. 'Take care of yourself and I'll pop down and see you again, before you leave here.' She leaned over him to kiss his cheek and a steamy heat seemed to emanate from her flushed skin. Estée Lauder's Beautiful enveloped him with its powerful fragrance. A moment later she had hurried away before he could see the mixture of hurt and defiance in her eyes.

Lucy struggled to her feet, batting the air in front of her with her good hand.

'Get *away*!' she cried out loudly. 'Oh, get away!' There was a hint of rising panic in her voice. Suddenly she heard footsteps pounding across the lawn.

'Stand still! I'll get rid of the little bugger!'

A moment later Simon had swiped away the angry wasp with a rolled up newspaper. He picked it up carefully by its wings and flung it into a nearby flower bed.

'You wouldn't want to tread on that with bare feet,' he announced cheerily, 'even though it's dead.'

Lucy sat down hurriedly again, pulling the brim of her straw hat lower over her eyes although she wore large dark glasses.

'Thanks,' she murmured. On the wicker table beside her chair was a bowl of fruit; Diana had thought it would be nice for her to have something to nibble as she relaxed in the garden.

'I think it's these plums that are causing the trouble. I've been plagued with wasps ever since I came out here this morning,' she remarked, keeping her face averted.

All Simon could see was the crown of her head and part of a scarf covering her cheeks.

'Why don't I take that fruit indoors?' he said easily.

'That's very kind.'

He noticed her empty coffee cup. 'I'm going to make myself some coffee. Could you use a refill?'

Lucy hesitated. She was thirsty and longing for something to drink, but at the same time didn't want to get into a friendly situation. Before she could answer, he spoke again.

'It's no trouble. Do you take milk and sugar?'

'Er – just milk, thank you.'

'No probs.'

Out of the corner of her eye she saw him move away. She reached for her book. If she was reading when he returned he was less likely to try and engage her in conversation.

'There you go.' His rich Australian accent was a change after Peter's clipped English tones.

'Thanks.' His hands, she noticed, as he placed her mug on the table, were large and tanned but the nails were well kept; they did not look like the hands of a manual labourer.

'I'll leave you to it, then,' Simon said, walking casually away across the lawn with his own mug. At the far end of the orchard, she saw him perch on the old stone wall. While he drank his coffee his gaze was fixed on the gentle landscape behind Susan's cottage.

Watching him covertly, she felt churlish. It wasn't his fault that she wanted to avoid the prying eyes of strangers. It struck her that he might be lonely, too, with his family so far away. And yet she wasn't ready to talk to anyone outside her immediate circle. The effort was too great. There was still so much that was unresolved in her own life, there was no room for anyone or anything else.

Lucy watched him on and off all morning but he kept out of her way, weeding the flower beds around the terrace and trimming the box hedge that divided the lawn from the kitchen garden, and she felt grateful that not once did he glance in her direction.

'There's a call for you, Lucy darling,' Diana said later that day, bringing the mobile phone into the drawing-room. A chilly breeze had come whipping across the South Downs after lunch and so Lucy had come indoors, leaving Simon to mow the lawns unobserved.

'Who is it?'

'It's Carol.'

'Oh, great!' Carol had been her best friend ever since the age of twelve when they'd been new girls at Heathfield and clung to each other in an initial paroxysm of home-sickness. Carol was supposed to have been her chief bridesmaid, too.

'Hiya,' Lucy greeted her eagerly. 'How are you? How was France? Did you have a great time? When did you get back?'

'An hour ago. Oh, Luce, how are you, sweetheart?'

'Ever seen *Daughter of Quasimodo*?' she quipped lightly. 'When are you coming to stay?'

'Whenever you like, but what's happening? Your mother told mine that you'd broken off your engagement? Is that true?'

'Yup. Peter's having a problem accepting my decision, but I'm definitely not marrying him. Not looking like I do now.'

'But you'll get better,' Carol reasoned. 'Anyway, I'm sure your looks will make no difference to him. He loves you, Luce. He's crazy about you. Why not just postpone the wedding instead of calling it all off?'

'He hasn't seen me,' Lucy said quietly. 'I'm making it easier for him this way. I just wish he'd understand instead of bombarding me with letters and calls – which I refuse to take – all the time.'

'At least you're home now. It must have been awful in hospital.'

'It wasn't a load of laughs. Listen, how about coming to stay tomorrow? Come in time for lunch. I'm going crazy with boredom and I want to hear all about France.'

'That would be great. Is there anything you want? I expect you've been deluged with books and magazines ... how about a silly game we can play like Trivial Pursuit? Something to keep the old grey matter ticking over before it rusts irretrievably?'

Lucy found herself laughing for what felt like the first time in years. 'Yes, I'd love that. And Carol . . .'

'Yes?'

'I want to warn you, you'll get a shock when you see me so be prepared. Miss World I'm not.'

'Sweetheart, I don't care if you look like a horse's arse! It's *you* I'm coming to see, and we'll have lots of laughs.'

Lucy felt cheered by Carol's call, but it was one thing to face a girlfriend, quite another to let her boyfriend, the man she loved and had hoped to marry, catch sight of her. His protestations that her 'scarring' in no way affected his feelings fell short of the mark. She was only too aware that, no matter how much plastic surgery she might have, her looks had to have been destroyed for ever. They could straighten her nose so that she could breathe properly, maybe stop her mouth being lopsided, build up her crushed cheekbones and fix her jaw, but at the end of it all, it would never again be *her*. This was inescapable and something she was going to have to come to terms with, sooner or later, but more than disfigurement itself, she realised that what she feared most of all was other people's reactions.

She walked slowly into the hall where there was a full-length mirror. As there was no one about, she gingerly removed her hat and the dark glasses which she wore all the time. Then she looked at herself, long and hard and dispassionately. How would *she* feel if she met herself in the street? For a while she regarded her reflection, turning her face this way and that. How could she expect any man to want to kiss her now, with her twisted mouth and knocked-in teeth? Who would even want to hold her close? She had lost so much weight she was all bones and sinews, her breasts as flat as a twelve year old's, and the arm that wasn't in plaster looked like a thin white stick protruding from her tee-shirt. It was the first time she'd seen herself full-length and she was shocked. If she'd been asked to identify herself, she'd have said she was looking at a starved creature from a concentration camp who had been kicked in the face until she was half dead.

'Why don't you put it on the hall table . . . ?' It was Diana's voice, and a second later she was leading Simon, who was carrying a gardenia plant in a Chinese pot, into the hall. 'It would look good here, don't you think?'

Lucy froze, glaring at them, caught in a moment of acute vulnerability.

'Oh, darling!' Diana exclaimed as if in apology.

Simon's eyes swept over Lucy candidly, and with a grin he spoke as if nothing was amiss.

'Hi there! Your ma's got me pot planting. Look at this little beaut! Straight out of the greenhouse. You haven't lived until you've had a sniff of this pong.' Without hesitation he offered up the plant to Lucy for her inspection, holding it inches away from her face. Among the dark shiny leaves were half a dozen perfect white blooms, the petals velvet soft and as smooth as a child's skin. Lucy looked at them and marvelled at their perfection.

'Have a good old sniff,' Simon said encouragingly. He was still smiling and his blue eyes were friendly. In that second she realised he was not regarding her with horror, or pity, or even curiosity. It was a straightforward look, as if he'd always known how she must look behind the dark glasses and wide-brimmed hat. Lucy leaned forward, breathing in the exquisitely heady perfume, finding it both sweet yet sharp.

'Umm. It's lovely,' she said, knowing that was a ridiculously inadequate thing to say. Then she inhaled more deeply. 'It's almost addictive, isn't it? I want to keep on smelling it.'

'Right on,' he agreed, and turned to Diana. 'You want it on the table here?'

She nodded. 'Are there any more ready to bring into the house?'

'There's one covered in buds, just about ready to open.'

Diana spoke to Lucy, who had put on her dark glasses again but not the hat. 'Would you like it in your room, darling? By your bed?'

She shook her head. 'No. I'm fed up with feeling like a patient. Can't we have it in the drawing-room? Then everyone can enjoy it. Carol is coming to stay tomorrow. I want to start living a more normal life again.'

'All right, darling.' There was a doubtful edge to Diana's voice.

Simon didn't say anything but he grinned at Lucy and gave her the hint of a wink, as if he was on her side. She smiled back, feeling as if they were conspirators.

A car with its horn beeping cheerfully came whizzing up the drive the next day, and with a flourish came to a stop beside the front door. Then a tall young woman with rippling corn-coloured hair jumped out of the driver's seat and waved to the figure standing at the ground-floor window.

'Carol!' Lucy shouted in greeting and, turning, rushed into the hall to meet her. Carol, who was taller and larger than her friend, enveloped her in a bear hug.

'God! You've lost weight *too*!' she exclaimed. 'You lucky thing. I've been on this new banana diet for a week now and I haven't lost an ounce.'

'There's nothing like a "crash" diet!' Lucy quipped instantly.

'Very funny.' Carol pretended to look severe.

'Come in. We'll unload the car later. How are you? I want to hear all your news.' Lucy led the way into the drawing-room, redolent today of the perfume of gardenias. Carol dropped into one of the big armchairs, her jeans-clad legs sprawled before her.

'What's with the disguise? Why the dark glasses and scarf and that absurd beach hat? You look like you're in Palm Beach, except you're not wearing enough jewellery.'

Slowly, Lucy took off the hat and scarf and glasses. 'There you are,' she said, facing Carol squarely. 'A pretty sight, isn't it?' There was no self-pity in her voice.

Carol looked steadily at her, determined to show no emotion. Inwardly, she was horrified. Lucy hadn't exaggerated the extent of her injuries; in fact they were far worse than Carol had expected. Fleetingly she could understand Lucy's refusal to see Peter. Outwardly she remained gently smiling.

'I can see that it must be awfully painful,' she said quietly. 'You've still got mammoth black eyes, and a lot of bruising. But I'm sure, when all the swelling has gone down, it won't look nearly so bad.'

'I'm probably going to America to have plastic surgery.' Lucy told her about the letter and kind offer from Amelia Harrow.

'Dr Kahlo? Why do I know that name?' Carol frowned in concentration. Then her face lit up. 'I know! There was a programme on TV about him. It mostly starred some bimbo starlet, false boobs and all, but he's *famous*. Wow! How much is that going to set you back? When are you going over there?'

'Not for a while yet. My face has to heal as much as possible before they can do anything.'

'Fancy Amelia Harrow writing to you! I can't believe it. I've always been a big fan of hers. I bet she's had her face redone, don't you think?'

'Bound to have.'

'At least it is a very bright light at the end of the tunnel,' Carol pointed out. 'I think you're going to be OK, babe,' she added, nodding slowly.

'You think?' Diana and Nigel had been rather negative about the whole thing, Lucy thought. Perhaps they hadn't wanted to raise her hopes.

'Isn't America the birthplace of cosmetic surgery?' Carol asked. 'I've always heard they're much more advanced than we are. This alters everything, doesn't it? You and Peter will get married now, won't you?'

There was a pained look in Lucy's eyes. 'I've made up my mind that's never going to happen. If the surgery isn't successful, how can I possibly expect Peter to be saddled with me for life? It wouldn't be fair on him and it wouldn't be fair on me. He could have any girl . . .'

'. . . and he's *bloody* lucky to have someone like you!' Carol retorted angrily. 'Don't you dare underestimate yourself. I can tell you one thing – he doesn't deserve you unless he sticks by you.'

'Oh, he wants to,' Lucy protested. 'This is none of his doing. It's my decision. He pesters me all the time but I don't want to talk to him. I've told him it's over, totally and finally, and I just wish he'd accept that.'

★　★　★

As the days passed, Lucy began to regain her strength. It was doing her good to be surrounded by her family and friends, and Carol always made her laugh, while Simon's laid-back manner made her feel less self-conscious about her looks. She still wore dark glasses all the time but only covered up when she was out in the garden.

Then came a set-back. Carol was awakened on the fifth night of her stay by screams. They were coming from Lucy's room, which was next to the spare room. Terrified that she might somehow have hurt herself, Carol threw herself out of bed and tore next door. The room was in darkness and Lucy was sitting up in bed, crying and sobbing hysterically.

'What is it, sweetheart?' Carol asked in alarm as she switched on the light.

Lucy shook her head, unable to speak. Her face was flushed and gleaming with sweat. Carol sat on the edge of the bed and put her arms around her.

'Have you got a pain, Luce?'

'I dreamed the accident was happening . . . I saw the car coming down . . . down on top of us . . .' she sobbed.

Carol hugged her. 'There, there. It's all right . . . You're safe now.'

Diana hurried into the room. 'What's happening?' she asked in agitation. 'I heard screams.'

'Lucy's had a nightmare,' Carol explained.

'I w-was going to be trapped under it,' Lucy wept. She still looked very frightened. 'I kn-knew I wasn't going to be able to g-get away.'

'Well, it's all over now, darling,' Diana said, trying to sound soothing but not succeeding. 'I'll go and make you some hot milk. Then you can go back to sleep.'

Lucy reached under her pillow for her handkerchief. She wiped her eyes and blew her nose.

'I'm scared of going to sleep again,' she admitted to Carol when her mother had left the room. 'You've no idea. It was so *real*. I was right there on the motorway with Peter driving, and then suddenly this car . . .' She broke off, shivering.

'Remember, it's over,' Carol said comfortingly. 'Nightmares are just nature's way of getting the shock of it all out of your system.'

The next morning, Lucy was tired but calm and cheerful again.

'Sorry about last night,' she said, grinning at Carol over her breakfast tray.

'Think nothing of it,' she replied airily. 'I thought you'd at least fallen down and broken the other arm or something.'

'No. Just made a fool of myself.'

'You did nothing of the kind. Listen, if you feel up to it, why don't we have a bit of a shopping trip today?'

Lucy looked stricken. 'Oh, I couldn't.'

'Why not? I wasn't thinking of whizzing down Bond Street; more like a quiet amble along Guildford High Street.'

'I don't want to be seen.'

'Who's going to see you – or recognise you – all swaddled up in scarves and hats and dark glasses? And if they do . . . so what?'

'I don't feel able to go out yet. I couldn't stand being stared at by strangers.'

Carol didn't pressure her. It was going to take much longer than anyone realised, she reckoned, for Lucy to recover psychologically. She'd already admitted that every night, while she was trying to go to sleep, she couldn't help picturing those last fatal seconds before the accident, as if they were on film. She talked of the terrible noise, like pistol shots, as the cars impacted. She recalled the way the world had turned monochrome, like an old-fashioned photograph. And she remembered thinking she was lying in the rain, only realising when she tasted it that it was her own blood wet upon her face.

That evening, after Lucy had gone upstairs, saying she was tired, Carol decided to broach the subject. Lucy's emotional state worried her much more than her injuries but neither Diana nor Nigel seemed aware that anything was wrong.

'Don't you think,' she began, looking at Diana, 'that Lucy ought to have counselling? I mean, her system's received the most enormous shock. Won't that have a lasting effect if she doesn't talk to someone now?'

'Talk . . . about what exactly?' Diana replied vaguely.

Carol glanced quickly at Nigel. 'Don't you think she ought to be in therapy?'

He nodded. 'Yes, I think she should.'

Over the lit candles, Diana's expression was scoffing.

'My dear Carol, I didn't know you'd been to America?' she said. 'Why should a sane, sensible girl like Lucy need to see a shrink? I've never heard such nonsense in my life.'

'Carol didn't say a shrink,' Nigel pointed out. 'Actually I think it's a very good idea. I thought of asking the doctor who looked after her at the hospital to recommend a counsellor.'

'They'll fill her with psycho-babble and give her a whole lot of hang-ups she never knew she had,' Diana retorted. 'There's nothing the matter with the poor little thing. Once her face has been straightened out, she'll be fine, and anyway, what is she supposed to talk *about*? Surely it's better she forgets about the accident as soon as possible? I think she's doing very well, myself. She never mentions it. She's not dwelling on what happened.'

Simon, who had been listening intently, spoke for the first time. 'That's the problem,' he said quietly.

Carol turned to him, glad of his support. 'Exactly. She's

being *too* brave. It must have been a horrific ordeal and it's bound to affect her subconsciously. I think she's either in denial, blocking the whole thing out, or it's going round and round in her head and she won't talk about it. She *must* be encouraged to talk.'

'You're right,' Nigel agreed.

'She's also being far too cool about breaking off her engagement to Peter,' Carol continued. 'After all, they've been together for two years, they'd planned to marry this summer, they'd found a new flat, and had their whole futures planned together. How can you let all that go, without suffering terrible regrets?'

Diana looked pained and helpless as she gazed down the table at Nigel.

'I thought it was only her face we had to worry about, Nigel,' she said.

Carol thought he looked immensely tired and careworn as he smiled patiently at his wife before replying. There was a sadness in his eyes she'd never noticed before and a certain grimness about the mouth.

'Nowadays, my dear, they take a holistic view,' he explained. 'The psychological effects of the accident may well be worse than the physical effects. Lucy *has* been too stoical, in my view. Actually I've been half expecting her to break down at some point. It would be healthier if she did.'

'But it'll make Lucy *think* there's something wrong with her mind if you take her off to a shrink.'

'I told you, a counsellor isn't a shrink,' Nigel said quite sharply.

'Can't she talk to us, darling? You and me, and Susan and Carol?' Diana suggested almost pleadingly, so deeply was she convinced that there was something shameful about psychiatric treatment. 'And Simon, too. She gets on very well with you, doesn't she, Simon?'

'But I'm not qualified,' he pointed out.

'We can all listen but none of us is qualified,' Nigel said.

'As she's bottling up everything, it needs someone who's trained to unlock the part of her psyche that she's shut off, to get her to talk in the first place. And when that *does* happen, none of us would know what to say. Then we might do more harm than good,' Carol said.

Nigel eyed her with renewed respect. 'Carol's hit the nail on the head. It's going to be difficult for anyone to shift the blockage in her mind.'

'That's because she doesn't *want* to talk, darling,' said Diana in mild surprise, as if they were all being silly. 'It's quite simple, really. I don't know what you're going on about. Lucy just wants to forget about the accident and I don't blame her.'

There was a moment's silence, and Carol and Simon exchanged looks.

'How can you be so *stupid*?' Nigel suddenly shouted angrily down the length of the dining-room table. 'You live in another world, Diana. You've no idea what the hell life is all about!' He spoke with such vehemence that Carol suddenly knew that this wasn't just about Lucy. There was something else, something that he'd kept locked inside himself, some intolerable burden of which his wife had no knowledge. It was true. Diana had always lived in a comfortable world of her own that did not extend much beyond running her beautiful house and bringing up her daughters as if they were still pretty little girls in party frocks.

'Goodness, look at the time! I think we should be getting back to the cottage,' Susan announced, getting to her feet and startling everyone. 'Come along, Simon. It's getting very late and you've got a heavy day in the kitchen garden tomorrow, haven't you?'

He got politely to his feet, pulling back her chair for her as he did so. 'Yeah. I've got a hot date with the potato patch,' he said lightly but looked confused by her sudden desire to leave. 'Thank you for a delicious dinner, Mrs Howard. I really enjoyed it.'

While Diana smiled graciously, Nigel, who had also risen, replied.

'It's very good to have you here, Simon, and I wish you'd call us by our first names. We don't go in for formality in this house. Anyway, being addressed as "Mr Howard" makes me feel a hundred!' he added, laughing.

'Let's take a trip together as soon as you're fit,' Carol suggested a few days later as they sat on the lawn in the cool shade of the spreading branches of a beech. She was due to return home the next day, and wanted to leave Lucy with something positive to look forward to.

'It's a great idea, but I've got to get back to work, you know,' she replied. 'I'm on compassionate leave at the moment, but how long am I going to be away? Another six months? Or more, with the corrective surgery? I'm so afraid City Radio will forget me. Everyone seems to want to get into television or radio and this couldn't have happened at a worse time in my career,' she added fretfully.

'You're still going to need a little trip,' Carol reasoned.

'I think going to America will be the only travelling I'll be doing for some time. I'm going to have to find a flat for myself now that I'm not getting married, and if my job's gone by the time I've recovered, I'm going to be broke as well as everything else. Oh, God! What a mess it all is.'

Lucy lay back and closed her eyes, longing for life to return to normal. On the ground beside her lay her discarded hat, scarf and glasses, but the minute she left the protection of the big old tree she knew she would have to put them on again.

'I'm sure they'll keep your job for you,' Carol said reassuringly. 'If not there are loads of other radio stations, aren't there? You could always get another job as a researcher.'

As they sat discussing the future they were unaware of someone coming up behind them from the direction of the house.

The first thing Lucy noticed was that Simon, weeding the herbaceous border, had suddenly stopped working and had straightened up to watch something intently.

'What's Simon looking at?' she asked curiously. Carol glanced up and they both turned towards the house to see for themselves.

It was Peter, dressed in a baggy grey track suit, hobbling towards them on crutches. His right foot, visible at the bottom of the trouser leg, was encased in plaster and supported by an iron instep rest. Although he walked with great difficulty his head was held high and he was smiling broadly.

'Lucy!' he called out triumphantly.

She leaned forward, aghast, realising her face was uncovered. Her hands flew up to cover her mouth . . . her nose . . . scrabbling frantically for her hat and glasses . . . anything to hide her injuries. But it was no use. Peter had seen her face, and he'd stopped and was staring at her as if he couldn't believe what he saw.

'Hello, Peter,' she said quietly, dropping her hands. She sat up, vulnerable and unprotected, looking levelly at him. A look of ill-concealed horror was spreading across his face.

'My God! You look *terrible*! You're scarred for life, aren't you?' he blurted out. The sudden sweaty pallor of his face reflected his shock. He shook his head in disbelief. 'I'd no idea you were going to look as bad as this.'

Lucy continued to sit rigidly in the deck chair, looking at

him. There was a silence in the garden as if all the countryside was holding its breath. Carol stood beside Lucy, saying nothing. Simon, by the flower bed, watched and kept dangerously still.

Peter shifted his weight, licking his bottom lip. It was obvious that he was desperately searching for a way of escape. Then he spoke.

'I . . . I came over to try to . . . umm . . . to try to persuade you to marry me, but now I can see why . . . you were right; there's no way we could get married now. Not with you looking like that.'

For what seemed an eternity the four of them remained stock still, characters in a tableau of such tragic intensity that Lucy felt herself grow icy. Then Peter turned away, crutches digging into the lawn like the claws of a crab intent on getting away before being engulfed by the incoming tide. He nearly tripped as he stepped on to the gravel path. Then he bundled himself through the drawing-room French windows and disappeared into the house. A minute later they heard the sound of a car driving away.

Lucy crumpled, sliding out of her chair and sinking down on to the grass, her plastered arm sticking out grotesquely in front of her, her other arm wrapped across her front as if to protect herself.

Carol gazed towards the house, her eyes blazing.

'The little bugger!' she roared. 'How *dare* he!'

Lucy couldn't speak. Wrenching sobs made it difficult for her even to breathe. Crouched on the ground, the life seemed to be draining out of her. Simon came bounding over, lifting her up with great care. Then he carried her into the house and laid her on the sofa in the drawing-room.

'It's OK,' he kept saying, reassuringly. 'It's OK. Let it out.'

'I thought he loved me . . .' she kept sobbing. 'Did you see his face? Did you see how he looked at me?'

Carol and Simon looked at each other and were unable to conjure up words of comfort. Appalled by the scene they'd just witnessed, they held Lucy's hands and hoped she felt their silent sympathy.

Diana rushed into the room. 'What's happened?'

'Who let him in?' Carol burst out, furiously.

Diana looked at her uncomprehendingly. 'Who?' Then she went over to Lucy and put her arms around her. 'What's wrong, darling?'

'Peter was here,' Carol explained, her face flushed with anger, long blonde hair dishevelled. 'He behaved terribly badly. I can't believe *anyone* would act like that! Christ! I wish I'd told him what I thought of him.'

'Peter? Here?' Diana looked around as if she expected to see him lurking in a corner. 'What was he doing? What did he say?'

Mrs Warren lumbered into the room at that moment, carrying as usual a duster in one hand and an aerosol of Pledge in the other as an indication of how hard she was working.

'What's going on?' she asked, her face alight with curiosity. 'I let Mr Beaumont in, if you wants to know. He came in a taxi and said as he wanted to surprise Miss Lucy. No one told me I shouldn't,' she added defiantly.

'It's all right, Mrs Warren,' Diana said in a pacifying voice. 'You weren't to know.'

'It's not all right at all,' Carol burst out rudely. Lucy was still sobbing, as if all the pain and shock she'd suffered had suddenly become too much to bear.

'Get her some brandy,' Diana was saying distractedly as she stroked Lucy's head with feverish intensity.

'She *needs* to cry,' Carol pointed out. 'I just wish, though, that it hadn't been that bugger who broke down her resistance.'

'But what *happened*?'

To their surprise, Lucy stopped sobbing and spoke brokenly through her tears.

'Peter was *repelled* when he saw me . . . he left . . . it was awful.' The tears ran down her cheeks and plopped on to the silk sofa cushions. Her swollen and distorted mouth trembled. 'In spite of breaking off our engagement, I had hoped . . . secretly . . . that one day we'd marry,' she wept. Then she looked up piteously, wiping her eyes with the back of her good hand. 'Do I look *that* terrible?'

'Darling, of course you don't,' Diana said hurriedly.

Carol plonked herself on the arm of the sofa beside Lucy, and gave her a comforting hug.

'I tell you one thing,' she said sturdily, 'at least you have the satisfaction of knowing that *you* chucked him! Don't let him get to you, babe. The little sod doesn't deserve another thought. I hope he rots in hell.'

'What did he *say*?' Diana asked, almost irritably. For some reason she resented the fact that Carol's words were having a better effect on Lucy than hers.

'He didn't say anything, really,' Lucy whispered. 'One look at my face and he was off. End of story.'

'Rotten little swine. I wish I'd broken his other leg!' Carol was still seething.

Mrs Warren came back with the brandy decanter and a tumbler. 'Here you go, love,' she said, shoving them at Lucy.

Simon stepped forward. 'Here. Let me.' Then he looked down at Lucy, his face filled with compassion. 'I reckon a cup of hot tea with loads of sugar would be better than this stuff.'

After Lucy had drunk her tea, and blown her nose several times, which caused a searing pain to shoot like hot needles through her sinuses, she clambered wearily to her feet, like an old woman.

Her mother watched her anxiously. 'Where are you going, darling?'

'To my room.'

'Can I get you anything?'

'No, thanks.'

They watched her go, a sad resigned little figure but with her head held high, respecting her need to be on her own for a while after the devastating humiliation of Peter's unexpected visit.

'He's going to pay for what he did just now,' Carol said vengefully.

'At least it's helped to break down her resistance,' Simon observed. 'She couldn't have gone on much longer being brave about everything. It wasn't healthy.'

Carol turned on him, protective of Lucy. 'But she's plucky by nature,' she informed him. 'She never even made a fuss about things when she was a little girl.'

Two days later Lucy received a letter from Peter. Recognising the familiar, neat handwriting, she snatched it up from the hall table, and hurried to her room where she could read it undisturbed. Her heart was hammering. She ripped open the envelope with shaking hands.

Dear Lucy,

Having seen you yesterday, I realise that I could never marry you, now. It wouldn't be fair to you, and it wouldn't be fair to me, either. I'll arrange for a removal van to collect your things from the flat and have them sent to your home. I don't suppose you're in a great hurry for them, are you? I'm off to convalesce at a health

farm for a few weeks which I'm greatly looking forward
to, having had quite enough of hospital life.

Yours, Peter.

Instead of keeping this letter, as she had the others, Lucy tore
it into tiny pieces as the tears streamed down her cheeks.
Peter was right about one thing: she wasn't in a hurry to have
her things back. Her belongings were part of a life that now
seemed to be most definitely over.

Seven

It was already autumn. The heat had gone out of the sun and the afternoons had begun to get chilly. Lucy could no longer sit in the garden so she took brisk walks with Muffie and Mackie, which Dr Sutherland said was better for her anyway and would help her regain her strength. Mornings were either taken up with visits to the physiotherapist, now her arm was out of plaster, or trips to the dentist, which had so far resulted in root canals being carried out on all her top front teeth.

'Apparently my teeth are suffering severe trauma,' she informed Tilly. 'Even the ones *next* to those that have been pushed in are dying in sympathy. That's why I'm having to have the roots removed.'

'Far out!' Tilly replied, deadpan. 'Poor little things. D'you think they need counselling, too?'

'Shut up!' Grinning, Lucy threw a cushion at her sister.

'What happens if your molars have a complete nervous breakdown?' Tilly demanded.

Meanwhile, Nigel was in correspondence with Mr Maurice Clark, the surgeon who had originally operated on Lucy, and Dr Dick Kahlo, in an effort to get the best corrective surgery for Lucy. Here, he had to tread carefully for fear of offending Mr Clark, who was an eminent surgeon in Britain and had originally taken it for granted that he would carry out any further operations on Lucy.

'I don't care what he thought,' Diana remarked, with unusual forcefulness. 'This is Lucy's face we're talking about, and Dr Kahlo has been strongly recommended to us.' She dropped her voice so that Lucy, in the next room, wouldn't hear. 'Mr Clark hasn't done a brilliant job on her face so far, has he?'

Nigel felt torn between his liking and respect for Mr Clark, and his natural wish to have everything possible done for Lucy.

'And I'll sell my bits and pieces of jewellery if necessary,' Susan intervened. In her opinion there was no question as to who should operate. She belonged to the generation who believed a girl's face was her greatest fortune, and Peter's behaviour when he'd seen Lucy had only served to reinforce this theory.

'Money doesn't come into it, we'll sell this house if it's *really* necessary,' said Diana.

'I agree, so let's go ahead with Dr Kahlo.' Nigel spoke decisively. 'She must have the very best for reasons of morale, if nothing else, and she seems to have great faith in him. Probably because he's known to have operated on a lot of famous and beautiful women.'

'Has he?' Susan asked. 'Such as . . . ?'

Nigel consulted the folder on his lap which was rapidly swelling with all their medical correspondence. 'According to Amelia Harrow, he's given facelifts to the wives of *three* United States Presidents . . .'

'Which ones?' Susan was fascinated.

Nigel smiled. 'Amelia's too discreet to say. He's also the top surgeon to most of Hollywood's film stars, male and female . . .'

'Do *men* have facelifts?'

'Apparently so. Now let's see what he says about Lucy.' He started to read aloud. '". . . Her face must be allowed to settle

132

before we can attempt corrective surgery. Please send me photographs of her before the accident, immediately afterwards and recently. I also want her X-rays, and copies of all her medical notes."' Nigel looked thoughtful. 'He sounds like the right man. I think the time has come to tell Mr Clark that we've decided Lucy should go to America, don't you?'

Ten days later, Nigel received a letter from Dr Kahlo that put a completely different aspect on the matter. As Lucy was the victim of a car crash and not just someone who wanted to be beautified, he intended to make a video film of every stage of her treatment which he would use when lecturing on plastic surgery. There would be no charges for the treatment. And her stay at the Kahlo Clinic would also be free, with the exception of phone calls or purchases she made in the clinic's boutique.

'In particular,' Dr Kahlo concluded in his letter, 'I have perfected new techniques of dermabrasion and laser treatment and it will be of great help to my students to see these methods being carried out on video.'

'How fantastic,' Diana exclaimed when Nigel had finished reading out the letter.

'Cool!' Tilly agreed.

'Thank God,' said Lucy fervently. 'I was really worried about the cost. I didn't want to bankrupt you, Daddy.'

'No risk of that now, darling,' Nigel said, looking at her fondly. 'And what ever the cost had been, we wouldn't have begrudged a penny.'

'I know.' Lucy reached up and slipped her arms around his neck. 'But I'm relieved all the same.'

'I'm quite excited in a way,' Lucy confided to Carol on one of their lengthy phone calls. 'Nervous, but excited. I mean, I can't look *worse* than I do now, so I've nothing to lose, have I?'

'He must be good if Presidents' wives go to him,' Carol agreed reassuringly. 'When do you think you'll go?'

'In about a month. We've sent this Dr Kahlo photos of me taken last summer and some horrendous ones Daddy took the other day. God! I do look frightening, Carol. If I met me in the dark in an alleyway, I'd have a fit.' In spite of her words her tone was upbeat, jokey even. In a strange way she now felt calm and resigned. Her appearance, how she was going to look for the next sixty years, was beyond her control and she felt quite relieved at the thought of being able to hand herself over to an expert. As she'd said, she had nothing to lose and hopefully a lot to gain. It had made her realise that life needn't come to an end because she'd lost her prettiness. Even if she only looked reasonably normal when it was all over, she'd be content; and she'd be more like herself once more. Peter's attitude had made her realise that he hadn't really loved *her* at all. Not her mind or her heart or her soul. For weeks she'd felt deeply bitter and upset but now she told herself she'd had a lucky escape. As Carol had remarked candidly during one of their conversations, a man like that was equally liable to go off you when you got fat and pregnant or old and grey.

'I should think it's Miranda's fault that he's so shallow,' she'd added. 'With a mother like that, what can you expect?'

Diana insisted on helping Lucy to pack the night before she flew to New York. Amelia Harrow was going to meet her at JFK airport, take her to her Park Avenue apartment for the night, and then fly with her by the local internal flight to Dr Kahlo's private clinic on Long Island.

'You'll need some warm clothes,' Diana advised. 'Would you like to borrow my white cashmere sweater? It would go awfully well with your red woollen skirt.'

'Thanks, Mum, but I'm going to take the minimum. The letter we got from the clinic said only nightclothes, things for the gym and a track suit were necessary. I'm not going to be *going* anywhere.'

'But what about staying with Amelia Harrow? You can't go around New York in a track suit. Supposing she takes you to a smart restaurant?' As she spoke, Diana was folding the new cotton pyjamas she'd bought for Lucy, and an extravagant silk dressing-gown.

'Amelia's not going to take me anywhere looking like this,' Lucy protested. 'I thought I'd buy a few things after it's all over, in New York.'

Diana brightened. For a moment there she'd thought Lucy had lost all interest in her appearance. 'What a good idea, darling, but why don't you take one decent outfit with you now? Just in case Amelia takes you somewhere nice.'

'Oh, Mum,' Lucy sighed, irritated by her mother's fussing, but for the sake of peace she stuffed her brown suit from Jigsaw with the long wrap-around skirt into her zip-up travelling bag.

'Is that it?' Diana looked faintly horrified.

'It's all I need,' Lucy said firmly.

Dinner on her last night was marred by an atmosphere of forced jollity. Nigel and Diana had wanted to give her a good send-off, and so they opened a couple of bottles of champagne in the drawing-room first, and Susan had cooked Lobster Thermidor, which was Lucy's favourite, but the trouble was nobody was in a festive mood. Diana kept bursting into tears because Lucy was going away, for probably six months Dr Kahlo had warned, and all the others seemed to be deep in various states of depression.

Susan was unusually low-spirited. Earlier she'd been talking about hoping she'd live long enough to see both Lucy and

Tilly settled, with nice husbands and children in their own homes.

Nigel was also downcast. Oliver's last words when they'd met for a drink kept repeating themselves over and over in his mind, driving him distracted. Could Oliver really be HIV positive? It was too dreadful a thought to contemplate. But surely he'd just been taunting him? Trying to make him feel guilty for ending their affair? On the other hand, Nigel kept waking up in the middle of the night, sweating with fear. Perhaps Oliver had been telling the truth? Maybe he should go and have a blood test himself? The implications if he *were* infected were too appalling to contemplate. But the agony of mind of *not* knowing seemed, at the moment, almost worse.

'Some wine, Simon?' Tonight he must do his best to appear the thoughtful host and happy family man.

'Thanks. It's a delicious wine,' Simon remarked, sipping it thoughtfully. 'What is it?'

Nigel topped up his own glass. 'Château des Annereaux. It's one of my favourite red Bordeaux. This is 1989. I laid down half a dozen cases because I think it's one of their best years.'

'Can I have some more, please, Daddy?' Lucy held out her glass. 'Although I think I prefer that stuff we had on Sunday. That was really good.'

Simon laughed. 'Full marks for tact, Lucy. That was an Australian wine, wasn't it?'

Nigel nodded. 'Penfold's Koonunga Hill Chardonnay.'

'I don't care what it is so long as it's alcohol,' Susan declared determinedly. 'So . . .' She held her glass aloft. 'Here's to you, Lucy! Bon voyage and . . .' Unexpectedly her eyes brimmed with tears and she was unable to continue. This set Diana off again.

'Yes, darling . . . here's to you,' she said, her voice quivering, a little sob catching in her throat.

'For heaven's sake!' Lucy exclaimed, looking incredulously at them. 'I'm not going away for *long*. You'd think I was emigrating or something!'

'Don't speak to your mother like that,' Nigel remonstrated, suddenly angry.

'I only said . . .'

Lucy looked round the table at them all; her mother and grandmother in tears, her father trying to hide his feelings by being cross. Only Simon seemed to be behaving normally.

As soon as dinner was over, Lucy rose, anxious to put an end to the evening. There seemed to be too much pain in this house now, and they'd all been huddled closely together for so long that the atmosphere seemed claustrophobic. It was time she got away and yet going was a wrench. It seemed as if in the last few months, by being forced to relinquish her independence, she'd been walking backwards into the past, so that she'd become diminished, but a shadow of herself.

'I'll give you a call at five-thirty, darling,' Diana said, struggling to smile through her tears, 'I suppose you and Daddy should leave for Heathrow by half-past six.'

'At the latest,' Nigel agreed.

'OK. See you in the morning.' Lucy kept it light. ''Bye, everyone.'

At the bottom of the stairs Simon caught up with her, his hand outstretched.

'All the best, sport,' he said. 'I hope it all goes OK.'

Pausing, she turned to shake his hand. 'Thanks, Simon.' She knew he'd found the type of job in engineering he'd been looking for and that he was about to leave Eastleigh Manor. 'I hope everything works out OK for you, too.'

'Thanks. Good luck.'

Alone in her room at last, exhausted by the strain of the

evening, Lucy went to the mirror above her chest-of-drawers and looked for a long time at her reflection. The bruising and swelling had gone but the scars were still livid, and when she smiled her face still screwed up on one side. Her nose was crooked and one of her cheekbones flattened, but worst of all was the left side of her jaw which seemed to hang much lower than her right. She tried to look at herself unemotionally. Certainly her grey eyes were nice, and her soft brown hair quite thick and glossy now she'd got her health back. It will be interesting to see what Dr Kahlo can do, she thought. And I must remember this moment and how I look now, because the next time I see myself in this mirror it will all be over.

Lucy looked back to give her mother a final wave as Nigel swung the car out through the gates of Eastleigh Manor. Diana, in a dressing-gown, was smiling bravely.

'Got everything, darling?' he asked, for something to say.

'Yes, Daddy. Everything, thanks.'

'Something to read on the flight?'

'I thought I'd get some magazines and a couple of books at the airport.'

'Have you got enough cash on you?'

It reminded her of going back to boarding school; her mother in tears, telling her she'd sewn name tapes on her new knickers, her father checking that she had enough money. Lucy chuckled. Did nothing change, no matter how old you were?

'I've got masses of cash,' she replied gently, feeling he needed her to be kind to him, 'and travellers' cheques, so I'm fine.'

As soon as Heathrow came into sight, Lucy put on her large black felt hat with the floppy brim, pulling it well down over her eyes, and then she popped on her dark glasses. Nigel glanced over at her.

'Is that necessary, sweetheart?' He'd got so used to seeing her at home, without what he called her 'disguise', that he forgot she hated strangers looking at her.

'You bet it is,' she replied cheerfully. 'Mustn't frighten the horses in the street.'

'As Mrs Patrick Campbell would have said.'

'Exactly. And, Daddy?'

'Yes, sweetheart?'

'Just drop me off when we get there, will you? No long drawn-out goodbyes. I'm a big girl now and I can see myself on to a plane.' For a moment she wasn't sure whether she was thinking about herself or him.

'What about your luggage?'

'I've only got my shoulder travelling bag and this.' She indicated a small zip-up bag between her feet.

He looked surprised. 'God! Talk about travelling light!'

'It's the best way, Daddy.'

When he drew up alongside the kerb by the Departures entrance, she kissed him quickly on the cheek, and then slid out of the car. The last glimpse he had of her was of a tall slender girl in tight jeans, a leather bomber jacket and that touchingly ridiculous hat, bent under the weight of her bright blue canvas bag as it hung from her shoulder. She turned to wave, he caught a flash of her poor little face which he saw through a blur of tears, and then she was gone.

'Staying with *you*?' Over the phone Miranda's voice rose in shaken surprise. 'Why have you asked her to stay with you, for heaven's sake?'

Amelia Harrow, reclining on the deep grey silk sofa in her living-room, with her first large cup of coffee of the day, frowned in irritation.

'Well, why not? It wouldn't be very kind to put her into a

hotel when I've got a spare room, would it? Anyway, I'm taking her to the clinic tomorrow, so it's far better she gets over her jetlag here.'

'When is she arriving?'

'This afternoon. I'm meeting her at JFK. I think this is her first trip to New York.'

'I'm *sure* it is. The girl hasn't been anywhere. So this Dr Kahlo is going to do her face, is he? God, he'll have a job. Peter was nearly sick when he saw her. I wonder what *can* be done actually?'

Amelia could only guess at the reason for Miranda's fury and chagrin, but she had a feeling it was to do with her not being able to afford to go to Dick Kahlo herself. For months now Miranda had been badgering Amelia to find out how much 'the works' cost at the Kahlo Clinic.

'Write to them,' Amelia had finally said, knowing full well that Miranda would not be able to afford to go but not wishing to embarrass her by revealing she knew this.

Nothing more was said and Miranda never mentioned Dr Kahlo again. That is until now when Amelia had foolishly let slip that Lucy Howard was on her way.

'How *is* Peter?' Amelia asked hurriedly, by way of a distraction.

'His leg is still troubling him but he's back at work. He's got a beautiful new girlfriend, too.'

Amelia could almost hear Miranda purring. 'Really? Is it serious?'

'Oh, you know the young, darling. He says he wants to marry her, but I think he should stay single for a bit longer. He's only twenty-nine and I'd like him to have a bit of fun before he settles down. Maybe the accident was fate! He'd have been married to Lucy by now, and I never did like her.'

'I'm not sure, Miranda, that you will ever like anyone Peter marries,' Amelia said drily.

'What do you mean? If he found the right girl, I'd be delighted,' she retorted huffily.

'Ah, yes. But who would be the right girl? You know,' she continued in a cosy confidential manner in order to mollify Miranda, 'I really am *very* glad I didn't have any children. All my friends have so many problems and such heartbreak over their kids . . .'

'Peter's never given me any problems,' Miranda cut in indignantly. 'It's how you bring them up that matters. Lucy and her family were extremely snobbish, you know. I also had my doubts about *him*.'

'Who?'

'Nigel. The father.'

'In what way?'

'You've never met him, have you?'

'No?'

'Quite.' Miranda spoke with knowing satisfaction. She'd turned the ability of deriving comfort from the failings of others into an art form. 'I'm sure he's really gay. Well, bi anyway. And his wife is so stupid I don't think she's got a clue.'

'So what? My first husband, Dale Catt, was bi-sexual. It never worried me,' Amelia replied calmly. 'At least he never looked at another woman.' She laughed suddenly. 'We used to have a private joke. He said, "Honey, you can have your lovers . . . and I can have them, too!"'

Miranda didn't wish to appear unsophisticated or prudish. 'How amusing,' she said in an unamused voice. 'I doubt if Nigel is as racy as that, though. They are actually a very boring couple. I'm glad Peter is no longer involved with any of them.'

When Amelia hung up it struck her that Miranda was a deeply unhappy woman. They'd been friends on and off for many years, although never close, but thinking back she couldn't recall a time when Miranda hadn't found something to complain about. She would hardly, Amelia reflected, have been an ideal mother-in-law.

'Beth?' Amelia called out to her black maid, who had been with her for nearly thirty years.

Beth appeared in the doorway, a small smiling woman with even white teeth, wearing a flowered overall. 'Yes, ma'am?'

'Is the spare room ready for my guest?'

'Yes, ma'am. I put those pink flowers you bought in the bedroom, and there's mineral water on the side.'

'Thank you, Beth. And we'll have dinner early tonight – I expect Miss Howard will be tired after her flight.'

'Yes, ma'am.' She grinned broadly.

Alone again. Amelia looked appreciatively around the living-room of her apartment and thanked God that out of three marriages she'd at least secured a roof over her head in the best part of town from one of her husbands. Otherwise, she'd lost out every damn' time. Dale Catt had left her with a mountain of debts, Mandler Scott had somehow managed to walk off with her house in Hollywood and most of her earnings from films, and Quentin Halpin had dumped her in a blaze of publicity for a seventeen-year-old nymphette, which had done her career no good. But at least she'd got this place out of the otherwise measly settlement. It had meant she'd still had to claw her way back up the financial ladder, and in her mid-forties it wasn't easy, but she'd managed. Just. She still had to graft and hustle for a living but she got by, and in comfort. But without those three husbands, she'd have been a millionairess many times over. Not, as she assured her many friends, that she was bitter. Everything had its price, and that was hers for falling in love with three bums.

After a light salad with a low-calorie dressing, a deliciously ripe pear and a glass of still water, for she still took great care of her figure and skin, she changed into a pale grey knee-skimming skirt and long jacket, teamed with pale grey tights and matching court shoes. It was time to leave for JFK. The chauffeur-driven limousine she'd ordered was waiting in the street below. But first she went to the long mirror in the hall to check her appearance with a critical eye. Slowly a smile of satisfaction spread across her perfectly preserved face. She didn't look a day over forty-five, she thought. Tall, slim, legs still shapely, and hair a soft shade of ash blonde, she really was defying the passing years.

'You're doing all right, old girl,' she murmured, adjusting the large rope of pearls around her neck. 'Who would ever guess you were really sixty-four?'

'Is there anything else I can get you?' cooed the air hostess for the umpteenth time. Lucy, in a window seat, pulled her hat down further and crouched lower, eyes hidden by dark glasses. This was the first time, apart from her family and friends and the people in the village, that she'd been seen in public and the shock her appearance was causing disturbed her greatly. She felt as if she had two heads or resembled Quasimodo, and didn't know how she was supposed to react. Should she acknowledge the startled looks she got? Smile reassuringly, perhaps? Should she ignore the stares of horrified fascination and pretend she hadn't noticed? Her walk around Duty Free was an agony of coming face to face with people who backed off, in spite of her dark glasses. In the end she bought some newspapers and held them up, pretending to read, until her plane was called. Once in her seat, she was sure no one would look at her, but then, she reflected with a stab of alarm, what would happen when she landed in New York? Amelia had said she was going to meet her. At least she'd *expect* her face to be scarred but was she prepared for just how badly, unless Dr Kahlo had warned her? A wide-eyed air hostess showed Lucy to her seat, gazing at her face all the time as if she couldn't quite believe what she saw.

'Can I get you anything?' she kept asking in a kind voice, but it was becoming more than Lucy could bear. Other passengers, walking up the aisle on their way to the loo, peered at her curiously, as if they'd already been tipped off about the girl in row K who had a face like a horror mask. When the lights were turned off for the film, she closed her eyes in thankfulness and slept from sheer exhaustion.

They were landing in forty minutes. The last chance to go to the loo before clasping her seat belt. Lucy rose, stiff from sitting for so long, and made her way up the aisle, keeping her head down. For the first time she had a deep longing to be safely tucked away in the Kahlo Clinic, where prying eyes could not search her out and she'd be in professional hands, as she'd been at the Guildford General Hospital.

There was a queue for the loo. Lucy stood, shoulders hunched, looking down at her feet.

'Are you all right? Is there anything I can get you?' It was the inquisitive air hostess again, talking to her as if she was a three-year-old child. Enraged, Lucy looked up, glaring straight into the eyes of the plumply pretty woman. Then she slowly took off her dark glasses.

'Is this what you want?' she shouted, voice choked. Then she whipped off her hat, pushing her long hair back behind her ears.

'Is *that* better? Can you get a good look at me now? You've been dying to see my face, haven't you? Sneaking up on me all the time, pretending to see if I wanted anything! Well, I do want something. I want you to bloody well leave me alone!' Tears were streaming down her cheeks and she realised that

144

almost everyone on the plane was craning round to see what the commotion was all about, but she no longer cared. Blushing, the appalled air hostess tried to help her back to her seat but Lucy lashed out in fury.

'Leave me *alone*! I don't want to go back to my seat, you stupid woman,' she sobbed. The plane hit an airpocket at that moment, and she found herself clinging to the back of somebody's seat in order to keep her balance. Several people gave little gasping screams and there was a sound of breaking crockery coming from the galley. Suddenly, everyone had forgotten her as their own safety came to the forefront of their mind.

'Will all passengers kindly return to their seats?' said the captain's voice over a loudspeaker. Lucy, putting on her dark glasses and hat again, glared at the air hostess.

'Kindly get out of my way,' she said. 'I don't care what anyone says, I must go to the loo.'

Amelia recognised her at once, of course. Cool and elegant-looking, groomed to within an inch of her life, she stood in the arrivals hall, having already secured a porter for Lucy's luggage.

'My dear Lucy, at last we meet!' she said, coming forward without hesitation. Her cheek was soft and scented as she kissed Lucy. 'Welcome to New York. I've been so looking forward to your arrival, I hope you're not exhausted by the flight?' Without waiting for a reply, she continued: 'Now, my dear, where's your luggage?'

Lucy grinned, liking her immediately. 'This is it.' She humped the travelling bag up higher on her shoulder, and indicated her hand luggage.

Amelia didn't show any surprise. 'Great.' She indicated to the porter to take the baggage. 'The car's outside, let's go!'

With a spring in her step that Lucy would later write to tell her mother was 'pretty amazing considering her age', Amelia led the way out of the airport, as if Lucy were royalty. Following behind in her crumpled jeans, she felt an absolute mess.

Once seated in the back of the limousine, Amelia continued to converse as if there was nothing odd about Lucy's face at all.

'I expect you'd like a quiet evening, so we're having dinner at home,' she explained, 'but if you're not too tired, how about we drive around the city so you can see some of the sights? I believe it's your first visit, isn't it?'

Lucy settled back in the soft leather luxury of the car and agreed there was nothing she'd like more.

'When this is all over, I really want to explore New York,' she said, 'and shop for clothes. I don't usually look like this but I've lost some weight and I need a few things.'

Amelia seemed to understand perfectly. 'It's much more sensible to travel in jeans than all dressed up,' she pointed out. 'Only those who never go anywhere put on their best clothes. And you're coming to stay with me again when Dick Kahlo has worked his magic, aren't you!' She clasped her gloved hands together, like a child who has been given a prize. 'What fun, my dear. I can get you a special discount at some of the best shops, and we can have a real spree . . . that is, of course, if you want me to go along?'

'Oh, I shall,' Lucy said fervently, glancing admiringly at Amelia's outfit. 'When this is all over I want a completely new look! A sort of major makeover!' Then she turned to the older woman and purposely took off her dark glasses. Amelia, she noticed, didn't flinch but continued to look at her with warm and kindly eyes.

'I can't thank you enough for going to so much trouble on my behalf,' Lucy said with sincerity. 'It's so wonderful of you to have me to stay and then take me to the clinic and everything. You've gone to so much trouble and I really am grateful, you know.'

Lucy couldn't be sure, but a mist seemed to pass across Amelia's eyes.

'My dear, as soon as Miranda told me what had happened, I knew Dick Kahlo was the answer. He's done some fantastic surgery and I've seen the results. Quite amazing, actually. One of his patients was a young woman who'd been in a fire and was terribly burned. Those are the most difficult operations of all, of course, and require skin grafts, but he did a fabulous job. When I last saw the young woman, you'd hardly know anything had happened. Then there was a model who was mugged on the New York subway and had her face slashed repeatedly with a razor blade; again Dick did a fantastic job.' Then she paused, frowning as if the memory was painful, before continuing: 'He's an artist, really. He had one patient who'd been in a riding accident. Her horse had thrown her and she'd landed against a stone wall.' Amelia shook her head and shut her eyes as if she couldn't bear the picture in her mind. Then her brow cleared again. 'By the time Dick had finished, the girl looked better than she had before. Men, women, children, he's the best.'

Lucy looked into the perfect face and longed to ask if Dick had performed his 'magic' on Amelia, too. Her jawline was firm and clear-cut, and there were no bags under her eyes or lines from her nose to the sides of her mouth. Even her neck looked smooth. She could tell that Amelia knew what she was thinking because she looked straight back at her before speaking.

'Dick Kahlo is an old friend of mine,' she said, as if to explain her knowledge of him. 'We go way back, to when I was a starlet and he was a medical student. I think you'll like him. He's a very compassionate and kind person. Now, I want you to watch ahead, because we're coming to one of the most exciting sights in the world.' If it was a way of evading any questions she might not want to answer, Lucy thought, it worked, because a moment later, as they crested a bridge spanning the East River into New York, a panoramic view of sky scrapers seemed to rise up out of the horizon and Lucy gasped with delight.

'Unreal!' she exclaimed.

Amelia beamed. 'Isn't it great? I still get a kick out of that view even after all these years.' Then she leaned forward to give the chauffeur some instructions.

Soon, Lucy was being shown the Empire State Building, Times Square, the famous Pan Am Building, then up Madison Avenue and down Fifth Avenue, while Amelia pointed out all the famous shops like Tiffany, Bergdorf Goodman, Van Cleef and Arpels, past the Trump Tower, Saks Fifth Avenue and then finally up Park Avenue to her apartment which was on Park and Sixty-ninth Street. As the car drew up to a palatial entrance, a uniformed doorman came forward to usher them into a small but glittering lobby and thence into a lift lined with mushroom-beige suede. Lucy trailed behind feeling like some poor émigrée from Europe.

'Let's have a drink, it must be nearly six o'clock,' Amelia said when they entered her apartment on the twelfth floor. Lucy looked around, and was immediately reminded of a stage set for a glamorous production of a Noël Coward play.

'Wine, darling? Or would you like gin, or perhaps vodka?' Amelia said, drawing off her kid gloves. Bowls of orchids, grey silk sofas with delicate tapestry cushions, subtle lighting and some fine paintings formed a perfect backdrop to her own brand of stage elegance.

'Wine would be lovely,' Lucy said, although she was longing

for a bath and a change of clothes. Thank God, she thought, her mother had forced her to bring at least one decent outfit.

As if she knew what Lucy was thinking, Amelia said, 'When we've had a drink, how about a little rest? We'll have dinner at eight, if that's OK with you?'

'That would be perfect,' Lucy replied, going over to the window to look out. New York had already got under her skin. There was such a buzz, so much life and activity and excitement, and immediately she thought, how Tilly would love it all! What a fun holiday they could have together when her sister was a bit older!

'I'm afraid the view isn't great,' Amelia remarked, handing her a cut crystal glass of white wine. 'The apartments overlooking Central Park are the best.'

Lucy's expression was radiant as she turned to look at her. 'But it's all so *alive*! I'd no idea it would be like this. Oh, I can't wait to come back.' Then she looked serious. 'Do you know how long my face will take? How long did the others have to have surgery before they . . . they looked normal?' she asked with a sudden rush.

Amelia smiled as if she understood. 'My dear, that all depends on how quickly you heal, and how much you bruise.' She eyed Lucy's glass of wine. 'Make the most of that, because you won't be allowed to drink once you're at the clinic.'

'Really? I don't drink much anyway so it won't worry me, but why is that?'

'Because alcohol in the blood affects your skin more than almost anything. You know how women who drink a lot of spirits end up looking? And Dick won't operate on anyone who smokes either, for the same reason. During surgery it leads to haemorrhaging, for one thing. He'll explain it all to you, though, and he'll be able to tell you how long it will take,' she added reassuringly.

'I *am* impatient,' Lucy admitted. 'If you'd seen how people looked at me on the way over here . . .' Her voice trailed off at the memory.

'How rude of them,' Amelia exclaimed. 'Anyway, anyone can see you're a lovely young girl who's had the misfortune to get bashed up in an accident, that's all. The main thing is you're lucky to be alive, from what I've heard, and Dick will soon have you looking as good as new.'

Lucy found she felt able to discuss her injuries freely with this woman she'd never met before. That was something she hadn't really been able to do with Carol, who was so anxious to cheer her up and bolster her spirits that there never seemed to be an opportunity for deep discussion.

'Do you really think Dr Kahlo can straighten me out?' she asked earnestly. 'I can't go through the rest of my life looking like this. Who will employ me? I hope the radio station I work for will give me my job back; at least no one outside the studio need see me, but I can't stay in hiding for the rest of my life.'

Amelia looked into Lucy's face and placed her hands on her shoulders. 'I promise you, Lucy, Dick can and will restore your face so that eventually no one will know what's happened. The man is a genius and because you are a special case I know he will take a particular interest. Relax, my dear, and be prepared to be patient. Have faith in him. You'll be thrilled by the time he's finished with you, I *know* you will.'

Impulsively Lucy hugged the older woman. 'Oh, thank you so much, and thank you for all you are doing. I really am grateful and I'll always be indebted to you.'

Amelia smiled. 'The best way you can thank me is by coming back to New York, when it's all over, and letting me go shopping with you! I'm just crazy about shopping. And we'll have a party, right here in the apartment, so I can show you off to my friends. Will you allow me to do that?'

Lucy laughed at Amelia's girlish enthusiasm. 'Try and stop me!'

'Then that's settled. We leave here tomorrow morning at eleven o'clock, and as the flight only takes thirty minutes, we'll arrive at the clinic in time for lunch.' She raised her glass. 'Here's to you, my dear. And to a dazzling future.'

From the outside, the Kahlo Clinic didn't look particularly inspiring and Lucy felt a sense of disappointment as she took in the plain grey stone façade, with its small square windows and unimposing entrance. It was a long low building, at the end of a drive lined with trees, and for a moment it reminded her more of a prison than a luxurious clinic.

As if she knew what Lucy was thinking, Amelia spoke.

'It doesn't look much from here,' she said. 'Dick likes the place to be inconspicuous from the road, because he has so many celebrity clients and has to guard their privacy.'

At that moment their car drew up to the entrance, and an English-looking butler, in grey and black pin-stripe trousers and a black coat, opened the door, as if he'd been lurking inside, waiting for their arrival.

'Good morning, Peters,' Amelia greeted him graciously.

'Good morning, ma'am.'

Lucy noticed that whilst greeting them with restrained warmth, he nevertheless managed to avoid eye contact; no doubt this was all a part of Dr Kahlo's famous policy of discretion which she'd heard so much about. They were led across a wide square hall, marble-floored, furnished with several large sofas covered in fondant-coloured linen, and a centre table on which stood a four-feet-high arrangement of exotic flowers. The room beyond, with windows from floor to ceiling, overlooked the sea. It too had sofas and chairs covered in pink and lavender, lime and pale yellow linen, arranged in seating areas around coffee tables, and there was a profusion of flowers and magazines which gave it a lived-in atmosphere.

'Dr Kahlo will be with you in a moment, ma'am,' Peters said respectfully.

Amelia sat down on one of the sofas, but Lucy, glad she was wearing her good suit today, went over to look out of the windows. A lawn, bordered on both sides by high walls, led down to a beach which the elements had swept into little drifts out of which tufts of rough grass were growing. It was impossible to see what was on either side of the walls and she realised the clinic must be a long, low building, with rooms looking out to sea. At that moment she heard footsteps and, turning, saw a balding man in his fifties, short and stocky, with a wise but sad face. Dark eyes swept penetratingly over her and she kept on her dark glasses, not yet ready for this intrusion into her inner self.

'Dick!' Amelia had risen, and was kissing him affectionately on both cheeks. 'How are you, my dear?' She extended a hand towards Lucy. 'Look what I've brought you, isn't she a darling?'

Dr Kahlo shook hands gravely with Lucy and again she was aware of her space being invaded. There was something very powerful about this small man, with his strong handshake and sharp eyes.

'Welcome to the clinic, Miss Howard,' he said formally. His accent was soft and his voice rich and attractive. 'I look forward to working with you in the months to come.'

'*With* me?' Lucy was taken aback.

'This will be a joint effort, Miss Howard. I cannot do anything without your co-operation, and the success of our little venture will depend as much on you as on me. A great work of creation cannot be achieved by one person alone.'

'Yes . . . yes, I see,' Lucy stammered. Dr Kahlo was nothing like she'd expected and Amelia seemed to sense her disquiet.

'Now stop talking like God, Dick,' she chided him gently, 'or you'll scare poor Lucy to death.'

He laughed then. 'OK! Let's have lunch. I suppose you want a glass of wine, Amelia, my dear?' He wagged his finger at her, and then reaching forward ran his fingertips along the line of her jaw. 'You've got to look after this, you know, and drinking doesn't help.'

'I'm not giving up my wine for you or anyone else,' she replied, smiling broadly. 'Come on, Dick, give me a break!'

Lucy followed them back into the hall, along a corridor and through a door into what looked like a private apartment. At one end of the living-room, a dining table laid for three was set into an alcove. Peters was hovering beside a drinks tray, ready to serve them.

'Miss Harrow will have white wine, Peters,' Dr Kahlo said. 'And you, Miss Howard? What can we get you?'

Lucy was beginning to feel like a child, taken on an outing by a couple of grown-ups who were excluding her from their adult conversation. The desire to assert herself suddenly became strong.

'I know I shall not be allowed to drink once the operations start,' she said coolly, raising her chin, 'but as that's not going to happen today, I'd like a gin and tonic, please.'

'Certainly, ma'am,' Peters said, busying himself with the tray. 'With ice and lemon?'

'Yes, please.' Taking off her dark glasses, she looked at the others with a touch of defiance. 'So when do we start my treatment, Dr Kahlo?' she asked.

He smiled, as if he approved of her show of spirit, and his manner became more straightforward.

'After lunch you will be taken to your suite, and this afternoon you'll be given the chance to settle in. Tomorrow morning you and I will meet for the first consultation and I will be assessing exactly how we should progress. Any questions you have, I will then deal with to the best of my ability.'

Lucy nodded, reassured. She didn't have to *like* this unprepossessing little man but she did have to trust him and be able, as he had said, to co-operate with him.

After Amelia left Dr Kahlo's personal assistant was summoned to take Lucy to her suite.

'This is Lauren Vincent. She will see you have everything you need,' he said by way of introduction. 'Have a pleasant afternoon and I will see you tomorrow.'

Thanking him, Lucy followed Lauren out of the private apartment, across the hall once again and then down a very long corridor which had doors down one side only. So far she had not seen anyone apart from the doctor, Peters, and Lauren Vincent, a quiet mousy woman in her thirties.

'Is the clinic quiet at this time of year?' Lucy asked conversationally.

Lauren smiled, a polite humourless expression that did little to relieve the plainness of her face, which was devoid of make-up.

'We make sure all patients have privacy and can stay here totally assured of complete anonymity,' she said rather primly. 'Many of them are famous celebrities, so of course they don't want their presence reported by the media.'

Lucy thought of the various Presidents' wives she'd been told had been here, not to mention the Hollywood film stars.

'I can understand that. It must be awfully interesting, working here and presumably meeting all these celebrities?'

Lauren, marching ahead, nodded. 'Yes, it is. I've only been with Dr Kahlo for the past three months, but I'm enjoying it.' She paused outside a door which had A18 in brass lettering on it. 'Here we are.' Unlocking the door, she led the way into a small lobby which had a hanging cupboard on one side, and an oil painting of a seascape on the other.

'As you know,' she continued, getting into tour guide mode, 'Dr Kahlo forbids mirrors in the clinic, and if you have brought one with you, I'm afraid it will be confiscated.' She paused to indicate the seascape. 'By the same token, all the pictures here are oil paintings, because any other type would require to be framed with glass, in which patients would be able to see their reflection.'

Lucy raised her eyebrows. 'Is that really necessary?'

Pale grey eyes looked into hers through gold-framed glasses. With her lank fair hair drawn severely back, and her beige skirt and blouse hanging limply on her thin frame, Lauren Vincent looked wan and exhausted and Lucy felt quite sorry for her. No doubt, she thought, she's at the beck and call of a very demanding man.

When Lauren spoke, her voice was hushed. 'Dr Kahlo feels it's necessary to stop patients worrying in the interim, before any scarring has healed. Some people are very neurotic, you know. Will you follow me, please?' She opened an inner door, and on a lower level reached by four carpeted steps was a large airy room, which would have resembled a hotel room had it not been for a hospital bed at one end. The furniture – a sofa, armchair, and a low table on which stood flowers, fruit and bottled water – was stylish and expensive-looking. Rugs, cushions and lavishly draped curtains were in muted shades of blue and green silk and through the large window Lucy could see a small high-walled garden leading on to the beach through a gate which was closed.

'The bathroom is through here,' Lauren said, going ahead again. Lucy inspected it. A large round pink marble jacuzzi stood in the middle, and all the other fittings were pink marble, too. There was a stack of fluffy white towels on a table, and a large white wicker chair, with pink cushions, stood by the bath. There was also a high narrow bed, with a pink blanket, in readiness for massage treatments.

Lucy looked around her with growing amazement. This place was more like a five-star hotel than a medical centre. She'd noticed a lap-top word processor as well as a fax machine and telephone on a desk in her room, and beside it an extensive menu to choose from. There was also a television set built into the wall with a combined video and a compact disc player. It seemed incredible she was getting all this and her medical treatment free of charge. Normally, she would have expected to have had to pay thousands of dollars a week, and yet Dr Kahlo was giving it all to her for nothing. The video he was going to make for the benefit of his students really must mean a lot to him, she reflected.

Eight

'Have you heard how Lucy's getting on?'

It was half-term, and Diana had picked up Tilly from the station, lugging with her a heavy case of dirty washing and a straw basket, out of which her school books and a pencil case kept falling.

'She's only checking into the clinic today so of course we haven't heard yet,' Diana replied as she climbed into the driving seat of the dark blue BMW Nigel had given her the previous year. 'It's still morning in America, too. She won't have left New York yet.'

'Oh, cool. I wonder what Amelia Harrow's like? She's had several husbands, hasn't she? I bet she's painted to the hilt, like Miranda. Honestly, these old women who try to look young – it's pathetic. They're a waste of space.'

Diana felt her mouth twitch. As they drove along, Tilly was wriggling out of her regulation grey skirt and reaching into her bag for a pair of pale pink jeans. The young, she reflected, instantly feeling she must be old because Tilly referred to them thus, saw everything in such definite black and white, with no shades in between. Had she been like that? she wondered. She could remember condemning a friend of her mother's for dyeing her hair blonde to disguise the fact it was turning white, and her mother saying: 'Wait until you grow old. You'll do more than just dye your hair.'

'Isn't that rather hard on Miranda, darling?' she asked.

'Get a life, Mum! She's a real dweeb.'

Diana blinked. 'Where do you get all these strange expressions from, Tilly?'

'Mum, *everyone* uses them. I say, what are we doing this weekend? It's going to be strange without Lucy, isn't it?'

Diana accelerated to overtake a car. The driver hooted back in annoyance. She put her foot down, knowing the country lanes as well as she did, and shot ahead.

'Wicked!' Tilly smiled in satisfaction.

'We're having a quiet weekend, I think,' Diana said after a minute. 'Daddy seems very tired these days so we're not planning to do much. I think the strain of the accident is really catching up with him. Granny insists on cooking Sunday lunch as it's Simon's last weekend, but I think that's about all.'

Tilly sat bolt upright. 'I'd forgotten he was going.'

'Yes, he's found a job with a big engineering company in Portsmouth. He's bought himself a flat there, and is moving in on Tuesday.'

'Far out! I'll miss him, though. He's a good sport.'

'I think we'll all miss him, and Granny in particular. She's really loved having him to stay. He's been great company for her.'

'He can come for weekends, can't he? He's not going to want to be stuck in a poky little flat in Portsmouth every weekend, surely?'

'Of course we'll invite him over, but I expect he'll soon make new friends of his own age.'

Tilly digested this disturbing thought with a puckered brow. 'I'm sure he'd much rather be with us. He's going to miss Granny's cooking, for one thing.' Then she sat hunched in silence for the rest of the journey home.

* * *

The telephone rang just as the ten o'clock news was starting on television. Nigel rose swiftly to his feet and hurried into the hall to answer it, a worried expression on his face. Diana watched anxiously, wondering why he'd been so on edge all evening. He'd arrived back from London later than usual, and hadn't wanted anything to eat, although she'd had a chicken casserole in the oven in readiness.

'I'm not hungry,' he'd murmured, his face tired and drawn-looking. 'I'll just have some fruit and a glass of wine.'

The only thing she could think of that might be worrying him was financial problems.

Turning down the sound with the remote control she strained to hear what he was saying.

'Darling! How are you feeling? How was the flight?'

With a sense of relief, realising it was Lucy calling from America, she hurried into the hall.

'I want to talk to her, after you,' she whispered to Nigel.

A few minutes later Lucy was regaling her with descriptions of her luxurious suite.

'Ma, it's like the Ritz!' Lucy said. 'I can't believe I'm really here. Amelia has been so kind and I've met Dr Kahlo; I'm having my first consultation with him in the morning.'

'That's wonderful, sweetheart. Have you met any of the other patients?'

She could hear Lucy laughing down the line, sounding more up-beat than she'd done for ages. 'No. I think one's going to be in solitary confinement, apart from the nurses, but I don't mind. I've got my own little walled garden overlooking the sea, the weather's fantastic and I feel like I'm on holiday.'

When they'd said goodbye and she'd hung up, Diana turned to Nigel and put her arms around him, pulling him close.

'Doesn't she sound happy, darling? Oh, I think everything's

going to turn out all right, don't you?'

He held her for a moment, his cheek pressed against her hair, and felt nothing but an icy numbness.

'As long as Lucy recovers,' he said. 'That's the most important thing.'

Earlier that day Oliver had phoned Nigel at the office. He could tell at once that something was wrong.

'I've got something to tell you,' Oliver said.

Nigel could guess, knew even before the words were said and his whole world started to topple.

'I'm HIV positive; I suspected it the last time I saw you. Now I've had it confirmed.' A simple straightforward statement, spoken without emotion. Nigel felt himself fragmenting inside and tried to hold his heart and his mind together.

'Oh, God! I'm sorry . . .' Inadequate words, he thought, to someone who had just told him they'd been condemned to death.

'I feel terrible . . . about you. Are you OK?' Oliver's voice was shaky now, as if he was trying not to cry.

'We were always careful,' Nigel said in a low voice, mindful of his colleagues at nearby desks. They *had* always taken precautions, always practised safe sex on his insistence, even so . . .

'I never thought it would come to this,' Oliver lamented.

'How long have you known?'

'Since yesterday. I got as drunk as hell last night. I don't know how it's all going to end.'

'But you're OK at the moment . . . ?'

'Yeah. It's not full-blown yet, but I don't know how long . . .'

'I'm really sorry, Oliver.'

'My own fault, playing around just once too often. Anyway, I must get on. I'm glad you're all right. Really glad. Take care, Nigel. Goodbye.' There was a click as he hung up.

Nigel sat at his desk for a long time, trying to take in the enormity of what he'd been told. Whatever Oliver had done, he didn't deserve this. No one did.

Later that night, as Diana lay beside him in their wide bed, Nigel turned on his side, away from her so she might not sense his anguish, even in sleep. The word that kept recurring in his mind was waste. It all came back to that: waste. Oliver had wasted his talents, his opportunities, and ultimately his life. Nigel found himself veering between violent anger and sorrow. What had the bloody fool been thinking of? How could he have been so careless? And how was Oliver's mother going to feel when she knew? But then . . . he'd loved Oliver once and this was something he wouldn't wish on his worst enemy.

The clock in the hall downstairs chimed one then two and the night grew colder and the country noises faded to silence, and he knew what he must do. He must get himself tested or he'd never have another moment's peace. Perhaps he *had* contracted this terrible disease from Oliver? Supposing Diana really insisted on making love one night, not that she was likely to because she hadn't seemed interested for several years, but just supposing . . .

He lay cold with fear and tears of bitter regret trickled down his cheeks on to the pillow. For all his care, he realised that the price that might be required of him for a few hours of lust was his life.

'If you want, I can give you a new face. Turn you into a great beauty.' Dr Kahlo's voice was kind and reassuring and his hands had a feathery touch as he traced the line of her cheek and jaw.

Lucy looked up at him, half excited but half fearful of letting her hopes be raised too much.

'You're very lucky your eyes weren't damaged,' he continued thoughtfully, lightly running his thumb along the line of one of her eyebrows.

She remained silent, shifting her gaze to the white ceiling of her room where she lay on her hospital bed which had been moved over to the window. His hands smelled of soap. His breath held a warm whiff of peppermint. His rotund body fitted comfortably into his white surgeon's coat.

A large and very bright light on a high stand had been wheeled in earlier, and he altered its angle, adjusting it so that he could examine her throat as well.

'You'll have to be patient, Lucy,' he observed softly. 'Rome wasn't built in a day but you will eventually be surprised by what I can do.'

What have I got to lose? she reflected. Aloud she asked, 'Will it hurt?'

'You will experience some discomfort but we will be working in stages so it shouldn't be too bad. I won't attempt to do everything at once.'

'How long will it take before . . .?' Lucy's voice faltered. It wasn't just the months of surgery that lay ahead which she dreaded, it was the fear that it would take so long to get back to her radio career everyone would have forgotten her.

'Before you can face the world again as a great beauty?' Dr Kahlo was beaming at her now, a wide fatherly smile that revealed even teeth and deep laughter lines around his eyes she hadn't noticed yesterday.

'I'll never be that, not in a million years,' Lucy replied drily.

He regarded her speculatively. 'Why do you say that?'

Her tone was candid. 'I was fairly pretty, I suppose, before the accident. Attractive, some people said, but in no way

beautiful. It would be nice if you could make me look normal
... well, presentable, but complete miracles I'm not expecting!'

Dr Kahlo chuckled, and then he looked out through the
window at the small enclosed garden and the sea beyond, as
if deep in thought. At last he spoke.

'You should have more faith in me, Lucy. I will not let you
down. In between the operations I want you to get really fit,
and I'm assigning to you my best personal trainer who will
help you get into shape again. Would you also like a counsellor
to assist you in getting over the trauma you've been through?'

'I've had some counselling and the nightmares have
stopped.' She paused thoughtfully. 'It would be nice to have
someone to talk to, though. I didn't want to burden my family
with my personal worries because there was nothing they could
say that really helped. We're all too close, I think. What I have
to come to terms with now is the fact that the man I was
going to marry was repelled when he saw me. It was I who
broke off the engagement but his reaction hurt me very much.'

'So there's no one in your life right now?'

'No one,' she replied firmly.

'Has Lauren been to see you this morning?'

Lucy nodded. 'She came to see me quite early.' Lauren
had arrived just as Lucy, sitting in her little private garden at
a table set under a striped awning, was finishing her breakfast
of cereal scattered with tiny wild strawberries, low-fat yoghurt,
toast and herb tea. (She'd already been told the night before
that ordinary tea and coffee were not served at the clinic
because they were stimulants, which was not good for the
skin.)

Lauren, a file on her knee, had sat down opposite Lucy
under the sunshade, her countenance was like an empty shell,
her eyes were expressionless as if her inner being had shrunk
to nothing and disappeared.

'I've come to make sure you have everything you want,' she began. 'A nurse will be coming to see you in due course, to get your medical history, take your temperature and blood pressure and all that, but meanwhile have you any likes or dislikes, food wise?'

'I don't think so. I can eat practically everything.'

'No allergies? To shellfish? Apples? Spicy dishes?'

Lucy shook her head and felt she must be rather boring.

'You will be given a very carefully balanced diet while you are here, but you're happy to have meat, are you? You're not vegetarian?' As she spoke she was scribbling away feverishly.

'Certainly not.'

'Good. I'm afraid Dr Kahlo doesn't allow patients to have any alcohol, and he's not too keen on fruit juice because of its sugar content, but you will be encouraged to drink up to eight pints of water a day. Do you prefer sparkling or flat?'

'Sparkling.'

'Were you warm enough in the night? Would you like an extra blanket? An extra pillow? A soft or a hard one? Is there a special bath oil you prefer? Which newspapers would you like each morning?'

When she'd gone through every possible like or dislike Lucy might have, Lauren went on to explain that each morning someone from the clinic's shop would visit her, asking if there was anything she needed.

'They stock books, magazines, lingerie and tights, dressing-gowns and slippers, toilet articles and tampons, writing materials and postage stamps . . .' The list seemed endless and Lucy switched off mentally halfway through, as Lauren rattled on like a robot in charge of a lift in a department store.

'Wouldn't it be simpler if I just strolled along to the shop to see what there is for myself?' she asked at last. 'Presumably it's in the building?'

164

Lauren looked faintly horrified, her eyes alert for the first time. 'Patients are *never* allowed to leave their rooms,' she explained. 'We would not want them bumping into each other, would we? To preserve everyone's privacy, the shop has trolleys which are taken around, on request, so that patients can make their purchases in their own rooms.'

For a moment Lucy felt stifled, sensing the almost prison-like atmosphere closing in on her.

'I shall certainly want to buy a lot of books,' she remarked with feeling.

Lauren scribbled that down too, her lips pinched in concentration. 'They sell cassettes, videos and CDs, as well.'

After she had gone Lucy lingered for a while over the remains of her breakfast, thinking what an extraordinary place the Kahlo Clinic was. Part medical centre, part five-star hotel, with overtones of a remand home, she wondered how she was going to cope with the smothering protectiveness that seemed to pervade the place. It almost felt as if she was going to be blanked out by a system that would drain away all her personality, and that at the end of the line she would emerge with a new persona, not to mention a new face as well.

'I will need to take some X-rays this morning,' Dr Kahlo announced on their second meeting. 'I think the first thing we need to do is straighten your broken nose and then reset your jawbone.' He smiled again, appraising her as if she were a fragile work of art. 'I'm also going to rebuild your cheekbone where it has been crushed.' He looked at both her cheeks as if comparing them. 'Maybe we could do a little . . .' Suddenly his tone changed, becoming brisk.

'In the meantime, you will be getting regular visits from our in-house counsellor, Suzy Durrell. She is a very kind, understanding woman and will help prepare you for the treatments and assist you in becoming acclimatised to life in the clinic during the coming months. There will be times, I know, when you are going to feel very frustrated and hemmed in, and it will require all your patience to stick with it. I can only say that at the end of the day you will not be disappointed by the results we will achieve.'

Later that day, after she'd been filmed on video from various angles, a middle-aged woman with straight grey hair cut in a fringe, and a clever but plain face, knocked on the door of her suite.

'Can I come in?' she asked, opening the door and stepping into the lobby before Lucy had time to say anything.

'Hi!' The woman strode across the room. She was wearing loose cream cotton trousers and a cream and white striped tee-shirt. 'I'm Suzy Durrell and I've come to see how you're doing?' Her handshake was strong and firm, and Lucy liked her direct manner. Candid pale blue eyes looked into hers with such unwavering intensity that for a moment Lucy forgot her face was a mess.

Suzy dropped into a chair by the window. A thin gold chain round her neck glinted in the sunlight. On her right hand she wore a large gold ring set with jade.

'I haven't come to analyse you,' she announced cheerfully, 'and I'm not here to give you psychiatric help because I can see you don't need it, but if there's anything about the surgery that worries you, or you have any misgivings about how you'll look afterwards, then I'm here to answer your questions.'

'I don't think I have any questions, right now, but of course I can't help feeling a bit nervous and apprehensive about the whole thing. On the other hand, I couldn't look worse than I do now, so I reckon I've nothing to lose.'

Suzy smiled understandingly. 'I can see you've got a positive approach and that's the most important thing of all.'

Lucy shrugged. 'I don't honestly have much choice.' She

grinned. 'I'm unemployable looking like this, and my love life is definitely on hold.'

'Tell me the most important thing you want to achieve out of all this?' Suzy settled herself back in the chair, her hands behind her head. She was watching Lucy with interest.

'Well . . .' Suddenly she couldn't find the words to describe exactly what she hoped for. 'To look normal again, I suppose,' she said lamely.

'Don't you feel normal now?'

'I feel . . .' Sudden tears sprang to her eyes and something bubbled up in her chest, threatening to erupt. Ever since the terrible scene with Peter she'd been quite stoical, but now it was as if a dam was bursting its banks and sweeping her away.

'I f-feel like a battered woman,' she sobbed. 'I look like the victim of battering. I feel as if I've been beaten up . . . and that's so *hard*.' She was crying uncontrollably now, and she had the mad notion of wanting to fling herself into the arms of this motherly woman with her clever face and understanding eyes, as if she was a little girl again.

'Did you feel like this right away?' Suzy asked after a few minutes.

'I don't think so. I knew my face was a mess and that I looked awful . . .'

'But you didn't feel like you'd been beaten up by another human being?' As she spoke, Suzy handed Lucy a box of tissues.

'Not at first.' She wiped her cheeks and blew her nose. 'But then I began to feel abused, as if I'd been brutalised. And . . . and I can't get rid of the feeling,' she added, her voice catching on another sob. 'I hope it will go when my face has been repaired.'

'You were engaged to be married, weren't you? Then I hear you broke it off. Was that because you felt you looked bad?'

Lucy nodded.

'How did your fiancé react then?'

'He . . . he still wanted us to get married. He said it would make no difference. That was until . . .'

Suzy leaned forward, intent on every word. 'Until what?' she asked softly.

'Until he saw me. Until he saw how I looked.' Lucy stared down at the floor, her shoulders hunched. She was tearing one of the tissues to shreds with hands that shook.

Suzy sat back, nodding in understanding as if a riddle had been solved.

'And that was when you first began to feel battered . . . because the hurt and pain he inflicted on you were actually worse than the pain you'd suffered in the accident?'

Lucy nodded again.

'I broke off the engagement because I didn't think it was fair on him. I didn't think I'd actually *repel* him, though. He was disgusted when he saw me. It was the worst moment of my life. But I find that even now . . . sometimes . . . I still hope we might be reconciled . . . Isn't that ridiculous?'

'You'll find these feelings will go after you've had surgery.' Suzy spoke in a practical no-nonsense way that Lucy found strangely comforting and reassuring.

'You'd be amazed,' she continued, 'at the number of women who have nothing wrong with their faces, but who still submit to surgery in order to erase some terrible memory. They might have been mugged, or the victim of domestic violence. Some have even been raped. As a result they've grown to hate the way they look, and the only answer for them is to change that.'

'Anyone would hate to look the way I do at present,' Lucy remarked. 'My greatest problem, apart from feeling I've been physically battered, is that I've lost something vital . . . myself.

And now I've got to find myself again. Someone I know and recognise. Right now I feel as if my face is a map, showing everything I've been through in the past few months, and none of it belongs to me.'

Suzy smiled understandingly. 'The treatment you're going to have in this clinic will help you make a new start and I'm here whenever you want to see me. I shall enjoy working with you, too.' She rose to go, her hands in her pockets, her movements relaxed and easy. 'I mostly have ladies who think a facelift will get their husbands back, or make a man twenty-five years younger fall in love with them, or that their whole lives will turn around, and they'll suddenly become rich, famous and happy.' She raised her dark eyebrows and shrugged. 'I tell them time and time again that all it will do is make them feel better about *themselves*, but sometimes it's kinda tough to get the message across.'

'At least I'm beginning to feel optimistic about the future,' Lucy admitted, dry-eyed now.

'You've every right to. While you're here, are you going in for breast augmentation? Or liposuction anywhere?'

Lucy looked shocked. 'No, I'm not.'

'Good. You don't need it anyway, you're skinny like a model, but it would be good for you to do the exercise programme. Have you met your personal trainer?'

'Not yet.'

'I expect they'll give you Richard. He's good. OK, kiddo, I'm off now, but I'll be popping in to see how you're getting on. If you have any problems, don't forget to ask for me.' With a wave, she climbed the steps to the small lobby and was gone. That night Lucy slept well, comforted by the thought that she'd met someone at the clinic who really understood how she felt.

* * *

Nigel watched as the dark red blood flowed from his arm into the cylinder of the hypodermic, so dark it looked almost black. What did it carry in its livid liquidity? The seeds of his death? He turned sharply away, unable to bear the sight of his fate seeping from his body into a container which would hold the answers. The white-coated laboratory assistant withdrew the needle and applied a small pad of cotton wool soaked in spirit to the pin-prick wound.

'Hold it there for a moment, will you?' she said. Her manner was friendly and she seemed unafraid to touch him, although of course, he reminded himself, she was wearing surgical rubber gloves.

'How long before I know the results?' His voice sounded strained and as if it belonged to somebody else.

'We'll call you as soon as they are available,' she replied cheerfully.

There were a million questions racing through his head, but he couldn't find the words to express himself or give voice to his fears.

'Thank you,' was all he could say. Then he left the AIDS clinic, sneaking quickly out of the door into the street for fear of being seen by anyone who was passing. A few yards away he stopped and stood quite still. *How bloody silly*, he thought. *I may have AIDS and if I do I'm going to die . . . and yet here I am, scared in case I'm seen leaving the building!*

There was a pub on the corner, the George VI. He went in and ordered himself a large gin and tonic although he knew it was going to take a great deal more than that to see him through if the result was HIV positive.

Within a few days Lucy began to settle in and feel more relaxed. There was little time for brooding, in any case. She'd decided, as she told her mother on the phone, to 'go with the flow,

Mum, as Tilly would say', and the hours seemed to pass in a fever of activity. At first, all Kahlo did was film her again from every angle, using different lighting and a variety of poses. Then he measured every dimension of her face and made copious notes. After that there were blood tests, X-rays of both her face and teeth, because she was going to have all her damaged front teeth crowned, and then began the operations, all of which were going to be recorded on video.

'Don't worry,' Dr Kahlo insisted. 'We're starting with your nose and we're going to put a cocaine-based jelly up each nostril so you won't feel anything.'

'Except high,' Lucy volunteered *sotto voce*. Dr Kahlo didn't have a sense of humour. She did however wake with a headache, eyes like a panda and a heavy plaster cast on her nose and forehead, but if she was going to end up with a dainty retroussé nose at the end of it then she wasn't complaining. The operation on her jaw was definitely more than 'uncomfortable', which was all Dr Kahlo had said it would be. As she told Diana on the phone, on a scale of one to ten, she'd rate the pain at around seven. But the treatment for her crushed cheekbone was even worse, especially as Dr Kahlo had insisted he had to 'do work on your other cheek as well, otherwise you'll look uneven'.

And at every stage they were filming her progress.

'I can't talk,' she told Diana afterwards, through lips that were swollen and stiff. 'It's too painful.'

'What's happening, darling?'

'My face is like a balloon,' Lucy whispered, feeling very sorry for herself. At moments like this she seriously wondered if it was all going to be worth it. 'They've made incisions on the inside of each cheek, and they've stuffed silicone implants over my cheekbones.'

'Oh, darling . . .'

'Mum, d'you think it's going to be OK?'

'I'm sure it will, sweetheart.'

There were moments when Lucy thought her mother didn't sound as sure as she was making out. No sooner had the swelling from that operation subsided than Dr Kahlo informed her cheerfully that the next stage would be an endoscopic brow lift.

'What's that?'

He smoothed the side of her face with tender fingers, and his smile was gentle.

'We just make two tiny incisions in your scalp at the front, behind the hairline so there will be no scarring, and then we insert a telescopic lens inside your forehead which will lift the skin and muscle around your eyes and eyebrows.'

Lucy looked at him in alarm. 'But there's nothing wrong with my eyes,' she protested.

'Nothing wrong with your eyesight,' he corrected, 'but the damage to your nose and cheekbone has affected the skin around your eyes. It's nothing, my dear Lucy. Thousands of women have this operation for mere vanity.'

Lucy supposed he knew best but the constant acute discomfort if not actual pain of all these operations was getting her down, as was the enforced bed rest for a couple of days afterwards, interspersed with Richard, her personal trainer, putting her through a strenuous series of exercises.

'When's it all going to end, Dad?' she wailed when Nigel phoned her one afternoon.

'I'm not sure, but according to Amelia Harrow, Dr Kahlo's delighted with your progress,' he replied. 'Has she been to see you?'

'No. I haven't seen her since she came here with me. They don't encourage visitors, you know. Anyway, that's enough about me. How are you and Mummy?'

Nigel's voice was more cheerful than she'd heard for a long time. 'I'm in terrific form, darling. Couldn't be better. And Mummy's fine. So are Granny and Tilly. We're all looking forward to having you home again. I'm sure it won't be all that long now.'

'I hope not.' She'd arrived at the clinic in October. Already it was December and it would be her first Christmas away from her family. By January, Dr Kahlo was rubbing his hands and talking about being 'nearly there'.

Lucy looked at him hopefully. 'How much longer?'

'We're going to get rid of this keloid next. That will make a big difference.'

'What's a keloid?'

He took her hand and smoothed one of her fingers over her cheek from the corner of her mouth to near her ear.

'Oh, I know,' Lucy said instantly. 'That dreadful scar that lies like a long thin pink worm on my skin.'

He patted her cheek and his smile was benevolent. 'What a way to describe your poor little scar,' he reproved gently. 'The newest type of laser treatment will take that all away, and then we will do a little fine tuning with your mouth to get it back in shape. I think we will take a little fat from your behind to enhance your lips surgically.'

January melted into February and then March while Dr Kahlo continued his 'fine tuning' like a sculptor perfecting a work of art. Richard kept Lucy in good physical shape. She also received regular visits from Lauren, who peered closely at Lucy's face through her gold-rimmed glasses and smiled wanly while enquiring if she had everything she wanted. And Suzy Durrell popped into her room twice a week to see if she had any problems and to ask if she was happy with the way everything was proceeding.

'I suppose so,' Lucy replied, not wishing to appear

ungrateful. After all, she was not being charged for anything, and she reckoned she was receiving hundreds of thousands of dollars' worth of treatment and care. 'I shall be glad when it's all over,' she added.

'Of course you will! It's been a very long haul hasn't it? And you've been amazingly patient.'

Then one morning, to her surprise, Dr Kahlo arrived in her room, accompanied by a make-up artist and hairdresser. He seemed excited as they stood in a row looking at Lucy, who was sitting up in bed, having her breakfast.

'Now we come to the finishing touches, my dear Lucy,' he said triumphantly, 'and I have a few suggestions to make which I think would enhance your looks even more.' He waved his hands expansively in introduction. 'This is Brett, one of Hollywood's top make-up artists, and this is Leroy, a famous hair stylist.'

Lucy grinned. This was more like it! Lipstick was more fun than liposuction and a good haircut would cheer her up more than dermabrasion, laser treatment and lashings of vitamin E cream to smooth away the last of the scarring.

'Great!' she enthused. 'When do we start?'

The three of them crowded closer, examining her from every angle, and praising her looks. Lauren joined them, making notes for the doctor. 'Fabulous', 'Amazing', 'Fantastic', were just some of the adjectives that flew around Lucy's room which had, for so long, been the setting for her pain and misery, tears, homesickness – especially at Christmas – acute boredom, the endless metallic taste of anaesthetic, the queasiness she suffered after every operation and the sensation of red-hot thread being pulled through her skin as the stitches were drawn out. Was it really all coming to an end at last? Would she be able to look in a mirror without fear and be free to go out into the world again?

For the next few days she felt like a film star as her hair was tinted glossy black – 'because it will enhance the colour of your skin more than brown' – before being expertly cut and root-permed to give it 'lift'. Then there were the experiments with make-up, closely watched by Dr Kahlo who kept making suggestions, which Lauren assiduously noted down for the commentary that was to accompany the video. Finally, he seemed satisfied except for one thing: the colour of her eyes.

Lucy stared at him, shocked. 'What's wrong with the colour of my eyes? They're bluish-grey.' She felt quite upset for a moment.

'Trust me, my dear. We are working towards total perfection here,' Dr Kahlo told her, squeezing her hand. 'Have patience. Tomorrow you will see yourself and I can promise you one thing – you'll be thrilled with the way you look.'

Nine

It was still dark when Lucy awoke, and suddenly, after all these months, she was consumed with impatience to see herself. The frustration of not having a mirror suddenly got to her. Whose face was it anyway? Clambering out of the high hospital bed, she switched on all the lights and pulled back the heavy curtains, hoping she could see her reflection in the floor to ceiling windows that overlooked the beach. But the dawn was already melting the night sky from dark pewter to pale pearly pink, and all she could make out was her general shape. Disappointed, she clambered back into bed. Amelia was coming to collect her at lunchtime and take her back to New York for ten days before she flew home.

'I'm giving a party for you, Lucy,' she'd announced when she'd phoned the previous week, 'and we'll do all that shopping for clothes we talked about and see a bit of the city. You probably feel as if you've been incarcerated for a very long time, like the Sleeping Beauty.'

'I *have* been incarcerated and it feels like forever!' she replied. 'I've lived in either track suits or pyjamas for so long, I've almost forgotten what it feels like to wear something nice.' And although she was longing to get home and see her family again, ten days in New York, staying in a fabulous Park Avenue duplex with Amelia Harrow, was a thrilling prospect after all she'd been through.

At nine o'clock Dr Kahlo came to see her. He looked very tired, she thought, and dispirited.

'So, you are off today, my dear Lucy,' he said sadly. 'I'm more indebted to you than I can say for allowing me to restructure your face. You have been a model patient and it's been a real pleasure to work with you. And thank you for giving me the opportunity to film the whole process for my students.'

'It's I who have to thank you, Dr Kahlo,' she said, feeling very sorry for this ageing man who suddenly appeared to her this morning an acutely lonely figure, talking as if he were regretting her departure and was going to miss her.

'I'm sure I'm going to be thrilled with my face . . . you've no idea how grateful I am,' she added with sincerity.

'I hope you will continue to be pleased,' he said, turning to go. 'I'm going to leave you in the hands of Brett and Leroy now, and my ophthalmic colleague will be coming to fit you with tinted contact lenses.' His eyes swept over her body as she stood in her leggings and leotard, ready for her workout, and he smiled indulgently. 'I'm glad to see you have put on some weight. Richard has done you a lot of good, hasn't he?'

It was true. Her muscles were firmer, her shape more defined and she definitely felt fitter.

'Yes,' she said, eyes shining. 'I'm going to join a health club when I get home, so I can keep up the good work.'

The next two hours seemed to fly past as Leroy and Brett did her face and hair, and the optician fitted her with contact lenses, and finally she changed into a lightweight pleated skirt with a long matching jacket which she'd bought at the clinic's boutique. Wearing matching shoes and tights, and a pair of pearl earrings, she felt both excited and nervous in equal measure. Whatever she looked like, she reflected, she *felt* enormously glamorous, but then who wouldn't with

Hollywood make-up artists hovering over her? A strong sense of unreality prevailed; if someone had come into her room and told her she'd got the starring role in a TV soap opera, she'd have believed them.

Then Dr Kahlo reappeared, and the others withdrew respectfully to the other side of the room. His appraisal of Lucy as she sat by the window was intent and as he continued to look at her, a smile of genuine pleasure filled his face.

'Magnificent, my dear Lucy,' he murmured. Then he turned to Lauren who had been watching intently.

'Bring in the mirror,' he commanded, and Lucy felt an icy frisson of excitement zing through her whole body.

Lauren, peering through her glasses, came back into the room with the nurse. Between them they carried a long mirror on a stand. It was covered with a white sheet. *What the hell ...?* Lucy thought, trying not to laugh. Talk about dramatics! Dr Kahlo evidently planned to unveil her reflection to her in a way that was pure theatre. The mirror was placed in front of her, no more than five feet away. Everyone stood in a silent group, with the exception of Dr Kahlo. The Ringmaster. The Magician. The Master Illusionist. The tension in the room was now almost palpable. Then he placed his hand on a corner of the sheet.

'Are you ready, Lucy?'

She braced herself, scared and apprehensive now. What in God's name was she going to look like? She closed her eyes for a moment and took a deep breath. She was shaking all over.

'Yes,' she said in a small voice.

The white sheet was whipped off. There was a gasp as she came face to face with herself for the first time in six months and Dr Kahlo beamed with triumph. Stunned, Lucy stared at her reflection. She was *beautiful*. A sob caught in her throat and she found it hard to believe her eyes. She was drop-dead beautiful. There were no scars. Her face was symmetric, both cheekbones high and rounded, her jaw now level on both sides, her nose straight and perfect. Her eyes seemed larger and wider and it was strange but rather fun to see how the contacts had turned her ordinary blue-grey eyes to a wonderful Elizabeth Taylor shade of violet. Nervously Lucy gave a little smile . . . and it was a balanced smile, full lipped and attractive, revealing even white teeth. Gone was the dreadful distorted lop-sided grin with the angry scar running up to her ear; gone were the scars along her jaw and on her forehead. She blinked and looked again. Her hair, which had been an ordinary shade of brown, was now black and cut with a fringe, hanging long and lustrous to her shoulders in a dramatic Cleopatra style.

'I don't know what to say . . .' she gasped.

'Your expression says it all.' Dr Kahlo beamed. 'Now, if you will allow me to take some final film of you our joint venture will have been completed.'

'I'm so grateful,' Lucy blurted out, as tears of emotion welled in her eyes.

Leroy, before he said goodbye, gave her the details of her tint, so she could do her own hair in future, and Brett gave her a make-up chart and a box of cosmetics.

'Just follow the diagram and you'll be able to recreate your make-up very easily,' he told her. The optician had already given her a spare pair of lenses. Then Richard came to give her a goodbye hug.

'Thank you so much for everything,' she said. 'I'll keep up the exercises, I promise.'

'Good girl,' he said, giving her a big kiss on the cheek. 'You've done well.'

After Dr Kahlo had filmed her from every angle for the last time, complimenting her on her choice of the cream suit because it went so well with her new colouring, she had to admit the manageress of the boutique had persuaded her to buy it.

'I've never worn cream before, because it made me look washed out,' she admitted.

Then it was time to say goodbye to her counsellor. Suzy had been away on her annual leave for the past few weeks, and so she hadn't been around to see the final touches to her appearance. As she swept into Lucy's room with her customary 'Hiya, Lucy!' she stopped suddenly, hands in the pockets of her trousers, and stared as if she couldn't believe her eyes.

'Lucy?'

In high spirits, she did a little twirl in the middle of the room, her pleated skirt flaring out around her knees.

'What do you think?'

Suzy sat on the edge of the bed. 'It's . . . it's amazing,' she said. 'Of course I've not seen you without dressings or bandages on some part of your face, or else you were all bruised and swollen. It really is remarkable,' she added.

'I can't believe what Dr Kahlo's done,' Lucy enthused. 'Wait until my parents see me! And my sister Tilly! God, I feel as if I've been reborn. Given a whole new start in life.' She seated herself on the sofa, a slim radiant figure with a face that Leroy had said would 'knock 'em dead!'.

There was a pause. 'And have you found yourself again?' Suzy asked.

Lucy laughed. 'I'm not sure, but I'll settle for this me for the time being,' she replied happily. 'It will take a bit of getting used to but I'm so bowled over by my own appearance that I don't think I care *who* I am, right now.'

There was a knock on the door. It was Lauren to say Miss Harrow had arrived and Dr Kahlo would like them to have a farewell drink with him in his private apartment before Lucy left.

'This is goodbye then,' Suzy said, giving her a hug. 'I've so enjoyed getting to know you, Lucy, and I wish you all the luck in the world. If you should ever need me, you know how to get hold of me. If there is anything I can do for you in the future, you only have to call.'

'Thanks. And thank you for all your words of wisdom over the months. I really am grateful.'

'Not my words of wisdom, Lucy. Your own ability to face the truth and deal with it – something a lot of people are unable to do. You've done very well and I'm proud of you.'

Dr Kahlo and Amelia were there waiting for her in his apartment, and as on the day she'd first arrived, Peters the butler was serving drinks.

'Ah, there you are, my dear Lucy,' Dr Kahlo exclaimed. 'You look magnificent. What do you think, Amelia? Doesn't she look fantastic? Would you believe that this was the little wounded girl you brought to me six months ago?'

Amelia's expression was frozen in a mask of shock, her mouth open and her eyes stricken. All she said was a whispered: 'Oh!'

The rapture left Lucy's face and she looked crestfallen. Dumbly, she stared at the older woman.

'Don't you like it?' She couldn't keep the disappointment out of her voice. She'd expected Amelia to praise her extravagantly as everyone else in the clinic had done. 'What's wrong?'

It seemed that Amelia had to conduct a terrible internal struggle with herself in order to get her face to smile again.

'Of course!' she said in an actressy voice, visibly trying to pull herself together. 'It's . . . it's *terrific*, darling! You look amazing! Well done. Are you pleased yourself?'

'I'm thrilled,' Lucy replied, looking at Dr Kahlo to see how he was reacting to Amelia's strange manner. But his expression was unchanged. He continued to smile and look proud of her.

'Let's drink a toast to you then, my dear Lucy. This was a joint effort so you are to be congratulated too on a magnificent achievement.' As Dr Kahlo spoke, Peters stepped forward with a small round silver tray on which stood three glasses of champagne.

Amelia's hand, Lucy noticed, shook as she helped herself to a drink, and her face was very white.

Dr Kahlo raised his glass. 'To Lucy . . . and her beauty,' he said. Amelia sipped her champagne but said nothing. Lucy took a gulp, and it seemed like the most wonderful drink in the world.

'Thank you, thank you so much,' she gushed, embarrassed by Amelia's obvious disapproval. Dr Kahlo seemed oblivious of it though as he continued to gaze with unconcealed pleasure at her face, as an artist will admire a sculpture or a painting he has executed.

'If you'll excuse me a minute . . .' Amelia said suddenly, and putting down her glass, she left the room, saying she must powder her nose. Lucy watched her go.

'What's wrong?' she whispered. 'Why is she behaving in such a funny manner?'

Dr Kahlo's smile was paternal. 'You mustn't let Amelia upset you, my dear. I have known her for over thirty years . . . nearly forty. You must realise –' his voice dropped to a whisper '– that it can be extremely hard for an older woman to see a beautiful young girl like you. It makes her remember how she once looked but will never look again. Amelia, in her youth, was one of the most exquisite women I've ever seen.' He gave a little shrug. 'I've done what I can over the years to hold back the ravages that time brings, but in the end age catches up with you and for a woman like her that can be a terrible tragedy. There is no turning back the clock beyond a certain point. I think Amelia came to realise that just now, and it is very, very painful for her.'

'Yes, I see.' Lucy hadn't realised how much it must have meant to Amelia to look youthful and beautiful.

'She'll be all right in a few minutes. Just ignore her mood. Her grudge isn't towards you personally. It's directed at the passing of time,' he added sadly.

They were talking about the video of his new operating techniques and how valuable it would be to other plastic surgeons when Amelia came back into the room. She was smiling with forced brightness now, but Lucy noticed that she avoided eye contact with Dr Kahlo as she finished her drink and then insisted they must off or they'd miss their flight back to New York.

The journey was awkward. Amelia hardly said anything, but twice Lucy caught her sneaking a sideways look at her face when she didn't think Lucy was looking.

'Are you sure it isn't a terrible bore for you to have me to stay for the next ten days?' Lucy said at last in desperation. If the atmosphere was going to be as frigid as this, she couldn't possibly stay.

Amelia blinked, and seemed to come out of a deep reverie.

'Of course I want you to stay.' She seemed surprised by the question. 'I'm giving a little party for you on Wednesday and then we'll go out to dinner. I've lined up several very nice young people for you to meet. And you want to go shopping, don't you? And see some of the sights?'

'If it's not too much trouble, but if you're busy I'll quite understand . . .'

Amelia clamped a grey-gloved hand over hers. 'I'm not too

busy at all. I'm looking forward to your staying. We'll have a great time, honey.' Her tone was sincere, Lucy thought. Perhaps it was going to be all right.

It wasn't until late that afternoon, ensconced in Amelia's spare room once more, that Lucy had a chance really to examine her face closely. There had been so many people around when Dr Kahlo had 'unveiled her', as he'd described it, and just how long could a person gaze at themselves in a mirror without being thought terribly vain? she reflected. There was a long gilt-framed mirror on the wall between the windows and Lucy stood in front of it now, unable to take her eyes off herself. It was a strange feeling, after all those months of not seeing herself at all, preceded by months of not being able to *bear* looking at herself. She had to admit that what she now saw in the mirror was fantastic. Dr Kahlo had really turned her into a young woman of stunning beauty. Of course the violet-coloured eyes and the dark dramatically styled hair would enhance any face, but the miracle was that all her scars had gone, her face was symmetrical, her mouth full and tilted up at the corners, and her skin a glorious golden shade, thanks to the make-up. Recognising that the resultant success was part surgery and part the illusion created by make-up, she still marvelled at Dr Kahlo's skill. For a moment she wished that Peter could see her now; better looking, in fact, than she'd ever been, poised, confident and generally in terrific shape thanks to Richard. A wide smile of delight spread across her face. Even her teeth seemed to look better than before the accident.

Amelia had said they were going out to dinner that night at a very popular Italian restaurant two blocks away.

'We'll leave here around seven, is that OK for you?' To Lucy's relief she had seemed more like herself once they'd got back to the apartment.

It was now five minutes to seven. Lucy slipped out of her room and went down to the elegantly furnished living-room below. As she passed Amelia's bedroom on the way, she heard her talking on the phone through the open door.

'. . . What are you playing at?' she was saying angrily. 'What sort of game is this, Dick?' There was a pause and then Amelia continued: 'I'm not worried about my commission. Yes, I know you'll give it to me just the same but I would *never* have brought the girl to you if I'd known . . .'

Lucy hovered nervously, gut feeling telling her they were discussing her surgery. But what had Dr Kahlo done that was making Amelia so enraged?

'. . . I was shocked when I saw her,' she was saying as Lucy strained to hear.

Lucy crept away, scared of being discovered eavesdropping by the maid. As she waited in the living-room for Amelia to join her she realised her heart was pounding uncomfortably and she felt uneasy. What had Amelia expected when she'd come to collect her earlier today? A plain Jane without the scars? Of course, Amelia had never seen her before the accident, so maybe she'd presumed she'd never been attractive in the first place? But why should she *mind*? That was what was so strange. She'd sounded quite furious on the phone just now . . . in spite of the fact she was 'still getting her commission' which Lucy thought an interesting point.

Amelia appeared a few minutes later, smiling and saying breezily it was time they left.

'We're being joined by some great friends of mine who have a son and a daughter around your age, so it should be fun,' she explained, swinging her beige mink-edged cape around her shoulders. She was wearing a dark chocolate brown chiffon cocktail dress with suede shoes to match, and in spite of her age looked every inch the film star. Lucy's first thought was, surely she couldn't be jealous of *me*? She was obviously too confident of her own appearance to be jealous of anyone.

'Let's go.' Amelia slipped her hand through Lucy's arm and hugged her to her side for a moment. 'You look gorgeous darling. You're going to break a lot of hearts from now on!'

Confused by this volte-face Lucy followed her down to the waiting limousine while Amelia chattered away, describing the shops they'd go to tomorrow, and the party she was giving for a hundred people in a few days' time.

'I wish your parents had come over because I'd love to meet them but I believe they're giving their own celebration party to welcome you home.'

Diana had mentioned this on the phone and Lucy nodded.

'I hope they recognise me!' she joked, wanting to draw out Amelia on the subject of her face. 'I'm not sure I recognise myself but I'm thrilled at what Dr Kahlo's done.'

Amelia didn't look at her, but continued to gaze out of the car window.

'He's a superb surgeon and artist,' she said quietly.

The restaurant was elegantly decorated with a lot of glass, mirrors, chrome and spotlights. Dazzling white table-cloths and scarlet flowers added a touch of drama, and as Lucy followed Amelia across the shiny black-tiled floor, she saw the rest of the party had already arrived and were waiting expectantly for them.

'Hello, darlings!' Amelia called out to no one in particular, and then as they rose to fawn over her sycophantically, she swooped around, kissing everyone on both cheeks, before introducing Lucy. There was a middle-aged couple called Pam and Serge Bowling with their son Ivan and seventeen-year-old daughter Fern, and another couple nearer Amelia in age, Nancy and Noel Messore. Lucy realised all eyes were on her and as she slid into her seat between Ivan, whom she took to be in his mid-twenties, and the elderly Noel Messore, she felt herself blushing uncomfortably. She also got the impression as the evening progressed that none of them knew what had happened to her. The conversation was general and she received a lot of compliments, especially from the men, but no one asked questions that led her to believe they knew she'd had plastic surgery and when she admitted this was her first visit to the States, Amelia added smoothly: 'Lucy and I got acquainted through mutual friends in Britain. Anyway, you'll all meet again at my party on Wednesday.'

Ivan, who was practically unable to eat he was so transfixed by Lucy, gazed at her throughout dinner and it was only when they got to the coffee stage that he spoke.

'Are you in films, too?'

'No, I'm a researcher for a London radio station,' she replied. 'What do you do?'

'I'm a commodity broker. Rather dull, I'm afraid.' He grinned self-deprecatingly.

At that moment Lucy felt a hand squeezing her shoulder and a man's soft husky voice murmuring in her ear. 'What a lovely surprise! I thought you were living in San Francisco? What brings you to New York, honey?'

Lucy spun round, startled. A tall deeply tanned man with clear blue eyes was gazing down at her and he was smiling broadly.

'I'm sorry . . . I'm afraid you've mistaken me for someone else,' she replied, smiling back.

'Hon-ey!' The man, greatly amused, drew out the term of endearment. 'Who d'you think you're kidding? How are you, Dagmar? You're looking great. How long has it been? Three . . . four years?'

Lucy shook her head. 'No, really. I don't know you. You've made a mistake . . .'

'Hey! What is this, sweetheart? You can't have *forgotten* me, for Christ's sake . . .?' A steely shaft made his eyes suddenly cold and his grip on her shoulder tightened.

'Look, I only arrived in New York today—'

Ivan suddenly cut in. 'Kindly leave my friend alone,' he said with youthful aggression. 'You've made a mistake. This lady comes from England.'

Amelia, who had been watching the interchange switched on her most radiant smile as she addressed the stranger. 'It's so easy to make a mistake . . . by candlelight . . . but my friend has never lived in America . . . and this is her first night in New York, so I'm sorry to say you *are* mistaken.' Her limpid eyes would have melted an iceberg, and the man stepped back, letting go of Lucy's shoulder. His smile was polite but unsure.

'Then I apologise,' he said doubtfully. He glanced at Lucy again. 'I really thought you were someone I used to know. Sorry to have bothered you.'

As he walked away, Amelia shrugged. 'What some men will do to meet a beautiful woman,' she remarked drily.

'*Two* beautiful women,' Noel corrected her.

She patted his hand. 'Ever the gallant gentleman,' she purred.

As the conversation became general again, Ivan turned back to Lucy.

'Have you been to see Wall Street?'

'I haven't had time to go anywhere yet.'

'Would you like to take a trip in a helicopter? It only lasts about twenty minutes but I'd be delighted to show you the sights. Perhaps we could have lunch afterwards?' There was no mistaking the admiration in Ivan's voice as he gazed into her eyes.

'Can I let you know? I'll have to take a rain-check with Amelia first because I'm not sure what her plans are,' Lucy replied diplomatically. She wasn't sure whether she liked Ivan or not and felt a strong resistance within herself to becoming involved, even remotely, with anyone at present.

'I'll see you at the party on Wednesday anyway,' he persisted eagerly. 'You can let me know then. I'm sure Amelia wouldn't mind.'

Lucy nodded politely and then turned her attention to Noel, who was picking his teeth surreptitiously behind a cupped hand. He immediately dropped his hands to his lap and turned the full force of his spinach-clogged smile on her.

'Do you like to go dancing?' he enquired.

Getting into bed that night, in the luxuriously decorated spare room of Amelia's apartment, Lucy felt vastly amused at how incredibly her life had changed in the space of twenty-four hours. There she'd been, confined to her gilded cage in the clinic, still feeling ugly though she'd been getting adjusted to that perception of herself over the months, and then – WHAM! Here she was, being taken to a top glitzy restaurant, and having men fawn over her like she was some model or pop star. The superficiality of it all was what struck her most. And how easily men were influenced by a pretty face. A few months ago they'd have shied away from her in disgust, as Peter had done. Now they wanted to whirl her around the skies and trip the light fantastic! And what would Peter do, she wondered, if he were to see her now?

At the party it was even more noticeable. Amelia had taken her shopping again in the morning, and Lucy decided to splash out and to hell with the cost. It was time to spoil herself. With Amelia's guidance, she bought several classic suits, three chic dresses that could be worn during the day or for drinks parties in the evening, a long white figure-hugging evening dress, and a beautiful cream silk dress with a low-cut back.

'That's the one you must wear tonight,' Amelia said as soon as she saw it. 'With cream tights and matching high-heeled shoes, and lots of pearls. You'll look sensational, darling.'

Lucy hadn't enjoyed herself so much for ages, especially as everyone knew Amelia and they were given VIP treatment in every shop. By the time they got back to the apartment, the boot of the car was loaded not only with all the clothes she'd bought, but shoes to match each outfit, handbags to match the shoes, scarves, belts and a range of costume jewellery that Lucy was assured would 'go with everything'. She'd spent nearly all her savings but felt heady with delight, if slightly guilty at spending so much on herself.

'How very English!' Amelia laughed. 'You deserve nice things after all you've been through. I can never understand this puritanical attitude the British have, like it's a sin to enjoy or indulge yourself. Be extravagant and have a good time, I say.' Then she looked critically at Lucy, her head on one side as if she couldn't make up her mind whether to say something or not.

'You do think this colour suits me, don't you?' Lucy asked, holding up the cream dress in front of herself.

'Brilliantly, darling. No doubt of that. I was just wondering though . . . do you intend to keep your hair that colour? I know Dick advised it . . . and of course it's stunning . . . but I quite liked your own colour, you know.' Amelia spoke diffidently, which was very unlike her, Lucy thought, and felt quite disappointed that her colouring didn't meet with her total approval.

'I think I'll keep it like this,' she replied, turning to look in the long cheval-glass in her room. 'It's supposed to go with the darker make-up he advised, and the violet-coloured contact lenses.' She peered at her reflection. She'd managed to recreate the eye make-up Brett had devised for her rather well, she thought, using black eyeliner, dark greyish-purple eyeshadow, and mascara brushed lightly into her eyebrows. Dr Kahlo had also recommended she have her eyelashes dyed at the same time as her hair and she loved the result.

'I'll let Mummy and Daddy see it first, but I think I'll probably keep it the way it is.' When she was alone she brooded on Amelia's remark. Was she really jealous of the way Dr Kahlo had made her look? On the phone that first evening she'd sounded more angry than anything else. Lucy shrugged. In just over a week's time she'd be home, ready to get back to real life again, and hopefully to her job at City Radio if they still wanted her back.

Amelia was already waiting for her guests when Lucy joined her in the drawing-room.

'Oh, you look wonderful,' Lucy said spontaneously as soon as she saw her standing in front of the fireplace sipping a glass of champagne. She was wearing a clinging dress of deep Parma violet silk and around her neck was a heavy necklace of amethysts and diamonds, with earrings to match.

'Thank you, darling.' She looked pleased by the compliment. 'So do you – cream really is your colour,' she added with genuine sincerity.

Waiters hovered by the bar which had been set up in the hall. The first of the guests began to arrive, and Lucy braced herself to be introduced to almost a hundred strangers who, according to Amelia, were longing to meet her. 'We love the English over here,' she explained.

The first couple were middle-aged New Yorkers, the wife chic in a black suede dress by Balmain, the husband oozing charm under the weight of a heavy wallet. Next came several nubile girls, bronzed, long haired, exuding a wide-eyed sweetness disguising a longing to get into films.

'Darling, I want you to meet . . .' Amelia was dragging her

off again, this time to meet a young man who quite obviously hoped he stood a chance with her.

'Champagne, Madame?' A waiter topped up Lucy's glass and she found herself being introduced to the head of a publishing empire, a charismatic man with dark curling hair and eyes like glittering coals.

'Tell me about your radio work,' he asked.

They were joined by an elderly couple, gushing and giggling like school children and holding out their glasses whenever a waiter came near. The room was filling up. Maids were having to weave their way through the crowd as they offered exotic canapés arranged on silver platters. A waiter opened some of the windows. The sound of popping corks in the hall was generic of the occasion. Several film stars of Amelia's generation made an entrance, slowly and purposefully as if they were still on a film set, and Lucy tried to remember their names to tell her mother.

Then the dinner guests from a few nights before appeared, with Ivan, flushed and eager, asking her how her trip was going and what about that ride in a helicopter?

'Lucy . . .' It was Amelia again, gaily grasping her hand and pulling her away. 'Come and meet one of the President's righthand men. He's Senator Arnold Ebner, and he's a *darling*.'

Lucy found herself face to face with a heavily built man in his sixties, his face reddened by a network of fine purple veins, his eyes hooded and his mouth full lipped.

'How do you do,' she said politely, stepping forward to shake his hand. He stared at her in a perplexed way before speaking.

'What did you say your name was?'

'Lucy Howard. I'm staying with Amelia,' she replied, almost having to shout above the din of conversation filling the room.

'Lucy Howard?' he repeated.

'Yes.'

'Humph!'

'Amelia tells me you're one of the President's righthand men; that must be so interesting,' said Lucy, trying to make conversation. The Senator half turned away as if wanting to find someone else to talk to, and Lucy looked around, searching for Amelia; where the hell had she got to? She'd been dipping and diving around the room, as if she were on roller blades.

Ivan popped up at her elbow. 'What are you doing after the party?'

The Senator had drifted away and the noise level was increasing. Lucy suddenly had the strangest feeling that she was not herself at all. When she caught sight of her reflection in the ornate gilt-framed mirror above the mantlepiece she wondered for a fraction of a second who the beautiful young woman with the long black hair and fringe was? Then she blinked and the stunning violet eyes blinked too, and she experienced a moment of panic. She'd changed so dramatically she literally didn't recognise the exquisite creature who looked back at her. It was also the first time in her life she'd been surrounded by people, and men in particular, who were all trying to get her attention, all showering her with compliments, all wanting to get to know her better, all wanting a piece of her. They clustered close, asking where she lived, what she did . . . surely she was a model? A film star? A pop singer? They couldn't *believe* she was only . . . did she say a *researcher* for a radio programme? Not even an interviewer or a presenter?

Lucy suddenly found it all too much after the months of isolation and sickness she'd been through. Excusing herself, she slipped out of the room and locked herself in the bathroom, where the small child that lurks inside every adult buried her face and wept because no one was acknowledging *her*. She wasn't a great beauty, just a sweet ordinary little girl, whom nobody noticed especially. No one thought there was anything special about her, except perhaps her parents, but *she* was the one who hurt; she was the one who felt bitterly rejected and knew she was only being made a fuss of now because of her new face.

The tears streamed unabated down Lucy's beautifully made-up cheeks and it took her several minutes to regain control of her emotions. It seemed she had lost so much and gained so much, but somewhere in the middle she had misplaced the person she used to be, and inside still was. Quickly repairing her make-up, she rejoined the party. There were cries of 'Where have you *been*?' and so she played them all at their own game, acting out the part expected of her. For a few hours she became the bright and brittle Lucy Howard from England, laughing at their silly jokes, accepting their banal compliments, tossing aside her great beauty with a nonchalant shrug, flirting outrageously, and only relinquishing the demanding role when she was alone, much later, in Amelia's spare room.

The urgent tapping on her bedroom door woke her up and for a moment Lucy felt completely disorientated. She couldn't even remember where she was. Then the door opened and the lights were switched on and there stood Amelia in trousers and a raincoat, her hair dishevelled and her face bare of make-up. For a moment Lucy thought she was dreaming, and then, as Amelia came over to her bed, she realised she was weeping.

'I'm so terribly sorry, Lucy, but I've just had very bad news. My elderly mother has had a stroke and I've got to go to her. She's in a coma and I'm not sure if . . .' She broke off, unable to continue.

Lucy sat upright, instantly awake. 'Oh, I'm so sorry! Is there anything I can do?'

Amelia shook her head and dabbed her eyes with a lace-edged handkerchief. 'Everything's under control. I'm catching the first plane to Dallas. Now you're to stay here, darling, just as we planned, and I'll fix for some of my friends to take you around, and I've already told my maid to look after you . . .'

'Please don't worry about me. I can easily get an earlier flight home so that . . .'

'I won't hear of it! I promised you this week and you shall have it. As soon as I get to Dallas I'll phone you. Of course, if the worst happens I'll be back . . .' Tears overcame her once again, and Lucy put her arms around her shoulders which seemed to have shrunk since the previous night. Then she went with Amelia to the front door of the apartment, where her chauffeur was waiting to drive her to JFK airport.

'Make yourself at home and help yourself to anything you want,' Amelia said, kissing her goodbye as she hurried off.

'Thank you. Take care of yourself. I hope you find things aren't too bad.'

'I daren't hope for that, darling. My mother's nearly ninety and she's been frail for a long time.'

After she had gone, Lucy turned to go back to her room and saw Beth, the maid, hovering in the hallway.

'That very bad for my lady,' she said sorrowfully. 'She always ask her mother to live here but the old lady wouldn't move. Now it is too late.' She shook her head and pulled her bright pink dressing-gown closer. 'You like some coffee, miss? Or a nice cup of tea?'

'No, thank you, Beth,' Lucy replied. 'There's some water in my room, I'll have that.'

It was a long time before she got back to sleep but while

she lay there she made one resolve. In the morning she'd go out and buy a guide to New York and explore the place by herself. She had a great need to be on her own right now in order to adjust herself to her new image. In order also, she realised, to stop being so protective of her former self. Last night she'd been shaken by the extraordinary sensation of actually being jealous of the way she now looked, compared to her appearance before the accident. What had been wrong with the old Lucy Howard? she'd asked herself, almost indignantly. Yet people hadn't fallen over themselves to get to know her then the way they had last night!

Dressing with care in a new green suit and with her face immaculately made-up, just as Brett had taught her, she set off to explore the city. It was a blue and gold day, with a light fresh breeze, and as she set off on foot for Madison Avenue she felt a surge of exhilaration.

It was as if she'd rejoined the human race after a long absence and it felt good.

Ten

'Is that you, Beth?'

Beth, who hated phones, clutched the receiver and pressed it hard against her ear. 'Yes, Miss Harrow.'

'Is everything all right?'

'Everything's just fine. How's your ma, Miss Harrow?'

'Not too good, I'm afraid.' Amelia's voice was husky and she sounded tired. 'Is Miss Howard there? Can I talk to her, Beth?'

'She's out, ma'am. Said she was goin' to see the sights. She left soon after breakfast.'

'OK, Beth. Will you tell her I called? And say there's no change in my mother's condition, so I don't know how long I'll be here . . . and will you cook dinner for her tonight, Beth? I don't suppose she'll want to go to a restaurant by herself.'

'Yes, ma'am.'

'Thanks. You've got my number here, haven't you?'

'At your ma's apartment?'

'Yes, Beth.'

'I expect so.' She sounded doubtful.

'I'll give it to you, to be on the safe side. Have you got a pencil?'

'Yes, Miss Harrow.'

Amelia enunciated with care. 'It's 214, that's the Dallas code, 661 7463. OK?'

Beth wrote down the numbers slowly and laboriously. 'Yes, ma'am. That's OK. Do you want Miss Howard to call you when she gets back?'

'No. The phone disturbs my mother. I'll check in tomorrow to make sure everything's all right.'

'Yes, Miss Harrow.'

Lucy didn't get back to the apartment until after six. She went straight up to her room, kicked off her shoes and flopped on to the bed, exhausted. But what a wonderful day she'd had! Partly walking and partly taking cabs, she'd seen the Empire State Building, gazed at some of the best paintings in the Metropolitan Museum of Art, watched people skating at the Rockerfeller Centre, popped in to Tiffany's where she drooled over the jewellery and the assistants seemed very anxious to sell her something, dashed down to Tribeca and looked in several art galleries, and finally wound up at Saks Fifth Avenue, where she bought Tilly the present of a short pink dress she could wear to parties.

What an exhilarating day it had been. So much to see. So much to do, and all the time it was like being at the bottom of deep ravines as the skyscrapers towered above her to dizzy heights.

A gentle tapping on her bedroom door awoke her just after she'd dozed off. It was Beth.

'Telephone for you, Miss Howard,' she said softly.

Lucy was instantly alert. She jumped off the bed, and ran in stockinged feet down the stairs to the phone in the hall, hoping it might be her parents; she wanted to talk to them but didn't like to make outgoing calls on Amelia's phone.

'Is that you, Lucy?'

Her heart sank with disappointment. 'Hello, Ivan.'

'How about that helicopter trip?' He sounded as eager as

ever. 'Are you doing anything tomorrow? I can take an extended lunch hour so we could take off at noon, and have lunch afterwards.'

Lucy hesitated for a moment. Ivan was a bit of a wimp but quite sweet and it would be nice to have an aerial view of New York with someone who could tell her about the various buildings.

'Thanks, that would be great,' she replied. 'Where shall we meet?'

Ivan sounded shocked. 'I'll come and collect you, Lucy. You can't go running around the city on your own.'

'Why ever not?' she said laughing. 'New York seems a lot safer than London these days, and I want to explore Times Square and take a stroll down Broadway in the morning.'

'Oh! Well, we could meet at the heliport, I suppose. It's at—'

She already had *Fedor's Guide to the USA* in front of her. 'Thirty-fourth Street and East River Drive,' she said.

'Yeah. That's right.' He sounded slightly miffed.

'OK. I'll be there just before twelve.'

Beth, who had been hovering in the kitchen doorway, came forward as Lucy finished the call.

'Will you be in for dinner tonight, miss?' As usual she was beaming broadly.

'Thank you, Beth. That would be lovely. Is there any news from Miss Harrow? How is her mother?'

'Madame says 'bout the same. She old lady, you know.'

Lucy nodded. 'It's very kind of Miss Harrow to let me stay on here.'

Beth smiled with silent delight and ambled back to the kitchen to make a fresh batch of chocolate cookies which she knew Lucy adored.

★ ★ ★

Ivan was waiting for her when she arrived at the heliport. He'd already bought their tickets and they were just in time to catch the next trip.

'Take the window seat,' he advised.

Lucy had never been in a helicopter before, and the sudden perpendicular take-off made her feel as if her innards were sinking out of her body and for a moment she felt quite dizzy. Then she looked down and the sight of Manhattan, spread below like a living map, made her gasp.

'It's amazing,' she said in wonderment.

Ivan was leaning over her, pointing out the skyscrapers and streets set out in a tidy grid pattern, with the exception of Broadway which slanted its way across the network of horizontal and vertical lines in a wayward route.

'There's Carnegie Hall, where all the best concerts are held . . . and that's the Eugene O'Neil Theatre. See that building over there?' He pointed with a long pale finger. 'That's Madison Square Garden and Pennsylvania Station.'

Lucy gazed down through the window, fascinated. Cars looked as small as ants, moving slowly along the roads, narrow as spaghetti. Pedestrians were mere specks of humanity who didn't seem to be moving at all. Then the helicopter swung to the right, and ahead lay the Hudson River, glittering like silver lamé in the sunlight, and beyond it the Atlantic.

'I really love it here,' she said impulsively. 'New York's got such a buzz, hasn't it?'

Ivan looked as gratified as if she'd paid him a personal compliment. 'Do you think you could live here?'

She smiled, aware of the note of hope in his voice. 'I'd never want to live anywhere but England because it's my home,' she replied with honesty, 'but I'd love to be a frequent visitor here, and if I'm ever seriously rich I'd like to have an apartment here.'

When the trip was over, Ivan suggested lunch at the Russian Tea Room. 'I feel like taking the afternoon off,' he added gazing soulfully down at her. 'Perhaps we could do something else? Maybe go to Radio City Music Hall?'

'Lunch would be great, but I do have various things to do this afternoon,' Lucy said gently. Ivan was a sweet young man and she didn't want to hurt his feelings but enough was enough. And if she spent the afternoon with him, he might take it as a sign of encouragement.

The traffic was so bad it took them half an hour to get to the restaurant and by the time they arrived it was early afternoon and the lunchtime rush was over.

'Yes, we have a nice table for two,' the manager assured them. He led the way to the front of the restaurant and Lucy followed, aware she was turning heads in a way she'd never done before but now she was becoming used to it. As Ivan followed, she suddenly heard a woman shriek. It was a cry of piercing indignation.

'Ivan! You louse! Goddammit . . . what are you playing at?'

Lucy spun round and saw Ivan cringing, scarlet in the face, hands shaking. Then the woman rose, charging over to where they stood. She was in her early twenties, with a harsh little face, long straight silvery hair, and so thin her knees seemed to be the widest part of her legs. Crisply dressed in navy blue and white, she was all sharp points and hard angles and her eyes were blazing with venom.

'Donna, it's all right. There's nothing going on. Let me explain . . .' Ivan was stammering and blushing so furiously his pale eyes were brimming with tears.

'Don't give me that!' Donna snarled, enraged. 'I'm outta town for a coupla days, and I come back to find you with this . . . this *broad*!'

The whole of the Russian Tea Room was agog now, ears

straining, eyes goggling, no one wanting to miss a moment of this unseemly drama.

Lucy stepped forward. 'I think there's been a misunderstanding—' she began calmly.

Donna didn't let her finish. 'The only misunderstanding I can see is you don't care whether you take someone else's fiancé . . .' She held up her hand. She flashed a large aquamarine surrounded by diamonds in Lucy's face. 'See *this*? You just leave Ivan alone. I'm not going to let . . .'

But Lucy had already turned away and was politely thanking Ivan for the helicopter trip.

'I've seen more of Manhattan than I ever knew existed, thanks to you,' she added drily. Then she walked with slow dignity out of the restaurant and into West Fifty-seventh Street.

The next day was Saturday and there was still no news from Amelia. Four more days remained before Lucy flew home and, feeling restless stuck in the apartment, she decided to do some more exploring. On her own this time. She still felt shaken by her encounter with Ivan's fiancée, and angry with him for allowing her to think he was unattached. What a jerk, she reflected, as she selected a red suit from her new wardrobe and brushed her hair until it hung, glossily, to her shoulders.

Today her plans included sending postcards to her friends and family and all her colleagues at City Radio announcing her imminent return. Then, saying goodbye to Beth, she set off, excited by the prospect of becoming a part of the surging mass of energy which she now associated with Manhattan. She'd meant it when she'd told Ivan how much she loved New York. From the dramatically rising skyscrapers to the bagel sellers on the streets, she breathed the air of enterprise and it gave her the feeling that anything was possible in this city.

* * *

When she got back to the apartment it was late afternoon. Laden with presents for the family, she went up to her room and decided to have a rest before dinner, which Beth had assured her was 'something special' tonight. Lounging on the bed, she switched on the large television in the corner. It had a huge screen and for a while she flipped from station to station, trying to find something interesting. There was little choice in spite of the enormous number of channels. It seemed to be either a variety of game shows where both the participants and the audience clapped to order at the least thing, like rows of seals, flapping their hands together, or else shopping channels where you could buy anything from a kitchen whisk to a diamond ring by phoning in with your credit card number. Finally she settled for the CNN news programme as that seemed to be the most interesting channel.

Almost immediately the announcer, in tones of suppressed excitement, began to give details of a murder that seemed to have taken place in New York just a few hours before.

'The body of Senator Arnold Ebner, who was fifty-six, has been found by a cleaner in the bedroom of what appears to have been a secret hideaway, on the twenty-seventh floor of the Southgate Tower apartment block, on Seventh Avenue and Thirty-first Street.' As he talked, the television camera panned up to the top of a very narrow skyscraper. In the background was Madison Square Garden and Pennsylvania Station. Lucy leaned closer to the set, fascinated. He'd been a guest at Amelia's party. She remembered speaking briefly to him.

Then the camera zoomed into a huge square lobby, with a bank of elevators and a long reception counter. Police were milling around now and an area, which was marked 'Emergency Exit' had been roped off. Having researched and worked on many such news items for City Radio, Lucy watched with keen interest. She knew that behind the scenes there would be chaos as the journalists scrabbled to amass as much material as possible for an audience always hungry for sensation and with deadlines to meet as well. It was hectic enough at a radio station; it must be ten times worse when visual footage was required as well.

'. . . It is not yet known why the Senator, who was shot through the head and chest at point-blank range, was in New York in the first place when his home, where he lives with his wife and their three sons, is in Washington,' continued the announcer. Shots of the Senator shaking hands with the President at the White House filled the screen and were quickly replaced with what Lucy thought was a typical clichéd group photograph with his wife and sons. Experience told her that a major story was breaking and for the first time since the accident she had a real longing to be back in the thick of things again, to be where it was happening and a part of the action. There was nothing as exciting as being at the centre of events when a big story was breaking. Turning up the volume she decided to stick with the CNN news programme, to see how they developed the story. Having met the Senator, she longed to know more about his murder – who would want him dead? And why?

The female news presenter, immaculately made-up and coiffured and wearing a smart navy suit, appeared on screen.

'At three o'clock this afternoon,' she announced, 'a cleaner at the Southgate Tower gave the alarm when she found the body of Senator Arnold Ebner sprawled on the bed. Senator Ebner is thought to have stayed there on a regular basis, although there is no record of the apartment being rented in his name . . .'

At this point a stretcher carrying a body in a rubber bag

was shown being carried out of the main entrance and into a waiting ambulance. The police were everywhere, and a large crowd formed a semi-circle outside the cordoned-off area.

'. . . The weapon has so far not been recovered.' It was back to the studio again, and this time a male announcer filled the screen reading the auto-cue. He was a smooth-looking grey-haired man in his forties, wearing a flamboyant silk tie. The shot flashed back to the scene outside the Southgate Tower, and a striking-looking man who was being introduced as Detective Mike Powling from the nearby Midtown South Precinct. He was in his thirties, blond, with strong features and a direct gaze.

'What can you tell us about this homicide?' the interviewer was asking, shoving a microphone to within inches of his face. Mike Powling looked grimly handsome, very obviously aware he was in the spotlight.

'We do have a description of someone who was seen leaving the apartment in question a few minutes after the estimated time of death of the victim,' he replied.

Lucy smiled to herself, recognising the speech mode from her own days of researching news items. It seemed the police talked in exactly the same sort of cautious jargon on both sides of the Atlantic.

'Are we talking about a male or female suspect?' asked the interviewer, pressing desperately for some real factual news that would keep the viewers at home happy.

'At this stage I do not wish to say but we do have shots of the suspect on the apartment block's security cameras so we are hoping to make an arrest very shortly.'

Then it was back to the studio, where the whole item was repeated once again from the top, with the added embellishment that the Senator's widow, Maisie Ebner, was reported to be 'shocked . . . grief stricken . . . unable to explain what her husband was doing in New York'. This last bit was read out while the screen became filled with a radiantly smiling face of a much bejewelled woman, which Lucy recognised as a stock 'mug-shot' from a picture library and entirely unsuitable for this particular occasion. That was one sort of embarrassment one was spared with radio, she reflected thankfully. Lucy watched for a while longer but there were no new developments, so getting bored she switched channels. Then Beth came to announce dinner. A place setting had been laid at the thick round glass table in the dining-room. She'd prepared a Mexican dish, hot and spicy with chillies and onions and herbs and there was a bowl of fresh fruit and a platter of cheese. Feeling hungry, not having stopped to eat all day, Lucy ate well, then felt so tired she had a bath and went straight to bed. By ten o'clock she was fast asleep.

The next day was Sunday and her stay was nearly at an end. She also realised that life outside the closeted environment of the clinic was proving more stressful and tiring than she'd expected. If she didn't pace herself during the next couple of days she'd arrive home exhausted. Working her way through the endless sections of the *New York Times* took up most of the morning, and as it was warm and sunny, she went for a stroll in Central Park in the afternoon and watched television in the evening.

Monday dawned grey and wet and as she looked out of her window, Lucy decided this was a day for going to the Museum of Modern Art.

As she put the finishing touches to her make-up – with practice she was getting quicker at doing it – her violet eyes gazed back at her from the mirror. It was weird to see this reflection of a person she didn't know and it was certainly going to take time to get used to her new glamorous image. A final brush of her now dark hair and she was ready.

There was loud urgent knocking on her bedroom door.

'Come in, Beth,' Lucy called out. Then the bedroom door opened, and a very frightened-looking face peered round it.

'Miss Howard, it's the police. They want to see you.'

Lucy turned slowly to look at her.

'The police?' she said stupidly.

'They here, miss. You come quickly.'

It could only mean one thing. Anxiety and fear kick-started her nervous system and she began to shake all over. The skin of her face felt tight and cold.

'Did they say what it was about?'

Beth shook her head.

'Oh God! Something must have happened at home . . .' Visions of her mother or father being in an accident filled her with horror. Was this how they'd felt when she'd had the car crash? But why were the New York police involved? Surely if something had happened her family would have phoned direct? Everyone knew where she was staying. Then she had another thought and instantly felt relieved. It must be Amelia they really wanted to see. Beth had got it wrong. They'd probably asked for the lady of the house. Lucy took a deep breath and hurried out of her room and down the spiral stairs of the duplex, followed by Beth who still looked terrified. In the hallway below, looking grimly up at her, were two uniformed policemen and a dumpy blonde-haired woman. The men wore navy shirts, trousers, and peaked caps with the city's coat-of-arms and their number in silver on the front. On their sleeves was the embroidered gold and blue shield-shaped badge of the NYPD, and strapped to their waists were sinister-looking revolvers in black leather holsters. The woman, by contrast, wore a tightly belted raincoat, heavy dark shoes, and had her hair cropped as short as a man's. There wasn't a trace of make-up on her face.

Lucy faced them coolly, hoping they wouldn't realise her heart was pounding nervously. Then the woman stepped forward, flashing her identity badge under Lucy's nose.

'I'm Detective Lee,' she snapped. 'We are arresting you on suspicion of homicide in connection with the death of Senator Arnold Ebner on the afternoon of Saturday May eleventh at approximately fourteen hundred hours.'

Lucy stared at them blankly, her mind spinning in freefall. This was some nightmarish mix-up; it wasn't happening. Of all the unreal situations she'd experienced in the past twelve months, this was the most bizarre.

'I'm afraid you've got the wrong person.' Her voice, after Detective Lee's, sounded very clipped and English.

One of the uniformed men spoke. He had a sour face and a deep cleft in his chin. Angry grey eyes stared into hers.

'What's your name?' he demanded roughly.

Lucy looked back at him, determined not to get ruffled.

'I'm Lucy Howard. I come from England and I'm staying here as a guest of Miss Amelia Harrow,' she replied succinctly.

'When did you arrive in the United States?'

Lucy hesitated. 'Just over six months ago, but I've only been in New York since Thursday.'

Detective Lee was scribbling everything down in her notepad. 'Where were you before you came here?'

'I was at the Kahlo Clinic. At Southampton, Long Island.'

'Doing what?' she demanded rudely. 'Have you a work permit?'

'I was a patient.' *What is this?* Lucy thought, with growing panic. *They're acting like they really think I've got something to do with this murder.*

'What was wrong with you?' Detective Lee's narrow face and beady eyes peered at her suspiciously.

'I had a bad car accident in England a year ago, and I was at the clinic for corrective surgery. You can phone them and ask them if you like,' Lucy added defiantly.

Lee searched her face disbelievingly.

'I don't see no scars.' Then she scribbled some more.

'Let's get going,' cut in one of the men impatiently. He looked like he wanted some real action and was still fingering his revolver, almost longingly.

Lee spun on him viciously. 'We'll go when I say it's time to go.' Then she grabbed Lucy by the arm and tried to steer her towards the front door. 'Move!' she yelled.

'Hang on a moment!' Lucy was seized by a mixture of alarm and fury. 'You've made a mistake. I don't even *know* the Senator.'

'Move!' Lee yelled again. 'You're under arrest, and if you don't come quietly we'll charge you with obstruction and resisting arrest.'

'But this is crazy . . .' Lucy tried to wriggle free but the woman's grip was like a tightening band of steel. *God! This is for real,* she thought in panic. *They don't believe me . . . what if they never believe me? What if they lock me up and I can't get hold of anyone? If only Amelia had been here . . . she would have explained that it was all a crazy mix-up.*

'You've *got* to believe me,' she begged in desperation. Beth was standing on the stairs watching the proceedings as if mesmerised.

'Beth!' she called over her shoulder. 'Get hold of Amelia . . . Miss Harrow . . . tell her what's happened! Tell her I need help . . .' Her words were cut short as Lee gave her another shove. Lucy managed to wrench her arm free but she was grabbed on the other side by one of the policemen. They'd got the front door open now and were trying to drag her bodily towards the elevators. She screamed and it flashed through her mind that this was more like being taken hostage than arrested. At that moment she felt the icy metal of cufflinks being snapped on to one of her wrists, then her other arm was seized and pulled behind her and both wrists were clamped together. Lucy screamed again.

'You can't do this . . .'

In silence, Detective Lee and the two armed policemen shoved her forward into the elevator and when they arrived in the lobby at street level, frogmarched her to the waiting police car. Press camera men let off flashes all around her. A crowd eager for excitement pressed forward. The nightmare had begun.

Detective Mike Powling, in the squad room for homicide at the Midtown South Precinct, had been put in charge of the case as soon as Senator Arnold Ebner's body had been discovered. His assistant, Detective Shelley Lee, swung into immediate action at his command and it wasn't long before he knew the murderer would be picked up very quickly, thanks to the security cameras at the Southgate Tower, situated on each landing. There were also three other cameras, positioned at various angles in the large square street-level lobby. It was going to be a cinch.

The initial examination of the body by a police surgeon had estimated the time of death at around two o'clock in the afternoon. It was Saturday and because of the weekend fewer cleaners were on duty which was why Amy, a cleaner from Harlem, hadn't got up to the twenty-seventh floor until the early afternoon. She was vacuuming the corridors when she heard the door of Apartment 536 slam shut. A moment later, apparently, a young woman with 'movie-star looks' hurried towards her from the direction of the apartment, and disappeared down the concrete emergency staircase that wound its way round and round a corner of the tower, all the way down to street level. Amy had wondered at this. It was a long way down, one mile she'd heard someone say, though she couldn't be sure. She'd had to walk down it herself once during a power failure and it had taken her twenty-five minutes. Of course she had no way of knowing if the suspect had got on to an elevator at a lower floor. But security cameras in the lobby had shown that the young woman emerged from the stairway twenty minutes later. So then Mike knew she *had* walked rather than risk being seen, close to, in one of the six elevators, which she most assuredly would have been on a Saturday afternoon when the majority of tenants were home.

An hour later Amy had entered Apartment 536 to clean around as she did each day and the sight that met her eyes sent her screaming down the corridor. The fifty-six-year-old Senator lay sprawled across the bed, the pillows stained crimson from the gaping wound in his head and the bedding soaked from bullet wounds in his chest and rotund stomach. He'd been shot seven times from point-blank range, and his open eyes and gaping blood-filled mouth bore testament to the terror he must have felt during those last few seconds before he was struck down. It reminded Mike of the violent killings he'd seen during the ten years he'd worked in the notorious 67th Precinct which covered South Brooklyn. Somehow he'd had the idea that life would be less turbulent in Midtown South, that the rich inhabitants of central Manhattan would settle their differences in a more civilised manner.

One thing was for sure, though. He'd never before come across such a distinctively featured suspect. Her beauty was breathtaking; her glossy black hair, long and thick and with a straight fringe, was dramatically stunning. But the face was extraordinary. The classic strength of the jawline, straight nose and high cheekbones was arrestingly beautiful, and he grinned to himself at the unintended pun as he examined the security camera's video. The perfect almond-shaped eyes and arched eyebrows could cause a man to go weak at the knees, he thought, as might the beautifully shaped mouth. No one looking like that could go around undetected for long. Once her face had been shown nationwide on TV and in the press she'd be picked up within hours. Even if she tried to disguise herself with a blonde wig and dark glasses she'd be spotted. Hers was one of the most sensational faces he'd ever seen. Forget Marilyn Monroe. Forget Audrey Hepburn. This girl was a real looker and he couldn't wait to interview her. Meanwhile . . . what was she doing with an ugly old bastard like Arnold Ebner?

Detective Shelley Lee had been in the police force for the past fifteen years and fourteen of those had been spent in the 67th Precinct, too, not that she'd worked under Mike Powling then. They'd been equals, both having joined the Police Academy at the same time, both graduating together, both intent on trying to make the world a safer and better place. Her transfer to Midtown South had taken place the previous year and to her disgust she'd been assigned as Mike's assistant. It was better than staying in the Flatbush area, she supposed, but there'd always been a sense of rivalry between her and Mike, and she felt pissed off that he'd got ahead and was now Chief of his own squad. The trouble was Mike had made the transition from the 67th to Midtown South without a blip, whilst she'd seen too much of the stinking under-belly of the city ever to fit comfortably into an affluent low-crime area again. She could never forget and never stop feeling that she was a part of an area that spilled its rotten guts out all over the goddamn' place, day after day, and night after night; it seemed that for the whole of her adult life she'd been running in hookers and chasing after drug dealers, picking up winos and pimps, and with her breasts crushed by a bulletproof vest, going after illegal immigrants, violent robbers and thieves, hoodlums with guns and plain crazy psychos who lurked in the dark ready to strike for no reason. Scum, the lot of them!

Surveying the savage killing of Senator Arnold Ebner was almost like old times. Arresting Lucy Howard, which Mike Powling had assigned her to do, was almost disappointingly easy. There'd been no real resistance. No dramatic shoot-out. Just one helluva rich babe who said in a mincing English accent: 'I'm afraid you've got the wrong person.'

Of course the stupid little bitch was as guilty as hell. Not only did they have her face on camera just after she'd left the Senator's apartment but the doorman also remembered seeing her coming down the stairs, which was unusual in itself, before she scuttled across the lobby and into the strcet. He'd even noticed her eyes were an unusual violet colour, 'like Elizabeth Taylor's.' That was why they'd been able to arrest her so easily, thanks to a taxi driver who'd been watching TV the previous night and remembered picking up the young woman who looked like 'that gorgeous dame' outside the Fashion Institute of Technology, which was only three blocks on Seventh Avenue from where Senator Ebner was murdered. More importantly he remembered dropping her off on Park Avenue and although he couldn't remember the number he was able to lead them to the right building. The doorman there informed them the young lady was a guest of Miss Amelia Harrow. What a breeze! Handed to the NYPD on a plate! Giftwrapped!

Now, with the prisoner safely locked in a cell in central holding, awaiting questioning, Detective Shelley Lee, thirty-nine, unmarried, unloved, and deeply bitter at the way life had worked out for her, sat down to file her report, due to be handed in to her superior officer, Detective Mike Powling, by lunchtime. She only hoped he'd give Miss Lucy fucking Howard as hard a time as she deserved, but because she had a pretty face, he probably wouldn't.

I do not believe this is happening, Lucy kept saying to herself as she sat on the edge of the bunk in the small cell into which she'd been unceremoniously pushed on her arrival at Midtown South Precinct's building. That had been two hours ago. No one had come near her since and she had no idea what was going to happen next. That was the worst part of all: frustration that no one would listen to her; no one would let her explain that she couldn't possibly have killed this wretched Senator whom she now hated irrationally although she hardly knew him. Why wouldn't they believe her? The whole situation was so absurd as to be laughable if it wasn't so serious. Sometimes, though, innocent people did get sent to prison, she reflected, as cold panic enveloped her. In the old days, in England, there were cases where blameless people had been hanged because they couldn't prove their innocence. Nothing like that would happen to her, of course, but there *was* Death Row and the electric chair in America, and . . . oh, God! If only Amelia had been home, none of this would have happened.

Lucy dropped her head into her hands, trying desperately to keep calm. She took deep breaths, her eyes shut, trying to force herself to be patient and logical. No doubt, in a few hours' time, she'd be back at Amelia's apartment, having a good laugh with her parents on the phone as she related her adventure. Wouldn't Tilly be fascinated? Want to hear every detail? What a story to dine out on for the next few years! 'There I was,' she could hear herself regaling her friends, 'putting the finishing touches of blusher to my perfect new cheekbones, when – WHAMMO! Policemen waving their guns around (well, a little embellishment was allowed in a case like this) and bursting into the Park Avenue apartment, and before I knew what was happening, I was accused of murdering a prominent US Senator. And then, as I was taken away in handcuffs, I found hundreds of photographers and TV crews waiting outside in the street and they all started shouting at me and going crazy. When I got there I was flung into this tiny filthy prison cell and then . . .'

It might make a riveting tale when it's all over, she reflected, coming out of her fantasy, but right now it was scary and it could be really serious if they didn't believe her.

Of course they'll believe me, she told herself sternly. In the first place, what would my motive be for murdering a man I'd only met briefly at a drinks party? This is a ludicrous mistake and no doubt they'll come any minute and say they're terribly sorry but they've arrested the wrong person. They'll *have* to, she thought as her heart gave an uncomfortable twist of apprehension.

The moment she set eyes on him she recognised him as the striking-looking detective she'd seen on television on the day of the murder, being interviewed outside the Southgate Tower, saying they had a description of the killer which he hoped would lead to an early arrest.

'I saw you on TV,' she said immediately, almost accusingly.

Detective Mike Powling regarded her with his steady gaze. His eyes, she realised, were a very pale blue so that the pupils were like large black full stops in the centre. His mouth, in repose, was full lipped and well shaped.

'Your full name, please?' he said politely.

Feeling more confident, Lucy replied almost perkily: 'Lucy Rebecca Howard.'

'Address?'

'Eastleigh Manor, Godalming, Surrey, England.'

'Age?'

'Twenty-two.'

'Status?'

Lucy frowned. 'How do you mean?'

Mike Powling pressed his lips together as if to suppress a smile. 'I mean, are you married or single?'

'Oh! Single.'

'Where were you Saturday afternoon between approximately two and three o'clock?'

'I was sightseeing, mostly. I bought two books in Doubleday, and then I looked around the shopping mall in the Trump Tower, and later I did a bit of shopping; presents to take home to my family, that sort of thing. Then I got a taxi and went back to Amelia Harrow's apartment where I'm staying.' As she spoke she realised the interview was being recorded.

'Precisely where did you pick up the cab?'

Lucy racked her brains, trying to visualise the scene. 'It was outside a big building . . .'

'All the buildings in New York are big, Miss Howard.' A flicker of sarcasm registered in his eyes.

Lucy ignored it. 'I remember now, it was the Fashion Institute of Technology. I nearly went inside but I was getting tired . . .'

'Whose apartment are you staying in?'

'I told you, Amelia Harrow. The film star,' she added defiantly, her expression daring him to say he'd never heard of her. Instead he actually looked impressed.

'What is the phone number there? I'll have to ask Amelia Harrow to corroborate your statement.'

'I don't remember the number and she's away in Dallas right now because her mother's very ill.'

'So you're alone in this apartment?' he asked with surprise.

'Completely alone, or do you have a . . . er . . . companion?'

'I am on my own,' Lucy replied, coldly now. 'That is, apart from Beth, the maid.'

'Has *she* got Amelia Harrow's number in Dallas?'

'I'm sure she has.'

Mike Powling lapsed into silence for a moment and then said almost sharply, 'What time did you arrive back at the apartment on Saturday?'

'About four o'clock, I suppose.'

'Can that be substantiated?' His pale blue eyes were searching deeply into hers.

She flushed. 'Yes. Beth saw me.'

Suddenly he leaned forward, resting his elbows on the desk that stood between them, his blond hair glinting in the overhead light like a smooth helmet.

'So tell me, Miss Howard, just how long have you been a . . . friend, shall we say? . . . of Senator Arnold Ebner?'

It was like a slap in the face after the routine questioning. *So he really does think I've done it,* she thought.

'I'm not a friend of the Senator. We met for a few minutes at a party given by Amelia Harrow last week, but that's all,' she replied with what she hoped was dignity.

'Come now, Miss Howard. Give me some slack. We know you were the Senator's mistress.' The black full stops seemed to pierce and impale her, holding her captive with their sharp enquiry, and the thought flashed across her mind that if she really had been guilty she would already have succumbed under the pressure.

'That is not true,' she said angrily. 'We talked for . . . oh, just a couple of minutes at Amelia Harrow's drinks party.'

Mike's voice was soft, almost seductive, as if he could wheedle the truth out of her. 'We know you were the Senator's mistress. We know you were at his apartment between two and three o'clock on Saturday afternoon. We know you walked a couple of blocks and then picked up a cab outside the Fashion Institute of Technology. We know where you are staying at present. We also know you were wearing a red suit that day . . . a very good colour which would have hidden any blood that might have splashed on to your clothes. We even have a statement from the cab driver who picked you up outside the Fashion Institute of Technology. This was a premeditated murder, ruthlessly planned. The message you left at the Southgate Tower for the Senator merely said you wanted to see him again, didn't it, for one last time?'

With each fresh accusation, Lucy started, flinching as Mike Powling's voice grew louder and angrier until he was almost bellowing in her face.

'And you kept that appointment, didn't you? He had dumped you but you wanted one last meeting . . . so you could get your revenge. Isn't that how it was?'

She shook her head violently. 'NO! No, absolutely not! I only met him for a few minutes. We didn't even talk, really. This is madness. And I was never even near the Southgate Tower.'

'Miss Howard,' he cut in, voice dropping to a deadly quietness, 'the Fashion Institute of Technology is three blocks from the Southgate Tower.'

Abashed, Lucy looked back at him. 'But you're mistaking me for someone else.'

'Then what about this?' He rose, tall and muscular, his white shirt and dark trousers sharply pressed and immaculate. There was a TV screen in the corner, linked to a video. He switched it on.

Lucy watched, intrigued. A moment later she let out a gasp, stunned, as she watched a film of herself hurrying along a corridor before turning sharply and disappearing down a staircase. But where was it? It didn't look like a shop and it certainly wasn't Amelia's apartment block. A moment later the screen was filled with a large square white marble lobby which she instantly recognised from having watched CNN news. It was the Southgate Tower. And there, walking towards the main door into the street was . . . herself. There was no mistaking her dark silky hair, cut long and straight and with a fringe, and her face, unmistakable with its dark arched eyebrows and almond-shaped violet eyes, straight nose, perfect mouth and clean jawline. And she was wearing her new red suit.

Aghast, she continued to look at the screen.

'But I've never been in that building in my life.' *She was innocent.* Why didn't he believe her? She'd obviously been set up, God knows by whom or why, but she could see it was going to be almost impossible to prove her innocence in the face of such evidence.

'You've got to believe me,' she said desperately.

Mike Powling didn't reply but continued to watch the TV screen as he pressed the rewind button on the remote control before playing the video once again.

Eleven

'Daddy? Oh, thank God I've got hold of you. Listen. I'm only allowed to make one call . . .'

Sitting in Detective Mike Powling's office, while he sat at his desk listening to every word, she tried to tell Nigel what had happened but kept stumbling on her words, gabbling in her haste in case she was suddenly cut off, not knowing how long she had to make this one plea to bring sanity to the situation.

'Daddy, *listen*,' she implored him as Nigel, dazed with shock, asked banal questions and seemed unable to grasp what was happening. 'Phone Amelia's apartment and get her number at her mother's house in Dallas from Beth the maid. Ask Amelia to fix for a lawyer to get me out of this mess.'

'Why isn't Amelia in New York? I thought she'd invited you . . .' he began, bewildered.

'For God's sake, Daddy! Her mother's very ill and she's had to go to Dallas. I need a lawyer. Fast. I've been arrested for *murder*, Daddy! I'm being held in a *cell*, for Christ's sake! I've got to get someone who can tell them I'm innocent.' Frustration and a searing sense of injustice brought tears of rage and fear to her eyes and made her voice croaky. 'They won't believe me, Daddy! And somehow they've filmed me leaving the building where the murder took place. I don't know what's going on and there's no one here

223

to help me,' she added, sobbing.

'Lucy, what's happening, darling? They've got to believe you. This is outrageous. Let me talk to someone . . .'

'It's no use, Daddy. I need an attorney. Please get hold of Amelia . . .'

'All right, darling. I'll get on to her right away. Now try and keep calm.'

After Lucy had hung up and been marched back to her cell, she felt reassured by her father's words. She knew she could depend on him. Now all she had to do was wait until a lawyer, or a criminal defence attorney as Detective Powling described it, got her out of this hell-hole. But how long would it take? It was now late afternoon, and her hopes of getting away that day were sinking fast. Did she really have to spend a night here? On this narrow bunk with a stinking blanket and stained pillow? With a small grille in the heavy metal door through which she could hear the shouts of abuse from the other prisoners?

At six o'clock the cell door was flung open and a prison warder marched in with a tin tray which he slammed down on the small wooden table before charging out of the cell again. It contained a metal plate of watery stew, a metal mug of strong tea and an apple. There was a spoon, but no knife or fork.

The irony of the situation was not lost on Lucy. This time last night she'd been relaxing in the guest suite of a luxurious two-million-dollar duplex in the smartest part of Manhattan, with a maid who'd been instructed to give her anything she wanted. Now here she was, held in a lock-up cell, accused of murder.

'What's going on, Nigel?' Diana asked in alarm. It was ten o'clock in the evening at Eastleigh Manor. Nigel had just come

224

off the phone from talking to Lucy and, in a stunned voice, was trying to explain what had happened.

'It doesn't make sense to me either,' he said, 'but she has been arrested for murder and I've got to get hold of Amelia Harrow.' He turned to go into his study and Diana trailed after him, still bewildered.

'But why Lucy?' she demanded.

Nigel seated himself at his large cluttered desk, quickly locating a blue folder marked 'Lucy's Medical File'.

Tilly, seeing them in the study, wandered in and draped herself along the length of the leather sofa by the fireplace.

'I thought you'd gone to bed,' she observed. 'What are you looking for, Daddy?'

'Ah! Here it is.' He withdrew one of Amelia's letters from the file. 'Tell her what's happened, Diana, while I get Amelia's number in Dallas from her maid.'

'Let's go into the kitchen and make some tea,' Diana whispered, as Nigel got through to Beth.

Briefly, Diana outlined the situation as she switched on the electric kettle. 'And apparently Amelia is visiting her sick mother,' she continued, 'so Lucy is alone, and desperately needs a lawyer to get her out of this mess.'

'Far out!' Tilly breathed in astonishment. 'Lucy accused of murder? Are you sure you've got it right, Mummy? Are you sure this isn't a wind-up?'

Diana shook her head. 'She spoke to Daddy herself. He said she was in a terrible state, and there's no one there to help her. We haven't any friends in New York either.'

Tilly leaned against the draining board, arms folded.

'Shit,' she said succinctly.

'Don't talk like that, darling. You know I hate . . .'

'. . . But, Mum! This is serious. What if they don't believe her?'

'They'll have to be *made* to believe her. Daddy will make sure she gets expert advice.'

Back in the study they found Nigel rubbing his face with both hands in a distracted manner.

'This is crazy,' he informed them. 'I've spoken to the maid *twice*, and she's given me the wrong number for Amelia. What the hell am I going to do now? She swears it's the number Amelia gave her, but when I got through it's an answerphone for a firm of bathroom fitters.'

'Get the right number from directory enquiries,' Diana suggested. 'We know from Lucy that Amelia's mother is in Dallas.'

Nigel raised tired and angry eyes. 'And does anyone know the name of Amelia's mother?' he demanded. 'Or her address? God, this is desperate. At this rate I'm going to have to fly to New York myself to fix a lawyer for Lucy.'

Tilly jumped up from where she'd been reclining.

'I know! Let's ring Miranda,' she exclaimed. 'She's a friend of Amelia's. She probably knows what her mother's name is.'

Nigel seized the phone again. 'Good thinking,' he said approvingly. Tilly gave a smug little smile and glanced in her mother's direction. She'd got to the age when she sometimes felt in competition with Diana for Nigel's attention and when she scored, took a secret delight in winning.

'Miranda? Nigel here.'

'Nigel? How are you? Everything OK?' Her husky gin-roughened voice sounded almost arch in its enquiry.

'I'm fine,' he retorted shortly. Fleetingly he felt glad that Miranda was history so far as becoming a part of their family was concerned; she'd always been too rich a mixture for him. 'I want to get hold of Amelia Harrow,' he continued, deciding to skip the explanations, 'but she's staying with her mother in Dallas, and I don't have the number. Would you by any chance know what it is? Or her mother's name?'

There was a pause, and a vision of Miranda, all tangled rusty-coloured hair and tight sexy leather trousers, flashed through his mind.

'I'm afraid I've no idea, Nigel,' she replied. 'It certainly isn't Harrow, because that's Amelia's stage name. I don't think I've ever heard her real name. Is it urgent?'

'Well . . .' He hesitated, unwilling to tell Miranda what had happened. She was a notorious gossip and if he did the tale of Lucy's arrest would be around London by dawn, no doubt in sensational and lurid terms.

'I just want to check something with Amelia,' he said evasively.

'You might be able to get it from her friend, Dr Kahlo. He's known her for years; kept her looking as young as she does, no doubt. Why don't you call him? Is Lucy still in the clinic? Is she looking normal yet?'

Nigel ignored the bitchiness. 'Yes, I'll call Dr Kahlo right away. Thank you very much.'

'Is there anything I can do?' She was obviously bursting with curiosity, sensing that something was up.

'No, thanks, Miranda.' Nigel made an attempt at sounding breezy. 'I'll call him tomorrow. Thanks, anyway.' Then he hung up quickly before she could say anything else.

'Wasn't that a bit rude, darling?' Diana asked anxiously.

'Fuck rude!' he snapped, dialling the clinic's number which he knew by heart, cursing himself for not thinking of it before. Diana and Tilly watched him in tense silence. When he got through he asked to speak to Dr Kahlo.

'I'm afraid he's with a patient. Can I connect you to his PA, Lauren Vincent?' the girl on the switchboard suggested.

'Thank you.'

A moment later Nigel was through to Lauren Vincent,

explaining his request but not saying why he needed to get hold of Amelia Harrow.

'She's checking to see if they've got it,' he whispered to Diana, hand cupped over the mouthpiece. There was what seemed a long pause. Then Lauren came back on the line.

'Yes?' said Nigel eagerly. They watched as his face fell into lines of disappointment. 'Well, thank you anyway,' he said politely. Slowly he replaced the receiver.

'No luck, Daddy?'

He shook his head. 'There's nothing for it.' Then he glanced at his watch. 'Diana, could you get on to British Airways and book me on the earliest flight they have in the morning? You can use the mobile. I've got to make some urgent calls to try and get the name of a good New York defence attorney.'

'But it's so late! You can't start ringing people at this hour,' Diana protested.

'I must,' he said firmly, 'because there may not be time in the morning.'

'I'll do it,' said Tilly, slithering off the sofa. 'Can I have your plastic? I'll put it on your Amex account, shall I?'

Nigel looked impressed and passed her his wallet. 'There you are.'

'Business class?'

'Anything you can get.'

'I suppose . . .' She tilted her head and looked longingly. 'I couldn't come with you, could I?'

'No way, sweetheart.'

'I could make myself useful, Daddy. And Lucy would like to have me there.'

For a second he longed to say, Yes, OK you can come. But Diana would need her support at home.

'I tell you what,' he said instead, 'I might take you and Mummy to the States when this is over.'

Tilly grinned. 'Wicked!' Then she flew off to the quiet of the drawing-room to call the airport on the mobile.

'Who are you going to phone now?' Diana asked, as he started dialling again.

'Geoffrey Morris, in the overseas section. He has a lot of dealings with our New York office. He's bound to be able to recommend someone. God, poor Lucy! As if she hadn't been through enough, without this disaster happening.'

Reaching across his desk for his address book, he dislodged a stack of papers and as they slipped sideways, about to topple on to the floor, Diana grabbed them and started to straighten them up.

'Don't touch those,' Nigel exclaimed. 'For God's sake, Diana, you know I can't stand the things on my desk being touched.'

'Yes, but . . .' Diana froze, gazing down at a letter that had caught her eye. She was reading it and her face had become white and pinched. Nigel looked up and to his horror saw what she was reading. It was written in green ink and the handwriting was as familiar to him as his own.

'Diana . . . I . . .' he began desperately, feeling the blood pounding through his head, and his heart racing.

The silence in the room was laden with impending disaster. The moment he had dreaded above all else had arrived and he had no excuses to offer.

'I don't understand,' she faltered. 'Who is Olivia?' Her gentle eyes were filled with agonised fear and Nigel knew the only way to deal with this was to tell her the truth.

Suddenly Diana turned away and flung herself down on the sofa as if she might faint. 'You're having an affair,' she burst out hysterically. 'Oh, God, Nigel, how could you? Who is this woman? How long has this been going on?'

He hurried over to where she lay, distraught for her and

for himself, realising that he might be about to lose everything he held dear.

'Listen to me, darling,' he said and his voice was louder than he meant it to be. 'Listen, Diana. It's over. In the past. And never for one moment was it a threat to our marriage. Never. I love you and I never had any intention of leaving.'

She was sobbing uncontrollably now. 'But who is she? How long were you . . . did it last?' She couldn't bring herself to say the word lovers. 'Where did you meet? Oh, dear God, I can't bear this. I always thought we . . .'

He took both her hands and held them tightly in his, his face full of anguish. Regret consumed him and made him feel hollow with guilt. It was now or never. If he didn't tell her everything he wasn't giving her the chance to understand what had happened, whether she eventually forgave him or not.

'Darling, there's something I must tell you. You're going to be shocked but I also hope it will help you to realise that this affair was never a threat to you,' he began gently.

Diana looked up at him, vulnerable and frail. Her whole world seemed to have collapsed and she wondered what he had to say that could possibly make things any better.

'It wasn't a woman called Olivia,' he said slowly. 'It was a chap called Oliver. He's in the army and—'

She looked bewildered. 'What do you mean . . . a man? What were you doing with a man?' It was obvious that in her confusion she didn't understand what he was saying.

'There have been times in my life,' he explained painfully, 'when I have loved men in the same way as I've loved women. I don't know why. It just happened. But it has never stopped me loving you. And it's over. I know it will never happen again. Oliver is out of my life for ever and you have absolutely nothing to fear.'

230

'You slept with a *man*?' she asked, dazed.

He nodded. 'It was much less of a threat to our relationship than another woman would have been, you know. I never stopped loving you for a single moment. You do believe that, don't you, sweetheart?'

Diana shook her head, shock stemming the flow of tears.

'I don't know what to believe,' she said, desperately hurt. 'I always thought we'd been faithful to each other. But with a man! How could you?'

'I'm more sorry than I can say, darling. I'd give everything I've got to be able to turn back the clock and spare you this pain. I never wanted to hurt you.'

'What's happened to him?'

Nigel took a deep breath. She had to be told in case the result of his blood test proved to be positive.

'He contacted me a while ago,' he said, unable to bring himself to look at her, 'to tell me he's been diagnosed HIV positive.'

Diana gave a smothered wail of horror. 'Oh, God!'

His grip on her hands tightened. 'I'm having a blood test but only as a precaution. I was always careful and I don't for a moment think we need to worry.'

Her grief was agonising to behold. He tried to take her in his arms, but she beat him off, arms flailing wildly. Then she jumped up off the sofa and fled upstairs to their bedroom, and he heard her slam the door shut.

For a long time Nigel sat with his face buried in his hands and it occurred to him that this couldn't have happened at a worse time. He rose shakily and went back to his desk to phone his colleague Geoffrey Morris. He couldn't bear the idea of leaving Diana at this moment, but there was Lucy to think of and he had to find her a good attorney as quickly as possible and he had to get to New York to sort out the mess she'd found herself in.

Geoffrey was helpful and immediately said he'd contact a brilliant attorney he knew. 'Give me all the details so he can get started. Where will you be staying?' he asked.

'I usually go to the Inter-Continental,' Nigel replied, feeling a great sense of relief as far as Lucy was concerned.

'OK. While you're flying over I'll set things in motion from this end,' he promised.

As Nigel was saying goodbye, Tilly came bounding back into the room, looking triumphant. He glanced at her warily, wondering if she'd heard Diana crying and rushing up to her room but she seemed oblivious to everything except her success at securing him a ticket for the first flight in the morning out of Gatwick to JFK.

Perhaps, he reflected sadly, it was just as well he was going away at this time. Diana would need peace and space in which to digest what he'd told her and, if they were to stay together, she'd have to readjust her thoughts and her feelings towards him and hopefully be able to understand and forgive. Always supposing, of course, his blood test was negative.

In the oval room of the White House, the President of the United States was still working late into the night. The murder of Senator Arnold Ebner was going to cause an almighty scandal and it was vital that a damage limitation campaign be set in motion immediately. So far the only question being asked by the media was, what was Senator Ebner doing in a New York apartment, rented in the name of Saul Schwartz, when he was supposed to be in Washington? The next thing they'd do was look into the details of his private life, and then God help them all! The President's normally bland expression was replaced by one of anxiety. Ebner had been a great politician, instrumental in getting several vital Bills through congress. He'd also been one of the President's most staunch supporters and his public image had always, miraculously, appeared to be unsullied. If the truth came out they'd all be branded with the same iron and, the President reflected, it would reflect badly on him. But how the hell were they going to stage a cover-up that would be good enough to convince the American people, let alone the eyes of the world which were also centred on Capitol Hill right now?

'We're going to have to go for the "set-up" theory,' he told his press secretary and advisors, who sat in a half circle around his desk, hanging on to his every word. 'The truth must not be allowed to come out. We must invent a scenario in which Ebner was set up by whoever, and it has to be a theory that will stick like shit to a blanket.'

Amelia held the thin white hands in both of hers as she sat on a low pouffe by the side of her mother's bed. Curled up into a foetal position, Rose opened her eyes and saw her daughter through a haze. She'd been like this for several days now, and Amelia had hardly left her side, although there were night and day nurses in attendance.

'When am I going to die, Amelia?' she asked at one point. Amelia struggled to keep her composure for she knew, had always known, that her mother feared death.

'You're not going to die,' she said robustly.

'Yes, I am.' Surprisingly, Rose's voice was stronger. 'I'm not scared any more. I don't mind dying now. It's just that . . .' She broke off and tears suddenly spilled down her sunken cheeks. 'It's just that I'm going to miss you so.'

Every ounce of acting technique that Amelia had ever acquired in her long career now came to the fore as she endeavoured to sound calm and cheerful.

'Oh, Mom, I'll be around, so don't you worry.' It struck

her then that this exchange should have been the other way round. But maybe not. She'd always believed in an after-life and that death was merely like going into another room. She would still be around and close to her mother after she had gone, and her mother would still be watching over her from wherever she was.

Rose seemed more peaceful then and closed her eyes. When the day nurse tiptoed into the room a few minutes later Amelia said: 'She's sleeping.' Then she asked for the telephone to be disconnected, so it wouldn't disturb Rose. 'And could you turn down the sound of the television, please?' she added. The set was in the next room and no one was watching it anyway.

'I'll turn it off,' said the nurse, creeping out again.

As the hours melted into each other so that Amelia lost track of time a change came gradually over her mother. It was almost imperceptible at first but gradually she seemed to shrink and grow paler, almost transparent, as if she might disappear altogether into the snowy linen of the bed.

Amelia couldn't be sure when Rose stopped breathing but the nurse came back into the room and said quietly: 'She's gone, dear,' and started to straighten the wasted arms and legs.

Although Amelia knew she was allowed to cry now and express her grief, somehow she couldn't. For a while she couldn't even take in that Rose had gone. Watching the laid-out body, serene, silent, with all the wrinkles on her face smoothed out, Amelia was convinced she could still see the chest rise and fall.

'Are you *sure*?' she asked doubtfully. Were her eyes playing tricks? Could Rose be just sleeping?

'Yes, dear. Quite sure. Very nice and peacefully she went, too,' replied the nurse, longing to be off.

There was much to do in the aftermath of death, and Amelia

decided she would hole up in her mother's house in Dallas until after the funeral. Most of her life had been spent working and pursuing her own interests; now she owed this time to her mother, who had asked so little of her in life.

Nigel's plane touched down at Kennedy Airport at seven o'clock, and by the time he arrived in Manhattan, crossing the bridge spanning the East River, the violet haze of evening was closing in on the multi-storey buildings, and in his imagination turning them into giant stalagmites rising out of a primordial swamp.

His room on the fifteenth floor of the Inter-Continental overlooked the Chemical Bank N.Y. Trust Building, the offices deserted and in semi-darkness now, but Nigel hardly noticed his surroundings, so anxious was he to get hold of the lawyer Geoffrey Morris had recommended as he was leaving Eastleigh that morning. He took the details out of his briefcase. The man's name was Joshua Goldberg, his office was at 576 Madison Avenue, and he lived in the apartment block on Park Avenue where the late Jackie Kennedy-Onassis used to live. He also probably charged an arm and a leg, thought Nigel, boldly dialling the attorney's home number although it was now late-evening.

'Actually I was expecting your call, Mr Howard,' Joshua Goldberg said as soon as Nigel got through. His voice was rich and relaxed and had the flavour of brandy and cigars. 'Geoffrey Morris has told me everything and I've been making enquiries into your daughter's situation. I shall be going to the Midtown South Precinct jail, where they are holding her, first thing in the morning. That is, of course, if you wish me to act on her behalf?'

'Yes, I do,' Nigel said with a mixture of relief and surprise that Joshua Goldberg had already started the ball rolling. 'Have you discovered what the hell's going on?'

There was a pause, then Goldberg spoke cautiously. 'Where are you staying?'

When Nigel told him, the lawyer suggested they meet right away.

'I know it's late but we have work to do,' he said. 'There's more to all this than meets the eye and we have to talk. I'll meet you in the bar in thirty minutes. Meanwhile, why don't you catch a look at CNN on television?'

Nigel switched on the set in the corner of his room. The screen sprang instantly to life. As he'd guessed, they were running the story of the Senator's death. He watched as the announcer recapped the details, and then he saw a shot of a stunningly beautiful young woman with long black hair being hustled out of a mansion block, her wrists manacled behind her back and her expression distraught, whilst two policemen pushed her roughly through a pack of jostling and shouting photographers and reporters and into a waiting police car. He barely heard the commentary but he caught the words: 'Lucy Howard, from Great Britain, was arrested within hours of the homicide and is being questioned about the Senator's death . . .'

Nigel sank on to the bed, shock making him feel suddenly weak. That was *Lucy*? He could hardly believe it. She was so changed! He felt quite breathless for a moment, wondering if they'd show any more pictures of her, but they'd gone on to another news item. Lucy . . . his poor battered-looking daughter a drop-dead beauty! Well, Dr Kahlo had certainly done his stuff, he reflected, trying to pull himself together. He honestly wouldn't have recognised her.

Glancing at his watch, he realised he had time for a quick shower and a change of clothes before he went down to the large opulent lobby with its incongruous gilt cage of twittering birds in the centre and adjoining bar. He placed himself at a table where he could watch the street entrance and ordered himself vodka and tonic. Twenty minutes later a very tall imposing-looking man appeared through the revolving doors. He was exquisitely dressed in a hand-made suit, with a white shirt and an Italian silk tie. He was younger than Nigel had expected; probably in his mid-thirties. After a quick glance around the lobby he made straight for Nigel.

'Mr Howard?' He shook Nigel's hand in a vast warm grip. 'I'm Joshua Goldberg.'

'Thank you for coming so quickly, Mr Goldberg. What can I get you to drink?'

'Mineral water, thanks.' He settled his large frame in the small chair opposite Nigel. 'Now, I'd like you to tell me everything you can about your daughter,' he continued without preamble. 'She's in a serious position, without an alibi, but also, very importantly, without a motive. I've been doing some research on Arnold Ebner. Of course the media are going bananas as you probably noticed if you watched the TV. I suppose they don't yet realise you've arrived in New York? Well, when they do you're going to be hounded by the press. The White House is going for a cover-up, of course; Ebner was a prominent Senator and a personal friend of the President. They're going to make out he's whiter than white. His widow, Maisie, is already hinting that he was killed because he stumbled on to an espionage plot to leak government secrets connected with dealings with the PLO.' Goldberg gave a short bark of ironic laughter. Then he withdrew a notebook from his breast pocket and a slim gold ballpoint. 'So tell me about your daughter Lucy?'

Fifteen minutes later Nigel had finished. There really hadn't been much to tell. In her twenty-two years Lucy had led a relatively ordinary life, with the exception of her accident twelve months before.

Joshua Goldberg sat in thoughtful silence.

'Will I be allowed to see her tomorrow?' Nigel asked anxiously.

'I'll arrange that you do. I'll leave you now, Mr Howard, to get some rest. You must be tired after your journey.' He rose to go.

'What's going to happen? Can we at least get Lucy out on bail while the situation is being sorted out?'

'I'll fix the arraignment for as soon as possible though bail may not necessarily be granted. A homicide charge is serious enough, but being charged with murdering a Senator is another matter. Can you fix sufficient funds? Or arrange collateral to cover bail?'

'Of course,' said Nigel positively, privately wondering how much Goldberg was talking about. Supposing he couldn't raise enough? Gritting his teeth, he decided that was something he'd worry about tomorrow.

'I'll call you in the morning,' Goldberg was saying, as Nigel walked him to the street door, 'and arrange for us to meet. I shall need to see the police report before I proceed, and . . . Oh!' It came out like an afterthought. 'Can you bring with you a cheque for fifty thousand dollars, made out to me for my fee? Once I appear in the Superior Court, to file for bail, I'm obliged to stay as the Attorney of Record, so I need half the fee before the arraignment. The other half will do afterwards,' he added almost casually.

As Nigel went up in the elevator to his room, he was wondering how on earth he was going to finance Lucy's defence. If Goldberg's fee was going to be a hundred thousand dollars, and there were bound to be extras, what was bail going to be set at? Whatever it cost, though, even if

238

it meant bankruptcy, he'd willingly give everything he had to help Lucy. He got into bed, but sleep evaded him. How had Lucy got herself into this position? he kept thinking. There was only one thing that stopped him from becoming hysterical during that long night, when the city seemed to consist of wailing canyons, police cars, ambulances and fire engines continually careering up and down them with their sirens screaming, and that was the knowledge that Lucy was innocent. That was all he had to hang on to. And if there was any justice in this world, she'd be proved innocent. In the meantime, though, he had to keep his head and do everything to help her. As soon as he got up in the morning, he'd start phoning around. Lying in the dark he made a mental list of the people he must contact. But first of all, he must find out the number of Amelia's mother . . . and his bank manager in England . . . and his accountant . . . the chairman of his company . . . his secretary . . . and, of course, Diana. She'd remained in her room that morning, after he'd spent a miserable night in the spare room, and she'd refused to see him when he left for the airport. He'd call her first thing to say he'd arrived but he wasn't sure how she'd react. Now, or in the future. The cold blue light of dawn filled his hotel room with melancholy as he finally dropped off to sleep at six a.m. When he awoke at eight, he realised it was already lunchtime in London.

'I didn't give you no wrong number.' Beth's indignant voice sounded like the squeal of tyres on hot tarmac.

Nigel tried to hold his temper in check. He'd rushed round to Amelia's apartment as soon as he'd had breakfast in an effort to obtain the correct phone number in Dallas and Beth was proving unhelpful. She stood in the doorway with her fat little arms akimbo, declaring that the number was right, and looked most offended when he told her flatly that it wasn't.

'Could I look at it, please?' he asked. He had the feeling that Beth had probably mis-read Amelia's handwriting.

'Look at what?' she said sullenly.

'The number. Where it's written down.' Time was getting on and he was seething with impatience. Joshua Goldberg would be phoning him at the hotel any time now, to say when he could go and visit Lucy, and he didn't want to hang about here, wasting time.

'But I gave you the right number. Why are you here? I can't help you no more.' Her voice had taken on a whining note.

'*Please* let me see where it's written down.' Nigel's face was red in an effort to overcome his frustration.

A moment later the beautiful mahogany front door was slammed in his face.

'What the hell?' he bellowed furiously, ringing the brass doorbell again. He felt more like kicking it. Then the door was flung wide and there was Beth, holding out a crumpled grocery bill. It was stained in one corner with what looked like coffee.

'What's this?'

'The number. It's on the back.' She looked at him as if he were stupid. On the reverse side some numbers had been scrawled in pencil.

'Thank you very much,' he said politely, jotting them down in his pocket diary. 'Do you know when Miss Harrow is returning to New York?'

Beth shook her head. 'She's burying her mother tomorrow.'

'Oh, I'm so sorry.' He felt embarrassed now. He didn't know the old lady had died. 'Thanks, anyway.' He was anxious to get away. In the elevator he compared the number with the one she'd already given him over the phone. It was exactly as he'd thought. In the telling Beth had transposed the 7463 to 4736.

Back at the Inter-Continental, he raced up to the reception desk to where an elegantly uniformed concierge was making notes.

'Are there any messages for me? The name's Howard?'

'I'll just see, sir.' He glanced at the rack behind him and withdrew a folded note from a little cubby-hole. 'This came a few minutes ago, sir.'

Nigel read the message, hands shaking: ARRAIGNMENT FIXED FOR FRIDAY. PLEASE CALL MY OFFICE, JOSHUA GOLDBERG.

Friday. Today was only Wednesday. God, he thought, Lucy will have been in prison for five days by then. Five days! She must be going out of her mind, wondering what was happening, unless Goldberg had already been able to speak to her? He flung himself on to his unmade bed, the chambermaids not having done his room yet, and set about making all his phone calls. Goldberg first, to find out when he could see Lucy. Then Diana, and after that Amelia. Of course he could understand now why Amelia hadn't come rushing back to New York when Lucy was arrested, but somehow he'd have expected her to get in touch by phoning them in England. Or doing *something*, even if her mother had died. CNN were running the story every half hour on television, which he'd watched again whilst having breakfast. It was major news, on the front page of the *New York Times* which had been delivered to his room. A large photograph of Lucy being driven away when she was arrested took up a quarter of the page.

His Lucy, he thought, though it didn't look remotely like her, this glamorous creature with the long black hair framing an exquisite face. He ached to see her now, and reassure her he was doing everything he could. And he knew Diana was going to go crazy when she found out that her daughter would have been imprisoned for five days by the time she was officially charged in court.

Seizing the phone, he dialled Goldberg's number. Perhaps they could bring the arraignment forward to tomorrow?

'Friday is the earliest I could arrange – the courts are busy,' Goldberg told him. 'I'm seeing your daughter this morning, and I've arranged for you to see her at noon. I'll meet you at Midtown South Precinct . . . it's on Ninth Avenue and Thirty-fifth Street. After you've seen her, we could go back to my office to discuss the whole situation.'

'Fine. I suppose you've no idea how much bail will be set at?' Nigel asked.

'Probably between two and three hundred thousand dollars,' Goldberg replied. 'Is that going to be a problem?'

It would probably mean raising a bank loan, getting a second mortgage on Eastleigh Manor and maybe selling his shares, but Nigel replied grandly: 'No problem. I'll set things in motion right away.'

'Great. See you at noon. Goodbye.'

Nigel ordered some fresh coffee from room service, and immediately the phone rang. It was Diana.

'What's happening, Nigel? How's Lucy? I've been waiting in all morning wondering what's going on. I tried to phone you earlier but they said you were out.' She sounded highly strung and edgy, and there was an unaccustomed coldness to her voice.

'Well, it's still only ten o'clock in the morning here,' he reminded her. 'I was round at Amelia's flat getting the right phone number for her mother.'

'Oh, God! Is she still away? I think that's too bad. She was supposed to be looking after Lucy and entertaining her

. . . she *must* know what's happened?'

'Her mother's died. The funeral is tomorrow. I've also met the attorney. Nice chap. He's arranged for me to visit Lucy at twelve o'clock today.'

'Give her my love. What does he think is going to happen? Why has she been arrested?' Diana was weeping now, but still she sounded hostile.

'That's what we've got to find out, sweetheart. Try not to worry. We all know she's innocent. I'll phone you later today. Is Tilly OK? And your mother?'

'Yes,' Diana sniffed. She didn't, he noticed, enquire how he was.

'I'll keep in close touch and phone you after I've seen Lucy,' he said.

'Yes, do. What did the attorney actually say? He can tell the police it's all a mistake, can't he?'

'I don't think it's as simple as that. She's being charged on Friday morning . . .'

'*What?* Oh, my God!'

'The murder is causing a big stir over here. CNN are running the story every half hour, showing Lucy being arrested, and she's on the front page of the *New York Times*.'

'No!'

'I'm afraid so. Listen, I've got to go, Diana. I've got to raise hundreds of thousands of dollars by Friday, and I must talk to the bank manager.'

'Nigel! Have we got that sort of money?'

'We're going to have to raise it, whether we've got it or not. Lawyers don't come cheap, you know, and because we don't live over here, I may actually have to produce the money for bail.'

'Oh, God! It gets worse every minute,' she wailed.

'Things will look a lot better when Lucy has been released.'

'But will it mean she can come home with you?'

'We'll be able to book into a hotel, but we won't be allowed to go back to England.'

'You mean, you'll have to stay in America?' Diana sounded appalled. 'For how long?'

'Of course we'll have to stay here until everything is sorted out,' he reasoned, sounding more patient than he felt. 'If we can prove that Lucy had nothing to do with the murder, then it'll be OK, but if we can't then God knows what will happen.'

'Oh, God . . .'

With forbearance, he told her once again not to worry before saying goodbye and hanging up. He had less than two hours before he saw Lucy and in that time he had to work financial miracles.

Lucy was awakened by the clanging of doors being opened and shut, and voices shouting to each other, but instead of feeling refreshed as she normally did when she first opened her eyes, she felt drugged and drowsy, sapped of all vitality, as if she'd drunk too much the night before and felt too heavy to move. This was her second morning in the central booking block so that meant it must be Wednesday. Where in God's name was everyone? Why was she still locked up? Incarcerated like a common criminal when she'd done nothing wrong? Anger overcame fear. She got to her feet and started thumping up and down the small confines of her cell, shouting: 'Hello? Hello? I want to see someone who can get me out of here!' She banged on her prison door with the flat of her hand. 'Will you listen to me!' she shouted, loudly and furiously.

For a moment there was silence as her clear English voice floated out into the corridor, and then an explosion of ribald jeers filled the air as the other prisoners expressed mocking derision at her accent, her words and her demands. They banged their metal mugs, swearing and yelling, so that she stood rigid with fear. It was a terrible sound and she could just imagine what would happen if she was let loose among that baying mob. Withdrawing to her bunk again she sat down hurriedly, overwhelmed by the seriousness of her situation. Suppose her father hadn't been able to arrange for someone to help her? *Where was Amelia?* She felt herself grow cold, the skin of her face stiff with anxiety. Two days now . . . two whole days. This isn't happening, she kept saying to herself. This can't be happening. It's one of those terrible nightmares that goes on and on and you know it's a nightmare but still you can't wake up . . .

Lucy started to breathe slowly and steadily in an effort to control the panic, wrought from fear and a sense of helplessness, that threatened to consume her. She kept repeating to herself that it would be all right in the end. Of course the police would realise their terrible mistake and let her go. They must . . . because she was innocent. As soon as they discovered she had nothing to do with the murder they'd let her out of this cell and tell her she was free to go. She clasped her hands together, interlocking her fingers so tightly to stop them from shaking that her joints ached. She clamped her jaw and closed her eyes, trying to concentrate her mind. Keep calm, she told herself. Stop panicking. Your family would never let you down. They will soon be coming to take you away from here.

The other prisoners had stopped yelling abuse at her through their grilles, but there was still a lot of clanging and swearing and the atmosphere was charged with hostility and the stench of degradation and squalor.

Please God, she prayed, eyes still tightly shut, help me to get out of here.

★   ★   ★

Joshua Goldberg couldn't keep his eyes off her. He didn't think he'd ever seen such a beautiful young woman in his life. The pictures he'd seen on television and in the newspapers didn't do her justice and she certainly bore no resemblance to her pleasant but ordinary-looking father. Sitting opposite her now, in an interview room at Midtown South Precinct, he had the unreal feeling that he was looking at some ancient goddess instead of an upper-class Englishwoman called Lucy Howard.

'My father's *here*? In New York?' She was pressing him to reassure her, comfort her, her almond-shaped eyes glittering almost feverishly with relief.

Joshua nodded. 'He'll be here in due course, but first I want you to tell me everything you can – and I mean everything. You'll be appearing in court on Friday where you will be formally charged with homicide and the charge put on record. We'll be asking for bail to be set, but I can't promise it will be granted.'

Lucy's eyes widened in terror, her momentary relief vanishing.

'You mean, I might have to stay in jail?'

'This is a very serious charge you're facing, and the political implications make it more serious than if Joe Schmo had been murdered. A date will be set for the preliminary hearing at that point.'

'But I didn't kill anyone,' she burst out distractedly. 'You've got to get them to believe that! I should never have been arrested in the first place. It's a ghastly mistake.' Her hands had started to tremble again and she looked at Joshua Goldberg beseechingly. 'You believe me, don't you? Daddy knows I'm telling the truth.'

There was something touchingly childlike in the way she said 'Daddy knows I'm telling the truth' and Joshua had no doubt at that moment that she was innocent. Not for a second did he think she'd killed anyone, but he'd seen the police report and the security video shot in the Southgate Tower, and the evidence, in his opinion, was stacked against her.

Drawing a yellow legal pad from his briefcase, he placed it on the table between them.

'Start at the beginning,' he said encouragingly.

'How far back do you want me to go? My arrival in New York last week? Or my arrival in America six months ago?'

'Tell me about your life in England, in the run-up to an accident I believe you had a year ago? Your father mentioned you were working as a researcher at a London radio station and that you were engaged to be married?'

Lucy nodded. Slowly and at times painfully she began to tell him about her job, her accident, Peter's reaction when he saw how badly injured her face was, and how his mother, Miranda Beaumont, had told Amelia Harrow what had happened and she in turn had recommended Dr Dick Kahlo.

Joshua raised his dark, clearly defined eyebrows and looked at Lucy closely again. So that was the secret of her remarkable looks; probably the secret of Amelia Harrow's beauty which he'd always admired, although she belonged to his mother's generation.

'Yeah. I see,' he said slowly, making a few additional notes to the pages of information he'd already taken down. 'So you arrived in New York last . . .?'

'Thursday. Amelia picked me up from the clinic, and we went out to dinner in the evening and met some friends of hers.'

'Can you give me their names?'

Lucy racked her brains, trying to visualise the group round the restaurant table.

'They were mostly older. I remember a couple called

Bowling and they had a son and a daughter, Ivan and Fern. Ivan took me on a helicopter tour of Manhattan on Friday and afterwards we went to the Russian Tea Room.' She paused, uncertainly.

Joshua looked at her closely. 'And?'

'We bumped into his fiancée. I didn't know he was engaged. It was very embarrassing,' she replied, flushing slightly.

'Who is his fiancée?'

Lucy shrugged. 'I don't know. He called her Donna. I left as soon as I realised the situation.'

Joshua made several notes on his pad. 'Who else was at this dinner?'

She remembered the spinach-clogged teeth leering at her. 'There was another couple. Noel and Nancy Messore. They were all old friends of Amelia.'

'What happened the next day?'

The flicker of a smile crossed Lucy's face. 'We went shopping.'

'What sort of shopping.'

'For clothes. I hadn't had anything new for ages, so I went on a spree.' She glanced down at the shapeless grey cotton prison uniform they'd made her change into when she'd arrived at the central booking department. 'I feel like I'm back in hospital or something in this garb,' she added, trying to sound jocular. The look of sympathy in Joshua's dark eyes nearly undid her at that moment. Biting her lip she looked away, fighting for control. If he noticed, he said nothing, but tactfully continued his questioning.

'Tell me about the drinks party Amelia Harrow gave. Did you know any of the guests?'

Lucy shook her head. 'No. She gave it so I could meet lots of people. I think she hoped I'd get invited to a few parties before I returned home.'

'Do you remember who was there? Can you recall any names?'

There was a pause and a flicker of anxiety showed in Lucy's eyes. 'Senator Ebner was there. I met him very briefly. That's not going to look good, is it?'

The dark eyebrows shot up again. 'How did he seem? Friendly? Relaxed? What did he talk about?'

Lucy frowned in concentration. 'I remember he seemed rather distracted. I tried to make conversation but he wasn't very friendly. I had the feeling he was looking around to see if there was someone more interesting to talk to.'

'Was he a great friend of Amelia Harrow?'

She shrugged again. 'I don't know.'

'Don't worry. I'll find out how well she knew him and also get a list of all the guests from her. That is, once she can be contacted.'

Lucy looked surprised. 'She's in Dallas with her mother. I told Daddy to phone her because I'm sure she'll be able to vouch for me. Haven't you spoken to her?'

'There's been a hitch on that. Her maid gave your father the wrong number, and now that he's got the right one, she doesn't seem to be answering her telephone. The operator says the phone has been taken off the hook.'

'What does that mean?' asked Lucy, perturbed.

'I'd say it means she doesn't want to talk to anyone because her mother just died, according to her maid who found a message on the answerphone when she got back from grocery shopping.'

'Oh, my God.' Lucy leaned against the back of her chair. 'She'll be so upset. How awful for her.'

Joshua Goldberg nodded, but he wasn't thinking about Amelia. Of greater importance to him was the line his defence was going to take. But first there were two vital things he had to do. The first was to find out who had set her up, and why. The second was to prove she didn't commit homicide by coming up with a fool-proof alibi for between one and three o'clock last Saturday afternoon, and as she was alone in the city, wandering around looking at the sights, that was going to be quite a challenge.

'Can you give me a list of people you came into contact with at the Kahlo Clinic?' he asked.

'Yes, but only the people who work there. The medical staff including the nurses, my personal trainer, the counsellor, beautician and hairdresser . . . those sort of people. You do realise I never met any of the other patients? Discretion is a priority at the clinic so no one knows who else is being treated. Will that be of any help?'

'We must try everything. Someone must have a motive for wanting to get you into trouble. What about your fiancé, Peter?'

Lucy looked at Joshua as if he were crazy. 'My *ex-fiancé*,' she corrected him. 'Why should he want to get me into this mess? It doesn't make sense. I honestly don't know anyone who would do a thing like that. I think the police have mistaken me for someone else.'

His smile was warm and full of admiration. 'Forgive my saying this, but you don't exactly look like anyone else.'

She shrugged dismissively, aware her new good looks were having an effect on Joshua Goldberg as they'd recently had on other men.

'So what are we going to do?'

'Tell me every single move you made on Saturday, the day Senator Ebner was murdered,' he replied. 'You must have an alibi of some sort. You must have been seen by someone, entering or leaving a building, going into a shop, catching a cab . . . apart from the one that picked you up near the Southgate Tower *after* the murder. Someone out there must have seen what you were doing early on Saturday afternoon, because our whole defence is going to rest on that.'

They sat looking at each other across the table and Lucy desperately tried to get her mind to work, but she felt so jarred, so nervous and confused, that she was having difficulty in getting her thoughts in order.

'Now *think*!' Joshua commanded her, almost sternly. He pulled a map of Manhattan from his briefcase. 'You started out from Amelia Harrow's apartment on Park Avenue. Did you walk everywhere? How many cabs did you take? Where did you go first?' He opened the map and spread it on the table. 'Now start working out the route you took, until you finally returned to her apartment in mid-afternoon. Everything depends on this.'

Twelve

Nigel followed the guard along a corridor and then into what reminded him of a glass-sided tunnel with heavy iron doors at each end. There was a row of wooden chairs beside telephones, and that was when he realised Lucy would be on the other side of the glass divide, looking in. Bitter disappointment filled him; he'd so wanted to give her a hug, hold her close and reassure her that, no matter what, everything would be all right. The guard consulted his clipboard.

'Here,' he said shortly, pointing to a chair. Nigel sat down, and then suddenly, looking startlingly beautiful and bearing no resemblance to his own beloved daughter, there was Lucy, clutching a phone and gazing at him through the thick glass with stricken eyes. Nigel grabbed his phone and spoke to her.

'How are you, sweetheart?'

'I'm OK, Daddy. I'm so sorry about all this. I don't understand what's happening or why they've arrested me . . .' Her voice broke, and he automatically reached out for her hand, but instead encountered the cold unforgiving glass screen.

'It's not your fault, darling. I think Joshua Goldberg's good, don't you? He'll do his damnedest to get you out of here.'

Lucy's eyes widened and he could see how frightened she was. 'God, I don't know what I'll do if he doesn't, Daddy.

And this is only a place for holding prisoners before they're charged. An actual prison is bound to be ten times worse. I *must* get out of here. Why do they think I killed this Senator? What are people saying? Does anyone really believe I did it?' The questions rattled out of her like machine-gun fire.

'Joshua Goldberg is the only person I've discussed it with,' Nigel replied. 'He knows you're innocent and he's going to do everything he can to prove it. How did you get on with him?'

'OK. He seems nice. He says the trouble is, I've got no alibi. There's no way I can prove I was only sight-seeing and doing odd bits of shopping on Saturday. I've racked my brains to think of anyone who might have seen me, around the time of the murder, but there's no one. And it's not much use that the doorman at Amelia's apartment saw me leave at ten-thirty that morning and come back at four is it?'

Nigel could tell by the way she was gabbling that she was near breaking point. Her hands were clenched into fists and her brow was furrowed, reminding him of how she'd been as a child when she was anxious about something. At this moment it was the only thing about Lucy he recognised. Her looks had changed so much and her appearance was so unfamiliar he found it hard to act naturally and bond with her again.

'If only Amelia had been home none of this would have happened, Daddy. I keep having this dreadful thought that she might have helped set me up. After all, it was Amelia who invited me to America and introduced me to Dr Kahlo. And then she introduced me to Senator Ebner. Do you think there's a link?'

He looked thoughtful. 'It has crossed my mind, I must say. It was Amelia who invited you over here and then insisted you stay with her after the operations, wasn't it? And it was she who gave this party where she introduced you to the

Senator. And now it seems she's vanished. It does seem a bit odd.' He looked into her eyes, wanting to say something to cheer her up. 'Dr Kahlo has done a wonderful job on your face, darling. Quite amazing. No one would know you'd had an accident.'

Her smile was wan. 'I look a bit different, don't I? I didn't recognise myself at first. They got me into wearing lilac-tinted contact lenses, and I've been taught how to do my make-up really professionally.' She smoothed her hands over her freshly washed face. Even without make-up, Nigel realised, there was not a trace of scarring on her pale clear skin.

'Amazing,' he said again. 'As soon as this nightmare is over we'll celebrate. I promised Mummy and Tilly a trip to New York. Shall I get them to join us, as soon as you're out of here?'

'I hope I'm out of here on Friday,' she said, alarm returning. 'You sound as if you think it'll be longer?'

'No, not at all. Of course you'll be bailed.'

'This has been worse than those first days in hospital. At least you and Mummy were there and everyone was being nice to me.' Her mouth drooped at the corners, like a child's. 'I just don't understand any of this.'

'Try not to worry. We'll get you out of here and this whole ludicrous situation as soon as we possibly can.'

'What worries me is . . .' There was a click as the line went dead. Lucy and Nigel looked at each other in dismay. The phones had been switched off. Their time was up. One of the guards was coming forward to escort Nigel out of the building. He rose reluctantly, never taking his eyes off Lucy. Then he blew her a kiss and felt as bad as on the day he'd left her at boarding school for the first time. She looked so slim and frail and her face had turned very white as he saw a warder taking her back to her cell.

Joshua Goldberg was waiting for him in the outer lobby, eyeing him speculatively.

'Everything OK?' he asked.

'We've got to get her out of here,' Nigel rejoined vigorously. 'I don't care what it costs, we've got to prove she had nothing to do with this murder. I think she's been made a scapegoat. Who is really behind all this? What sort of a man was this Senator, for God's sake?'

'Let's get to my office and we can run through the whole thing. I've got a car waiting,' Joshua replied. 'Believe me, I'm not letting a stone go unturned. We have to go into every eventuality. Someone wanted Senator Ebner out of the way, whether for private or political reasons. The question is, why? Once we know some more about him we'll have a much clearer picture of what's going on. It's obvious that your daughter was in the wrong place at the wrong time.'

'But she says she was never *in* the Southgate Tower,' Nigel protested vehemently.

Outside the precinct the crowds had grown in the hour since Nigel had arrived and in the front line, five deep, were the press photographers, journalists, and TV camera crews, all surging forward immediately clamouring to get a picture, an interview, even a sound-bite from the father of the girl who'd been accused of killing one of the country's leading Senators. This was a big news story, possibly the scandal of the decade, and although the White House Press Office had issued a statement in which they suggested the murder was the work of a subversive political group, no one believed it. Supposition was rife and every possible theory being expounded. Members of the late Senator's family, brothers, a sister, even a cousin, were freely giving television interviews in which they claimed Arnold Ebner to have been 'a wonnerful human being' who would not have hurt a fly, and they 'felt sick to the stomach' that a great man like him had met with such 'a truly terrible end'.

'What's your daughter saying, Mr Howard?'

'How does she feel today?'

'What have you got to say about your daughter?'

'Is she going to plead guilty?'

'Have you talked to Lucy today?'

'What are *you* feeling about this murder?'

'What does it feel like to have a killer for a daughter?'

Nigel recoiled as if he'd been punched in the chest. Faces crowded close, voices seemed to be baying almost angrily. He felt trapped, vulnerable, caught up in a maelstrom from which there was no escape. For a moment he panicked and then he heard a strong and steady voice in his ear.

'Ignore them. Say nothing. The car is straight ahead so just push your way through,' Joshua advised.

Nigel pressed forward, avoiding eye contact with the journalists who clustered ever closer like locusts ready to strip him bare to his soul. He pressed his lips together and tried to look tough, but he was being jostled and pummelled and squashed, and a scuffle broke out to his right as a photographer stepped back on to the foot of a camera man. Then he felt a kick on his left ankle as a lens zoomed close to his face and flashbulbs practically blinded him. For an awful moment Nigel thought he'd be knocked down and trampled underfoot before he reached Joshua's car but suddenly a policeman seemed to appear from nowhere, the car door was opened and he felt himself being pushed inside with such force that he thought he'd pitch forward on to his knees. Joshua jumped in after him, the door slammed shut, and still surrounded by shouting and flashing lights, the car pulled away from the kerb.

Nigel looked at Joshua, stunned. 'Jesus Christ! That was awful! Did you know it was going to be like that?'

'I'm afraid the news got out that you were visiting Lucy this morning. I'm sorry about the commotion, but you have to realise this is a sensational situation. Everyone thought highly of Arnold Ebner; he was the President's best friend. The news of his murder is bound to cause an explosion of media interest.'

As Nigel settled back in the luxurious chauffeur-driven limousine, he realised he was out of his depth. Nothing like this had ever happened in his life before and his orderly existence of commuting from the country up to London each day was like comparing a galactic trip in a rocket to driving along a country lane in a horse and cart. It was not surprising, he reflected, that Joshua charged such enormous fees. The pressure must be intense. Even more impressive than the car were Joshua's offices, at 576 Madison Avenue. Situated on what he described as the second floor, but which by English definition was the first, Nigel found himself in a panelled room, dominated by a partner's desk, on which were arranged a maroon leather blotter, the bronze figurine of a horse, a silver-framed photograph of two little girls, and, unlike his own desk at home, a couple of neat stacks of files. Maroon leather-covered chairs, several good paintings, and a low square coffee table set in front of a sofa gave the room an air of masculine comfort and opulence which Nigel found reassuring.

Joshua motioned him to take a seat while he positioned himself behind his desk, and opened a blue file which had Lucy's name on it.

'Your daughter has told me everything about herself but I wondered if you had any ideas? It seems inconceivable that Lucy should have enemies, don't you agree?'

Nigel nodded vehemently. 'She's always been very popular, apart from which she doesn't really know anyone over here.'

'That's a thin line of defence but it's the one we're going to have to go for on Friday in the absence of any alibi, although I'm still hoping someone will have seen her on Saturday afternoon around the time of the murder who will be prepared to make a statement.' As he spoke, he was riffling through the file as if for inspiration.

'There is one thing,' Nigel began, almost diffidently.

Joshua looked up sharply, his eyes bright with interest.

'It seems odd,' Nigel continued, 'that within days of Amelia's being called away to be with her sick mother last Thursday morning, Senator Ebner is murdered and no one has been able to get hold of Amelia since. She *must* know what's happened to Lucy. The case has been featured constantly on TV and in the newspapers, I don't see how she can have missed it. Why hasn't she come forward, if only to offer Lucy who was, after all, her guest in the apartment, her support? How come the phone at her mother's house is off the hook? Why does no one seem to know her mother's name or where she lives, apart from the fact that it's in Dallas? Is her maid covering up for her?'

Joshua nodded. 'We're doing all we can to get hold of her, but if she'd already left New York on Thursday morning, she won't be able to provide an alibi for Lucy on Saturday afternoon, will she?'

'That is, if she really did leave town.'

When Nigel finally left Joshua's office two hours later, he felt no more reassured than when he'd awoken that morning. As he returned disconsolately to the Inter-Continental, once again in Joshua's car which he'd been lent as protection from pursuing journalists, he feared that unless Joshua Goldberg could pull something out of the hat, Lucy might well be denied bail at the arraignment on Friday morning. Maybe the British Consul could help? Or perhaps he should contact the British Ambassador in Washington? Something drastic had to be done or he'd be letting Lucy down, and for that he would never forgive himself. Back in his room he phoned his bank in England to make sure they'd transferred three hundred thousand dollars to the Chase Manhattan Bank. Joshua had warned him that if Lucy were granted bail he'd have to pay the bailbondman's fee up front before they'd release her. Failure to do this would mean they'd keep her in jail until the case went to trial. He shuddered at the thought and, driven by panic, dialled the number in London.

Amelia woke on the morning of her mother's funeral feeling, to her surprise, quite calm and serene. It was to be a small and private affair for which she was deeply thankful: just a few of Rose's old friends and neighbours and the nurses who had looked after her during her last few days. Sometimes, Amelia missed the publicity and glamour she'd known when she'd been a big star in Hollywood, when everything she did and said and wore was reported, and she was followed everywhere by scores of photographers, but today she was thankful that her farewell to her mother would go unnoticed and unreported. It was what Rose would have wanted because she'd always chosen to stay in the background, proud of her only child, so dazzling in the limelight, but preferring for herself the anonymity of the shadows.

Many years before, when Amelia's father had died, Rose had bought the adjoining plot in the local graveyard for herself.

'We will be together in heaven,' she'd told Amelia with total conviction, as if they'd booked a suite in some paradisaical hotel. 'But we should also lie together, as we did for the forty-seven years of our marriage, so make sure I'm buried beside your father.'

Amelia derived great comfort from the belief that her parents were together again, and that today she would merely be making sure that their discarded earthly remains would lie for ever, side by side, under the rich soil. And, when it was all over, she would lock up Rose's house for the time being, and go away to some quiet spot for a couple of days, in order to grieve alone before returning to New York. She'd felt badly about abandoning Lucy Howard, alone in her apartment with only Beth to look after her, but was sure Lucy would have understood because she was such a sympathetic young woman. In any case, she'd be home in England by now, reunited with her family. Amelia vowed to write to her next week, to say how sorry she was and invite her to stay again the next time she was in New York.

At that moment the hearse arrived, bearing the pale oak casket. It looked so small. On the lid a profusion of white Casablanca lilies trembled delicately, their heady perfume filling the air with a poignant sweetness.

Amelia, dressed in a plain black suit, make-up and jewellery left behind, and accompanied by two of Rose's oldest friends, climbed into the following car. Any thought of Lucy was forgotten.

Diana hadn't slept for two nights and everyone presumed the reason was because she was worried about Lucy. In some ways she was actually grateful to have something to hide behind because how would she otherwise explain her constant tears, her distress and her obvious exhaustion?

She knew she was still in shock at learning Nigel was bi-sexual and she didn't know how she was going to come to terms with this dreadful knowledge, but sooner or later she was either going to have to ask for a divorce or stay with him. Mostly, she felt a deep sense of hurt and rejection. She'd failed him. That was obvious. Otherwise why had he turned to someone else? And a man, too? Not even another woman?

That was what she found so hard to understand. And had there been others, apart from Oliver, whose affectionate letter was forever stamped before her inner eye?

There were moments when her misery about Nigel and her worry about Lucy collided in her mind and she felt as if her head was going to explode and throw her into a nervous breakdown. What was she supposed to do?

It was a comfort to know her daughter was in the hands of a professional lawyer and that everything was being done to ensure her release; and she was grateful that Nigel had dropped everything to go to New York to be with Lucy, but who was there to comfort and advise her? She couldn't tell anyone what Nigel had confessed. It seemed too shaming. What would people say? Could she bear to witness the pity on other people's faces if it became known that her own wonderful husband liked sleeping with other men? And how would her own mother react?

Thankful that Tilly had gone back to school, Diana found herself enveloped in the most appalling misery she had ever known. Doubts filled her mind night and day. Hadn't she satisfied Nigel in bed? Had she become boring? Did she no longer attract him? Diana spent her nights sobbing into her pillow, feeling as totally bereaved as if she'd been widowed. The man she loved had gone and she didn't know what was going to replace the love they'd shared. Looking back, she realised their relationship had become so comfortable and cosy over the years they'd hardly had sex at all, and it hadn't worried her until now. Was that why he'd had an affair with Oliver? Because she'd shown no interest in him physically? Round and round her thoughts tormented her and she began to think it would have almost been easier to bear if Nigel *had* died. At least everyone would have been sympathetic.

On the third morning after Nigel's departure, she crawled

down to the kitchen feeling sick and wretched. Her mother was sitting at the table, chopping mushrooms.

'Look at these?' she said brightly. 'I was up at dawn and picked them from the field next door. I thought you might like a mushroom omelette later on.'

Without replying Diana slumped on to a kitchen chair, her eyes puffy with crying.

Susan looked at her sharply. 'What you need is a nice cup of hot coffee. I'll make you some.' As she busied herself around the kitchen she continued to talk in a reassuringly calm manner. 'You mustn't expect miracles, you know. Nigel and this lawyer will be doing their best to get Lucy out of prison, but it's not going to happen overnight.'

'But she must be so frightened,' Diana said dully, 'and she's been through so much, already. Why have they arrested her for the death of someone she's only met briefly?'

Susan laid a sympathetic hand on her daughter's shoulder. 'I know, darling. Life can be terribly unfair.' She glanced out of the kitchen window to the gates where a television crew and several photographers and news reporters hung around hoping for an interview with Diana.

'Don't forget that Tilly needs you, too,' Susan continued.

Diana blew her nose. 'I haven't the heart for anything until I know Lucy's out of prison,' she said listlessly.

Susan spoke briskly. 'Now come on, darling. Tilly is your daughter, too, and she'll be home again at the weekend. She's been pushed into the background for the past year and does need a little attention.'

'America is so far away,' Diana pointed out in a small voice.

'Not by Concorde it isn't,' Susan retorted drily.

'Suppose no one believes Lucy's innocent? Suppose she's been deliberately set up so that it looks as if she did it and she's no way of proving she didn't?'

'And supposing the moon's really made of Stilton cheese?' her mother snapped. 'Now stop all your supposing and drink this coffee.'

Suddenly Diana burst into tears, with her face buried in her hands as she rocked back and forth.

Susan looked at her for a moment and then taking the seat opposite, leaned forward and spoke in a gentle voice.

'What's really wrong, darling?'

Diana continued to weep and didn't answer.

'I know you're frantic with worry about Lucy, we all are, but there's something else, isn't there? What is it, Diana? Why have you been so distraught these last few days?'

'You wouldn't understand.'

'Try me, sweetheart. I understand a great deal more than you might imagine, you know.'

Diana drew a deep sobbing breath and then it all came bursting out: the letter from Oliver, Nigel's confession, her own feelings, her doubts about the future. Susan listened quietly without saying anything, and then she reached across the table for Diana's hand.

'Darling, I've known about this for quite a while,' she said when Diana had stopped speaking.

'You *knew*?' Diana was stunned. 'You *knew*,' she repeated. 'Why didn't you tell me, for God's sake? How could you keep something like this from me?'

Susan's voice was filled with compassion. 'I didn't keep it to myself to protect Nigel, I did it to protect you from finding out, from being made unhappy . . .' Her voice drifted away and she shrugged helplessly. 'I found that damned letter, too. I can't think why Nigel kept it among his papers, unless he'd forgotten about it. I suppose I hoped you'd never know.'

Diana picked up a tea towel that was lying on the kitchen table, and wiped her eyes. 'I don't know what to do.'

'Everything depends on how much you love him.'

'But what's wrong with me? Why haven't I been enough for him?' she wept.

'Listen to me,' Susan said urgently. 'You *are* enough for him. You're his wife, the mother of his children, you look after him and nurture him, he's a very lucky man and I'm convinced he knows it. But this is something quite apart from you. It's like saying someone likes chocolate best, but sometimes they fancy ice-cream instead,' she added, as if she were talking to a child.

Diana shook her head. 'I'm so scared, Ma. I had absolutely no idea he was interested in other men, and there's something else which terrifies me.'

'What's that?'

'This man – Oliver – he phoned Nigel to tell him he was HIV positive. Nigel's had a test but he won't know the results for a while, and now he's gone to the States, so I don't know when he'll find out.' She shot her mother an anguished look. 'What will happen if Nigel's got it?'

Susan's face was a study of self-controlled calm. 'I have to ask you this, Diana, but when did you last sleep with Nigel?'

There was a long pause and then Diana sobbed: 'So long ago I can't even remember. That's what worries me. He's obviously bored with me and that's why he's found consolation with . . . with . . .' but she couldn't continue.

'If he'd been bored with you he'd have had an affair with another woman,' Susan said firmly. 'This is something different, darling. And it's no threat to you. Do try to understand that for your own good. At least we can rule out the possibility of you being infected with the AIDS virus. And next time you talk to him on the phone, remind him to get the results and let you know what they are.'

'I don't believe this is happening, Ma.'

'It happens to a lot more women than you imagine,' Susan pointed out. 'You're not alone in finding out you're married to a bi-sexual. Not that it's any consolation to you at the moment,' she added drily.

'It's the shock of it all that's got to me. It's the last thing on earth I'd have thought Nigel would do, and I can't help feeling terribly betrayed.'

'More betrayed than if he'd had an affair with another woman?'

'I don't know.' Diana gazed out of the kitchen window, seeing the garden through a film of tears. 'I thought we were such a perfect couple.'

'This needn't make your relationship any less perfect. Up to now, you've only known a part of Nigel. Now you have the chance to get to know the man as a whole, and eventually it could bring you closer together.'

'You think so? Right now I feel so disillusioned. I keep asking myself *how could he?*'

'I expect he's asked himself that a million times, too.' Susan rose to put on the kettle again. 'It doesn't make him any less of a man, Diana.'

'Doesn't it?' She sounded doubtful. 'I always thought—'

'Times have changed,' Susan said briskly. 'When I was a young woman homosexuality was an offence for which men were sent to prison. Nowadays, there's a greater understanding and a realisation that whilst it might be impossible for you or I to go to bed with someone of the same sex, to others, it is entirely natural. For someone like Nigel, who has inclinations both ways, it is perhaps more difficult, but if you love him enough, you'll work it out.'

'And supposing he's HIV positive?' Diana whispered.

'Then you'll work that out, too.'

'Oh, God!' She buried her face in her hands. 'I don't think

I'm brave enough for all this. I don't think I'm going to be able to cope.'

Susan went and put her arms around her daughter's hunched shoulders. 'God never sends you more than you're able to cope with,' she said with vigour. 'You've never been forced to be brave in the past, but you can do it. And you will. Meanwhile there's Lucy to think about. And Tilly. It's your turn to be the strong one now, darling, if you are going to hold this family together.'

Diana sat in dazed silence, not answering. Then Susan spoke again.

'Nigel doesn't know I found the letter from Oliver and I think we should keep it that way, don't you?'

It was Thursday morning. By this time tomorrow, Lucy reflected, as she sat on her bunk, she could be out of here for ever, bailed by her father. And even unable to return to England, at least she'd be free. Able to go out and about. Able to get some undisturbed sleep. The past three nights had been hell because of new detainees. These included winos, panhandlers, footpads and vagrants, all of them noisy, picked up on sight as part of the new anti-crime philosophy that by clearing the streets of petty criminals, major crimes would decline in number. She remembered one of Amelia's guests at the drinks party last week – was it only last *week*? – remarking proudly how safe New York had become as a result of a massive clean-up campaign inaugurated by the Chief Commissioner of the NYPD.

'This used to be one of the top twenty most dangerous cities in the United States,' the elderly man had expounded to the group surrounding him. 'And d'you know what it is now? One hundred and thirty-sixth! How about that? The Commissioner came down heavy on everyone from police officers who didn't agree with his policies to graffiti artists who covered the subway with their daubings, and it worked! Law-abiding citizens can walk the streets in safety. Tourism is up. Crime levels are down. The core of the Big Apple is no longer rotten.'

Lucy had wondered at the time who this man was and it did not surprise her to hear from another guest that he was running for Mayor at the next election.

In spite of being exhausted though, and longing to sleep, she felt too strung-up to relax. Her body was tense, her nerves jangling at the least thing. Most of the time her head ached and when she managed to doze, which offered a blessed though brief escape from reality, she soon awoke again and the nightmare of her situation came rushing back to engulf her with anxiety. Worst of all was the frustration of not being able to convince anyone except Joshua Goldberg, and naturally her father, that she was innocent. Mike Powling had interviewed her again yesterday afternoon after Nigel had left, and had remained sullenly cynical and disbelieving as he'd tried to get her to admit she was guilty and she'd sworn she was not. Never, in her whole life, had anyone accused her of lying or thought her a liar. Her parents had instilled in both her and Tilly the vital importance of telling the truth and had gone so far as to lessen the punishment for a childish misdemeanour if she and her sister admitted everything immediately. To tell the truth and be believed was as intrinsic to her experience of life as it was to breathe.

There was nothing to do, either, as the hours dragged by with intolerable slowness. There were no newspapers, magazines or books to read. Nothing to distract and occupy her mind except the mental challenges she set herself, like trying to see how much she could recall of Tennyson's 'The Lady of Shalott'. Most of that day, her fourth in central booking, she wanted to shout and scream and kick her cell door while raging against those who held her captive so unjustly, but she didn't because she'd been brought up to be self-controlled. However, if she wasn't released after her arraignment, she wasn't sure how she was going to be able to stand it a moment longer.

'Where was this note found?' Mike Powling demanded. A plastic bag of items that had been overlooked in Arnold Ebner's apartment had been brought to him and he was furious not to have received it sooner. Among the personal effects was a gold lighter, several restaurant receipts, a few copies of the *New Yorker* and *Penthouse*, and the torn and screwed-up remains of a typewritten letter.

'Under the bed.' Shelley Lee sounded defiant. 'What's the big deal? It nails Lucy Howard once and for all, doesn't it? It's a death threat, isn't it?'

Mike spread out the crumpled sheet of paper, the bottom part of which was missing.

Don't think it's all over. You're going to realise this was the biggest mistake of your life and I'll make sure that you pay for what you've done.

'There you go!' Shelley said breezily when Mike had finished reading it. 'We've really got her now.'

He looked at her coldly. 'But it's unsigned.'

Alone in his Park Avenue apartment, Joshua Goldberg poured himself a glass of wine and tried to relax. He was used to being on his own since Mara had left him the year before, taking with her their two small daughters, but tonight he felt restless, his thoughts returning again and again to Lucy

Howard. He knew she was innocent, would bet his life on it, but how had she gotten into this position in the first place? She was British, a newly arrived visitor in New York, and had only briefly met Senator Ebner, notorious among those in certain circles as an incorrigible womaniser. So what was the connection? Who wanted him out of the way? And why had they chosen Lucy to be the patsy?

Joshua wandered around his living-room, glass in hand, trying to solve a riddle for which there didn't seem to be any clues. And all the time the memory of Lucy's exquisite face was in the forefront of his mind; her almond-shaped eyes alert with anxiety, her slender hands continually pushing her long black hair behind her ears as she leaned forward, desperate to make him understand the charges against her were grossly false. In all the years he'd practised he'd never got emotionally involved with a client. It was something one simply didn't do. Unprofessional, confusing and as taboo, to his mind, as a doctor falling in love with a patient. Yet he couldn't get Lucy Howard out of his mind, and knew he was kidding himself by thinking his obsession arose from the complexity of the case. The case had nothing to do with it. He'd got clients out of tighter corners than this. It was Lucy herself, with her touching mixture of strength and vulnerability, who had affected him profoundly from the moment he'd set eyes on her. She also seemed much older than twenty-two but that might be because of the suffering she'd endured after her accident. Whatever it was, she was always *there*, filling every corner of his mind for the past two days, making him feel unusually protective. And somewhere in the middle of his ribcage there was a strange sensation, a tenderness that almost hurt.

It was late now, and he knew he should get some sleep because he wanted to be fresh in the morning for the arraignment, but he lingered a while longer by his living-room window, looking out at a spangled city and indulging in a fantasy in which Lucy felt the same way about him. Lucy naked. Lucy in his arms, her mouth soft and gentle beneath his. Lucy crying out with pleasure as he gave himself to her with all the fevered passion of a very young man. For a moment he leaned forward, pressing his forehead against the cool pane of glass, and ached at the emptiness of his life. Maybe he was just lonely and not really in love at all. He fervently hoped that was the case. He'd been surprisingly unmoved when Mara left because their marriage had become a sham, and since that day had given no thought to being on his own again. After all, he had a lot of friends as well as his work and hardly knew the meaning of loneliness. Until now.

Nigel looked at the breakfast tray he'd ordered from room service and felt nauseous. As it was going to be a long and stressful day he'd ordered eggs and sausages, fruit juice, toast and coffee, but now he felt too nervous and sick with apprehension to eat a thing. He hadn't slept at all, and was so stressed his hands had begun to shake. It occurred to him that if he felt this racked with anxiety, what the hell must Lucy be feeling?

Joshua Goldberg had told him to get to the courtroom by ten o'clock. It was now only seven-thirty. What was he going to do in the meantime? It would only take him half an hour to get across town by cab at that time in the morning, so what was he going to do during the next two hours?

He wished with all his heart that Diana was with him now. Loneliness swept over him like a cold tidal wave. Had he lost her? And what in God's name would be the results of his blood test, due in any time now? Filled with despair and the beginnings of panic, he paced the room once more and then switched on the television. Anything to distract him and the more banal the programme the better.

Forcing himself to try the coffee and a slice of toast, he sat on the edge of the bed and watched a cartoon film, wishing he'd been able to snatch a couple more hours' sleep. Throughout the night he'd lain awake, alert and apprehensive, trying to find a comfortable position until unbearable restlessness had forced him to get up and walk up and down his room, before hanging out of his window to watch the traffic far below. Only the knowledge that the human mind and body could not withstand this degree of pressure for long kept him from going crazy. Sooner or later, no matter what happened, he knew a delicious sense of emotional numbness would take over and just wished it would happen soon.

The coffee tasted bitter but he persevered, his thoughts a tangled web, one minute thinking about Diana and how she must be feeling, the next concentrating on Lucy, alone and afraid in her cell. Maybe he'd have a long bath. *Supposing Lucy wasn't granted bail?* He turned on the taps and water splashed forcefully into the tub. *Supposing Joshua was unable to prove her innocence?* Nigel heard the phone by the bed ringing through the roar of the water. He dashed back into the bedroom and grabbed the receiver.

'Hello?'

It was Joshua Goldberg and his voice was reassuring. 'Just calling to check you're OK for ten o'clock?'

'I'll be there in good time.'

'The court's very overscheduled this morning. It may be a long wait for the charge against Lucy to be put on record so don't worry. I'll be there and we'll talk afterwards.'

Nigel felt his heart lurch and his stomach tighten nervously and could hardly believe this was all happening.

'We'll be able to take Lucy with us, I imagine, when it's over?'

'Let's get through the arraignment first. Then we can sort everything out.' Was it Nigel's imagination or did Joshua sound dismissive? Cool, even? Fear pricked him all over. Had something gone wrong?

'What will there be to sort out?' he demanded more sharply than he'd intended.

'Look, I'll see you in court. I must go now,' said Joshua.

When Nigel hung up, his hands were shaking. He gulped the remains of his coffee. By now it was cold.

'Oh, God,' he said under his breath, as he went back to the adjoining bathroom. He'd never felt as bad as this in his life. His stomach was upset and his heart pounded and he wondered how he was going to get through the next few hours.

Lucy entered the courtroom with a guard to each side of her. Nigel saw with a pang that her face was as white as ivory and there were deep blue hollows under her eyes. She'd been allowed to wear the suit she'd had on when she'd been arrested, a dark green skirt and fitted jacket that enhanced her black hair and made her look rich and sophisticated and older than her years. From a distance of twenty-five feet Nigel would not have recognised her, and he recalled how stunned he'd been when he'd first seen her on television. It was only close to, looking into her eyes and hearing her voice, that he was sure she was the daughter he'd loved for twenty-two years. *This has to be a case of mistaken identity,* he thought. He started scribbling madly in the back of his diary before tearing out the sheet and, leaning forward, handing it to Joshua Goldberg who was watching Lucy with an impassive expression. 'She used to look different before her operations,' Nigel had written. 'Can't you use that in her defence?'

273

This thought, incomplete but surely a propos, kept bugging him throughout the next few minutes of court procedure. It was surely the explanation for this whole bizarre affair? He now had it fixed in his mind that if Lucy had still looked as she'd used to look before the accident, none of this would have happened. He knew it didn't make sense, but he couldn't get the notion out of his head that this was the unexplained link that had led the police to her instead of to the real murderer. Tensely he watched Joshua as he read the note before laying it down on top of the papers before him. Nigel craved a look of encouragement, a nod from the attorney that signified he found Nigel's theory the most likely explanation, but there was none. Somebody was saying something; wildly Nigel tried to gather his wits together and concentrate on what was happening, his eyes darting from Lucy's set face to the judge, then to Joshua . . . and then the shock, the utter heart-stopping moment of horror, the falling of an emotional guillotine that severed all feeling as he heard the judge speak.

'Bail is not granted. A preliminary hearing will be set to take place in three weeks' time.' A pause so brief that Nigel could not even take a breath and then the words: 'Next case, please.'

Bail not granted. Lucy, her face stiff with dismay, was being led away by the two guards. Nigel rose slowly as if he were an old man, and as he followed Joshua out of the courtroom he felt as if he were walking waist-deep in treacle. It was unthinkable. Too appalling to take in. The world had gone mad and Lucy was the victim of this madness. Nigel gripped Joshua's arm as they reached the lobby.

'Why wasn't she granted bail?' he gasped.

Joshua looked grim, his mouth tight, eyes glittering dangerously.

274

'I wish to God I knew, but I'm going to find out,' he replied, his voice husky. At that moment he caught sight of Mike Powling as he came marching out of the courtroom, looking similarly grim-faced. Neither man spoke but the look they exchanged was explosive.

Back at Midtown South Precinct, Detective Shelley Lee felt good. The morning had gone well. The fact that Lucy Howard had been refused bail made her believe that at the trial she'd be found guilty and would end up with a life sentence. No jury in the world, as far as Shelley was concerned, was going to let Lucy walk. The evidence was too damning, too irrefutable. Especially when it got out, as it undoubtedly would, in spite of the White House's attempt to whitewash the affair, that Senator Arnold Ebner was an old lecher who had secretly rented an apartment in the Southgate Tower under the name of Saul Schwartz for the past seven years and stayed there whenever he could get away from Washington and his wife.

Bitterly, Shelley reflected that Mike was so besotted with Lucy Howard he had secretly hoped she'd be granted bail. What the fuck was he playing at? He was a Chief in charge of his own crime squad, and supposed to be out there hustling for convictions, not talking about 'insufficient evidence'. There *was* sufficient evidence. The trouble was, Mike was just unwilling to admit it. Shelley slumped angrily behind her desk and gazed with eyes blinded by jealousy across the busy room, where phones and faxes rang continuously and there was a constant buzz of activity. Why did little tramps like Lucy Howard always attract the men, for Christsakes? They only had to smile and look pathetic and cross their legs, and the men were fawning. She'd thought Mike was above that sort of juvenile behaviour, but obviously not. Shelley's bitterness became a pain which turned inward so that at moments she hated herself for not being pretty and sexy and appealing to men.

At that moment Mike entered the room. He looked stunned as he made his way to her desk.

'There was a message waiting for me when I got back from court,' he announced. From his expression she couldn't be sure whether or not he was pleased. Then he placed a fax before her.

'Take a look at this.'

It was from the Miami police. Frowning, Shelley read it through twice.

'Interesting, huh?' Mike remarked.

Shelley looked up at him, disbelief written all over her face. It didn't seem possible but the Miami police were stating that as a result of the repeated showing on television last Sunday and Monday of the suspect leaving the Southgate Tower after the murder of Senator Arnold Ebner, they'd arrested a woman of twenty-seven, called Tamsin Fraser, who exactly fitted the description.

'Jesus!' Shelley groaned. 'This can't be right. Have you seen the mug shot of the suspect they've picked up?'

'There you go,' Mike said casually, dropping another fax on to her desk. Shelley snatched it up. She found herself looking at a picture of Lucy Howard.

Miranda Beaumont stared at the picture on the front page of the *Daily Express*, her mind refusing to believe what her eyes were telling her. Lucy Howard? It couldn't be the same Lucy Howard her son had been engaged to, surely? How the hell could even the best plastic surgeon in the world turn a girl who'd been reasonably pretty, in a very English way, Miranda reflected disparagingly, into a sensationally beautiful young woman?

Miranda had just returned, with Roger in tow, from three weeks in Mauritius, and this was the first newspaper she'd seen for ages. Fascinated, she reread the account of the Senator's murder and how Lucy had been refused bail and was being held in a New York prison. Staggered, she held out the newspaper to Roger, who was lying on her bed, admiring his deep suntan.

'Look at this! God, Peter's had a lucky escape, hasn't he? I always knew there was something odd about that girl . . . but to commit murder! She must have been having an affair with this man,' she exclaimed in satisfied tones.

Roger read the piece and then said mildly: 'She hasn't been tried yet. She may not have had anything to do with it.'

'Oh, don't talk nonsense. Of course she did it. The article says she was seen leaving the block of apartments where he lived,' Miranda rejoined crossly. 'I bet she was hoping to marry him.'

'Well, she's certainly a great looker now,' Roger remarked, studying Lucy's picture. 'With that face I reckon she could have anyone she wanted.'

Miranda rose abruptly and went over to her dressing table. She'd really worked at her tan in Mauritius, and she'd jogged along the beach every morning while Roger slept. As a result, her body was in great shape, her upper arms and thighs firm, her stomach flat. But her face was old, old, *old*, compared to that damned Lucy Howard. Dr Kahlo had done a fantastic job on that plain little thing, Miranda thought as she peered into her hand mirror. Her sense of misery and jealousy increased, overlaid with the now familiar fear that soon even Roger wouldn't want to hang around, in spite of the restaurants, the trips abroad and the clothes with which she indulged him. There was nothing for it. She must book herself in to the Kahlo Clinic and get her face restored. She didn't care how much it cost. Her husband had left her a couple of valuable paintings, which he said were to be passed on to Peter eventually, but Peter could do without; she needed to look young and desirable if she was to be happy. There was no other way.

Rising, she lifted the newspaper off the bed and threw it face down on to the floor. She regarded Roger with eyes that held promise.

'Supposing we celebrate our homecoming with a little champagne?' she suggested huskily. She ran a blue-veined hand down his thigh. 'I was thinking we might go to America next time? I've got to go there on business quite soon, but you could join me, couldn't you, darling? We could have a couple of weeks in Hollywood? That would be fun, wouldn't it?'

Roger didn't reply. He was gazing at the discarded newspaper. He'd enjoyed looking at the gorgeous face of Lucy Howard and was thinking what a nerd Peter had been to break off their engagement.

At Eastleigh Manor it was late afternoon and Diana was waiting to hear the result of Lucy's arraignment as she sat in the drawing-room tidying her desk. Tilly, home for half-term, lay full length on the sofa, reading a magazine with the deliberately maddening calm of a teenager, as if it were an everyday occurrence for one of the family to be charged with murder.

'I wonder when Daddy will phone,' Diana remarked, glancing at the gilt carriage clock that ticked sedately on the mantelpiece. It was nearly five o'clock. Allowing for the time difference, Nigel should be ringing with news at any time now, she reflected.

'Chill out, Mum,' Tilly said. 'There's no way Lucy's *not* going to get bail. I bet the whole case will be quashed! It wouldn't surprise me if Dad and Lucy didn't fly home tomorrow.'

'You're right. Wouldn't that be marvellous? Thank goodness Daddy found a brilliant lawyer to represent Lucy.'

Tilly looked up at her mother with mild surprise. It was a long time since she'd heard her sound so positive.

Diana, tearing up old letters, Christmas cards and shopping lists, crumpled receipts and cooking suggestions cut from newspapers, dusty postage stamps, dog-eared labels and guarantees for kitchen equipment dated ten years ago, was finding the job of clearing away the clutter of the past very therapeutic. It was like sweeping clean the cobwebs from her mind although she was aware it was going to take a lot more than tidying the little drawers and pigeon holes of her desk to do that, but it was a start. And as the wastepaper basket at her feet overflowed on to the carpet, she felt calmer, almost cleansed of the appalling sense of despair that had threatened to overcome her during the past few days. What she had to do was learn to accept the reality of life, instead of living in a naive world of her own making. It was going to be hard. Nothing was as she'd imagined it to be. But if she could just make the best of what was left, maybe something could be salvaged.

Susan popped her head round the door at that moment, breaking into her thoughts. 'I've just put a steak-and-kidney pie on the kitchen table for dinner tonight. Is there any news?'

Diana shook her head. 'Not a thing.'

'It will be OK though, Granny. I know it will,' said Tilly, uncoiling herself from where she lay and standing up to stretch long arms above her head. 'Lucy hasn't done anything wrong so it's bound to be all right.'

Susan put her arms around Tilly's shoulders and kissed her firm young cheek. 'Of course it will, my lamb,' she said, marvelling at the faith of young people.

'Shall I make us some tea?' Tilly offered, unexpectedly.

'That would be lovely, darling,' Diana said gratefully.

'You'll find your favourite lemon sponge cake in the big blue tin,' Susan called after her, as she bounded off to the kitchen. 'I made it this morning so it's beautifully fresh.'

Alone, Diana and Susan exchanged a look of understanding.

'Tilly's making a determined effort to stay cool, as she'd call it,' Diana observed in a low voice.

'And so are you,' Susan replied gently. 'How are you feeling?'

'I'll survive.' She smiled wrily. 'But life is unrelenting, isn't it? Being a parent is pretty demanding, too. Just when you think your children are grown-up and off to lead their own lives, you find they need you more than ever.'

'Being a parent is a commitment from the moment they are born until you die. It never comes to an end. Your children always need you, no matter how old they are, and you always have to be there for them.'

'Like you, Mum. I don't know what I'd do without you.'

'What would I do without all of you?' Susan said briskly. 'Learn to play Bridge? Run the local Women's Institute? Lucy and Tilly keep me young, too. And in due course, so will *their* children, I hope.'

When the phone rang a few minutes later, Diana jumped to her feet, and ran into the hall to answer it.

It was Nigel. 'How did it go?' she asked without preamble.

Tilly came dashing out of the kitchen and stood watching Diana's face with anxiety. 'What's happening?' she whispered.

Diana's face was white. 'They've refused Lucy bail,' she mouthed as she continued to listen to what Nigel was saying.

'Oh, shit!' exclaimed Tilly, bursting into tears. 'What's going to happen now?'

Thirteen

Shelley Lee stared at the fax, unable to believe her eyes. 'This has to be a joke,' she said heatedly.

'I don't think it is,' Mike Powling replied, his smile amused. He knew she'd formed a personal hatred of Lucy Howard, just as she always took against any woman who was pretty, and slim, and sexy. Sallow-skinned, overweight and with bristling bright yellow hair, he sometimes wondered if Shelley didn't deliberately make herself look as ugly as possible. How much easier to think to oneself, of course men don't look at me because I deliberately don't make myself attractive – than to make an effort to look good and *then* be ignored.

'Let me have another look at her details,' he said, refusing to acknowledge her chagrin. He picked up the fax again.

'"Twenty-seven,"' he read aloud. '"Owns a boutique in Miami. Unmarried. Fits the description exactly." I'll have to get them to send me more details than this.'

'I bet it's just a coincidence,' Shelley grumbled. 'All these glamorous bitches look alike. They all copy Hollywood movie stars and end up looking as if they came from the same frigging mould. Are they bringing her to New York to be charged?'

Mike shrugged.

'When this gets out it will really be the talk of the town, won't it?' Shelley said with a malicious smile. 'The Press Office at the White House are going to go crazy trying to make out

281

this was a political murder now. How many women did Arnold Ebner have visit him in his hide-away apartment, for Christ's sake?'

'Dozens,' Mike replied, only half listening. If this other woman, Tamsin Fraser, was another suspect, it would certainly take the heat off Lucy Howard, he thought, secretly realising that this was what he very much wanted to happen. As it was, in his heart of hearts he found it difficult to convince himself that Lucy had committed a felony. In his experience she just wasn't the type . . . although that could be a dangerous line of thought. So could having the hots for a suspect, and the trouble was he couldn't get Lucy out of his mind. Woke up thinking about those incredible eyes and that sexy mouth. Fell asleep fantasising about her breasts and what it would be like to fuck her. God help him, he thought, going back to his own desk, just thinking about her gave him an erection. But then? Was that the effect she'd had on Arnold Ebner, too? He didn't find it a pleasant thought.

Exhausted by the stress of her arraignment, Lucy slept on Friday night, dead to the world from the moment her head hit the pillow until the noise of the other inmates awoke her at six the next morning. Then she remembered what had happened and the shock and disappointment of the previous day came rushing back, pushing her to the edge of frustrated despair. What was Joshua Goldberg doing, for God's sake? And her father? They'd been to see her briefly when she left the court, but despite the usual assurances that they were doing everything possible to get her freed, she was still stuck here and had been told that later on today she'd be transferred to a regular prison to await her preliminary hearing. Was the nightmare never going to end?

Hour after hour dragged by and nobody came near her,

except with food, and nobody told her anything. She was left floundering in her own distress, desperate to shout from the roof-tops that she was innocent; that she'd never been inside the Southgate Tower; had only met the Senator briefly at Amelia's party. Round and round in her head she kept going over the events of last Saturday . . . A week today! she reflected, appalled that a whole week had passed. She thought back to the moment she'd got up and had a shower and dressed in her red suit to go sightseeing until she'd returned mid-afternoon. Over and over she retraced in her head everything she'd done; everywhere she'd been, straining to recall any particular incident when someone might have remembered seeing her. The trouble was, when she'd been arrested, she'd been in such shock she'd never thought to take her handbag with her. Maybe there was something in her bag . . . and then, with growing excitement, she remembered that she'd stuffed a receipt for a scarf she'd bought her mother at Saks Fifth Avenue early on Saturday afternoon into her handbag. She'd got into the habit of keeping all her receipts when she'd worked for City Radio, because they refunded any expenses she incurred when she was researching a project. This time it might just save her bacon. It would be dated but more importantly it would also provide proof as to the time of purchase.

Lucy jumped to her feet and started pacing the tiny cell, squeezing and rubbing her hands together in frustration at not being able to do anything. Daddy? Where the hell was Daddy now that she desperately needed him? And why hadn't she thought of that receipt before now? It could be the absolute proof she needed. Oh, God, she must get a message to Joshua Goldberg . . . but where was he? Angrily, she wondered why on earth he hadn't thought of her shopping as an alibi? No doubt he was charging her father a fortune so why the hell wasn't he doing something? She gave a strangled shout of fury, not caring if it brought one of the warders running. *What am I doing here?* she raged in silent fury. *How dare they lock me up on a trumped-up charge when I had nothing to do with the death of that man?* Suddenly her fury overflowed.

'I want to talk to someone!' she shouted loudly through the grille in her door. 'I want to talk to someone *now!*'

Nigel awoke with a start, and instantly remembered that yesterday Lucy had been refused bail and he had received a call to say that today the results of his blood test would be through. For a moment he lay still, gripped with anguish, his eyes tightly shut. Then, in the dim light of a New York dawn, he peered at his bedside clock. Six o'clock was too early to do anything to help Lucy, but it was eleven o'clock in London. Not too early to phone the AIDS clinic. With shaking hands, he reached for his Filofax and looked up the number. Better get it over and know the worst . . . or the best, he reflected grimly.

It seemed an age before anyone answered and he tried to prepare himself for bad news, but how did anyone react when they were given a death sentence? For a moment his head spun dizzily, thinking of Diana and his daughters. How would he tell them? How would they cope with the devastation such news would bring?

'Warfside Clinic, can I help you?'

He gripped the receiver. 'I'm phoning to find out the results of my blood test, an HIV test,' he stammered. 'The name's Howard. Nigel Howard.'

'Just a minute.' The woman's voice was pleasant and cheerful.

He waited in the silence of his hotel room, for what seemed like a thousand years. Then he heard a click.

'Hello, Mr Howard?'

'Yes.'

'I have the results of your tests—'

'Yes?'

'They're negative.'

'Are you sure?' he asked urgently. The possibility of a reprieve from hell was almost too great to accept. Although he and Oliver had always practised safe sex, he hadn't been a hundred per cent certain he'd escaped infection.

'Quite sure, Mr Howard.'

'Thank you. Thank you so much,' he said gratefully.

He lay back against the pillows, his heart hammering. That particular nightmare was over and the relief he felt was enormous. He could get on with the rest of his life, devote himself to his wife and daughters, and do everything he could to repair the damage he'd done to his marriage. Thank God. Thank God, he repeated to himself, but as he did so, he thought of Oliver, realising the terrible suffering he must have endured when his test proved positive. Then he reached for the phone again and dialled Eastleigh Manor. Diana answered.

'Have you seen Joshua Goldberg yet?' she asked immediately.

'It's too early, here. I've got an appointment to see him later this morning. I'll let you know what his plans are for Lucy as soon as we've worked out what to do next. Meanwhile,' he continued without pausing, 'I'm ringing to let you know that the results of my blood test are negative. I've just been on to the clinic and I'm in the clear.'

There was a pause and then he heard her draw a sobbing breath.

'Oh, thank God! Oh, Nigel . . . I've been so frightened. Thank God you're all right.'

'At least we've nothing to worry about on that score now,

darling. I wish I was at home with you—'

'Lucy needs you more at this time, Nigel,' she said firmly, surprising him. 'I've got my mother and Tilly but Lucy has no one but you.'

'I know. I'm doing all I can, and we're lucky to have Joshua Goldberg representing her, but yesterday was a disaster. I still can't believe she was refused bail.'

'Poor Lucy. Will you call me later to tell me what's happening? Or shall I call you?'

'I don't know when I'll be back at the hotel so it's better I ring you. Are you all right, otherwise, darling?' he asked gently.

'I'm fine. And I'm so glad about the results of . . . of the test,' she added hurriedly, as if embarrassed to say the word AIDS.

After he'd said goodbye and hung up, Nigel lay in bed for a while longer, deep in thought. Diana's composure after her first emotional gasp had amazed him. She'd sounded so calm, so in control. It was going to take time and dedication on his part to restore her trust in him and, even then, he wondered if things would ever be the same again between them?

'They've picked up another suspect for questioning,' Joshua informed Nigel without preamble when he arrived at the attorney's office for a meeting at noon.

Nigel's jaw dropped at the implication of this. Then his eyes blazed with triumph.

'So the police realise it wasn't Lucy?' he exclaimed excitedly.

Joshua shook his head, indicating where Nigel should sit, while he himself sat down again behind his imposing desk.

'Something odd is going on. That son-of-a-bitch Detective Powling tried to keep the wraps on this, probably because he thinks he's got the case all buttoned up, which makes him look good, but I've got my sources of information in the police department, and they called me a few minutes ago to let me know about this new development.'

'Tell me,' Nigel breathed, not daring to let himself think that this could mean Lucy would be released within hours.

'It's a young woman in Miami, called Tamsin Fraser. Apparently she owns an up-market boutique, and on the face of it has no more of a motive for murdering Ebner than Lucy. At this stage I don't know if she was even in New York last Saturday or not.'

Nigel looked baffled. 'Then what's the link? Why do they think she killed him?'

'Because she's a dead ringer for Lucy.'

'You mean she looks just like Lucy?' Nigel sounded incredulous.

'Apparently she was arrested because she looked like the girl seen leaving the Southgate Tower in the video. The Miami police weren't aware the New York police department had already arrested Lucy as their suspect. Strange, isn't it?' Joshua gazed thoughtfully at Nigel, feeling sorry for this gentle Englishman who was so obviously distracted with worry about his daughter.

'But I don't understand!' he protested. 'Nevertheless, it must be good news for Lucy? If they think they've found another suspect, it must mean they're not certain that Lucy is guilty.'

Joshua smiled wrily. 'I have a feeling it's not going to be as simple as that, but I'll certainly take that angle. Is there any news from your friend Amelia Harrow? Is she back in New York yet?'

'I ring her flat three times a day,' Nigel groaned. 'All I get is her maid saying she doesn't know where Miss Harrow is and doesn't know when she'll be back. I *think* she's telling the truth,' he added doubtfully.

'I need to speak to her. I must find out how well she knew Senator Ebner and if she invited him to the party so that he could meet Lucy.' Then he looked directly at Nigel. 'Tell me more about your daughter's job with the radio station in England. What was it called?'

'City Radio. They're one of the up and coming new stations and Lucy was a researcher for them. She's hoping to get her job back when she gets home.'

'As a researcher, did she have contact with guest speakers? That sort of thing?'

Nigel nodded, remembering how she'd amused them all with tales of the various celebrities she'd met at the studios.

'Part of her job involved interviewing guests to find out what they had to say before recommending them to the producer. It was a sort of screening process. Of course it didn't apply to well-known people who were accustomed to broadcasting, but she got to meet everyone on the programme she worked on.'

'Do you know if Lucy was ever involved in interviewing anyone in American politics?'

Nigel was taken aback, but immediately realised what Joshua was getting at. 'I've no idea. You'd have to ask her that yourself. It's quite possible, though.'

'I have to think of every angle. What about this man she was engaged to? Could he figure in any of this?'

'Not in a million years. Peter's a weak little shit. It was he who finally walked out on her when he saw how badly disfigured she'd become. He hasn't the guts to fight his way out of a paper bag.'

Joshua's eyes clouded. 'She must have been very hurt. Very demoralised.'

'By Peter's reaction? She was devastated. She was doing him a kindness by withdrawing from his life; it was quite another thing when, metaphorically speaking, he kicked her in the teeth.'

'Has he seen her since her operations?' Joshua asked curiously.

'No.'

'She's certainly very beautiful now.' For a moment it was as if he were talking to himself, thinking aloud.

'It's not enough just to be beautiful, I want her to be happy too,' Nigel said quietly.

Back at the Inter-Continental by mid-afternoon, Nigel ordered a club sandwich and coffee from room service. Depressed because he hadn't been allowed to see Lucy today because she was being moved to another prison, he had no idea how long all this was going to take. So far the finance company he'd been with for the past twenty-three years had been very understanding, but there was a limit even to their generosity, especially as he'd already had so much time off when Lucy had been in hospital. Not that he had any intention of leaving until he could take her home again. At least she knew he was here, doing all he could to get her off this ludicrous charge . . . which reminded him . . . he reached for the phone, and knowing it now by heart, dialled Amelia's number. *Please God, let her be in* . . . He heard it ring with a distinctive pe-e-e-p which always took him by surprise after the metallic purring of the phones back home.

''Ullo?' It was the scared and cautious voice of Beth.

'Is Miss Harrow back yet?'

'No. She's not back.'

'Have you heard from her?' He asked the same questions every time, and every time the answer was negative.

'I'll try again in the morning,' he said and hung up. There was no point in leaving another message, it would only confuse

Beth whom he felt was already confused enough by the events of the past week.

For a while he lay supine, gazing up at the beige ceiling of his beige and blue room, racking his brains until it felt as if his head would explode, pinning his hopes now on the second suspect that had been picked up. Surely she was the one they should have arrested in the first place? Leaning forward, he switched on the television to see if there was any further news. Perhaps this other girl, Tamsin something, had confessed? For a moment he allowed himself to day dream . . . of the real murderer being charged, of Lucy being released . . . He tuned in to CNN, his favourite station, and found them describing an horrific air crash in North Carolina. There were shots of the scattered wreckage of the plane and the newscaster spoke those fatal words: 'It is feared there are no survivors.'

At least Lucy is alive, he reflected gratefully. She could have died in the car crash, but thank God she didn't. Comparing the plight of the aircraft's passengers to Lucy's being wrongfully accused of homicide made her current position seem less terrible. We'll get through this, Nigel said to himself. It isn't an arm or a leg and it's not the end of the world as it is for the families of those who perished in North Carolina.

He was still thinking about the disaster when he heard Lucy's name and saw the now familiar video of her in the Southgate Tower fill the screen.

'. . . has been charged and the preliminary hearing will take place in three weeks' time,' the smart-looking female announcer was reading off the autocue. 'Meanwhile two more arrests have been made in the past twenty-four hours . . .'

Two? Nigel held his breath, scared of missing a word.

'Yesterday a young woman was arrested in Miami, answering the description of the killer. She is Tamsin Fraser . . .'

I've heard all this, he thought impatiently. Who's this other suspect?

The newscaster was continuing with the smooth delivery of an experienced announcer: 'Earlier today a former *Vogue* model, Dagmar Allen, was arrested in San Francisco where she lives with her husband and small daughter. It is thought . . .'

Nigel didn't wait to hear any more. He grabbed the phone again and punched out Joshua's home number. The answermachine was on. Nigel left a breathless message and then felt useless because he didn't know what else to do. This whole thing was crazy. How the hell could there be three suspects, all looking alike? It didn't make sense. Frustrated, he decided to phone Midtown South Precinct. Surely they'd have to change their mind about Lucy now?

Amelia finished her packing, glad now to be going back to New York. Her few days of being cut off from the world as she rested in a remote guest house on Rhode Island had restored her, physically and spiritually. Allowing herself the luxury of grief, something she'd never before done because she'd always been working when there'd been a crisis and directors soon got fed up if the star of the show kept collapsing with sorrow, she now felt herself cleansed by tears, restored by the complete isolation, and strengthened by the rest. The owners of the small guest house had respected her desire for peace and privacy with masterly diplomacy, leaving her alone and only going near her when she requested to have food or drink sent to her room. It had been a time of healing and now she felt wonderfully refreshed, promising to return next time she felt in need of a complete break.

The flight to New York was uneventful, and she'd ordered a car to meet her at the airport and take her home.

'How is everything, Beth?' she asked when she got back to the apartment.

Beth's face was a mixture of misery and confusion.

'Miss Howard . . . she's still in jail! And her father is very angry. He rings twice, three times a day to talk to you!'

'What are you talking about?' Amelia asked, aghast. 'What's happened, for God's sake?'

With the words tumbling out incoherently, Beth tried to explain what had happened but all that Amelia could understand was that the police had come for Lucy, that her picture was on television all the time because she'd killed an important man, and that her father was very angry.

'What's his number, Beth?'

She wrung her hands and tears rolled out of her eyes. 'He don't say,' she wept, clearly frightened. 'He says he'll ring again.'

'But where is Lucy?'

'I tell you, in prison. I don't know anything else.'

Bewildered, Amelia hurried into her living-room and turned on the television. It wasn't that she didn't believe Beth, but on the other hand it seemed inconceivable that Lucy Howard had actually committed homicide. Lucy Howard was supposed to have left for England nearly a week ago; she shouldn't even still be in New York. Beth followed Amelia at a respectful distance, her apron wound round her hands like a security blanket. She fixed her olive-black eyes on the screen as if willing it to confirm her words. Amelia sank on to one of the grey silk sofas, watching intently.

'. . . In a ruling that strengthens free-speech protection for advertisers and casts doubts on the present administration's proposed restrictions on cigarette promotion . . .'

The newscaster was in full flow. Amelia pulled off her pale grey kid gloves and laid them beside her over the arm of the sofa.

'When did all this happen, Beth?'

'Last Monday, Miss Harrow.'

'Last Monday?' Amelia repeated in astonishment. 'Why wasn't I told about it sooner, for heaven's sake?' Then she remembered she'd asked the nurses to disconnect the phone so it wouldn't disturb her mother, and then she hadn't wanted to take any calls in the immediate aftermath of Rose's death. And after the funeral, of course, she'd flown to Rhode Island and given instructions to the owners of the guest house that she didn't want to be disturbed. It was quite a shock, she reflected, to realise she'd been uncontactable for nearly a week.

'. . . The number of Americans on welfare has fallen by nearly one point three million in the last three years . . .'

'Are you sure it's on TV?' she asked, frowning.

Beth nodded emphatically. 'All the time. Pictures of Miss Howard leaving the apartment block where the homicide happened, and pictures of her leaving this building, with the police.'

'What about the newspapers? Have you kept them? I must find out exactly what's going on.' Amelia felt increasingly agitated. It was obvious from Beth's manner that something awful had happened.

'Yes, I kept the newspapers. I'll fetch them from the kitchen.'

Then Amelia gasped as at that moment the video that all America had been watching repeatedly for the past week, of Lucy leaving the Southgate Tower, flashed on to the screen.

'I don't believe it!'

'. . . three young women have now been arrested in connection with the murder of Senator Arnold Ebner . . .' Amelia listened, stunned. Arnold Ebner! Whom she'd known for years . . . !

'Earlier in the week a young English woman called Lucy

293

Howard was thought to be the only suspect, having been identified as the woman seen leaving the Senator's apartment on the security cameras, but police in Miami and San Francisco have since picked up two more women answering to exactly the same description. They are Tamsin Fraser, a twenty-seven-year-old boutique owner, and ex-model Dagmar Allen who . . .'

'I'll kill him for this!' Amelia shrieked, jumping to her feet. 'The demented old fool. I *told* him, every time, that he had to stop . . .'

Beth came back into the room, holding several crumpled newspapers. She halted, shocked, as Amelia stamped her feet and punched the air with her fists whilst raging aloud.

'The goddamn old fool! He's gone too far! That's it! I don't give a fuck what happens to him now. He's got to be made to stop ruining other people's lives!'

Beth watched, stupefied by her mistress's outburst. She'd never seen the cool reserved Amelia Harrow like this, raving and ranting in agitation.

When the phone suddenly rang it startled both of them. Amelia, with unaccustomed agility, made a grab for it.

'Yes?' she snapped curtly.

'Is that Amelia Harrow?' The man's voice sounded strained and anxious.

'Who wants her?'

'This is Nigel Howard. I've been trying to get in touch . . .'

'Oh-h-h!' It was a long drawn-out sigh, laden with a dozen nuances. 'My God! I've only just heard what's happened, Mr Howard. I've been away—'

'I know,' Nigel cut in, 'and I'm very sorry to hear about your mother.'

'Thank you. Is Lucy all right?'

'She was refused bail and—'

'What? Oh, that's dreadful. Oh, I can't tell you how sorry I am. Can you come round to my apartment right away?'

'I certainly can. Was this Senator a friend of yours, then?'

There was a pause before she replied. 'Yes. He was a very old friend. He was only here a couple of weeks ago at a drinks party I gave for Lucy.'

'So I've heard.'

'But I think I do know what happened. Can you come round right away?'

Tamsin Fraser, held in a lock-up in the Miami jail house, knew that her partner, Sorcha Keitel, would never be able to raise enough money to bail her out. The boutique was doing well, but they weren't making big bucks yet, and she already had a large bank loan. Too large for comfort. So what was she going to do? She sat curled up on her bunk, sick with apprehension, waiting for further questioning. Knowing all the details of her past were going to come out, things she'd never wanted her parents in Atlanta to know about. They didn't even know she lived with another woman; how were they going to handle that?

Tamsin came from a very strict southern background, where prayers were said before every meal and she had to be home by ten o'clock at night. There wasn't much money, she was one of five children, and the claustrophobic atmosphere that pervaded her home was so stifling she'd felt like running away most of the time. Nothing ever happened. Every day was the same, but Sundays were the worst. Her father made them read passages aloud from the bible, after they'd been to church in the morning, and in the evening they had to sit in the parlour reading what he called 'decent' books until it was time to go to bed at nine o'clock.

One day, when she was fifteen, she decided she couldn't

stand it a moment longer. Stealing some money from her mother's purse, and stuffing a few clothes into a rucksack, Tamsin got on a bus to Tampa.

For the next four years she waited tables, became a stripper, and finally a hooker, and all the time she was saving her money, so that one day she could make her dream come true. Ever since she'd been a little girl, playing with her dolls, she'd wanted to own a dress shop. Then she'd met Sorcha Keitel, a beautiful black model, who also turned a few tricks. Her clients were more up-market than Tamsin's, but as their relationship deepened and they became lovers, they frequently offered their services to men who went for threesomes. At one point Senator Ebner was one of their regulars; he said that being in bed with a black girl and a white girl, watching them making love to each other before they turned their attention to him was the biggest turn-on he'd had in years. Then tragedy struck. One night, in the Senator's apartment, a candle was knocked over, setting fire to the bed, where Tamsin lay in a deep sleep. Sorcha was at home that night with a heavy cold, and the Senator, fearful for his reputation, grabbed some clothes and ran out of the apartment, leaving Tamsin alone. By the time she woke up, she was engulfed in flames. Later, as she lay in hospital, the Senator contacted Sorcha and told her that as long as his name was kept out of the enquiries as to how the fire started, he'd pay all Tamsin's medical expenses.

Five years later the girls had saved enough money to open their own boutique in Miami, and at last make their dreams come true. They were in profit after the first year, with Tamsin looking after the business side, while Sorcha did the buying. Everything should have been perfect, except for one thing. Tamsin had never recovered from the way the Senator had run out on her to save his own skin.

When Sorcha, watching television, saw the video of the

woman suspected of killing Arnold Ebner leaving the Southgate Tower her heart seemed to stop for a moment. She yelled to Tamsin to come and watch.

'That's kinda scary,' Tamsin agreed, staring at the screen. 'Same hair and even cut in my style, too. I wonder who she is?'

Sorcha looked up at her with a troubled expression.

'You were in New York last weekend, weren't you? For your brother's wedding?'

'Yeah. So?'

'So nothing. You must have a double, honey,' Sorcha remarked quietly.

For the next few days they'd been so busy they hadn't referred to the news again until the Miami police came into the boutique on Friday morning, charging Tamsin with homicide.

'Just 'cause she look like the dame on the TV?' Sorcha exclaimed loyally. 'I'm telling you, mister, you're making a big mistake!'

Sorcha was given a caution about her abusive manner, but Tamsin had been taken away to await her arraignment in two days' time, leaving her friend with more doubts about what had happened than she liked to admit, even to herself.

Dagmar Allen, incarcerated in a lock-up in the San Francisco Hall of Justice, covered her face with her hands and wept bitterly. It was more than she could bear to be parted from Tara, who had only turned four last week, and she kept wondering how her daughter was faring with Judy, a neighbour who had a little boy of the same age. Tara had often gone to play at Judy's house, assured that Dagmar would pick her up again after a couple of hours, but now she might think she'd been abandoned! All the 'ifs' in the world were whirling through Dagmar's tortured soul. If only, in the first place, she'd never met that old lecher, Arnold Ebner, when she'd been modelling in New York some years back; if only she hadn't let him pay for her medical expenses after she'd been mugged in the subway. But most importantly, if only he hadn't written to her, after all these years, suggesting they get together again, offering her an apartment of her own in Manhattan, a car, jewellery, everything any woman would want, if she'd only go back to him. She'd said no, of course; what about her husband, Jim, and how could she bring up Tara in the way she wanted if she was going to let Arnold keep her? He'd written again, and she'd only just managed to hide the letter under a sofa cushion, when Jim came home early one evening. But with the determination of a stalker, Arnold Ebner had kept on writing and phoning, obsessed by her and his desire to be with her again. Jim had been looking at her strangely recently and she wondered if he suspected anything. When he'd taken off for a business trip to Europe ten days ago, all she'd felt was relief.

The tears poured down her beautiful face as she pushed her long black hair behind her ears. What in God's name was Jim going to say now? Judy had promised to get hold of him, tell him of her arrest and get him to find her a good attorney but he was going to go crazy when he heard what had happened. He knew so little about her past, because he'd always lived in San Francisco and they'd met when he was on vacation in Hawaii and she was doing a fashion shoot for *Vogue*. It had been love at first sight for her, and for the past five years she'd done everything to make their marriage work. Until now. Thinking about her life in New York as a model, how could she tell Jim about her days of popping uppers when she was at the top and every photographer wanted a piece of her; her nights on the party scene, after a liberal intake of vodka laced with speed so she could dance all night; her abortion, three years before she met him; her frantic bed-hopping while she searched for love and never found it . . . until she met him. And then there was Tara.

Oh, Jesus! Dagmar turned on her side, drawing her knees up in a foetal position, toes curled under, hands clenched in tight fists above her head. Oh, God! She was rigid with misery, sick to her stomach, her brain about to explode. Jim and Tara had been her life for the past five years . . . and then Arnold Ebner had come back on the scene and his existence had threatened to ruin everything.

By the time Nigel arrived at Amelia's apartment she had changed out of her travelling clothes and slipped into cream-coloured linen trousers and a pale blue silk shirt. Her hands shook with nervousness. How was she going to explain to Lucy's father what had happened? She felt responsible and yet it wasn't directly her fault. There was no way she could have known what was going to happen.

'Beth,' she called to her maid, 'can you make some coffee? You'll have coffee, Mr Howard, won't you?'

'Thank you.' Nigel looked around, struck by the glamour of Amelia's sitting-room, trying to imagine Lucy in this glitzy setting before her arrest.

Amelia sat facing him, taking at once to this gentle-looking man, instinctively knowing there was a feminine side to his make-up. In her long career in films she'd come across many such men; they made loyal and kind friends but their sexual ambivalence was hard to deal with if you were in love with them.

'Mr Howard,' she began.

'Nigel, please.'

'Nigel. I feel I owe you an explanation about Lucy.'

He blanched and his eyes widened. 'What do you mean?'

'I think it would help if I started at the beginning,' she said, 'and I hope you will believe me when I say I had no idea this was going to happen to your daughter. I'd never have . . .'

'Do you know who murdered the Senator, then?' he cut in urgently.

Amelia looked directly into his anxious eyes and could see how much he was suffering.

'At this stage I'm not sure who committed the murder,' she replied with honesty. 'But I'm sure it wasn't Lucy.'

'She hasn't got an alibi,' Nigel fretted. 'That's the trouble. You were away . . . not that I blame you, but it did mean Lucy was here with only your maid, and the police have only got her word for it that she spent the day shopping and sightseeing.'

'I understand what you're saying, and I do feel badly about not being here to look after her but . . .'

Nigel raised his hand in protest. 'No, please. You had to go to your mother. Anyway, Lucy's not a child. I'm just desperate to find out *why* the police think it's her, and what about these other suspects? How the hell can three women all look the same?'

Even at moments of real-life crisis Amelia's theatrical sense of timing did not fail her. There was a pause and then she said dramatically: 'The answer lies in the hands of Dick Kahlo.'

'Dr Kahlo?' Nigel stared in amazement. 'What has he got to do with it? Was the Senator a friend of his?'

'I want to tell you everything from the beginning. I think it would help you to understand,' Amelia said. 'Ah, here is Beth with the coffee. Let me give you a cup and then I'll tell you what I think happened.'

Nigel frowned in irritation. He wished she'd just get on with it and cut out the dramatic crap. Pointedly he glanced at his watch and instantly felt ashamed at his own discourtesy. If she noticed his rudeness she gave no sign, but with beautifully manicured hands poured the coffee from a silver pot. In silence he took it, refusing sugar.

'Now,' she began, 'years ago Dick was married to a very pretty woman called Rita. It was a love match at the beginning, and as she came from a poor mid-west background, she was dazzled by this clever and successful doctor who was making a name for himself as a plastic surgeon. They moved to New York to start with, and only expanded to Long Island when he built the Kahlo Clinic fifteen years ago. As I said, Rita Kahlo was pretty and she did have potential – something Dick recognised right away. Gradually he started performing little operations on her, perfecting her looks bit by bit.'

'How macabre!' Nigel exclaimed. 'Why did she let him do that?'

Amelia looked slightly pained. 'Every woman wants to look her best, and no woman is born perfect,' she said. 'I knew Rita well, and she was enormously grateful to him for turning her from a pretty girl into a drop-dead beauty! He did her nose, several times to get it just right, and widened her eyes, slightly rounded her chin and gave her higher cheekbones . . .'

As she talked Nigel suddenly grew suspicious. This is what he's done to Lucy, he thought. So what in God's name is the connection?

'Rita helped Dick become quite famous,' Amelia was saying. 'A pioneer in the art of surgical improvement, Dick is an artist. His approach is that of a sculptor. Then her sister, Silvie, went on television, to say that Dick's surgery had helped her career in films.'

'But Lucy went to him because she'd been badly injured and scarred,' Nigel protested. To his puritanical way of thinking, God gave you the face you'd got and it was like cheating at games to have 'improvements' carried out.

The flicker of a smile crossed Amelia's face. 'I know, Nigel, and I think you'll agree he's done a brilliant job? There's not a sign of a single scar.'

He nodded, slightly embarrassed. After all, if it hadn't been for Amelia, they would never have had an introduction to the doctor or afforded to have had Lucy's face restored to such a degree of perfection in the first place.

She continued, 'Everything was fine between Dick and Rita until she fell in love with a nineteen-year-old beach bum.'

'Did they divorce?'

'Eventually, yes. But meanwhile Dick had a nervous breakdown, because she was his life. Not just his work; not just a living, breathing, moving advertisement of his skill and brilliance, but his *life*. He worshipped her, was obsessed with her. She was his wife, lover, colleague, friend and companion, but she was also like his child. Someone he had created. A great beauty whom he had fashioned with his scalpel. Do you understand what I'm saying?'

Nigel nodded, remembering Oliver. Amelia continued: 'When Dick recovered, he went back to work and we all thought everything was fine. He was treating more patients than ever, with brilliant results. Then, one day, a case was referred to him from the Patients Hospital here in New York. She'd been mugged on the subway, which she'd foolishly gone on because it was raining and there were no cabs, and her face had been repeatedly slashed with a razor blade. Her name was Dagmar Allen.'

'My God! One of the women who's been arrested?'

'Exactly. She had a rich lover at the time, and I believe he paid Dick to restore her face. But of course Dick did more than that. He couldn't resist the temptation to recreate the object of his obsession: Rita. When Dagmar finally left the clinic, she was like a clone of Dick's wife.'

Nigel was aghast. 'Then he's made Lucy look like his ex-wife, too? And the third woman who's been arrested!'

'Tamsin Fraser? Yes. She was badly burned in a housefire. That was when Dick was able to show the world how brilliant his skin grafts could be, as well as demonstrating all his other skills,' Amelia said drily.

'And you allowed him to get his hands on Lucy!' Nigel exploded. He was outraged, almost speechless with fury. Lucy had been *used*, to feed the dementia of a sick old man whose wife had run away and left him. Unchecked, he was recreating her likeness again and again and again . . . What in God's name did Kahlo want with these clones? he asked himself, as a whole series of terrible thoughts and realisations surged through his brain. Did he try to sleep with them, fooling himself Rita had returned? And what about the murder of the Senator? Jesus! Nigel jumped to his feet. Lucy *had* been set up. No wonder the police were confused. But whilst Kahlo, maybe with Amelia's connivance, had set Lucy up to appear the guilty one, whom had he really been protecting? Dagmar the model? Or Tamsin the boutique owner? Nigel couldn't wait to tell Joshua of this incredible situation. He turned on Amelia who was calmly sipping her coffee.

'Do you realise this means there are three identical women walking around, all being accused of the same murder?'

'Four.'

'What do you mean, four?'

'You've forgotten the original model, Rita Kahlo.'

Nigel sank back on to the sofa, and covered his face with his hands.

'This beggars belief! This is madness. Why in God's name did you recommend him to us, knowing what he'd do?' Nigel's voice shook with anger. 'It was utterly irresponsible of you. Apart from this, Lucy won't want to look like a clone of someone else . . . no, I'm wrong, *a whole bloody group of people*!' He was shouting now and striding up and down the room again.

'Nigel.' Amelia sounded severe. 'I give you my word I would never have recommended Dick if I'd realised he was still obsessed in this terrible way. He promised me, after he'd done Tamsin's face, that he'd never try to recreate Rita again. He realised it was wrong. He *knew* that these girls should be restored to their original looks, but somehow . . . I don't know . . . in a funny sort of way he felt he was doing them a favour. He felt he was giving them a special present. He once said to me that a beautiful work of art was so special, who could refuse the opportunity of looking like Helen of Troy or Cleopatra?'

'When did you find out what he'd done to Lucy?'

'When I went to collect her.'

'You had no idea beforehand?'

'None, I promise you. I was deeply shocked. I think Lucy realised I was horrified. I heard her ask Dick what was wrong, and he told her I was jealous because I was getting old and losing my looks.' She shrugged and smiled wrily. 'There was a tiny bit of truth in that, I suppose, but I was very angry with him, and he knew it. I phoned and told him so when Lucy and I got back here.' Then her tone changed, became more positive.

'Having said all that, Nigel, if Lucy hadn't got involved in this dreadful murder, would you have objected to the way she looks now? I never saw her before her accident but I think you have to agree she looks stunning. When I introduced her to my friends they were bowled over, couldn't take their eyes off her. When this is all over and you're home again, won't you be glad Dick's done such a wonderful job?'

Nigel hesitated, trying to analyse his feelings. Then he said bluntly: 'The trouble is . . . she doesn't look like my Lucy any more. I can't find her in this new person, except for the expression in her eyes and her voice, and I miss the way she was before. I've watched her grow from the moment she was born and now I've lost that point of reference. Just looking at her, she might be anybody's daughter,' he added regretfully.

Amelia smiled. 'How like a man,' she said with tender tolerance. 'You've lost your little girl and have yet to make friends with your grown-up daughter. Believe me, I think she's thrilled with the way she looks.'

Nigel ignored the remark. He wasn't sure how Lucy felt about her face, and of course neither he nor Diana would ever tell her she looked anything but beautiful, but right now there were more vital considerations.

'We've got to get on to my attorney, Joshua Goldberg, and he must tell the police everything you've told me. I wonder which of them killed the Senator? Tamsin Fraser or Dagmar Allen?'

'Or Rita Kahlo,' Amelia added darkly.

Joshua, summoned to Amelia's apartment although it was Sunday afternoon, listened intently as she repeated everything she'd told Nigel.

'This alters everything, doesn't it?' Nigel asked eagerly when she'd finished.

'Of course,' Joshua agreed, 'but I'm afraid it doesn't mean they'll release Lucy. She's still the prime suspect. We don't even know at this stage if these two other women were in New York last weekend. I'll go and see Detective Powling this afternoon, providing he's on duty, and tell him what you've told me, and tomorrow I'll visit Lucy. There's no doubting this new situation takes the heat off her. I'll also contact Dr Kahlo; we'll need him as a witness. He may also be able to tell the police where they can find his ex-wife.' He turned to

Amelia. 'You say you've lost contact with her?'

'I haven't seen her for years. I believe she and her boy-friend went to Los Angeles. She hoped to get into films there. That was the last I heard of her.'

'I don't remember there having been a case like this before, where we've had *four* identical suspects,' Joshua remarked, shaking his head in amazement.

'Will you act for all four of them? Try and get them all off the hook?' Amelia asked.

'My only concern is Lucy,' he replied softly. 'The sooner I can get her out of that hell-hole, the better.'

A flash of understanding flickered in Amelia's eyes. So the great Joshua Goldberg, powerful criminal defence attorney to the rich and famous, was already in love with Lucy. It wasn't surprising. She was not just sensational-looking, she was a great girl with that mixture of strength and vulnerability that men find irresistible. Amelia couldn't help reflecting on the impact Lucy would have on the film industry if she were to go to Hollywood. The same sort of excitement Amelia herself had created thirty years ago, no doubt.

'. . . if you could let me have Dr Kahlo's phone number?' Joshua was asking her.

Amelia came back to reality unwillingly. Her whole life had been given over to the world of make-believe and she found it a much nicer place to be. 'This is his private line,' she said as she scribbled the number on a snakeskin-covered notepad she'd picked out of her handbag.

'Thanks.'

'You can use the phone in my little study next door, if you like?'

'Thanks,' he said again. Amelia watched him as he turned to leave the room, a tall broad-shouldered man with a handsome tanned face and eyes alight with intelligence. Lucy was a lucky girl, she reflected. Then she gave a little inward sigh. It had been a long time since a man like Joshua Goldberg had fallen in love with her.

Alone with Nigel again, who by comparison seemed to be blurred at the edges, an altogether softer version of manhood, she smiled politely.

'You've got a good attorney there. I'm sure he'll be able to clear Lucy's name very quickly, once he's placed all this new information in front of the police.'

'I hope so,' Nigel said fervently. 'God, I can't wait to get her home.'

At Eastleigh Manor they waited anxiously for news. Tilly rather enjoyed the media attention as journalists and photographers hung about the main gates of the drive, trying to way-lay the family with a barrage of questions and flash bulbs every time they passed.

'Lucy's *so* famous!' she exclaimed as the case of the English girl accused of murdering an eminent US Senator made almost daily headlines in the tabloids.

'Notorious, more like,' Susan snorted, growing exhausted and frayed at the edges as the days went by. The stress of Lucy's ordeal was taking its toll and she was longing to be at peace again, in her little house at the bottom of the garden – a wish she knew would not be granted until Nigel brought Lucy safely home again.

'But you're not really worried about her, are you, Granny? I mean, if she were *guilty* it would be awful, but as it is, I bet when she gets back she'll be invited on all the TV chat shows to give her version of what happened, and they'll serialise her story in the newspapers. She's bound to get promoted to being a presenter on City Radio, too! Think of it, it'll be really cool!'

Susan eyed her younger granddaughter with something akin to envy. How long it was since she'd been that carefree and insouciant herself. She could barely remember what it felt like.

'We should give a party,' she said, relenting, and surprising herself in the process.

Tilly's face lit up. 'Granny! That's the *greatest* idea! After all, Lucy and Dad might be home any day now more suspects have been discovered! Wow! How wicked! What shall it be? Oh, let's have a party at night and we can all wear evening dress and—'

'What are you two up to?' Diana asked smilingly, coming into the room at that moment.

'Granny was suggesting we hold a party when Daddy and Lucy come home.'

Diana's eyes lit up. 'What a good idea,' she exclaimed. 'A big welcome home party is just what we all need.'

'It is?' Susan asked stunned. In the past couple of days Diana had seemed much more cheerful and positive. They hadn't talked about Nigel again, but Susan had the feeling that her daughter had come to some sort of a decision, though she had no idea what it might be.

'Why not, Ma?' Diana said. 'I can't remember when we last gave a party, except the barbecue that had to be cancelled when Lucy had her accident.'

'Wicked!' Tilly looked thrilled. 'Can it be an evening party? Can I have a new dress for it? A long one?'

Diana smiled again. 'I expect so, darling, but hold your horses for a bit. Lucy hasn't been freed yet and it may still take a while before she is, in spite of the fact there are three other suspects now.'

Tilly rushed to get pencil and paper. 'Let's make a list of guests, though. And we must invite Simon. Perhaps he could stay with you for the weekend, Granny? It's ages since we saw him.'

'He phoned me yesterday, actually. He was horrified when he read in the papers what had happened.'

'How is he?' Diana asked. 'Does he like his new job?'

'He seems to but he said he missed my cooking,' Susan replied, amused.

'While you're making the list, I'm going to get some vegetables from the garden for lunch,' Diana remarked. 'See you later.' Her mind was filled with the conversation she'd had on the phone with Nigel last night. It had been wonderful just to hear his voice, making her realise how much she missed him, she reflected. There was still so much to resolve though, and she had to learn to accept this other side of him that she'd had no idea existed, but at least they were able to converse as friends, and that was a start.

When he told her that Dr Kahlo had made Lucy look like his ex-wife she'd been deeply shaken.

'He has made her extraordinarily beautiful, though,' he'd assured her, 'and she's thrilled with the way she looks so don't spoil it for her by comparing her to Rita Kahlo.'

'Of course I won't,' Diana had promised. 'Have they found her yet?'

'Not yet. They're making enquiries in Los Angeles, where she was last known to be, but they haven't turned up anything yet. They have, though, eliminated one of the women from their enquiries because she's got an alibi.'

'Oh, God! Which one?'

'Tamsin Fraser. She was at her brother's wedding in Queens, so she's got over fifty witnesses who can testify she was there all day. They released her this morning.'

'But they're still holding Lucy?' Diana had asked, voice heavy with disappointment.

'Yes, but she's told us she remembers shopping in Saks around the time of the murder. No one has come forward to say they remember seeing her, not even the girl on the scarf counter where she bought a present for you, but Lucy says she kept the receipt and it's in her handbag at Amelia's apartment.'

'Well, then!'

'She can't find it,' he said flatly. 'Both Amelia and Beth have been through all her things, and there's no sign of it. I'm afraid she may not have left it in her bag, but put it on the dressing table or bedside table, and Beth has thrown it away when she was cleaning the room.'

'Oh, God! Surely Saks will have a record of her purchase? Or someone must have seen her shopping at that time?'

'We're doing everything we can. Joshua Goldberg is pulling out all the stops and Lucy knows we're working like hell to get her off this charge.' He sounded tired and deflated.

'Poor you,' Diana had said sympathetically. 'I hope you're eating properly and looking after yourself?'

'I'm fine,' he replied, but she didn't think he sounded it. It was only after they'd said goodbye that Diana realised that for the first time in their marriage she hadn't leaned on him for comfort and reassurance. It was quite a shock. It had never struck her until now that her reliance on him must have been a burden, and yet he'd never said a word. Her problem, she realised, sprang from the fact that she'd never had to be independent, because she'd always had her mother around to look after her. Even when she'd married, Susan had lived only a hundred yards away, always on hand to babysit, or produce a meal in an emergency, or turn up a hem, or do some shopping . . . And all the while Nigel had shielded her from bills and bank managers and all the nightmares of the late-twentieth century, which she didn't even want to understand, until at last he was unable to shelter her from the worst thing of all: his sexuality.

'What's up, Mum?' Tilly had wandered into the garden, breaking into Diana's thoughts as she picked some early runner beans.

Diana straightened her shoulders. 'I was thinking about Daddy and Lucy's homecoming. It will be wonderful to have them back, won't it?'

Tilly flung her arms around her mother and pressed a soft kiss on to her cheek. 'Lucy *will* get out of prison, won't she?'

Diana hugged her. 'Of course she will, darling. Daddy will see to that. What we have to do is keep everything going here so that when they come home we can all get back to normal, again.'

'I've almost forgotten what "normal" is like!' Tilly remarked wistfully. 'It seems years since I've seen Lucy. Did Daddy say she looked really beautiful now?'

'Yes, he said Dr Kahlo's done a wonderful job. All her scars are gone.'

'Wow! And she doesn't mind being one of four look-alikes? It must be a strange feeling, like being one of quadruplets. I'm not sure I'd like it.'

'Daddy said we should play that side of it down when we see Lucy again and I think he's right. After all, the other three live in the States, so she's not likely to bump into them again.'

'Thank God for that!' said Tilly, rolling her eyes in mock horror.

'But I insist, Nigel,' Amelia said firmly. 'Of course you must stay here until we get Lucy released. It's the least I can do after what's happened.'

She'd invited him to supper, and an hour before he was

due had phoned him at the Inter-Continental to tell him to bring his luggage with him.

'Thank you very much,' he'd replied gratefully.

He packed and checked out of the hotel, leaving instructions to give callers his phone number at Amelia's, and caught a cab. Another day in New York was over. Another day of anxiety and apprehension which had left him drained. There were moments when he wondered if this nightmare was ever going to end. The worst part of all was the frustration and sense of helplessness. If he could only get Lucy out of prison . . . The thought hammered away in his head all the time, driving him crazy, and he felt as if he'd swallowed a pint of warm lead and it was sitting in his stomach, weighing heavily on his organs.

As soon as he arrived at Amelia's apartment, Beth took his luggage and Amelia came forward with outstretched arms to greet him.

'My dear Nigel! You must be exhausted. Come and sit down and let me give you a drink,' she said, smiling warmly.

He found himself enveloped in heady perfume, soft lights, soothing music, and a minute later a sharply iced gin and tonic was in his hand as he lowered himself on to one of the softly cushioned sofas.

'Now you're to make yourself at home while you're staying here,' Amelia was saying, as she poured herself a glass of white wine. 'Ask Beth for anything you want, and give her your laundry . . . she's so good at ironing! Feel free to use the phone or the fax, and if you want to hold meetings here, with Joshua Goldberg or anyone else, just go right ahead.'

'You're too kind,' he murmured. 'I really don't want to be any bother. Somewhere to sleep is all I need.'

'You need to be looked after, Nigel. You've been under enormous stress and I bet you haven't been eating properly. When you've finished your drink, why don't you have a shower and then we'll have dinner? You'd probably like an early night, too.' Her tone was kind but firm; a woman used to having her own way, he reflected.

The first thing he noticed in the guest suite was all Lucy's things, just as she'd left them that Monday, over a week ago, when she'd been arrested. Her make-up and perfume and hairbrush were on the dressing table, several pairs of smart shoes were placed by the built-in cupboards in which hung, to his surprise, a couple of dozen suits and dresses, all brand new, and all rather glamorous and theatrical in style to his untrained eye. He was used to seeing Lucy in tweed skirts or maybe jeans, with shirts and sweaters, Barbours and flat shoes. Then he smiled indulgently. She deserved some nice new things after all she'd been through, and she'd always been more of a town girl than a country bumpkin.

Amelia had filled the room with fresh flowers and on the table by the bed were a stack of interesting-looking books and the latest magazines. In the adjoining bathroom he found a neatly folded pile of fluffy white towels, and a basket for guests containing items they might have forgotten, ranging from toothbrush and toothpaste, to deodorant, shampoo, after-shave, and even aspirin.

Standing under the tingling hot shower, Nigel felt the strain slide away, like butter off a hot plate. He wouldn't have believed that the comforting environment of Amelia's apartment could have restored him to a sense of well-being and optimism so quickly. He felt invigorated, full of resolve again. He *would* get Lucy's innocence proved, and quickly, too.

Beth had conjured up a feast of smoked salmon with juicy wedges of lemon and brown bread and butter, followed by roast beef with tiny young vegetables, fresh pineapple, a selection of strong cheeses, excellent wine and then brandy and coffee. Throughout dinner Amelia kept the conversation light and uncontroversial, as the red candles flickered gently around them, lighting the dining-room so that it glowed, warm and relaxing, protective and safe as a womb.

'This is really most good of you,' Nigel said, as he sipped his glass of brandy. 'It was pretty miserable alone in my room at the hotel with only my thoughts . . .'

'You certainly shouldn't be alone at this time,' she agreed.

'I do feel I'm imposing, though. If this business drags on, God forbid, I will go back to a hotel. I can't expect you to offer me this incredible hospitality for . . .'

She cut him short by raising her manicured hand, on the fourth finger of which blazed a tear-shaped diamond ring.

'Nigel! I insist you stay here until we have Lucy released and her innocence proved. Not only do I feel I owe it to you, because it was I who fixed her up with Dick Kahlo, but also because you're doing me a favour by being here.'

He looked at her, surprised. 'How come?'

'I don't want to be alone right now,' she replied quietly.

Nigel nodded slowly, understanding.

'My mother was my last living relative. I had no brothers or sisters. Sadly, I had no children either. I'm alone in the world, and to tell you the truth . . . rather scared.' Her voice broke but she remained dry-eyed and composed.

'I'm sure you have a great many friends?'

'I have a lot of friends, but few who are close to me. Few I feel I can really trust. And when you're in my position, that's important. There are those who could make a fortune by selling some of my . . . personal secrets, shall we say? Those moments of indiscretion that one regrets afterwards but seemed highly desirable at the time.'

Nigel thought of Oliver. 'Tell me about it,' he said with feeling.

Amelia looked at him. 'You're lucky, though, in that you're not a household name. Even a has-been one,' she added with a little smile. 'Nevertheless, I have no wish for people to know about some of the things I've done, and if anyone *is* going to tell the world then it should be me. Not that I ever will. I don't believe in autobiographies. They either wash the writer's dirty linen in public or they're plain boring.'

'I'm inclined to agree with you, although I would have thought the story of your amazing career would fascinate people.'

'But once you open the lid of Pandora's box, everything jumps out, doesn't it? If I could write about what the studios were like in my hey-day – Paramount, MGM, Columbia – then that would be great. It was a different world and I was privileged to have been a part of it. But I know my private life would make a far more fascinating story, though it's one I don't intend to make public.'

The candles were guttering low by the time she'd told him about herself; her love affairs and her marriages; her rape by a famous film producer who threatened to ruin her career if she told anyone; her two abortions, arranged by the studio she worked for because her pregnancies would have wrecked their filming schedules; her pills-and-liquor phase when she took everything she could lay hands on to alleviate her misery; and her suicide attempt when she realised her second husband had gone through all her money.

So at ease did Nigel feel with Amelia, almost as if he'd known her all his life in fact, that he suddenly found himself telling her about the first time he'd fallen in love, not with a girl but with a fellow student at Oxford. Amelia listened intently, smiling from time to time in understanding.

'Then there was Michael,' he continued, 'just before Tilly was born. He went to live abroad and I thought I would die from grief. At the time he seemed to be everything I'd ever wanted.'

'How did your wife cope?' Amelia asked curiously.

'She had no idea. It never entered her head that I might be bi-sexual.' Nigel smiled wrily.

'That must have been a great strain for you, having to lead two separate lives.'

He nodded. 'You'd think I'd have learned, wouldn't you? But, no, it happened again. All that excitement and joy, and then hell and anguish. He was in the army. His name was Oliver.'

They sat in silence. A candle spluttered and then the wick became engulfed in melted wax and went out.

'What happened?' Amelia asked softly.

Nigel looked at her and she saw the agony in his eyes.

'We broke up and then he phoned me to tell me he's HIV positive.'

'Oh, my God, I'm sorry.' It was said with a genuine rush of compassion and sympathy. 'How sad. And how awful for you. And your wife still doesn't know about it?'

'Yes, she does, now. She discovered a letter from Oliver in a folder on my desk; I told her everything then.'

'How did she take it?'

He looked pained. 'She was shocked, wouldn't believe me at first, and she was terribly upset, of course. And obviously scared that I'd contracted the AIDS virus.'

'And have you?' she asked, concerned.

'Thank God, I'm in the clear. I've only just had the results of the test and I phoned her immediately to tell her.' He paused, deep in thought. 'I thought it would be OK because I took precautions, but it was still a relief to find out I had nothing to worry about on that score. She was very relieved, too, although she was never at risk because the physical side of our marriage ended some time ago.'

'So you're reconciled?'

'I hope so.' He took a nervous sip of his brandy. 'I still don't know if she'll want to stay with me. I realise it's a part of me she never knew about and that it's going to be very hard for her to accept.'

'Do your daughters know?'

'God, no! Now that it's all in the past I'd prefer them not to know. I have a feeling my mother-in-law has guessed, though. She's extraordinarily perceptive and intuitive, and there are times when I feel she can almost read my mind.'

Amelia reached for the decanter and refilled Nigel's brandy balloon.

'Mothers-in-law can be difficult; do you get on with her?'

'Remarkably well. Both my parents died some years ago so Susan has been like a surrogate mother to me.'

'Then I'm sure you can rely on her support.'

'I hope so.' He drew a deep sighing breath and looked at Amelia with gratitude. 'So there you are. My secrets,' he concluded. To his surprise he felt enormously relieved at having unburdened himself. It made him realise that he'd been carrying this around since he'd been eighteen, unable to confide in anyone, unable to trust a living soul. A lifetime of living a lie. Nearly thirty years of deception.

'Thank you for listening,' he said at last. 'I'm so glad to have got all that off my chest.'

She smiled at him, her expression warm and compassionate. 'Secrets fester if you keep them to yourself. I'm lucky in having Dick Kahlo as a confidant. He's been a friend for the past forty years and he's never let me down. You need someone like that, Nigel.'

'You're right. There have been times when I've longed to talk to someone.'

'If you want, you can always talk to me, you know. I fly to England several times a year, and I'm always at the end of a phone. If you need an outlet, I'm here. It's dangerous to bottle things up.'

He looked at her with gratitude. She was an amazing woman, still beautiful and elegant, and although she was not his type, there was something graciously alluring about her, an infinitely seductive appeal that made him feel good. There was something else too. Judging by tonight, she was versed in the art of entertaining a man; for someone to have Amelia as a mistress would indeed be a recipe for being well looked after.

'Thank you,' he replied. 'I'll probably take you up on that, though I pray to God I'll never get involved with anyone else like Oliver again. I don't think my nerves could stand it.'

'Falling in and out of love is exhausting,' she replied, laughing. 'I hope it never happens to me again either!'

Soon after they left the dining table, blowing out the last of the candles as Amelia assured Nigel that Beth would take care of clearing away in the morning.

'Thank you for everything. I've enjoyed the evening so much,' he said as she bade him goodnight in the hall.

'Dear Nigel, I've enjoyed it too, and it's wonderful to get to know you like this. I'm so fond of Lucy, and I promise you I'll do everything I can to help get her out of this mess.' She reached up to kiss his cheek, and he was very aware of the sheen of pearls, the warmth of smooth skin and the scent of jasmine.

Fourteen

'Dad, how much longer, do you think?'

Nigel was visiting Lucy at the downtown women's prison near the New York County Court House and this was the ninth day of her incarceration. Once again they spoke by phone, seeing each other through a perspex screen.

'The police are still trying to trace Dr Kahlo's ex-wife Rita,' Nigel explained, 'but they've had no luck.' He saw Lucy's face cloud with disappointment so he hurriedly continued. 'I don't think she's got anything to do with the murder, though. I have a feeling it's Dagmar Allen, who lives in San Francisco.'

'Isn't she the model? Why do the police think it's her? San Francisco is a long way from New York. Did she fly in on the weekend of the murder?'

'I don't know, but the point is she's admitted she knew Arnold Ebner. Was his mistress, in fact. He even paid for her to go to Dr Kahlo, after she'd been mugged on the New York subway.'

'Wow!' Lucy's face lit up with excitement. 'That's it then, isn't it?'

'It could be.' He sounded cautious. 'They've released Tamsin Fraser and eliminated her from their enquiries because it turns out she had an alibi after all. Dagmar Allen swears she took her child to visit friends over in Marin County on the day of the murder, but she hasn't been able to prove it yet because the police can't get hold of these so-called friends. She says they've gone to Mexico City for a few days. Strikes me as a very unlikely story. I don't suppose they even exist.'

'Oh, God, Daddy! This is all so uncertain, isn't it? Is there any news from Saks? Have you got their own copy of my shopping receipt?'

'Yes, but it doesn't prove anything unless we've got your receipt, but we're doing everything we can. Joshua is practically *living* at Midtown South Precinct, in order to keep in touch. Oh, there's one piece of good news.'

'What's that?'

'Detective Powling, the one who—'

'I know. I hate him! He questioned me for hours after my arrest, but most of the time his eyes were on my breasts,' she said angrily.

Nigel was taken aback. 'Well . . . I have to tell you that he confided to Joshua he doesn't think you're guilty.'

She sat upright. 'Really? Then who does he think did it?'

'Dagmar Allen, I suppose. I don't know, really. Let's hope they can find some evidence which will prove she . . .'

'Does she really look like me?' Lucy cut in. 'Could it have been her on the security video, leaving the Southgate Tower? Wearing a red suit, too? God, it's creepy, isn't it, to think there are other people out there, who look exactly like me?'

'It's probably more of a general impression,' Nigel said, trying to comfort her. 'I expect if you were lined up in a row, you'd all look quite different.'

'Obviously not different enough!' she said caustically, with a return of her old spirit. 'Thinking back,' she continued, 'Dr Kahlo was meticulous in the way he measured my nose and my jawline, even my cheeks. He was obviously reconstructing my face to exactly the same dimensions as his ex-wife's.' As she spoke she smoothed her fingers over the planes of her face. 'I'm not as exclusive-looking as I thought,' she added with a wistful smile.

'There won't be another like you in the whole of the world,' Nigel reassured her robustly, 'but that isn't what matters. It's having *you* home again, well and happy, that counts.' Through the cold impersonal perspex barrier he looked into her eyes, searching for the Lucy he knew and loved, longing for that moment when he truly recognised the very essence of her and knew that behind the exquisite exterior, his beloved daughter still existed. Lucy looked lovingly back at him, and suddenly it was there. The four-year-old girl who'd come running in from the garden one dewy summer's morning, telling him the grass was crying; the teenager who'd pranced into his study one evening on her way to a party to show him her new dress; and then the young woman, grown-up and serene, assuring him that although she was marrying Peter, he would always be her special darling Daddy.

Tears gathered behind his eyes threatening to spill over, and his throat felt tight. He and Lucy had always been particularly close. Joy at finding her again overcame him for a moment, and she smiled, understanding. Then she spoke.

'Daddy, I know you're doing your best to get me out of here, and I can't tell you what a difference it makes just having you here in New York, but what about Mummy and Tilly? And your work? Shouldn't you be getting home, soon?'

'Darling, I'm staying here for however long it takes to get you out of prison and the case against you dismissed. Amelia has asked me to stay in her apartment, did I tell you? I'm in your room, actually. She's being extremely kind and supportive.'

'She is nice, isn't she? Thank God she came back to New York when she did. Daddy, will you let me know when . . .?'

As had happened on previous occasions their time was up

and the phone had been switched off. Lucy grimaced and spread her hands in a gesture of helplessness, but as she blew him a goodbye kiss it seemed to him that she was in better spirits. The news about Dagmar Allen was hopeful, of course. Once the murder could be pinned on her the worst would be over.

Dr Kahlo looked pained. 'I don't see how I can help you,' he told Mike Powling as they sat in the living-room of his private quarters at the clinic. 'I haven't spoken to my wife for several years. I've no idea where she is.'

'Your ex-wife, you mean? I believe you and Rita Kahlo are divorced,' he pointed out.

'That is irrelevant,' the doctor replied stiffly.

'We do need to talk to her,' Mike persisted. Dr Kahlo had resisted being interviewed at first, seemingly wishing to wash his hands of the three look-alikes he'd created in the image of Rita, but Mike wasn't listening to any excuses. This was a major homicide incident that had triggered off international interest and his own reputation was on the line. His boss, the Chief Commissioner of the NYPD, was looking to him to secure a conviction, and whilst all the evidence pointed to Lucy Howard, he had this gut feeling she was innocent . . . or did he just want her to be because he had the hots for her?

Something wasn't right though. The answers, Mike felt, were here at the Kahlo Clinic, and if Dagmar Allen wasn't guilty of the murder, then Rita Kahlo must be. It even crossed his mind that Dick Kahlo could be involved himself and that he had deliberately set up Lucy, Tamsin Fraser and Dagmar Allen in order to confuse everyone and protect himself. Or was it to protect Rita with whom he was apparently still obsessed? And what could Dr Kahlo and Rita have against Arnold Ebner? Powling took a deep breath as he tried to hold all these theories in his head whilst conducting a seemingly innocuous interview.

'Is it possible that Rita has remarried?' he asked.

'How should I know? I told you, I haven't seen her for years.'

'You don't seem very interested in her either?' Mike needled.

'Why should I be?' Kahlo's dark eyes were icy.

'Yet you were interested enough in her to remodel three other women to look like her?' Mike shot back. 'Why did you do that?'

Kahlo shrugged. '"A thing of beauty is a joy forever",' he quoted. 'I created Rita in the first place. She would have been nothing if I hadn't spent all my time and talent turning her into a perfect specimen. I was doing the other girls a favour. They should be grateful to me.'

Mike looked at him, chilled by his words. Someone had likened him to Frankenstein; in his opinion Kahlo was worse, because in the case of Lucy he hadn't even asked her permission before cloning her to look like his wife.

'So tell me about these other girls – Tamsin and Dagmar and Lucy?'

'What do you want to know? I can't tell you anything you probably aren't already aware of. Dagmar Allen came to me first; it was at the height of her career as a top model. She'd been mugged in the New York subway and her face had been slashed repeatedly with a razor. Two years later I met Tamsin Fraser. She'd been badly burned and required extensive skin grafts before I could do much. Otherwise she's an ordinary sort of girl – prefers women to men; owns a boutique at which rich ladies with stretched faces buy their clothes. Lucy Howard, my most recent patient, was, as you are no doubt aware, injured in an automobile accident.'

'Who paid for their surgery?'

There was a silence. Shafts of sunlight, laden with drifting dust motes, slanted into the room through the venetian blinds. The soft hum of the air-conditioning was like the sound of distant traffic.

Dr Kahlo spoke. 'I never divulge private information of that sort.'

'I have to remind you that this is not a newspaper interview or some idle enquiry,' Mike reminded him sharply. 'I know for a fact that Senator Ebner paid for Dagmar Allen's treatment.'

'In that case, why did you ask me?' Kahlo's bottom lip stuck out obstinately and his beautifully manicured hands gestured in protest. 'I do not have time to waste, Detective Powling. I have patients to see to. If Dagmar Allen and Senator Ebner were friends, then that is her concern.' He rose from his chair, smoothing his white surgical coat as he did so. 'Now, if you'll excuse me? I have work to do.'

Mike rose also but he wasn't giving up that easily.

'I'd like to talk to the members of your staff,' he persisted. 'They might remember something about either Dagmar Allen or Lucy Howard that would help. We've dropped our charges against Tamsin Fraser as she has an alibi.'

Kahlo looked disinterested, even bored as he walked towards the door. 'We have a lot of people working in the clinic, but I'll get my assistant, Lauren Vincent, to arrange it. Kindly wait here.'

Mike waited, looking around the room more closely as he did so. If these were the personal quarters of the doctor, they were the most sterile he'd ever seen outside a hotel suite. There wasn't a single picture or photograph or book of a personal nature lying around. The room could have belonged to anyone. To add to the strangeness, Dr Kahlo's English butler reappeared at that moment to offer Mike either tea or coffee.

'Coffee, please. Milk but no sugar. Thanks,' he replied, rising to stretch his legs. A moment later an unprepossessing young woman in glasses and a severe hairstyle came into the room.

'Detective Powling? I'm Dr Kahlo's assistant, Lauren Vincent. I gather you wish to question members of staff?' Her manner was prim though pleasant, he thought as he mentally gave her nought out of ten for looks.

'Yeah. Thanks. I'd like in particular to talk to all those who came into contact with three of Dr Kahlo's patients.'

She looked wary. 'Which three? You know we go to great lengths to protect the privacy of patients here.'

Mike smiled drily. 'Lady, these three women have already been arrested for murder. I somehow don't think they've got much privacy left.'

Lauren Vincent was unamused. 'Very well, Detective Powling. Who would you like to question first? The anaesthetist? The theatre staff? The nurses? The personal trainers? The counsellors? The beauticians and . . .'

'Hold it there, Miss Vincent,' Mike exclaimed.

Pale grey eyes looked enquiringly at him through gold-framed glasses. 'We do have a large staff. You had better use my office as it could take you some time, and Dr Kahlo will want to come back in here again shortly. Who would you like to see first?'

'How about you? You must have met Tamsin Fraser, Dagmar Allen and Lucy Howard? What can you tell me about them?'

Lauren Vincent pursed her lips fastidiously. 'I've only been with Dr Kahlo a little while. I'm afraid Lucy Howard is the only one I've met.'

Three hours later, Mike Powling left the Kahlo Clinic and made the return journey to New York by police helicopter. As far as he was concerned, he'd drawn a blank. He'd learned nothing more about Tamsin and Dagmar, and nothing he didn't already know about Lucy. Lauren Vincent and the rest of the staff had been helpful and co-operative, even letting him see the list of distinguished patients they'd had over the years, but he'd still not turned up anything of importance. The clinic was clean, the staff impeccable with excellent references which he'd have checked later, but which he felt sure would reveal nothing sinister. As for Dr Kahlo himself, he was obviously a highly skilled surgeon with an obsession: to make other women in the image of his wife. But there all contact with them had ended. That left Rita Kahlo or whatever she was calling herself these days.

'Any messages?' he asked, as soon as he got back to the precinct.

Shelley Lee's smile was malicious. 'The family in Mexico City have turned up.'

Mike looked at her blankly. 'What family?'

'The family Dagmar Allen said she spent the day with in Marin County, at the time the Senator was murdered.'

'Shit!' He thumped his desk with his clenched fist. 'Have they been questioned? Are you sure there's no mistake?'

Shelley shook her head, her double chin wobbling slightly. 'Apparently they returned home yesterday. The San Francisco police were waiting for them and they've been questioned. Dagmar Allen and her little girl drove to Marin County on the Saturday morning, and spent the day with these people. They've made signed statements. They're releasing the suspect.'

'Shit!' Mike exclaimed again.

'What's the big deal?' she asked slyly.

His jaw tightened and he looked away. He was not going to give Shelley the satisfaction of knowing just how much he cared.

'No big deal,' he replied loftily. 'I still want to interview Rita Kahlo, though. We can't eliminate her without questioning her first.'

'There's no news on her whereabouts. We've got searches going on, but she seems to have vanished off the face of the earth.'

'No one with a face like that vanishes,' Mike protested. 'If she's as beautiful as the others, she'll be found somewhere.'

Joshua regarded Nigel with sympathy. 'We're not having much luck. There's no sign of Rita Kahlo in spite of constant TV appeals, and with both Tamsin Fraser and Dagmar Allen in the clear, the bulk of the evidence is pointing to Lucy again.'

'I realise that.'

They faced each other across the expanse of Joshua's tidy desk and the attorney was aware of the grief in Nigel's eyes. He seemed to have aged since he'd arrived in New York, and the lines on either side of his mouth had deepened. He swallowed as if his throat was sore and spoke harshly.

'What can we do? You have a system of plea bargaining over here, don't you?'

Joshua nodded. 'The problem is we have nothing to bargain with. It's not as if Lucy were able to dish the dirt on Arnold Ebner. Apart from his womanising, he's clean. If she were to plead guilty, she'd probably get life rather than the electric . . .' He broke off, seeing the horror on Nigel's face.

'Dear God!' For a moment he thought Nigel was going to faint, so drained of blood did his face become. 'It won't come to that, will it?' he asked hoarsely.

Joshua forced his features to remain impassive. 'We must prepare ourselves by considering every angle. Nothing is certain and everything depends on the jury. But we're jumping ahead. A lot depends on the prosecution, and remember, there's only one witness, the cleaner, who saw Lucy's look-alike leaving Ebner's apartment; at the initial hearing the judge may even think there's insufficient evidence to proceed. He could kick the whole case out of court . . .' Joshua knew he was talking nonsense but he had to do something to allay the fears of this devoted father and wipe the look of sheer panic off his face.

'Are we going to tell her the suspect in San Francisco had an alibi, after all?' Nigel asked miserably.

'I see no point in that. We've got to keep her morale up, whatever happens. Try not to worry too much, Nigel. If Rita Kahlo can be traced, I'm certain it will get Lucy off the hook.'

'You think she did it?'

'Who else is there? We know for certain there were originally four look-alikes. Two of them have alibis and Lucy is innocent. That only leaves the ex-wife. It *has* to be her.' He spread his large hands and his dark eyes sparked with determination. 'Believe me, if it's the last thing I do, I'm getting Lucy off this charge.' Something in his vehement tone made Nigel look at him afresh and at that moment it dawned on him, with a sense of shock, that Joshua Goldberg was in love with his daughter.

'I think I know where Rita Kahlo lives.' The woman's voice at the end of the phone sounded as if she lived on cigarettes and liquor. Mike Powling gripped the receiver and felt his stomach contract with excitement.

'Can you tell me your name?' he asked, trying to keep his voice steady.

'Whaddya want *my* name fer?' Her tone was querulous.

'I need to know your name and address, please, ma'am,' he replied with elaborate politeness.

'I'm not giving you my name! I've got nothing to do with

it! I'm doing you a favour but if you don't want it, you can frigging well do without it.'

Alarmed, Mike changed tack. She sounded like she might hang up if she wasn't handled right and this was a chance he couldn't let slip through his fingers.

'So where is Rita Kahlo?' he asked bluntly.

'She's here.'

'Where is here?' he enquired carefully.

'In New York, of course. Where d'you think?'

He'd met the type many times before. When drunk they became belligerent, and this dame sure was drunk. Her speech was slurred and then there was a crashing sound and silence and he knew she'd dropped the phone.

'Are you there, ma'am?' Christ! He hoped she hadn't hung up. 'I believe there's a reward for information leading to the whereabouts of Rita . . .'

Her voice came back at him so loudly he jumped.

'She lives on Bleecker Street.'

'Have you a street number for that?'

There was much shuffling and snuffling and whispered oaths on the line and he presumed the woman was going through some papers.

'Do you have it?' he asked again.

'Have what?' Suddenly she sounded as if she had no idea what he was talking about.

Mike realised he was sweating. 'The number in Bleecker Street where Rita Kahlo lives?'

'Why? D'you know her?'

Jesus Christ! He closed his eyes and took a deep breath. 'Will you please give me the full address of Rita Kahlo?'

It came as if from far, far away, in a voice that was fading under an ocean of alcohol.

'249 Bleecker . . . Street . . .' A final click heralded total silence. Whoever it was had gone, but Mike jumped to his feet, triumphant.

'Yeah,' he yelled, punching the air with his fist. 'Got it!'

Shelley Lee looked up from the report she was writing and stared at him. 'You're looking mighty pleased with yourself?'

'Yeah!' he said again. 'I've found out where Kahlo's ex-wife lives. Right here in the city. She's obviously been in hiding but now I know where she's hanging out, I'm going to fix a warrant for her arrest faster than shit through a goose!'

The news spread fast. Within minutes Midtown South Precinct was buzzing with the fact that another suspect for the homicide of Senator Ebner was about to be arrested.

'If this leaks to the media . . .' Mike said warningly.

'Chill out,' Shelley said, archly. 'At this rate you might get the promotion *and* the girl.'

He pretended he hadn't heard. Goddamn Shelley for guessing how he felt about Lucy Howard. Shrugging on a dark jacket over his white shirt and stone-coloured trousers, he hurried down to the street and the waiting police car. One of his squad from Homicide, Detective Jack Maxwell, was already sitting in the front seat, talking into the police radio. Mike jumped into the back, charged with an adrenalin rush, his face red and eyes wide. He leaned forward and spoke to the driver.

'Drop us off at the beginning of Hudson Street. I don't want the suspect to see the blue and white, so follow us at a distance and park up a side street. OK?'

'Yes, sir.'

As they shot down Ninth Avenue towards Greenwich Village the driver threw the siren switch. The 'blue and white' screamed past almost stationary vehicles which swerved, huddling together at one side of the road, to be out of their path. The radio crackled; something was about to happen and the warrant for the arrest of Rita Kahlo felt good in Mike's pocket. This was one of his better days. He wished there were more like them.

At the end of Ninth Avenue the driver took a half left, crossing West Fourteenth Street, and then they were in Hudson Street, dwarfed by the last few towering skyscrapers before the skyline dropped, softening to two- and three-floor buildings and the altogether more tranquil atmosphere of the Village.

Mike and Jack Maxwell climbed out of the car and set off on foot to cover the short distance to Bleecker Street, two men in casual clothes whose presence in the neighbourhood went unnoticed as they studiously looked ahead whilst at the same time taking everything in.

Number 249 was an old house which had been divided into apartments. Not smart enough to have a doorman or a security guard, a series of bells by the street door listing the names of the occupants was the only way of finding out who these were. Mike's eyes skimmed down the crudely written names, his heart pounding. Connors. Kibbler. Yeboah. McCoy. Kahlo . . .

'Yeah!' The relief was incredible. Mike punched the bell and shot Jack Maxwell a triumphant glance. If Rita Kahlo proved to be the one and Lucy was released . . . well, he didn't want to flatter himself, but he thought he was in with a good chance. Lucy looked like she could be hot, under the right circumstances.

A woman's voice broke into his thoughts. 'Hello?'

Mike spoke. 'Mrs Rita Kahlo? We'd like to have a few words with you.'

She sounded suspicious. 'Who is that?'

'Detective Mike Powling and Detective Jack Maxwell, from Homicide, New York Police Department.'

There was a long silence.

'Mrs Kahlo, are you there? I have a warrant for your arrest. Unless you let us in, we will have to make a forced entry . . .'

'OK. OK.' She sounded weary, defeated. 'Come on up. Fourth floor. I was kinda expecting you. Sooner or later.' A loud buzzing noise followed, like an angry wasp trapped in a glass, as she pressed the button of the entry phone and Mike pushed open the door. The smell of cat's pee hit him as he stepped into the gloomy hallway.

'Christ! I expected better than this,' he muttered as they climbed the steep stairs that led to the upper floors. 'She must have fallen on hard times, by the look of it.'

On the fourth floor there was only one door, marked APT E in black lettering. It was closed. Mike rapped loudly on it with his knuckles. After a moment it opened, and an elderly woman with grey hair and a skin raddled and lined by too much sun stood gazing at them. Her face and arms were the reddish-brown of chestnuts, and she wore a wrap-around ankle-length skirt and halter neck top, more suited to the beach than the town. At a glance Mike reckoned she must weigh eighteen stone.

Mike was completely taken aback. Somehow he'd expected Rita Kahlo to open the door herself. This, he deduced, must be her mother.

'I want to see Rita Kahlo,' he said sharply.

She stood to one side. 'You'd better come in.'

The living-room of the apartment was a messy, not-too-clean clutter of dilapidated furniture that looked as if it had been retrieved off a tip, piles of magazines, dirty glasses and empty whisky bottles, and a long-haired tabby cat who glowered at them with angry yellow eyes from his perch on top of a cupboard.

Mike looked around quickly. 'Where's Rita Kahlo?' he

demanded, a trace of anxiety in his voice. If she'd skipped out the back way . . .

'Right here,' said the woman complacently.

Mike swung round, frowning. 'What do you mean?'

Her smile was amused as she lowered her bulky frame into the only solid-looking armchair. 'I'm Rita Kahlo.'

'You're . . . ?' Fuck it! he thought. They'd gotten the wrong woman. That crank who had phoned and told him where Mrs Kahlo lived, had been referring to the *wrong Mrs Kahlo*. Red in the face now, Mike glared into the sun-darkened face with its double chins and puffy eyes.

'I'm sorry,' he began, humiliation and disappointment making him feel as if he'd been punched in the stomach. 'My informant obviously got it wrong. You're not the lady I'm looking for.'

She raised her eyebrows. 'Are you sure?' Then she ran her pudgy fingers through the grey strands of her hair as she watched him with a playful expression. 'Are you sure I'm not the woman you want?'

For a dreadful moment he wondered if she was coming on to him. 'What do you mean?'

'You're looking for the ex-wife of Dick Kahlo?'

Mike looked at her uneasily, his eyes narrowed. 'Yes,' he said tersely.

She smiled broadly. 'Well, isn't this just your lucky day? You've found her. Not quite what you expected, huh?'

'I don't understand . . .' He shook his head, stunned.

'You were expecting a slim, beautiful young woman with long black hair and eyes to die for, huh? Like the pictures on the TV of the woman who murdered the Senator?'

Mike shifted from foot to foot, not looking at Jack Maxwell. 'Well . . . er . . . yes,' he admitted finally.

'That's why I didn't bother coming forward. I knew it wasn't me you wanted, it was one of those dames my crazy ex-husband cloned as my look-alikes.'

This seemed to amuse her greatly, and as she looked around and finally located a glass half-full of whisky which she picked up and drank deeply from, Mike realised she was drunk. Probably never really sober, by the look of her. He sat down gingerly on the edge of the sagging sofa and peered closer into her face. It was just possible to see, beneath the fat and the wrinkles and the puffiness, the structure of a perfect nose, high cheekbones, and wide-spaced eyes . . . that were the colour of dark violets.

'My God,' he said, shocked.

'What did you want with me anyway? You've got the girl who did it, haven't you? The most recent of Dick's victims? That English girl?'

'We had to see you in order to eliminate you from our enquiries. We've already interviewed two others,' he replied, thinking he could do with a strong whisky himself. It was almost unbelievable that the old, bloated, grey-haired woman sitting opposite him had once looked like Lucy Howard. Of course he knew she was older, forty-eight in fact, but even so; if he'd seen this woman in the street he'd have put her down as at least sixty-five.

'If you're looking for someone to punish, you should go for Dick,' Rita continued expansively. 'Lock him away before he ruins any more lives, the crazy old bastard! Turning all those women into clones of me. Sick, I call it. And he never even asked them first!' She finished her drink, draining the glass to the last drop before reaching for the bottle of whisky which stood on the floor behind her chair. Filling her glass, and obviously in a talkative mood, relishing the embarrassment of the two detectives, she spoke again.

'Know something? Dick moulded me into the fantasy

woman of his dreams, but I got fed up with being regarded as a work of art . . . *his* work of art, mind you.'

The cat, startled by her vehemence, jumped down from the cupboard on to her lap where he proceeded to sink slowly between her vast thighs as if standing on quicksand.

'So I left him!' Rita announced, stroking the cat absent-mindedly. 'I walked out on him and his clinic, and I flew to Hollywood with someone called Jeff. He'd been one of Dick's patients; having his nose straightened for the movies, that sort of thing.' She shrugged. 'After Jeff, there were a lot more guys until I finally ended up here. They all left me in the end, because they just wanted to fuck a famous beauty, not me at all. I'm on my own now. And do you want to know how I *really* punished Dick for turning me into a plastic doll?'

Mike nodded, mesmerised. Jack stood behind him, wondering what the hell was going on.

'I set out to *ruin* my looks!' Rita announced triumphantly. 'I gained all the weight I could pile on, and I baked my skin in the sun, and I stopped dyeing my hair and having my teeth fixed. And if I'm not happy, at least I know he's not happy either.' Tears splashed down her cheeks, forming rivulets in the wrinkles on either side of her nose, and she took a quick gulp of her drink with lips that trembled.

There was silence in the room until Mike rose.

'I'm sorry,' he said awkwardly.

'So I'm not the woman you're looking for?' Her voice was thick with grief and whisky.

'No, you're not. We'll be on our way now. I'm sorry to have disturbed you.'

As they left the room she spoke again.

'Tell the English girl . . . whatever her name is . . . that I hope Dick hasn't ruined her life, too.'

'I'll do that, ma'am,' Mike replied politely as he shut the door after him.

'Do you suppose Dr Kahlo knows what Rita has done to herself?' Jack asked, once they were back in the car and returning to police headquarters.

Mike shrugged. 'He's probably always regarded her as a painting or a statue, not really a person at all, so I'm not sure how he'd feel. I guess the guy's such a screwball he enjoys creating the look-alikes more than he prizes the finished product. Lucy Howard never suggested he tried to seduce her or anything after he'd finished, did she? I don't suppose he cares a damn about the person, just his skill in turning them into his fantasy woman, like Rita said.'

'So Lucy Howard is the one who committed the crime, after all? You got the right dame first time around? Boy, the Commissioner's going to be pleased with you.'

Mike gazed out of the car, seeing nothing. 'Yeah, I guess so,' he said hollowly.

Fifteen

Hope was slithering away from Nigel's grasp like water through his fingers and there didn't seem to be anything Joshua could do to stem the flow. The shattering revelations about Rita Kahlo had left him stunned. Now all their options for finding the real killer had gone and unless a miracle happened, the case would go ahead and Lucy would be charged with murder in the first degree. Unable to sleep, he went over and over what had happened, and how his hopes had been raised when it was discovered there were supposedly three other women who looked exactly like Lucy. It was such a bizarre situation in the first place that anything seemed possible, and he'd been so convinced that *one* of them must have committed the murder that he'd phoned Diana to say the end was in sight.

Now they were back to square one and he felt despairing. How was he going to tell her, for one thing, that if found guilty their daughter could get the death sentence? He'd spent hours with Joshua discussing the possibility of Lucy's being extradited back to England, to be tried by a British court, but the attorney thought it unlikely in view of the seriousness of the crime. They were just going to have to sweat it out for the time being, Joshua told him, while he prepared the defence. Nigel began to worry afresh. Was Joshua the right man for the job?

Alone in Amelia's apartment, while she lunched with

friends, Nigel sat in the living-room and tried to read the *New York Times*, but frustration and anxiety made him restless. There must be something he could do? When he'd visited Lucy the previous day he'd seen panic in the depths of her eyes as she'd searched his face for a hopeful sign, and then her expression had clouded, her mouth drooping at the corners, and she'd looked crushed when she'd realised there was no news.

It reminded him of the time he'd forgotten to get her the bicycle she'd wanted for her sixth birthday, and she'd rushed into their room at dawn asking excitedly where he'd hidden it? Diana's expression of reproach had been hard to bear but Lucy's heartbroken little face when she realised he'd let her down had haunted him for months. Yesterday, that feeling of having betrayed her came back. She still trusted him and he was letting her down.

In desperation he rose, flung down the newspaper and went to the guest room. The shopping receipt from Saks Fifth Avenue *must* be somewhere. Beth had sworn she'd thrown nothing out and no one else, apart from Amelia, had been in the room. It had to be somewhere, and if it took him all day he was going to go through everything meticulously again; books, magazines, clothes, handbags, make-up, boxes of costume jewellery – he was even going to remove the lining paper in all the drawers in case it had got accidentally tucked underneath. If he could only find it there was just a chance it might prove to be the alibi Lucy needed.

Two hours later, Amelia returned from lunch, glamorous in a Parma violet dress and long jacket with matching accessories, even to her amethyst earrings and bracelet. She knocked on the guest room door.

'Are you in, Nigel?'

He opened the door looking hot and dishevelled. The room behind him was a mess, with drawers and cupboards flung open and clothes strewn everywhere. Her eyes widened as she looked around.

'I'm sorry, Amelia, I'll clear up everything in a minute but I've been having another go at trying to find that shopping receipt.' He shook his head dejectedly. 'It's simply not here. God knows what Lucy did with it.'

'Oh, darling! I'm so sorry.' She took his arm and led him gently back to the living-room. 'Come and sit down and I'll get Beth to make us some herb tea. She can clear up in here. You need to rest.'

'It's hopeless, Amelia.' He felt near to tears. 'I feel I'm letting her down. I feel so helpless . . .'

At that moment the phone started ringing. She answered it immediately and, after a friendly exchange, handed it to Nigel.

'It's for you, darling. It's Joshua Goldberg.'

Nigel grabbed the receiver. 'Hello?' he said, voice sharp with anxiety.

'This may not be important,' Joshua began, 'but I've heard on the grapevine that they've found fresh evidence. Detective Powling is dealing with it right now . . .'

'What sort of evidence?'

'I couldn't get anything out of them except that it was something that had been overlooked at the Senator's apartment. I'll let you know when I hear anything definite. Homicide don't want any leaks at this stage, because they've been made to look foolish as it is, chasing up all these look-alikes and not being able to pin anything on them. It looks as if they don't know what they're doing – which just about sums up the situation.'

'Christ, I hope it's something good,' Nigel said with feeling.

'So do I. She deserves a break. I'll keep in touch.'

'Thanks.' He hung up and turned to Amelia. 'Joshua says

the police have found fresh evidence in the case but he doesn't yet know what it is.'

'Well, it can't be bad news, Nigel,' she reasoned, 'because Lucy's innocent. The only news there can possibly be *must* be good news, darling!' She grabbed his hands and looked up earnestly into his face with sparkling eyes.

'Hope, Nigel. It's the most important thing in the world. Without it we're all finished.'

He gripped her hands in return. 'I honestly don't know what I'd do without you, Amelia,' he replied. 'You keep me going and stop me losing heart.'

'That's what friends are for,' she said simply.

Earlier that day, a call had come through to Midtown South Precinct from the chief security officer at the Southgate Tower. He was immediately put through to Mike.

'We've had workmen fixing the air conditioning in Apartment 536, where Senator Ebner was . . .'

'Yeah? So what gives?'

'They found some snapshots. In an envelope. They'd fallen down behind the ventilation unit, under the window. I don't know whether they belonged to the Senator but I thought you might want them.'

'What sort of snapshots?'

'Pictures of dames. One in particular.'

'I'll get someone to pick them up right away. Thanks.'

Twenty minutes later a white envelope containing between twenty and thirty snapshots was delivered to Mike. He went through them swiftly, pausing to examine several of them closely before flipping them down on his desk, one by one. Then he reached for the phone and ordered a police helicopter.

'Right away,' he added.

'What's up?' Jack Maxwell asked, from his desk opposite.

'We'll need a search warrant,' Mike replied almost to himself as he gathered up the photographs and stuffed them into the inner pocket of his jacket.

'Why? Where are we heading?'

Suddenly Mike grinned, ignoring the avid curiosity of Shelley Lee as she looked from one to the other of them, hoping to glean something.

'The Kahlo Clinic,' he replied succinctly.

'Your attorney is here to see you,' the prison warder informed Lucy later that afternoon. 'Come this way.' Without another word he led her from the cell, along a narrow corridor with grey-painted walls and strip lights in the ceiling, to a small room, entered by a door with a glass panel covered in wire mesh. The room contained a table and two upright chairs and sitting on one of these was Joshua Goldberg.

'Hello,' Lucy said eagerly, glad to see a familiar face. 'Is there any news?' She sat facing him, pale and beautiful despite the lack of make-up. He noticed she'd lost a lot of weight and her black hair was lacklustre. But her eyes were wide and clear, the whites a startling contrast to her thick dark lashes.

Joshua regarded her for a long moment, wishing his heart would stop pounding. Then he spoke.

'There's no news as such, but Detective Powling has gone rushing off to the Kahlo Clinic – for the second time. Apparently some new evidence has been found in the Senator's apartment, though I haven't been able to find out exactly what it is.'

'New evidence?' she repeated excitedly. She leaned forward, hands clasped tightly together. 'What sort of evidence? Something that definitely gets me off the hook?'

'I don't know, Lucy. I wish to God I did. I wish I could say to you, It's OK, they've found the killer.' He sighed. 'Unfortunately I can't.'

'It couldn't be . . .' She paused, frowning. 'I don't trust anyone these days. What if this "evidence" is something that has been planted, in order to make it look as if I'm guilty? Have you thought of that? Doesn't it seem odd that they've only just made this discovery? Why didn't they find it at the time? What if the murderer, realising the other look-alikes have alibis and so couldn't have committed the crime, has planted something that will *really* make it look like I've done it?' Fear flickered in her eyes again as she looked beseechingly at Joshua. 'Oh, God, I'm scared. This thing is closing in on me, Joshua,' she added, her voice shaky.

'I didn't mean to frighten you,' he explained gently. 'Personally, I believe this is a positive sign. I have a feeling they've found something that will expose Arnold Ebner for what he was. Trust me, Lucy. I'll get you off this charge if it's the last thing I do. I know you're not guilty, and I'm going to make damn' sure everyone else knows it, too.'

'You can't be sure of getting me off. No one can. I'm being realistic, Joshua. This is the worst thing that has happened to me; worse than the accident, worse than the six months of surgery, worse than my fiancé rejecting me. *This* could be the end of everything, rock bottom, wiped out.' Her emotions were under control now, and she was looking at him candidly. 'I don't want to be lulled by fairy stories of getting off, in case it doesn't happen.'

'I *will* get you off, Lucy,' he said forcefully and continued to gaze at her for a moment.

'You want to search these premises?' Dr Kahlo looked incredulously at Mike Powling. 'That's out of the question,' he snapped.

342

Mike stood in the middle of the clinic's elegant lobby, with his feet planted wide apart. He did not look like a man who would willingly budge.

'I'm afraid you don't have a choice in the matter, Dr Kahlo. I have a search warrant. If necessary I can, and will, strip this place bare.'

'But my patients! I have to protect their privacy. We have several eminent people staying here at the moment. I cannot possibly allow you to disturb them, or to go into their rooms,' Kahlo said angrily.

Mike could see the doctor was genuinely concerned. He raised his hands in mock surrender.

'It's not your patients' rooms I'm particularly interested in,' he explained.

'Then what . . .?'

'I want to search all staff quarters, bedrooms, offices, kitchens and bathrooms, including your own.'

Dick Kahlo looked from Mike to Jack Maxwell, his dark eyes registering amazement. 'Staff quarters?'

'That's right, and I'd appreciate it if you'd let us get on with it right away.'

'You won't find anything of interest in the staff rooms,' Kahlo protested. Then shrugged. 'Go right ahead. We've nothing to hide here.'

Mike nodded to Maxwell, and at a signal from him, six uniformed policemen, who had travelled in the helicopter with them, surged in through the main door from where they'd been waiting in the drive. They looked alert and ready for anything.

'I'll get Lauren to show you the staff rooms . . .' the doctor began, but Mike cut him short.

'Thanks, but I already know where to look.' He turned to Maxwell and the others. 'OK. Let's go.'

* * *

'Diana? Oh, Diana, thank God you're still awake!'

It was nearly midnight in Eastleigh Manor, and Diana, unable to sleep, was sitting up in bed reading when the phone rang. Its shrill tones set her nerves jangling.

'Nigel! What's happened? What's wrong? Is Lucy all right?'

'Yes, darling. Yes.' Nigel sounded breathless as if he'd been running. 'Something fantastic has happened and Joshua Goldberg is arranging for her to be released first thing in the morning. Oh, God, what a day it's been!'

'Released? Oh, thank God. What *happened*?'

'They've arrested the person who murdered the Senator. They've even got a signed confession. During the afternoon I heard from Joshua that the police had found some new evidence but he didn't know what it was. Apparently, some intimate photographs of a young woman were found in Senator Ebner's apartment and also some letters. The moment the detective in charge of the case saw them, he recognised the woman. Her name is Lauren Vincent and she works at the clinic. He'd actually spent some time with her when he went to interview Dr Kahlo, originally.'

'Why did she kill him?'

'Apparently they had an affair and she got pregnant. He'd told her he was going to leave his wife so they could get married, but instead he merely offered to pay for an abortion. I gather that led to her having a breakdown but as soon as she recovered she was out for revenge. She wanted him dead.'

There was a stunned silence. 'So there was *another* look-alike wandering around, that the police didn't know about?' Diana gasped.

'No. I haven't seen this woman but I gather she doesn't look anything like the others. That's why no one suspected her until these compromising photographs of her were found.

And her letters begging him to leave his wife because she was having a baby.'

'It sounds as if she went crazy.'

'Yes. I hear that when she went to work at the clinic, one of the nurses told her about Dr Kahlo's obsession and how he'd turned two other patients into carbon copies of his ex-wife. When Lucy was being treated, and Lauren realised he was cloning his ex-wife again, it gave her the idea of confusing the police by pretending to be one of the look-alikes,' Nigel continued.

'But I don't understand!' Diana swung her legs over the side of the bed and sat on the edge, frowning in concentration. 'If this woman, Lauren, doesn't look like the others . . . who was the woman picked out by the security video? Seen leaving the apartment just after the murder? The woman who looks like Lucy?'

'Oh, God, it's so complicated, darling. It was Lauren Vincent but she *disguised* herself with a latex mask and make-up and a wig when she went to murder the Senator. On the security cameras she looked exactly like Lucy. Even I thought it was her when I studied the television. Then today the police found the wig and everything, including the murder weapon, in this woman's room in the Kahlo Clinic. Isn't it unbelievable?' Nigel was stumbling over his words now with excitement.

'It's the most extraordinary thing I've ever heard,' Diana said incredulously. 'And is Lucy really being freed tomorrow?'

'Yes, sweetheart, she really is. I tried to get her released this evening but there's the usual bureaucratic red tape to be got through before they can actually let her go. But she's been told she's in the clear. Jesus, what a nightmare the whole thing has been!' Now that he'd told Diana everything he suddenly felt tired and almost deflated. He'd been living on adrenalin for the past couple of weeks and now had the strange feeling of not knowing whether he wanted to laugh or cry.

'You'll be able to bring her home now,' Diana was saying.

'I know, it'll be marvellous.'

After they'd said goodbye, she put on her dressing-gown and went down to the kitchen to put on the kettle. Sleep was impossible. In a few days Lucy would be home after all these months. And she would have to decide whether to stay with Nigel or not . . . A minute later Tilly came stumbling sleepily through the doorway, her long dark hair tousled, eyes puffy with sleep.

'What's up, Mum? The phone woke me and then I heard you coming downstairs. Is everything all right?'

'Oh, Tilly! The most marvellous news.' Diana flung her arms around her and hugged her close. 'Lucy's being released in the morning. They've found the real murderer.'

'Wicked!' Tilly replied, grinning with delight. She hitched herself up on to the island worktop and swung her feet.

'When are they due back?'

'Daddy didn't say. I expect he'll ring us again tomorrow. Oh, the relief! I feel I've aged twenty years in the past few weeks.'

'Tell me everything Daddy said. No, wait!' Tilly jumped down again. 'I'll see if Granny's awake. She'll be furious if she misses all the excitement.'

Diana unhooked three mugs from the dresser, and took the large brown teapot out of the cupboard. By the time Susan came hurrying across the lawn, her hand-torch lighting the way, with Tilly jabbering excitedly beside her, the tea was ready.

'Well?' Susan demanded, settling herself by the kitchen table. 'Tell us exactly what's happened.'

They continued to talk into the small hours, as Diana repeated everything Nigel had told her. At last, Tilly, with her eyes drooping, shambled off to bed again, saying she couldn't keep awake any longer. Diana made a fresh pot of tea, too strung-up to relax, thankful to have Susan with her for company.

At last a pale streak of light splintered the dark horizon, and a faint twitter heralded the dawn chorus of birds which nested in the garden.

'Have you thought any more about your future with Nigel?' Susan asked gently, breaking the silence that had fallen between them.

'I've been thinking about it night and day,' Diana replied.

'And have you decided what to do?'

Diana gazed out of the window at the widening crack of light. 'There's nothing to decide.' She spoke with finality.

Susan looked at her anxiously. 'Are you going to tell him before he gets back? You should resolve the situation before Lucy returns with him, shouldn't you?'

Diana rose, tightening the sash of her dressing-gown. She shook her head. 'No. It's not something I can discuss over the phone.'

'So you're going to end it, are you?'

Diana turned to look at her mother in surprise. 'Of course not. I love him, Ma. He's been my life for the past twenty-four years. I can't possibly break-up our marriage now.'

'And you're able to accept what he is?'

'I have to,' Diana replied simply. 'I really have no option. I must say, I don't like the idea of him and . . .' She paused as if she was having difficulty finding the right words to express what she was feeling. 'I felt bitterly hurt and jealous, at first. What had these men got that I hadn't?'

'Of course it isn't like that.'

'I know, Ma. I know. That's what Nigel said but it still hurts to realise that anyone could mean as much, or more, to him, than me. But . . .' She took a deep breath before continuing. 'I love him so much, Ma, that if I can't have the whole cake, at least I'll have half and that's better than nothing.' Her eyes suddenly brimmed, but she raised her chin and her voice was determined. 'He's getting older. Maybe there won't be another Oliver, but I'm prepared to do everything I can to keep Nigel with me in the future. And that's not just for the sake of the girls.'

'A wise decision,' Susan said softly. 'One that I'm sure you won't regret.'

'I hope not. Anyway, I'm willing to try, if he is. Who knows? In a strange way all that has happened may bring us closer, eventually.'

Lucy stepped gingerly from her cell, not daring to believe that she was really about to be freed. It had happened so suddenly, so unbelievably, that she was afraid it was all a mistake and they'd suddenly turn round and tell her she was going to be put on trial after all. A warder led her to an ante-room where Detective Mike Powling was waiting for her. He was holding her release papers and looking at her with eyes that seemed to glitter like a fish's.

'Congratulations,' he said immediately. 'You'll be glad this is all over and you're free to go.'

'I am,' she said, sinking on to the chair he'd indicated.

'I see you've already got your own things back?' He stood before her, only a few feet away, and indicated the smart suit and shoes she'd been wearing when she'd been arrested.

Lucy nodded, wishing she was out of this place, wishing her father or even Joshua were here to take her away.

'So . . . were you surprised? Had you suspected anything when you were at the Kahlo Clinic?' he asked conversationally.

'There are so many things I still don't know or understand.'

'Lauren Vincent is a complex woman.'

'But she was so quiet. Such a mousy person. I'd never have suspected her of murdering anyone in a thousand years,' Lucy protested.

Mike spoke succinctly. 'Revenge is a deadly motive and a woman scorned is even deadlier. She followed you to New York, you know, when you left the clinic.'

Lucy looked perturbed. 'That's creepy.'

'On the day of the murder she saw you leave Amelia Harrow's apartment, and then she went straight to Bergdorf Goodman and bought a red suit almost identical to the one you wore that day.'

'She had the whole thing planned then . . . to set me up?'

Mike nodded knowingly, relishing this opportunity to show her how smart he'd been to solve the case and get her off.

'Lauren Vincent started out as a TV make-up artist, did you know that? That's how she put the whole thing together. She struck lucky on the day she bumped off the Senator, too, because unwittingly you played into her hands by going shopping in the vicinity of the Southgate Tower.'

Lucy felt quite sick. Another woman, imitating her, had gone into an apartment block and repeatedly shot a man to death, while deliberately making it look as if it was her. Lauren Vincent would have got away with it too, if photographs of her and her letters to Arnold Ebner hadn't been discovered.

'What happens now?' she asked faintly.

'I escort you off the premises,' Mike replied. 'You're free to go. I believe your attorney is here to meet you.'

'Oh, good.' Lucy jumped to her feet, eager to be off. The detective, with his glittering eyes, made her nervous and she hated the way he looked at her.

Outside on the sidewalk her father stood waiting, Joshua beside him.

'Daddy!' she exclaimed, running to fling her arms around his neck. Joshua watched them as Nigel held her close.

'Are you all right, darling?' Nigel asked, feeling her cheek wet against his.

'Oh, yes,' Lucy replied, her voice caught on a sob. 'Yes, I'm all right now.'

It took a lot to make Amelia Harrow angry and she hated losing her temper because she felt it reflected unflatteringly on her face, but today she could not contain her fury. As soon as Nigel left the apartment to collect Lucy from the prison, she picked up the phone and dialled the number of the Kahlo Clinic with hands that shook. There was nothing for it. If she didn't say her piece her rage would fester inside her and she'd have a headache by lunchtime.

'I'd like to speak to Dr Kahlo, please,' she announced crisply when she got through.

'I'll see if he's available . . .'

'Tell him to *make* himself available! This is Amelia Harrow calling and I want to speak to him now.' She drew on a blue satin and ecru lace peignoir over a matching nightdress and then sank gracefully and dramatically on to the chaise-longue at the foot of her bed. She knew exactly what she was going to say as thoroughly as if she'd learned lines for some Hollywood epic.

'Amelia?' Dick Kahlo's voice held a hint of surprise. 'How are you, my dear?'

'I'll tell you how I am! I'm ashamed, mortified and utterly disillusioned by the way you turned a nice young girl, whom I recommended to go to you, into one of your sick clones of Rita! You have put this girl and her family, not to mention me, through absolute hell because of your self-indulgence, and I will never, ever, recommend you to *anyone* ever again. And to compensate Lucy's poor parents for this ordeal, *you* will pay all her father's legal fees, flights, hotel and other expenses. Do you understand?'

'Yes.' He sounded tired and defeated. 'My career is at an end anyway because of this. No one trusts me now, although the miracles I performed on Tamsin, Dagmar and Lucy are living proof of my skills.'

'No one's doubting your medical skills, Dick, it's your crankiness that's scaring people to death!' she said scathingly. 'Anyway, your original idol doesn't look anything like the Rita you created, according to the photographs of her in yesterday's newspapers.'

'I can't help that. I made Rita perfect. I made the others perfect, too. I don't understand why they aren't grateful. Lucy was pleased when she first saw the results,' he added dolefully.

'But you can understand why she isn't exactly thrilled, now, can't you? As for me, I've just run clean out of compassion. You've put me in a terrible position and I wouldn't blame Nigel Howard if he wanted to sue you for millions.' Privately, Amelia knew Nigel was not the litigious type, but she did not intend to let Dick off the hook so lightly. 'I'll find out what all this has cost him and let you know.'

Just as Amelia was putting the finishing touches to her toilette, Lucy, Nigel and Joshua arrived, bounding in excitedly, filling the apartment with a buzz of voices and an atmosphere of celebration. There was much hugging and kissing, and then the champagne corks were popping and Lucy was shouting excitedly into the phone as she talked to Diana and Tilly, and Joshua was inviting them all out to lunch at La Grenouille, and Nigel and Amelia were indulging in harmless flirtation; even Beth cheered up, face gleaming with pleasure as she opened a large tin of Beluga caviar and set it on a bowl of

351

crushed ice on a silver tray, surrounded by miniature mother-of-pearl spoons.

Joshua hardly took his eyes off Lucy, watching her every movement, smiling at her every time she looked in his direction. At last she went to change before they went out to lunch.

'And I won't be wearing my red suit again,' she remarked, grinning. Twenty minutes later she returned, and for the first time Nigel felt the full impact of her new appearance. She'd put on make-up and her violet-coloured contacts, brushed her hair until it gleamed like black silk around her shoulders, and was wearing a new caramel silk dress and jacket.

Joshua nearly fell off his chair and his mouth dropped open as he looked at her, awed. Amelia, watching both his and Nigel's reactions, smiled. Dick *had* done a wonderful job on Lucy's face. There wasn't a trace of a scar, her teeth were perfect, and she was altogether unrecognisable from the severely injured young woman who had arrived in New York nearly seven months before.

'Here's to you.' Joshua raised his glass to Lucy, as he rose to his feet.

She flashed him a radiant smile and then looked at her father. Nigel had noticed the exchange between them, and for a moment felt a sharp pang as he realised he might be about to lose her again. From the moment Joshua had set eyes on her, Nigel had realised, he'd become besotted and now it looked as if Lucy might be returning those feelings. Then he chided himself for being selfish. She deserved to have someone in her life again after all she'd been through including the heartbreak caused by that bastard, Peter. She was young, healthy and beautiful, her life before her. Nevertheless, he sighed inwardly, America was a long way away.

* * *

After lunch Amelia said she must get back to the apartment because she had things to do, and Nigel decided he'd go with her because he had to fix their return flights to London, so Joshua asked Lucy if she'd like to take a stroll in Central Park?

'I'd love to,' she said readily. 'I've been cooped up in a cell for so long, I began to feel I'd lose the use of my legs.'

The park was lushly green and quiet as they walked along the tree-lined paths towards the crescent-shaped lake at its centre. People were walking dogs, jogging and skimming silently past on roller blades, but Lucy barely noticed them. She was marvelling at the fresh air, taking deep breaths and holding it in her lungs, smelling the grass and lime trees and warm earth. To be free, to be out in the open, to be able to do anything and go anywhere she wanted, was so marvellous she knew that if she'd been alone she'd have taken off her shoes and run and danced on the cool grass for the sheer joy of being alive.

She realised Joshua was looking at her.

'You must be thankful it's all over,' he said gently.

Lucy raised her face to the perfect blue of an unclouded sky. 'It's so fantastic, I can hardly believe it.'

'You're definitely going back to England with your father?'

She looked shocked. 'Of *course*! I can't wait to get home, it's been such ages.'

Joshua nodded as if he understood but his eyes clouded and his mouth was slack with disappointment.

'But you'll come back?' It was more a statement than a question and uttered anxiously.

'I'm sure I will. Daddy's promised Mummy and Tilly a trip to New York so I'm sure I won't be able to resist coming along too.'

They walked slowly in silence for a few minutes then Joshua

spoke again. 'I'd hoped that perhaps . . . we could become closer, now that the case is over?' He stopped, taking her hand and turning so that he was facing her, looking down into her eyes. 'You're so beautiful . . .' His voice was husky.

Lucy looked away, averting her gaze. 'It's too soon for me to become involved with anyone,' she said, and to her own ears it sounded like a feeble excuse. 'So much has happened,' she continued, 'and right now I want to go home and . . . sort of . . . *collect* myself. I feel I'm a different person from the Lucy Howard who used to work in radio and was getting married and had a nice safe little life.' Then she looked directly at him.

'I'm afraid I can't give you an answer, Joshua. I've honestly no idea what the future holds for me but I hope that at least we can remain friends. I'm so grateful to you for all you've done . . .'

He let go of her hand and his face looked stern and pale as he started walking again. 'I shall always be here for you, Lucy. If you need me. Now let's go find a cab. I expect you want to be with your father. You must have a lot of catching up to do.'

When he'd put her into a cab, saying he was going to walk back to his office, she saw him smile and wave. But as the taxi drew away from the kerb she caught the final look on his face. It was composed and smiling, but the eyes were seared with pain.

'What does he want?' Lucy looked petrified for a moment. 'Nothing's gone wrong, has it?' She looked beseechingly at her father as he gave her the message that Mike Powling had phoned and wanted her to ring back.

'No, everything's fine,' Nigel assured her.

'But how do you know? Oh, my God, supposing Lauren

354

Vincent has withdrawn her confession? I simply couldn't bear . . .'

Nigel gripped her by the shoulders. 'I *promise* you, Lucy, everything is all right. I actually checked with him. He said it was nothing to do with the case. Here's the number. Why don't you call him right away and get it over with?'

Reluctantly, she went into Amelia's study and dialled the number. Mike answered immediately, making her realise he'd left his home number.

'I believe you wanted to speak to me?' she said, voice clipped and English because she was nervous.

'Yeah. Nothing to worry about.' He sounded different, not so sure of himself. 'I just wondered . . . umm . . . are you planning on staying in New York for a bit?'

'No, I'm not. Why?' she asked, puzzled.

'Well . . . I was wondering if you'd consider . . . you know, having dinner, or even a drink with me, one evening.'

'Actually, my father and I are flying back to England, tomorrow,' she replied truthfully.

'Oh, gee, that's a real shame. Any chance of you coming back some time?' he added hopefully.

'I don't know. One day, perhaps.' She longed for the conversation to end but didn't want to appear rude. Across the room, Nigel, gathering what was going on, winked at her in amusement.

'I must go now,' she finally said. 'I've got to do my packing.'

'You'll have to get used to it,' Amelia remarked later, when Lucy, still amazed, told them about Joshua and Mike.

'A beautiful woman is always desired by men. You'll have more passes made to you than you ever dreamed of, and quite a few proposals of marriage as well, I've no doubt,' she added smiling.

'And there speaks a woman of experience,' Nigel remarked.

'But I hate hurting people. And it's so embarrassing when they like you more than you like them,' Lucy protested.

Memories of all the rejected swains of the past filled Amelia's mind, in a glorious parade of handsome men who had clamoured for her affections.

'You'll soon learn the art of the gentle put-down,' she assured Lucy matter-of-factly. 'Just remember to do it graciously, kindly, and then tell them you'll always be there for them, for the rest of your life – not as a lover but as a friend. That way they leave without feeling bruised and with their egos intact.'

'How wise,' Nigel said, 'and how clever.'

'But how shall I know when it *is* the right person?' Lucy asked in tones of bewilderment.

Amelia and Nigel exchanged a look of understanding.

'You'll know,' Amelia said.

'Oh, yes. You'll know,' Nigel echoed.

Sixteen

As Lucy emerged from customs at Heathrow with Nigel by her side, a barrage of photographers and TV camera crews surged forward, regardless of all the other people waiting to greet those also arriving on the overnight flight from JFK. For a moment she stood still, stunned by the attention and horrified to find herself the object of such avid curiosity.

'Just keep going, darling,' Nigel murmured, gripping her arm. He'd expected this media circus because Lucy had been approached by three British tabloid newspapers while they'd still been in New York, all of them anxious to get her to tell her story exclusively to them and in her own words for an 'undisclosed fee'. She'd turned them all down. Now it was a free for all, and as they walked steadily towards the nearest exit, where Nigel knew a hired car would be waiting to whisk them away to a private reunion with Diana and Tilly, microphones were being pushed in her face, flash bulbs were blinding her and clamorous voices were demanding answers to their questions.

Smiling politely, she remained silent, finding the attention overwhelming and almost scary. Had *she* ever pursued someone like this when she'd been working for City Radio? she wondered. Pushing the trolley piled high with their luggage, Nigel managed to cut a swathe through the crowds, for ordinary members of the public, alerted by the actions of the media, were now also crowding round, most of them wondering who they were supposed to be looking at. Was this ravishing beauty a pop star? A Hollywood film actress? A topline model?

Lucy flung herself into the back of the car while Nigel and the driver unloaded the trolley in record time. Then they were off, threading their way through the traffic, hoping not too many would follow them in determined pursuit.

'God, that was awful!' Lucy exclaimed, sliding down low on the back seat. 'I feel *notorious*. There aren't going to be more at home, are there, Daddy?'

Nigel looked grim. 'I'm afraid there will be. Mummy said on the phone yesterday that they're practically camping outside the main gate.'

'I never thought it would be like this.'

'You've been through a unique experience, darling.'

'Yes, and I know only too well it makes a terrific story,' she agreed gloomily. 'Me and three look-alikes, all wanted for a murder none of us committed.'

'And all along it was a plain Jane, disguising herself to look like one of you.'

Lucy nodded. 'I wonder what they're thinking at City Radio? I had hoped to get my job back, once the dust had settled.'

'I should think they'd love to have you back, if that's what you want to do.'

She looked thoughtful. 'The trouble is, I don't know what I want to do any more. My world has been rather turned upside down and I haven't really got any plans for the future now. I'm not sure I want to go back to the radio station, after all.'

'You need time to get your bearings again, and take stock, before you decide what to do.'

'Perhaps I should get a flat in London, and try to get into

television journalism, but I don't like the idea of living alone. I've never been on my own,' she added. When she'd first gone to London she'd shared a flat with two other girls and then she'd moved in with Peter. Suddenly Lucy felt tearful and insecure, which, she told herself sternly, was ridiculous; she'd survived a near fatal car crash, her face had been restored and she had her health back, and the nightmare of the past few weeks was over. Now she was on her way home, with her father beside her and a loving family waiting to welcome her. She had no earthly reason to feel depressed and yet she couldn't stop the tears as they poured unchecked down her cheeks.

Nigel reached out and gripped her hand.

'It's all right, darling. You're suffering from delayed reaction, you're over-tired and suddenly it's all too much. I know the feeling. Here.' He handed her the large white handkerchief from his breast pocket. 'There are going to be lots more tears before the end of the day, so don't worry about it. Your mother, for one, is going to turn on the taps when she sees you, and I shouldn't wonder if even your grandmother doesn't get the sniffles.'

Lucy giggled through her tears and it came out like a hiccup. 'Oh, Daddy! It is going to be all right?' She wasn't sure whether she meant the rest of the day or the whole of her future life, but she was in the grip of wanting to howl her eyes out and couldn't understand why.

Nigel's grip tightened and his manner was both sympathetic and robustly assuring.

'It's going to be fine, Lucy. It's going to be what you make it and you always have made the best of everything. I suggest you stay at home for a while and don't even attempt to get into the main stream at first. Don't put any pressure on yourself. You may have been lying around for six months at the Kahlo Clinic, but a holiday it certainly wasn't. My advice to you is just to vegetate in the security of Eastleigh Manor, safe with us.'

For ten days Lucy revelled in the tranquillity of the English countryside, going for long walks with Diana, accompanied by Muffie and Mackie who had been hysterical with joy at seeing her again, sitting up until late into the night gossiping with Tilly, who had matured a lot in the past year, and watching Susan as she whisked around her little kitchen, cooking all Lucy's favourite dishes. Gradually she began to feel more like herself as she grew accustomed to her changed appearance, allowing the black hair dye to grow out and soften its shade in the sunlight knowing it would take on the tones of her original warm brown colour, and only occasionally wearing her violet-coloured lenses.

Then one morning she received an invitation from one of her old flatmates, whom she hadn't seen for a couple of years.

'Jennifer's getting married! Isn't that marvellous?' she exclaimed as she scanned the thick white folded card. The rest of the family, enjoying a leisurely Saturday morning breakfast in the kitchen of the manor, looked up with interest.

'Who's she marrying?' Diana asked. 'She was such a pretty little thing.'

'*Was?*' Lucy asked, jokingly. 'Still *is*, I imagine.' She read the elegant Palace Script typeface. 'Someone called Julian Herniman.'

'Where is the wedding?' Nigel said.

'St Paul's, Knightsbridge, and then the Hyde Park Hotel.'

'Oh, very swish!' Tilly commented. 'What will you wear? You've got all those gorgeous clothes you bought in New York . . . and Daddy, you *promised* to take Mummy and me there sometime. But you'll need a hat, Lucy.'

She nodded. 'I'll go up for the day. It'll be fun to see the old gang again!'

Nigel wandered blindly through the orchard, his hands in his pockets, his mind reeling with shock, pain and regret that cut so deep he felt as if he had been run through with a knife. The letter had arrived that morning. He'd instantly recognised the handwriting, although the green ink was missing. Habit made him take it to his study where he could read it in private, and he was glad because his cry of anguish at the contents would have deeply upset Diana, who'd been so understanding and loving towards him since his return from the States.

It was a rambling letter but the gist of it was that Oliver was now in hospital, suffering from AIDS related pneumonia.

    . . . I've been unwell for some weeks now, but this thing is really closing in on me now and I don't know how long I've got left. Sometimes I hope it will be quick, rather than a long drawn-out ending; there are chaps here who have been seriously ill for years. I pray to God I haven't given it to you. Please let me know so that I can die in peace. It would be nice to see you, one more time, but I will quite understand if you'd rather not. The nurses here are wonderful . . .

The tears in Nigel's eyes blurred his vision and he couldn't read on. Stuffing the letter into his jacket pocket he walked into the garden and it seemed that by getting nearer to nature he would also be getting closer to Oliver. It was a beautiful morning with clear skies and a warming sun, and the trees and the smooth lawn were the clean fresh green of spring. It was just the sort of day Oliver loved and Nigel's heart ached for the man whom had once meant so much to him. Leaning against the old stone wall at the bottom of the garden, he looked at the tranquil landscape and tried to come to terms with his grief.

'What's the matter, Nigel?'

It was Diana, walking across the lawn towards him. He decided to tell her the truth.

'I've had some bad news. Oliver is in hospital. By the sounds of it, he may not have long.'

Diana turned pale and she searched Nigel's eyes anxiously as if trying to gauge the depth of his grief.

'I'm sorry.' She spoke hesitantly. 'That's awful. He's quite young, isn't he?'

'Thirty-nine.'

She shook her head, her brow furrowed. 'That's no age at all. How very, very sad.'

'Diana . . . ?'

'Yes?'

'He's asked me to visit him at the Brompton Hospital. To say . . . goodbye, I suppose.' His eyes were dry now but his voice wobbled dangerously. 'Would you mind terribly if I go and see him?'

'Of course not, Nigel. You must go, I can see that.' Then she paused before saying in a small voice: 'Is there anything I can do?'

'Nothing, my darling, but thank you for being so understanding. I want you to know that my feelings towards him are only those of a friend, nothing more. A dear friend to whom I must say goodbye.'

Diana's eyes filled with sudden tears. She spoke with a rush. 'I do understand, Nigel. Really I do. It must be awful for him, knowing he's going to die; and awful for you, too. When will you go?'

'Lucy's going up to London for a wedding tomorrow, isn't

she? I think I'll drive her up, go and visit Oliver, and then give her a lift home again afterwards.'

'That's a good idea. Then you won't be alone on the journey.' She put her arms round him with a protective, maternal gesture and pressed her cheek to his. 'I'll be thinking of you,' she said softly, then she turned and hurried back to the house, her emotions so mixed she needed to be by herself for a while, so she could try and sort out the confusion in her mind.

Lucy saw him immediately. He was escorting a tall blonde girl in a pale pink suit and one of the ushers was showing them into a pew on the bride's side of the church. The girl's large straw hat, crown circled with pink roses, hid her face from the side, so that Lucy couldn't see what she looked like, but he looked well – tall and tanned and elegant in his pearl grey morning suit with a pale blue cravat held in place by a small sapphire tie pin. Oh, yes, Peter looked well as he smiled and nodded to people around where he sat. He didn't look in her direction and she was thankful. Her heart had almost ground to a standstill when she'd seen him and she felt cold and stiff as she remembered that dreadful day he'd arrived unexpectedly at Eastleigh Manor and found her in the garden.

Lucy was hardly aware of the arrival of the bride and the Wedding Service that followed. If the accident hadn't happened, she kept thinking. If she hadn't been so badly injured . . . Peter was exchanging little knowing smiles and nudges with the girl by his side, and the congregation were singing 'Lead Us, Heavenly Father, Lead Us' and Lucy wondered if she hadn't better duck out of the reception. So many of her . . . she corrected herself, *their* old friends had been invited, all the people who'd been on her own wedding list. What a fool she'd been to come today! Why hadn't she thought it through? It was inevitable that Jennifer would ask Peter; he was always round at their flat until Lucy had gone to live with him. Everyone in her set knew Peter and he knew everyone; the only unfamiliar-looking girl was the one by his side today.

The organ was swelling to the notes of Widor's Toccata and Jennifer, glowing with happiness in a cloud of white lace, with Julian holding her arm, was coming down the aisle, smiling broadly, followed by both sets of parents, the mothers self-conscious in their unaccustomed finery, the fathers looking fatuously proud, with white carnations sprouting from their lapels.

Then, Lucy looked past them, and realised that Peter was staring at her. Their eyes locked and his mouth fell open. He looked as if he'd had a tremendous shock. Lucy stared back and then averted her face as if to watch the bride leave the church, deciding she couldn't possibly go on to the reception.

'Lucy! I hardly recognised you,' said a shrill voice just behind her. It was Miranda, in a white silk suit, which made her skin look like dark-brown leather. Her cloud of russet hair swelled out from under a large hat decorated with daisies, and she was staring at Lucy's face with incredulity. 'You do look good,' she said grudgingly.

'Thank you, Miranda,' Lucy replied politely. She'd never realised before that the woman who might have been her mother-in-law could be so catty.

'I'm looking for Peter, have you seen him? We were supposed to meet for lunch but I was late . . . and he didn't wait.' Her eyes were darting left and right, eager to find her son among the crowds leaving the church.

'I think he's over there.' Lucy nodded to where she'd seen Peter minutes before. Miranda pushed her way in the direction she'd indicated and a few minutes later there they were, just ahead of her. Peter was talking almost angrily to his mother.

'What's all this rubbish about you going to America?' he demanded.

'It's just a trip, darling.' Miranda sounded evasive but Lucy didn't hear any more because she found herself, surrounded by old friends, caught up and swept along the short route to the Hyde Park Hotel.

Once in the ballroom, with a glass of champagne in her hand, she decided she'd just have to do her best to avoid bumping into Peter. It shouldn't be difficult. Jennifer had invited three hundred guests and the room was soon packed. She glanced surreptitiously at her watch. It was three-thirty. Her father wasn't picking her up for another hour. She launched herself into a group of old schoolfriends who were thrilled to see her again, and squealed with delighted amazement at her looks, which only made her wonder if they'd thought her unattractive in the first place? Once again she began to feel she didn't belong inside this new exterior, and, worse, it was causing people to treat her differently.

'Lucy.'

She felt a hand on her shoulder and the voice was instantly recognisable. Turning slowly, she regarded Peter from under the brim of her new navy blue straw hat.

'Hello, Peter.'

'It's so good to see you again. How are you?' he enthused. The blonde in pink was absent from his side, she noticed.

'I'm very well indeed,' Lucy replied crisply. 'And you're obviously fine.' She noticed that his eyes were searching every centimetre of her face with a growing look of amazement.

'Looking for the scars?' she enquired lightly.

He turned scarlet. 'You look wonderful . . . there's not a trace of . . . you're *beautiful*, Lucy. I'd no idea they could . . .' His voice faded as he realised he was getting deeper and deeper into a quagmire of embarrassment.

'No idea I could be turned around from looking like a gargoyle into something resembling a human being?'

'No! No, I didn't mean that . . . I mean, well, I'm so thrilled to see you again, and to know that you're all right. It was all so terrible at the time. I was blaming myself for the accident, and feared I was going to be crippled for life so I . . . so I sort of lost my head, I'm afraid.' He'd started to sweat.

Lucy looked at him in silence.

'I'm so terribly sorry for the way I behaved,' he continued in low rapid tones as he moved closer, gripping her elbow with his hand. 'I think I went a little crazy . . . I certainly couldn't cope. My mother will tell you that. And d'you know something? Every day, ever since . . . well, you know, I've regretted the fact we broke up.' He shook his head dolefully and she noticed the hand that held the glass of champagne was shaking. 'I was a complete fool. We had so much going for us . . . and then that damned accident happened.'

Lucy continued to regard him calmly as he floundered and blushed and gradually a wonderful warm feeling spread through her body, lifting a weight from her shoulders and casting away a dark cloud that had hung over her ever since that day when he'd come to Eastleigh Manor unexpectedly. She'd been so hurt by him, so utterly devastated by his reaction to her injuries; now here he was, gazing at her with undisguised admiration, adoration even, regretting what he'd done. It was like a gentle balm to her spirit.

'You've no idea how marvellous it is to see you again,' he was saying, almost breathless now. 'Oh, Lucy. Darling. Can you ever forgive me? I never, *never* meant to hurt you. I just couldn't cope, that was all. I've always been devilishly weak over things like blood and needles, and we'd both been through so much . . . but is it too late? Can't we turn the clock back, darling? If you'll just forgive me?' His eyes were sincere as they gazed longingly into hers. His grip on her arm tightened as he tried to pull her closer. The last little bit of grey cloud slipped away from her mind so quietly it was there one minute and gone the next.

'Oh, I'll forgive you, Peter,' she said smiling easily, 'but I never want to set eyes on you again.'

It was even worse than Nigel expected. In the AIDS ward the patients had their own private rooms, but because there were so few visitors and the condition of many of the AIDS victims was critical, their doors were kept permanently open so the nursing staff, situated in a central working area, could keep an eye on them all. As Nigel walked past these rooms the sight that met his eyes was so horrifying he felt he'd stepped into a world of dark powers and terrible suffering. Never before in his life had he seen human beings so disfigured, so skeletal, so utterly damned and without hope. And yet the nurses looked cheerful and there was an atmosphere of camaraderie.

'Hello! Can I help you?' a rosy-cheeked, dark-haired nurse asked him when he arrived.

'I've come to see Oliver Stephens.'

He was directed to the last room on the left. Bracing himself, he made his way along the passage, clutching the magazines and fruit he'd brought. At that moment he had no idea how he was going to handle the situation.

'Nigel!'

Oliver was propped up on pillows, looking ivory-skinned and emaciated. Drips were fixed to both arms, and there was an oxygen mask attached to a large red cylinder by his bedside.

'You've come,' he exclaimed, his voice filled with gratitude and his eyes burned bright with fever.

'Of course I've come,' Nigel replied, trying to act naturally.

There was no question of embracing; too much medical apparatus was in the way. 'Here's something to read, and a few grapes.' Awkwardly, he placed them on the bedside cabinet before sitting in the narrow armchair which was drawn up beside the bed.

Oliver reached for his hand, his grip hot and dry. 'I'm so glad you're here, Nigel. I wanted to make it right with you.'

'How's it going? How are you feeling?'

'Dreadful. I'm having a problem breathing. They drew a litre of liquid from my left lung this morning.'

'Jesus, I'm sorry. You don't deserve this, Oliver.'

'No one deserves it.' There was a pause as his eyes searched the ceiling, in an effort to fight back the tears. 'Every time something goes wrong they treat it and it goes away for a while and then something else starts up. It's like plugging a hole in a dyke and the minute you do, another leak springs out from somewhere else. Last night three people died.' He made a sickly attempt to smile. 'They've nicknamed this ward death row.' Then he started coughing, a rasping desperate sound that lasted nearly a minute and left him exhausted.

'Can I get you anything? A glass of water?' Nigel asked, watching Oliver struggle for air.

He shook his head. 'I'm scared,' he whispered.

'Of course you are,' Nigel sympathised, knowing Oliver well enough to realise he wouldn't want to be duped by false denials. 'The only consolation is realising we're all going to die one day. The only thing we don't know is who's going first.'

Oliver nodded. 'You haven't got it, have you? I couldn't bear it if . . .'

Nigel's grip on his hand tightened. 'I'm fine. My test was negative.'

'Thank Christ! I didn't know I was HIV until after we met

that last time, in that pub at Richmond, but I had a horrible suspicion I might be. I wondered if you'd guessed?'

'No. It didn't cross my mind until you mentioned it.'

'I'm sorry I threatened to tell your wife.'

'As it happens, I've told her everything myself. She knows I've come to see you today.'

Oliver's eyes widened in surprise, and then he became overcome with another bout of coughing. A moment later the pink-cheeked nurse hurried into the room.

'What you need is a whiff of oxygen, my love,' she said, putting the mask over Oliver's nose and mouth.

Nigel didn't stay long. Oliver was obviously weak and easily tired, but he promised to visit him again.

'That is if I'm still here,' he remarked, pulling off his mask for a moment. Then he winked and for a split second Nigel saw a flash of the old Oliver he'd first found so attractive, before he retreated behind the mask once more and closed his eyes, as if shutting out the world.

As Nigel and Lucy drove home that evening they were steeped in their own thoughts, for each, unbeknown to the other, had said goodbye to an important person from the past. For Lucy it was a wondrous relief, Peter had not been the right man for her, as his shallowness today had proved. She need no longer hanker for lost love, or feel sadness for what might have been. Now, she felt free to go forward, to make a new life for herself with a confidence she would not have previously thought possible.

For Nigel the day had brought about the end of an era, and a final deliverance from constant anxiety. Never again would he be living a secret life, away from Diana; a life of lies and fear of being found out. Glad that he'd been to see Oliver, he nevertheless felt pity and compassion at the waste of a life.

God moves in mysterious ways, he reflected, and it is not for him to question. For Oliver's sake he hoped the end would come painlessly and quickly.

Muffie and Mackie greeted Nigel and Lucy with ecstatic delight when they arrived at Eastleigh Manor, but otherwise the house seemed silent and empty. Then Susan appeared in the hall on her way in from the garden.

'Had a good day?' she asked. Nigel had gone up to London on the pretext of doing some shopping. She turned to Lucy. 'How was the wedding?'

'Great,' Lucy replied enthusiastically. 'I met a lot of old friends.'

'There's a surprise visitor in the garden,' Susan announced. 'We're just about to have drinks.'

'Who is it?' Nigel asked.

'I'm not sure I like surprises,' Lucy remarked.

'How do you know until you see who it is?' Susan retorted.

'Yeah. Well, OK.' Reluctantly Lucy turned and went into the garden and across the lawn, followed by Nigel. Diana and Tilly were there, and someone else, too. He rose as soon as he saw Lucy and then came towards her, arms outstretched.

'Simon! What are you doing here?' she asked, astonished, as he swept her up in a bear hug.

'I thought I'd drive over and see you all! I tried to make it last weekend but I couldn't get away, there's so much work on.'

'It's so good to see you again,' she exclaimed, looking into the friendly and familiar face. She had the feeling that if she'd last seen Simon ten years ago or last week, everything would still be the same.

'You've been away a long time,' he observed as they strolled over to join the others. 'I've been reading all about the terrible time you had in New York. I don't suppose you want to go back there in a hurry.'

'I'm just glad to be home,' she said fervently.

'I think everyone's very glad to have you home,' he replied, smiling.

Much later, in the kitchen, for Simon had been invited to stay for the weekend and Susan had observed he didn't need any persuading, Lucy was helping her mother prepare dinner, and then she made a remark that startled her mother.

'Do you know something, Mum? Simon is the only person who has treated me in exactly the same way, right from the beginning. No matter how I looked. My face was at its worst when he first saw me, and he didn't blink an eyelid. And this evening, when he saw me again, it was the same. He sees *me*. The person inside. He always has, and that's what's so marvellous.' She was chopping parsley as she spoke, bringing the blade down decisively on the wooden board.

'So how have other people treated you?'

Lucy gazed thoughtfully out of the kitchen window, at a violet dusk that was gently enveloping the garden, etching the trees like black lace against the skyline.

'Everyone is much nicer to me now I'm prettier,' she said bluntly. 'Especially men. I'm sure Joshua Goldberg wouldn't have worked so hard to try and get me off if he hadn't fancied me. It was even the same with the detective in charge of the case. Then there were all the people Amelia introduced me to. It was quite embarrassing the way the men fawned over me.' She paused, and scraped the chopped parsley into a bowl.

'Peter was at the wedding today,' she continued casually.

Diana spun round to look at her. 'Oh my God! What did you do?'

A smile appeared on Lucy's face. 'Nothing much, I was just *there*. He came over and tried to make it up with me.

371

Wanted us to get together again, in spite of the fact he had a girl in tow.'

'And?' Diana held her breath.

'I told him I never wanted to see him again.'

'You were quite right.'

'I know I was.'

'You deserve better, darling.'

'All I want is to be liked for myself.'

'And you think . . . ?'

Lucy's smile was radiant now. 'Oh, yes. I'm sure of it. I'm so glad he's staying for the weekend.'

'I think the time has come to organise the big party I promised we'd give, to celebrate your homecoming, and Daddy's too,' Diana added, her cheeks flushing suddenly.

'What's that about a big party?' Tilly came bounding into the kitchen. 'Can I have a new dress? Can we make it a dance? With a disco? Oh, wicked! I can hardly wait. Let me go and tell Simon. I think he loves dancing.'

Diana had decided to make it a really big party with a marquee. 'We can have at least a hundred and fifty people then,' she explained, thoroughly enjoying the organising of the occasion. Nigel watched with delight as she set about planning the evening. No longer did she lean on him for every decision, or cling to him for constant reassurance as she'd done in the past. Caterers were hired, menus chosen, champagne and wine selected. Pink and white flowers were ordered to harmonise with the pink and white lining of the marquee, a discotheque from London was booked, and then Diana set about arranging for guests to stay with various friends in the neighbourhood, and a coach to transport those who didn't want to drive down from London.

'What am I going to *wear*?' Tilly kept bleating. 'And I'll

need new shoes; high-heeled ones.'

Lucy offered to take her to London for the day. 'I'll help you choose something.'

'Don't let her buy anything too sophisticated, darling,' Diana pointed out.

'Mum, she is seventeen. She's not going to want to wear a party frock.'

Later that day, as Diana checked the list of acceptances she confided to Nigel that she only had one worry about the party.

'But you seem to have everything under control,' he said.

'Everything except the feelings of our youngest daughter,' she said with a wry smile.

'Tilly? Why? What's the matter?'

'I'm afraid she's got a crush on Simon,' she explained, 'and the trouble is, so has Lucy.'

'But Tilly is only a child!' he protested, laughing. 'She can't be serious.'

Diana gave him an old-fashioned look. 'D'you want to bet? I'm so worried in case she gets hurt.'

Nigel, greatly amused, told her not to worry. 'They'll work it out between themselves,' he assured her.

It was the warmest summer evening anyone could remember. The air was so still the flaming torches, lining the drive, barely flickered and a full moon bathed the orchard in a silvery light.

Nigel and Diana, looking radiant in a long red satin dress, welcomed their guests in the drawing-room, for a champagne reception, before they went into the marquee for dinner by the light of hundreds of pink candles.

Tilly, in a slinky black dress, cut low at the back, which Nigel announced made her look twenty-five, seemed to be here, there and everywhere, looking after her own young friends. Lucy, wearing a white dress she'd bought in New York, helped her parents introduce the guests to each other.

'This is a night to remember, isn't it?' Susan kept saying to anyone who would listen. 'And don't Lucy and Tilly look marvellous?'

'Do you think it's going all right?' Diana asked Nigel, as the guests seated themselves for dinner at the round tables for ten, in the marquee.

'It's going with a great swing,' he assured her. 'Everyone, including your mother, or should I say *especially* your mother, is having a great time.'

Later in the evening, when the air was filled with the loud beat of dance music, and Diana was making sure everyone was being looked after, she slipped in to the house to touch up her make-up.

'Where's Simon?' she asked Nigel in a low voice. Her tone held a note of concern for the first time that evening.

'On the dance floor with Lucy,' he replied, 'having a ball.'

'Then where's Tilly?'

He took her hand and led her towards the study, where a bar had been set up for the older guests who wanted some respite from the loud music. A deep, leather sofa had been pushed back against the wall. Under a tangled heap of dinner jackets Diana caught a glimpse of Tilly's long legs, emerging under three young men who all appeared to be sitting on her lap. Suddenly there was a commotion and Diana caught the words: 'Look out! My mother's here!' as the three young men leaped off Tilly, like flies being shooed off a honey pot, before standing in an uncertain circle, grinning sheepishly.

'Hi, Mum!' Tilly called out gaily.

'I don't think,' Nigel remarked, as he tried to contain his laughter, 'that you need worry about your younger offspring.

374

She seems to be able to look after herself in no uncertain way.'

Diana was laughing, too. 'Well, thank God for that,' she replied succinctly. She linked arms with Nigel and they strolled back to the marquee, closer than they'd been for many years, brought together by all that had happened in the past fifteen months.

'Enjoying yourself, darling?' he whispered, thinking how lovely she looked, her face glowing and her eyes sparkling with happiness.

She turned to look into his eyes. 'Very much,' she murmured. 'Only two years to go and we can give another big party.' Her smile was teasing. 'We're going to have to celebrate our silver wedding anniversary.'

'I'll drink to that,' he replied fervently, slipping his arm around her waist.

On the dance floor, Simon was holding Lucy close, as they moved in harmony to a slow romantic number. Every now and then he looked down into her eyes and smiled at her and she smiled back, feeling happier than she could ever remember being in her life. With Simon she knew she'd found herself and, at last, felt comfortable in her own skin. Others might fawn over her because of her outer beauty, but Simon would always recognise and love the person inside.

'Let's go into the garden,' he whispered. Hand in hand they left the crowded marquee and wandered into the silvery orchard which seemed imbued with magic on this still, moonlit night. Then he pulled her gently towards him and kissed her, tentative at first, but with growing tenderness as she responded. She knew that this time, without any doubt, she'd found someone who loved her for herself.

False Promises

The spellbinding novel of intrigue and suspense
from the author of A GUILTY PLEASURE

'A smoothly readable thriller' *Daily Telegraph*

Una-Mary Parker

Toby and Liza Hamcroft share a life of wealth,
privilege and marital bliss. Parents of three adorable
children, members of Lloyd's of London, and part of
England's elite – not a day goes by without Liza
counting her blessings. Then her life is thrown into
turmoil when Toby disappears without trace.

Lloyd's, where Toby is a successful broker, is
suffering huge insurance losses and as the syndicates
start to crash, Liza realises the implications could be
catastrophic for those involved. Disaster for her
brother Freddy whose wife Melissa is only after his
money; ruin for Sir Humphrey and Lady Rosemary
Davenport who put their trust in Toby; and humiliation
for her parents who are set to lose everything.

As the days go by, Liza frantically searches for clues
to Toby's whereabouts. But who can she turn to for
help? Toby's colleagues show concern, but can they be
trusted? When events take a more sinister turn Liza
realises she must take the law into her own hands if she
is to find her husband before it is too late . . .

FICTION / GENERAL 0 7472 4874 5

SERENDIPITY

Only when they have made peace with the
past, can they make plans for the future . . .

Fern Michaels

As a naïve seventeen-year-old, Jory Ryan found
herself pregnant by one of Philadelphia's most
eligible young bachelors: lawyer Ross Landers.
But their marriage brought neither of them
happiness, and a miscarriage only added to the
couple's pain. In desperation, Jory fled to Florida
and built a new life for herself. Now, six years
later, Ross wants to finalise their separation
with a divorce.

Jory returns to Philadelphia as an independent,
sophisticated woman, and Ross begins to regret
his decision. But for Jory there's no looking back
– particularly now that Ross's best friend Pete
'Woo' Woojalesky has re-entered her life. She
decides to move into her family home, setting
down roots and rekindling friendships she
thought were long gone.

But Jory cannot cut herself off from the Landers
family forever. And events that take place,
including a bitter power struggle for control
of the family business, an ongoing feud and a
tragic accident, link them together with
unexpected consequences . . .

FICTION / GENERAL 0 7472 4995 4